Also by John Boyne

THE ELEMENTS

THE ELEMENTS

A Novel

John Boyne

Henry Holt and Company
New York

Henry Holt and Company
Publishers since 1866
120 Broadway
New York, New York 10271
www.henryholt.com

Henry Holt® and Ⓗ ® are registered trademarks of
Macmillan Publishing Group, LLC.
EU Representative: Macmillan Publishers Ireland Ltd., 1st Floor,
The Liffey Trust Centre, 117–126 Sheriff Street Upper, Dublin 1, DO1 YC43

Library of Congress Cataloging-in-Publication Data

Names: Boyne, John, 1971– author.
Title: The elements : a novel / John Boyne.
Description: First edition. | New York : Henry Holt and Company,
2025.
Identifiers: LCCN 2025009245 | ISBN 9781250410368 (hardcover) |
ISBN 9781250410276 (ebook)
Subjects: LCGFT: Novels.
Classification: LCC PR6102.O96 E44 2025 | DDC 823/.92—dc23/
eng/20250417
LC record available at https://lccn.loc.gov/2025009245

Our books may be purchased in bulk for specialty retail/wholesale,
literacy, corporate/premium, educational, and subscription box use.
Please contact MacmillanSpecialMarkets@macmillan.com.

First Edition 2025

Published in the UK in 2025 by Transworld

Designed by Gabriel Guma

Printed in the United States of America

10 9 8 7 6 5 4 3 2 1

This is a work of fiction. All of the characters, organizations, and events portrayed
in this novel either are products of the author's imagination or are used fictitiously.

For Bill Scott-Kerr

Contents

WATER

1

The first thing I do when I arrive on the island is change my name.

I've been Vanessa Carvin for a long time, twenty-eight years, but I was Vanessa Hale for twenty-four years before that and there's an unexpected comfort in reclaiming my birthright, which sometimes feels as if it was stolen from me, even though I was complicit in the crime.

A few minutes later, I change it again, this time to Willow Hale. Willow is my middle name, and it seems prudent to take a further step in separating the woman I am now from the woman I once was, lest anyone here makes the connection. My parents were unremarkable, middle-class people—a teacher and a shop assistant—and there were some who thought them presumptuous in calling their daughter Vanessa Willow, which summons images of a Bloomsbury writer or a painter's wan muse, but I was always rather pleased with it. I had notions about myself back then, I suppose. I don't have them any longer.

My next task is to shave my head. I've kept my hair shoulder-length and blond for as long as I can remember, but I purchased an electric razor before leaving Dublin and plug the device in to charge for half an hour before easing it around my skull, experiencing a feverish delight in watching the clumps tumble into the sink or fall on the floor around my feet. Standing in the cascading tendrils of my femininity, I decide not to make myself entirely bald for that would draw too much attention, and I don't have the head for it anyway, unlike the famous singer who looked like one of God's angels when she first appeared on our television screens. Instead, I shear myself down to the uncomplicated blunt crop of a hardworking country woman, someone far too busy to concern herself with indulging the physical. The blond is gone now, replaced by a darkish gray that must have been lurking inside me all the time, like a benign cancer. I wonder how I will look when it starts to grow out again and rather hope that it won't. The truth is, it would be more convenient if it just gave up the ghost with the cruel efficiency it inflicts on men.

I explore the cottage and find it suitable to my needs. The photographs I saw online did not lie about its austerity. The front door opens onto a living room that houses a kitchen. Or, perhaps, a kitchen that houses a living room. There's a single bedroom with a single bed—how strange it will feel to sleep like a child again—and a small bathroom with no shower. An unappealing rubber attachment is squeezed plumply around the tap spouts, and I pull it away, relocating it to a cupboard beneath the sink. The roof must be sound, for there are no damp spots on the stone floor that have fallen from above. The simplicity, the monastic nature of all of this, pleases me. It is so far from what I am accustomed to.

When I first made inquiries of the owner, a man named Peader Dooley, I asked about the Wi-Fi, and he told me a pub on the island offered it but that very few of the houses had access yet and his was not one of them.

"I suppose that'll rule the place out for you?" he asked, disappoint-ment in his tone, for this was not the type of cottage to draw many offers, and certainly not for an open-ended lease.

"On the contrary," I told him. "If anything, it makes it more appealing."

When I turn on the taps, the water emerges brown at first before clearing its throat in the pipes and running clear. I place my hand beneath it, and it is shockingly cold. Taking a glass from the shelf, I fill it and drink. I cannot remember when I last experienced such purity. I drink more and feel something inside me spring to life. I wonder, could a person get drunk on this water?

Moving from room to room, I check the light switches and am relieved that they're all in working order since the island at night is sure to be darker than any place I've ever known. The wallpaper is bleached of its color and looks as if it remains on the wall out of habit more than anything else; one good tug, however, and I imagine the sheets would fall away without complaint. Something is missing, and it takes me a few moments to realize what it is: there is no television set. I'm not disappointed. If I am to live this hermetic existence, then it is best that nothing intrudes upon it. It will be a rare privilege to be so willfully ignorant of the outside world and all its nonsense.

There is, however, a radio, an old-fashioned one with an aerial folded down. I turn it on but receive only static. Pulling up the copper spike, I rotate the dial and soon find myself tuned in to RTÉ Radio 1, where Joe Duffy is displaying admirable patience while interrogating one of his listeners about the latest indignity that has befallen her. For years, I listened to Joe's show every day, but I turn it off now. Over the last twelve months, Brendan and I were the subject of debate on many occasions and, masochist that I am, I couldn't stop myself from obsessively listening as strangers called in to denounce us both.

"And as for her," they would say, vicious in their moral superiority. "Sure, you only have to look at that creature to see that she was in on it all along. Like attracts like."

I've sworn that I won't pay attention to these merciless commentators anymore, and so I remove the batteries from the device and bury them in different parts of the back garden, smoothing over their graves so I won't be able to find them again.

Food. That will be an issue. The taxi driver, the only one on the island, a man named Mícheál Óg Ó'Ceallaigh, brought me and my suitcase from the dock to the cottage and told me there was a "grand little shop" only twenty minutes' walk from where I would be staying, between the pub and the church. The old pub, he added, not the new pub. I shall enjoy walking. They say that exercise is good for one's mental health, and mine is in a low place. Right now, however, I'm not hungry, and, even if I was, Mr. Dooley must have an agent somewhere nearby, for a fresh loaf of bread has been left on the table and there's butter, ham, eggs, and cheese in the fridge, as well as a small sack of potatoes slumped like a weary traveler by the front door.

When I unpack my suitcase, I'm surprised to find that I included a toiletries bag bursting with makeup, the zip straining against the pressure of a lifetime's commitment to hiding the truth. I don't remember including it. Perhaps it was simply an unconscious gesture after years of packing for holidays and Brendan's work trips. I spill its contents onto the bed now and look them over. There must be a thousand euros' worth of deception here, promises of youth decanted into white tubes, glass bottles, and plastic containers. I sweep the lot back into the bag and throw it all in the bin. Rebecca, my younger daughter, would have a fit if she witnessed such waste. Some years ago, when she was fourteen, she turned into something of an eco-warrior and was forever scolding me for throwing things away when there was still life in them, just as men do with their first wives. Anyway, it's no longer an issue for I intend to embrace a plain complexion here. I'll wash my face with soap, dry it with a rough towel, and let the elements do their worst.

I didn't bring many clothes, so it doesn't take long for me to hang them up in the wardrobe. A few pairs of jeans. Some T-shirts. Underwear. A couple of heavy woolen jumpers. I anticipated the Atlantic cold and rather liked the idea of walking along the cliffs like an actress in a television advertisement, staring out to sea and contemplating the ruins of my existence. Only two pairs of shoes. The ones I'm wearing, which are really just a comfortable pair of trainers, and a second pair that aren't much better. I should have brought some hiking boots, I suppose. I wonder if there might be a place to purchase some here, as I have no intention of returning to the mainland during my self-imposed exile. If not, I will simply have to survive with what I have. People always used to. Plenty still have no choice.

The front door is ajar, and a cat marches in, pausing for a moment in surprise, her front right paw held in midair. She stares at me in outrage as if I, and not she, is the intruder.

"I have a rental agreement," I tell her, and her eyes narrow at my insolence. "Do you want to see it?"

I'm not much of an animal person and hope that she'll take umbrage at this infringement of her rights and leave, but no, she simply emits a resigned meow before making her way to the armchair and springing onto it before promptly falling asleep. Emma, my elder daughter, wanted a dog when she was a child, but Brendan claimed to be allergic, another assertion I never really believed. The truth was that he valued order and felt that having any sort of pet around the place would lead to chaos. Toys everywhere. Baskets. Water bowls. Urine on the floor tiles. I regret that now. We only have our children with us for a short time. It seems churlish not to give them the things they ask for, particularly when they're asking for something that might love them unconditionally.

I allow my mind to drift to my ex-husband for a moment. Well, he's surrounded by chaos now, I tell myself, wondering whether I should smile at the irony but being unable to. Although he's technically not my ex-husband at all yet. I just think of him that way. One day, I will summon the energy to speak to a solicitor, but right now I have had enough of the legal system to last me a lifetime, and, who knows, maybe he'll die, or be killed, which would save me both the bother and the expense.

With nothing left to do in the cottage, I step back outside and look around. It is a fine day, neither cold nor warm, without even the whisper of a breeze in the air. There are a few other houses in sight, each one located at some distance from mine. A dozen or more cattle and sheep dot the fields of my closest neighbor, whose farmhouse stands atop a hill, perhaps ten minutes' walk from my door. "This is where I live now," I say aloud, and my voice doesn't sound like my own. Perhaps it's something in the island acoustics, an inharmonious meeting point between water, earth, fire, and air. It's hard to believe that I've landed in such a place.

Earlier, on a whim, I checked the calendar on my phone to see where I'd been on this day last year, and it turned out to have been the morning that Brendan and I had an audience with Pope Francis in Rome. The Irish Ambassador to the Holy See had introduced us, telling His Holiness that this was the great Brendan Carvin, who was known and admired the length and breadth of the country, and if Brendan had been blessed with feathers, he would have spread them wide and enclosed us all within his colorful train. *And this is his wife*, the ambassador added a moment later, not deeming me worthy of a name, and I performed a sort of curtsy in the black dress I'd bought for the occasion in Brown Thomas, which hung between my knees and ankles, my face hidden behind a veil, presumably to protect the Pope from any temptation.

Francis's was not the first papal hand that either Brendan or I had shaken—there were two others—but it will certainly be the last.

I look at my watch. Three o'clock now and already I'm not sure how I'll fill the rest of the day. I've brought a few books with me—classics, mostly—but amn't in the mood for reading. I'll go to the shop, I suppose. Explore. Build up an appetite and see what they serve in the pub, assuming they have a menu at all. Maybe I'll get drunk and dance on a table. It would be quite something to be barred from one of the island's two pubs on my first night here.

I remember my phone now and go back inside to retrieve it from my handbag, touching the screen to bring it to life, and to my surprise I have five full bars. So, no Wi-Fi, but plenty of coverage. Opening my messaging service, I scroll to Rebecca's name, rereading our last conversation, which took place more than a week ago, and glance toward the top of the screen. With no regard for her privacy, it tells me that she is online.

I've arrived, I tell her. I'm on the island. And then, despite having no reason to believe this, I add: I think you'd like it here.

I send the message and watch as a gray tick appears next to it, then another. A moment later, they turn blue. She's reading it. A rare moment when I know exactly what my daughter is doing.

The word *typing* . . . appears below.

She's replying.

But then it disappears. She's changed her mind.

The picture on her profile vanishes too. I know what this means. That she has blocked me. Temporarily, at least. She does this quite regularly, usually in the immediate aftermath of my contacting her, but I always wake the next day to find her picture restored.

I set the phone down on the table. There is only one more thing I need to do before I head to the village, and that is to take the small, framed photograph of Emma, Rebecca, and me from my suitcase and place it on the table, in full view of the sofa. It was taken years ago when the girls were ten and eight respectively. Brendan isn't in it, of course. If he had been, I'd have burned it. But he remains a presence, after a fashion, for he must have been the person behind the camera. I consider smashing the frame on the floor and tearing the photograph to shreds, because of his ghostly presence, but if I do this, then I will have no pictures of my daughters at all. True, Rebecca will have restored hers by tomorrow morning but there'll be no more of Emma in this lifetime. My failures as a mother have ensured that.

"What do you think?" I ask the cat, who opens a lazy eye and, as if rethinking her earlier fearlessness, leaps from the armchair and marches out the door. I'm not far behind her.

2

It doesn't take long for the people of the island to become intrigued by the stranger who has appeared in their midst. I suppose they rarely encounter outsiders, except during the summer months when the tourists arrive, a prospect I'm already dreading. Holidaymakers from Dublin, after all, might recognize me, so I will need to keep my wits about me then. I'm conscious of my arrogance in assuming that no one on this small atoll could possibly identify me, but I feel reasonably confident that they won't.

A rumor spreads that a woman from the mainland, which usually means Galway, Mayo, or Clare, has rented Peader Dooley's cottage and, in each shop I enter, I am asked to confirm that I am the refugee in question. When I do, I'm greeted with a mixture of excitement, alarm, and, above all, concern for my safety. The general feeling is that my new home is not sufficiently insulated and that, if I remain there, I will surely die from hypothermia.

"It's actually quite warm," I tell the fifth or sixth islander to prophesy my demise, and my Cassandra is preparing to contradict me, to assure me that I'll be dead within the month, when her husband interrupts to say that no, the Dooley cottage was constructed with good bricks.

"Most aren't," he observes, scratching his stubbly chin. There is more hair growing from his ears, nose, and eyebrows than from his head, and it's a disconcerting sight. "Not anymore. And cheap blocks will let the cold in every time. But a cottage with good bricks? They'll protect you. Do you know himself at all?"

"Who?" I ask.

"Your man Dooley."

"No," I tell him, shaking my head. "We conducted our business over email. He doesn't live here, I believe."

"Away across," he replies, nodding in the general direction of the mainland. "'Twas his father, Shay Dooley, built that cottage. Put it together with his own hands. People did, back then. Now, they wouldn't know how. Sure, the old skills are long gone."

I'm trying to imagine the work that must have gone into the construction. Where did the bricks even come from? Or the mortar? How deep are the foundations? And, while he was about it, would it have killed him to have installed a shower?

"You're a writer, I bet," says the woman, with a confident smile on her face. "I'd put a pound to a penny that you are."

"Why do you say that?" I ask.

"It's the sort of thing writers do, isn't it?" she says. "They rent some oul' cottage in the middle of nowhere when they're working on a book, and then off they feck when the thing is finished and go on Pat Kenny or Ryan Tubridy to tell everyone listening how the place changed them. I'm right, amn't I?"

"I'm afraid not," I say, amused by the idea. I have a story to tell, it's true, but I lack the inclination to tell it.

She seems disappointed, as if she had hoped that I was importing a little celebrity to island life and I have thwarted her. Perhaps she envisioned lectures or workshops. A reading in the church. A book group. Anything that would alter the monotony of her daily existence.

"Then what is it you do?" she asks, irritated now, as if I'm being deliberately obtuse by not being a writer.

"I don't do anything," I tell her.

"But before you came here? You must have done something."

"No, nothing at all," I reply, and I hear how ridiculous this sounds, but, after all, it's the truth. I did nothing. I'm an able-bodied, intellectually curious woman of fifty-two years who hasn't drawn a paycheck in almost three decades. What a thing to admit.

Still, for all their prying, I enjoy talking to the islanders. They are, for the most part, a friendly group. And, whatever curiosity they feel, they have the decency not to ask too many questions about why I have exchanged a city of around one and a half million people for an island of four hundred. I had expected more of an inquisition. One or two extract the information that I am from Dublin, and they wrap their arms around themselves then, shaking their heads in wariness, as if they've heard nothing but bad about that place and would no more visit it than journey to the moon.

I develop a routine to my days. I wake at seven and take a long walk along the cliffs, enjoying the feeling of the early-morning wind in my face, before returning to the cottage, where I eat a light breakfast and check when Rebecca was last online. I feel a sense of relief when I see that it was relatively early—say around eleven p.m.—but much later than that and I start to worry. On the rare occasions when I see that she is still using her phone at three or four o'clock in the morning, I grow concerned and wonder what she might be doing. Is there a boy, perhaps, keeping her awake? She's never liked to confide in me about her romantic life but, aged twenty-four, it would be perverse if she hadn't had some experiences in that area. I've only met one who might have been considered a suitor, and that was the young man who took her to her Debs six years ago. Colm, or Colin, or Colum. Something like that. A face still troubled by acne, with a mop of shiny red hair and an air of uncertainty about him. Thin, bony fingers. Brendan behaved as if he was Spencer Tracy in *Father of the Bride*, all gruff and authoritative, but the part didn't suit him. Colm, or Colin, or Colum told me that he wanted to be an entomologist and I think I surprised him, disappointed him even, when I knew what that word meant and he didn't have the pleasure of explaining it to me. It was a job, I thought, that would suit him. Anyway, I never saw him again after the Debs, and if I raised his name, Rebecca would pretend she didn't know who I was talking about.

I have occasionally wondered whether she might be more interested in girls than boys, but no, on reflection, I don't think that's the case. I've noticed her, in unguarded moments, casting glances toward handsome men in shops or restaurants and, anyway, she's not the type to hide a marginal sexuality, as if it was something shameful. If anything, she would revel in it. And she knows it wouldn't matter to me in the slightest who she brought home, although, if I'm honest, I'd prefer it was a boy, just to keep things simple. I'm aware that expressing a sentiment like that can get a person in trouble these days, but life, I feel, is hard enough without adding another layer of difficulty. And to be fair to Brendan, I think he would have felt the same way. Although, whatever she is, he won't be the one walking her up the aisle, should such a day ever come.

And Emma, of course, died before she could fall in love with anyone, so there are no stories there.

The mornings pass quickly. I take a bath, washing my head by submerging myself in the water and blocking out the silence. I clean things that I cleaned the day before. I talk to the cat, who has grudgingly accepted my presence but will not be denied her armchair. I read. I look out the window. I think about the morning when the Gardaí arrived at our front door in Terenure. I tell myself not to think about the morning when the Gardaí arrived at our front door in Terenure. And, in this way, the hours pass and, before I know it, it's almost lunchtime and I can walk down to the village.

There's not much to do there, but it's important to get out and speak to people, not to be seen as the mad Dublin woman hiding out in the cottage above. Also, I have a fear that if I am seen as a recluse, some well-meaning but pushy neighbor will invite me for dinner and then I'll be passed from house to house till they strip the past out of me and I'll have no choice but to up sticks and move again. No, better to be seen as available but standoffish. Whenever I notice one of the islanders looking in my direction, I smile and engage them in conversation. The weather, of course, for where would we all be without conversations about it? The longer stretch in the evenings. The possibility of a storm. They talk of the tides, of their unpredictable ways, but I know little of this subject, even if it does fascinate me.

I go to the new pub for lunch—a sandwich and a bowl of soup—and keep the old pub for when I drop down at night, on the occasions when the isolation gets to me and I need some alcohol in my bloodstream to stop me from slitting my wrists, or to give me the courage to do so. I don't buy any drink for the cottage. That's a slippery slope.

The old pub and the new pub are alike in most respects and are officially named after their owners, but everyone refers to them in this way. The old pub has been serving liquor on the island since 1873 and the current owner is the great-grandson or great-great-grandson of the original publican. The new pub, on the other hand, has only been in operation since 1956 and has changed hands several times in the intervening decades. The current proprietor is a man in his fifties who looks as if he would like to talk to me, but I make sure to carry a book to defend my privacy and this seems to put him off. He's not unattractive, but I have not come to the island in search of romance, and I don't want to encourage him by being too friendly. There's a ring on his finger anyway. I looked, despite myself.

Of course, it's only my vanity that makes me assume he's interested in me, for I am accustomed to being admired, but then I go to the bathroom and, while washing my hands, examine my face in the mirror and continue to be surprised by the changes I see there. The brutal haircut, for one. The skin beginning to dry out now that I no longer apply a succession of daily serums and moisturizers. A decent body, yes, but it's hidden beneath my various layers. There's no particular reason why any man would look at me twice, other than out of loneliness. But, again, I'm not looking for passion from the new pub, just a sandwich and a bowl of soup.

I've only been on the island a week when I am stopped in the street by a man who introduces himself as Fr. Onkin but who invites me to call him Ifechi. May God forgive me, but the first thing I think when I see him is that this man is as black as the ace of spades, a phrase my mother always used but which I have more sense than to say aloud now. He's no islander, that's for sure, but he has a smile that warms me and the most perfect set of teeth I have ever seen on a man. He's young, no more than thirty, and seems genuinely pleased to make my acquaintance.

"And you're Mrs. . . ." he asks, raising an eyebrow, and I almost say the name from which I have unshackled myself but catch myself in time.

"Miss Hale," I tell him, aware how spinsterish this sounds, like a lady's companion in an E. M. Forster novel. "But please, call me Willow."

"What a beautiful name," he says.

"As is yours," I tell him. "Ifechi. I've never heard it before."

"It means the light of God," he replies.

"Appropriate, then."

"Yes, although it was not my choice, of course. My parents', naturally."

"And, if you don't mind my asking, Ifechi," I say, "where do you come from?"

He tells me that he was born in Nigeria, in a place called Benin City, the traditional home of the Edo people. I don't know who the Edo people are and think that I might look them up on Wikipedia when I get back to the cottage, but then remember that I have no Wi-Fi. Perhaps I will search on my phone the next time I'm in the old pub, assuming the promise of a connection there is true. Curiously, the new pub has none. Although it does have a pool table.

"You're new here," he says, half a question, half a statement, and I admit that I am. "We don't get many new people."

"No, I wouldn't imagine so. I suppose everyone is gossiping about me."

"Everyone and their mother," he replies, then breaks into a cheerful laugh, which makes me laugh too. He is a comfortable presence and I like him. "Will we see you on Sunday, Willow?" he asks.

"In the church? I'm afraid not, Ifechi. I'm not that way inclined."

I don't tell him that I've met three popes.

"Of course," he says, and, to my relief, makes no attempt to convert me. "But should you ever feel like a few moments of peace and quiet, the church is open throughout the day and mostly empty. It can be a good place to catch one's thoughts, away from the world. You can talk to God, talk to yourself, or talk to no one at all. If you feel so moved, you can even have a snooze in the pews." He laughs at the rhyme, but this time I just smile. I feel it's a rehearsed line, often repeated.

The truth is, I've never been religious, although I was brought up a Catholic and Brendan insisted that we attend Mass every Sunday when the girls were young. I was happy enough to do so—everyone else did, after all—and stood and knelt at the right moments, shaking hands with neighbors and incanting prayers while never, for even a moment, thinking about the words. Brendan, on the other hand, liked to feel that he was not just part of the community but one of its leaders.

Occasionally, he read the lesson on a Sunday, and it could be embarrassing how much effort he put into the nuance and characters of the Bible stories, adopting ridiculous voices that made the girls blush in mortification, and regularly served as a minister of the Eucharist, dispensing Holy Communion to parishioners when the church was too full for the priest to feed us all on his own.

The church, I might add, was on the grounds of Terenure College, an all-boys school that had, for generations, presented itself as a bastion of rugby and Catholicism. Brendan did not attend that school as a child, but he liked to be seen there on a Sunday morning. He was friends with the school librarian, Fr. Odran Yates, and invited him over for dinner from time to time, the pair of them sitting in our good room talking about rugby and swimming and GAA as if I wasn't even present. If we'd had a son, he would doubtless have been a student, but, fortunately for the child, we did not. The school must feel a debt of gratitude to my husband. Across the last year, he has pushed it off the front pages.

Still, despite my lack of religious scruple, perhaps I will call into Ifechi's church some day. He makes it sound welcoming and it's not as if I have a busy schedule. We shall see.

"You've made quite the sacrifice," I say before we part, and he looks at me quizzically.

"Sacrifice?" he asks. "I don't understand."

"Living here," I tell him. "In such an isolated spot. And, of course, there's the celibacy issue too. That can't be easy." I pause. Why I'm interested in the poor man's sex life, or lack thereof, is anyone's guess. "Forgive me," I say. "I don't know why I said that. It's none of my business. I've only just met you."

"Celibacy is a curse," he says, reaching for my hand, and I allow him to take it. His palms are soft, and, for one strange moment, I wonder how it might feel for them to move across my breasts or between my legs. "But you must understand, there is only one thing in the world that I love more than women."

"And what is that?" I ask.

"God."

"But God won't keep you warm in your bed at night, will he?"

Later, when I too am alone in my single bed, I wonder whether God is looking over me and, if He is, what punishment He will send my way next. A dead daughter. A husband in jail. My family's reputation shattered. An entire country convinced that I was complicit in all of it. What more can He do to hurt me?

"Are you there, God?" I whisper into the darkness, remembering a book title from many years ago. "It's me, Willow."

But, of course, it's not Willow at all. I can call myself Willow Hale till the cows come home but, underneath, I'm still Vanessa Carvin. I just can't let anyone know.

3

Soon, I find myself embroiled in an argument.

It's late morning and I'm reading one of the books I brought with me, a biography of Joan of Arc, when a loud, aggressive rapping sounds on the front door of the cottage. Before I can rise from the sofa, it's flung open, revealing a person of around sixty who, I think, might be a woman, although it's not immediately obvious. She must pay as little attention to her appearance as I do. While my decision to neglect my looks is still new, however, hers seems to have been a lifetime's work.

"There you are, you wee scut," she barks, although she is not looking in my direction. "I knew I'd find you here."

"Who are you?" I say, jumping to my feet, alarmed by this extraordinary intrusion. "What do you want?"

"I've come for bananas," she says, turning to me now, her face red with rage. "You've been feeding bananas, I know you have, so don't deny it." She raises a thick finger and jabs it in the air. "You're not here a wet weekend and you think you can just do as you like?"

I stare at her in bewilderment and glance toward the kitchen area in search of a weapon, should this belligerence turn violent. Unfortunately, there's nothing there but an empty cup and a teaspoon, neither of which seems likely to prove useful should I need to defend myself.

"I don't know what you're talking about," I protest. "I don't have any bananas. I don't even like bananas."

"Bananas!" she roars, before pointing at the cat, who has risen to her feet, and appears to be considering a quick dart out the front door. "You've been feeding Bananas!"

"Bananas is the cat?" I ask, understanding now.

"Of course Bananas is the cat! What else would Bananas be?"

"Well, I don't know her name, do I?" I say, raising my voice for the first time. "She didn't introduce herself when she invited herself in."

"Bananas is a tom," she grunts, and the cat descends from his throne before strolling nonchalantly over to his mistress, delighted to be the center of an argument between two women, thus establishing his sex beyond any doubt.

"I'm sorry," I say, hoping to defuse the situation. "I thought she— he—was a stray."

"There are no strays on the island," she says. "Everyone and every-thing is accounted for." She glances toward the kettle now. "Well, are we having a cup of tea or not?"

I scurry over to the sink and fill the kettle, not daring to protest. The woman has already removed her coat and gloves and is settling herself into the armchair, Bananas' erstwhile retreat.

"You can't feed him," she tells me. "He has irritable bowel syn-drome."

"He wasn't wearing a medical bracelet," I reply. "Anyway, I've only given him a few bits and pieces. Some leftover chicken. A few saucers of milk."

"And he's lactose-intolerant."

A cat with such refined notions seems absurd to me but I choose not to argue. The sound of the water bubbling to a boil fills the room and I take down two mugs from the shelf.

"How do you like it?" I ask.

"How do I like what?"

"Your tea."

"The way God intended. Milk and three sugars."

I wait by the sink, deciding that when I sit, I will take my place at the table, which is a comfortable distance from this extraordinary crea-ture. I glance over at Bananas, who is licking his testicles. How did I never notice them before? I wasn't looking, I suppose.

"Well, I'm sorry," I say, putting a couple of tea bags into the pot and filling it with hot water. "I didn't know. But I do now. So I'll stop."

"He's a wee scut," she insists. "The lads who stayed here before you, they used to feed him too, so he marches over every morning in hope. I'd say he couldn't believe his luck when you showed up."

"What lads?" I ask, bringing the pot over and setting it down on the table. "I thought the cottage was empty before I arrived?"

She waves this away, her expression suggesting that she can't quite believe how stupid I am. "It was three years ago," she says. "They only stayed a month. Queer fellas. We ran them."

"Do you mean strange?" I ask, uncertain how contemporary her vocabulary might be. "Strange in what way?"

"Strange enough," she replies. "Partners, as they say." She makes inverted-comma symbols in the air and rolls her eyes. "Did you ever hear the like?"

"Then you mean they were gay," I tell her. "Not queer."

"Oh, is that what I mean, is it?"

"It is," I tell her. She unsettles me, this woman, but I'm not willing to let her away with such language. There's a lengthy pause while she stares in my direction, getting the measure of me, I suppose, before she replies.

"Gay, then," she concedes, and I realize that I have no reason to be frightened of her, after all. She's just a bully. And like all bullies, one only has to stand up to them and they fall like dominoes. "One of them called himself a painter and the other said he was writing a play, but I didn't believe a word of it."

"Why not?"

She shrugs her shoulders and mutters something that I don't catch.

"They were the last ones to stay here," she says, clearer now. "I don't know if Peader told you."

"He didn't," I admit. "But then, it's none of my business really, is it? Why would I care?"

"I like to know where I'm sleeping," she says.

Now it's my turn to roll my eyes. Perhaps I'm being narrow-minded, but I suspect this woman has never slept in any bed other than her own, on this tiny island, since the day she was born.

"Right," I say, thinking about my small bedroom and wondering how two young men could have slept in that single bed, because it has clearly been a fixture of the cottage for many years, and not something purchased in advance of my arrival. Maybe they enjoyed the closeness of it. Maybe it made them love each other even more. In all my years of sleeping with Brendan, after a brief cuddle when the lights were turned off, we tended to keep as much space between us as possible.

"And how did you run them, if you don't mind my asking?"

"Do you have a slice of cake to go with this, no?" she asks as I pour the tea and hand her a cup.

"I don't," I say.

"Very hospitable."

"How did you run them?"

"A delegation showed up at their door," she says. Now it's her turn to challenge me. She's not going to let a blow-in like me look down her nose at her. "That door there, if you please." She nods in the direction of the front door. "And they were told what was what. We couldn't be having it. Not here. Not on the island."

"Disgraceful," I say. "A mob bullying two young gay men away? What is this, the 1950s? Don't they have as much right to be here as anyone?"

"You make a very weak cup of tea," she replies, ignoring my question. "You should let it brew longer. Did your mammy never teach you that?"

"No," I say. I want to learn more about the bullying of the two boys but find that I haven't the energy to ask any more questions. Rebecca, if she was here, would be dragging the woman out by her ears, but she's young and doesn't yet recognize that life can get in the way of principles. We grow too tired to fight. And so, I limit myself to this: "We have a gay Taoiseach, of course. I'd imagine he'd have something to say about that sort of thing."

"He can say what he likes, that fella," says the woman, and I can tell that she's only a heartbeat away from spitting on the floor at the mention of his name. "But he's never set foot here, has he? I'd say he'd have difficulty finding the island on a map. Go on so. Tell me your name. If you're going to be living here, we might as well be acquainted."

"Are you the census taker?"

"That's a joke, is it?"

"I'm Willow Hale," I tell her, sighing a little, exhausted by her belligerence. "And you?"

"Mrs. Duggan."

"No first name?"

"Mrs."

"Well, I'm pleased to meet you, Mrs. Duggan. Tell me, do you always break into houses unannounced? Most people prefer to be invited in."

"Only vampires," she says and, again, I'm surprised that she would know such a thing. Will I spend my time on this island realizing that all my presumptions about people are wrong? "And I didn't break in, did I? Sure, didn't I see you sitting there through the window? Reading your book. You're one of those, I suppose."

"One of what?"

"Readers."

I don't know how to respond to this remark, which appears to be some form of accusation. I enjoy books, yes, but I'm far from a bibliophile. In Terenure, I was a member of a book club, but that was mostly because I could find no way out of it. My friends were involved, and Brendan liked the idea of the National Swimming Federation wives socializing in civilized or philanthropic ways. We ran fundraisers. Spent a night out on the streets before Christmas to support the homeless. And, yes, we read contemporary novels and sat in each other's living rooms and discussed them. It was never something I enjoyed, if I'm honest. In general, I don't like talking about books. I prefer simply to read them.

"Willow Hale," she says when I haven't replied, mulling over my assumed identity. "You know Nora Hale, I suppose?"

"I don't," I tell her.

"Ah you do," she says irritably, as if I'm just being difficult. "Nora Hale. From Galway. You're one of her people, I'd say?"

"I'm not. I've never heard of her."

"A nice enough woman," she says, considering it, and I suspect this is the greatest compliment she can pay anyone. "But her husband is the devil incarnate."

I say nothing, even though it's obvious that she wants me to ask. But I have no interest in the misadventures of strangers' husbands. I have enough on my hands dealing with the misadventures of my own. Tired of being ignored, Bananas, from the corner, meows, and Mrs. Duggan informs him, in no uncertain terms, that he would be well advised to hold his tongue.

"Have you come far?" I ask finally, aware that I sound like the late queen.

"From over there," she says, nodding in some vague direction that might be anywhere.

"The farm with the cows?"

"That's the one."

"So, we're neighbors."

"For now."

"What does that mean? Do you intend to run me too?"

She smiles, and to my astonishment her face lights up when she does so, and then she throws her head back in laughter. I can't help myself. I laugh too. I taste my tea and offer a further concession.

"You're right," I admit. "It is weak."

"Will you be with us long?" she asks.

"I've taken the cottage on a month-by-month basis. I'll decide in time."

"You don't have parties, do you?" she asks. "We can't be doing with parties."

I stare at her, wondering how she could possibly imagine that I would. *Who would I invite?*

"No. No parties," I assure her.

"Good. The queer lads had their music blaring half the night. Mr. Duggan wanted to come over but was frightened of what might happen if he did, so I had to do it instead. I read them the riot act, have no fear."

"What was he frightened of?"

"That they might try to have their way with him."

I smother a laugh. If Mrs. Duggan is anything to go by, I suspect that her husband would be of no interest to either of them, whose side I have taken in this historic row.

"And you'll be from Dublin, I suppose," she continues, employing a tense that I'm not sure exists in the language.

"I am," I say.

"What part?"

I'm surprised by the question. I can't imagine she knows Dublin at all.

"Terenure," I say.

"The rugby players," she replies, astonishing me even further.

"You mean the school?" I ask.

"I do. Sure, they're always winning cups, aren't they?"

"I'm surprised you'd know such a thing."

"I read the papers," she says, sitting up straighter now, apparently offended. "And I'm what you might call a sports aficionado."

She pronounces the word slowly, carefully in syllables, as if she wants me to be impressed by the extent of her vocabulary.

"It means a person who has an enthusiasm for a subject," she clarifies.

"I know," I say.

"We have little enough of it on the island, of course," she says. "A few good hurlers, I suppose. But they do say that Evan Keogh is as good a footballer as anyone has ever seen."

"Who's Evan Keogh?"

"The Keogh lad," she replies, which clarifies nothing. "Charlie Keogh wants him to go off to England and get a trial with a club over there. But, from what I hear, Evan isn't keen. Charlie's a bitter piece of work, though. Wanted to be a footballer himself but wasn't good enough. Still, I'd bet everything in my pockets on him getting his way in the end. But keep that to yourself, you. I don't want him hammering on my door some evening with a flea in his ear."

"No, I can only imagine how annoying that would be," I say, wondering with whom I would spread such gossip, even if I was interested in it, which I'm not.

"And where, pray tell, is Mr. Hale?" she asks now, raising her voice and looking around, as if a man might unexpectedly appear from the fridge or drop down from the ceiling, like Tom Cruise in that film.

"There is no Mr. Hale," I reply, which is true, for there isn't. There's a Mr. Carvin, of course, but he's nearly two hundred kilometers away in Midlands Prison.

"You're not married?" she asks, raising an eyebrow in disapproval.

"I'm divorced," I say. A lie, but near enough to the truth.

"Marriage is for life," she tells me. "What God joins together, may no man split asunder. You're married."

"I'm divorced," I insist.

"Have it your way. But you're not. We had a divorcée on the island before. She came over after her husband cheated on her and tried to get in with poor Denny Albright."

I have no idea who poor Denny Albright is either, and don't ask.

"And what happened to her?" I ask.

"We ran her."

It occurs to me that I was fortunate not to meet Mrs. Duggan on my first day here. The warmth of her welcome might have undone me entirely.

"And you and Mr. Duggan," I say. "How long have you been married?"

"Forty-five years," she tells me. "We got married on my sixteenth birthday."

"That's very young," I reply. "How old was he?"

"Thirty-one."

There's so much I'd like to say, so much I'd like to know, but, like Bananas, I understand that it's best to remain silent.

"Do you have children?" I ask.

"Of course we do," she snaps, as if even the question is ridiculous. "Eight. Four of each. They're all away now, save Luke. We keep him here to help out on the farm."

"I think I've seen him," I say, for on my perambulations I've been vaguely aware of a figure in the distance, calling out to the cows and herding them around the fields. It disturbs me to hear her speak of the boy as if he's a possession. Doesn't she know that you should love your child, want to spend every moment with them, because you never know when they'll be taken from you?

"Don't get any ideas about Luke," she says, glowering at me now. "He's a good boy and we'd like to keep him that way."

"I'll do my best," I say.

"Do more than your best."

The tea has turned cold now, and I hope that she'll stand up and leave, taking the troublesome cat with her, but she shows no desire to go. Instead, she asks the question that I knew was coming next. The one I had hoped to avoid.

"And you?" she asks. "Do you have any children yourself?"

4

I was never what you might call a natural mother, but I loved my daughters and did everything I could to ensure that they enjoyed a happy and secure childhood. My own had been untroubled and, having come through it without any noticeable scars, I simply emulated my own mother's behavior. Businesslike and efficient, without being overly sugary.

I am, I suppose, part of that last generation of Irish women who did not recognize that they had the right to a career outside the home, and the courage to demand one. I just took it for granted that, one day, I would meet a suitable man, marry, bear children, and live a standard middle-class existence. I didn't expect or ask for more.

When Brendan and I married, he was keen to start a family immediately, but, as I hoped to wait a few years, I made the mistake of suggesting that we use the condoms that were finally accessible in Ireland. Too embarrassed to go into a chemist's and ask for them from a judgmental pharmacist, I had made my way into Trinity College, where I'd half-heartedly completed an undergraduate degree in English literature a few years earlier, and where enthusiastic, priapic students handed them out free of charge to all and sundry from large plastic tubs, a kick to the governments and clergy that had controlled the state for so long. There was something erotic about accepting a handful of prophylactics from a handsome, grinning boy only a few years younger than me, who smiled as if to say, *You're doing it, then? So am I! We could do it together, if you like?*, but when I presented a trio of foil-encased liberators to Brendan, he looked at me as if I was the Whore of Babylon and insisted that I throw them away.

"What did we get married for if not to have children?" he asked, and I couldn't think of a good answer to his question, which is to neither his nor my credit. So we went about things in the usual way, five or six nights out of seven, but, try as we might, no baby was conceived.

Despite his old-fashioned tendencies, I was happy with Brendan during those early years. His unconscious disdain for women seemed no different to that of most Irish men, although not, perhaps, the sensual boy who had given me the johnnies under the shade of Front Arch, his fingers stroking my palm as he did so, and whose face, for some inexplicable reason, remained in my mind for years afterward, occasionally supplanting Brendan's at the moment of climax. No, that boy looked like he loved, adored, and worshipped women. As if he couldn't get enough of us. But, a decade older than me, Brendan was more attuned with the previous generation than his and didn't care for the tide of change that was decanting across the land. He would switch channels whenever President Robinson appeared on the news; her voice, he claimed, gave him a headache. He had an inexplicable hatred for Hillary Clinton, who had only recently risen to prominence. And while he addressed all the boys who were making their way through the junior ranks of the National Swimming Federation by name, those lacking in a penis were simply called "The Girls," a homogeneous and indivisible collective.

As head of that organization, at a time when swimming was becoming a more high-profile sport in Ireland, Brendan thrived on his minor celebrity status, embracing every opportunity to appear before a camera or microphone. He was a regular contributor to radio programs and, once in a while, would be invited as a guest on *The Late Late Show*, where I would sit in the audience and play the part of dutiful wife. Perhaps it was his growing arrogance that proved the reason why he was loath to confide in a doctor our failure to conceive, particularly when the doctor in question was a woman.

Her name was Dr. Jennifer Soren, and, at our first meeting, she asked what I assume was a perfectly standard set of questions about our sex life. Naturally, I felt a little awkward answering them, but I recognized their necessity. Brendan, however, found them intrusive, and when she asked whether I had been sexually active before meeting my husband, he practically leaped from his chair in outrage. This, in fact, had long been a bone of contention between us, for when we were dating we had revealed our sexual histories to each other, and it turned out that while I had had three previous lovers, two of whom had been one-night stands, Brendan was still a virgin. Although this might seem a little bizarre for a thirty-four-year-old man, in 1995 Ireland it was not quite as eccentric or worrisome as it would be today. And I rather liked the fact that he was an innocent. It suggested to me, wrongly, that he respected women and did not see us as creatures who existed purely to satisfy his needs.

The truth was that his parents had instilled a fear of sexuality in him from an early age, convincing him that he should be ashamed of his natural desires. I never knew them well—within five years of my meeting Brendan, they were both dead—but I always felt they believed there was something distasteful about their son having a girlfriend at all, let alone a wife. The day he moved out of their home, which coincided with our return from our honeymoon, was an exercise in mortification, his mother crying at the kitchen table and his father despairing over who was going to cut the grass from now on.

Repression was their legacy to their son, who struggled with my inconsequential sexual history, and I teased him about being so conventional until I recognized that he did not appreciate the joke. It was a subject that soon became out of bounds for us, but, when we argued, he could always be relied upon to suggest that he should be congratulated for taking me as his wife when other men would have walked away. The implication, of course, being that I was a slut. But, in the minds of men like Brendan, all women are sluts and are to be treated as such. The words might have changed over the years, each one replaced by something more toxic and violent, but there is always one in common parlance, mostly uttered by men, but sometimes by handmaiden women, each one designed to make us understand how deeply men's desire for us makes them hate us even more.

Things grew more difficult when, having conducted a series of tests and found nothing amiss, Dr. Soren invited Brendan to produce a sperm sample for analysis. He was enraged by the suggestion that our inability to conceive could have anything to do with him and, at first, refused, which led to the first great argument of our marriage.

"I think you've been dishonest with me," he said as we sat at home, Brendan fuming at the indignity of being asked to masturbate into a cup, especially as he knew that he would ultimately have no choice but to submit to the doctor's request if we were ever to have a baby.

"In what way?" I asked.

"I need you to tell me the truth, Vanessa," he said. "Those fellas you were with before me. Did you get pregnant by one of them, is that it? Did you go across the water?"

"You can't possibly imagine that I would keep something like that a secret from you," I said.

"Well, what else am I to think?" he roared. "I've read about it. Women who don't keep themselves tidy, then take the boat to Liverpool to have the baby sucked out of them, and then they can't get pregnant afterward. Sure, their insides are all destroyed."

"Dr. Soren has already said that there's nothing wrong with my 'insides,' as you put it," I replied, trying to control my temper. "I've never been pregnant, I've never had an abortion, but if I had, I would have told you, and I wouldn't be ashamed of it."

"That doesn't surprise me," he said. "Sure you had no shame about riding those other lads before me, did you?"

"Not a bit," I said, wanting to hurt him now, just as he was hurting me. "You're just jealous, that's all, that you didn't get your share when you were younger. I'm surprised you're so offended at the idea of wanking into a cup; you must have spent years playing with yourself in your mammy's upstairs room."

He didn't like that one bit, but it was the truth, I knew it was. We didn't speak for days afterward, and something shifted in our relationship then. Eventually, however, fuming and discomfited, he submitted to Dr. Soren's requests. And, as it turned out, there was nothing wrong with him either. We were just being unlucky. The only advice she could give us was to keep trying, which we did, and then, in time, I fell pregnant with Emma.

I should add that unpleasant moments like this were the exception between us and not the rule. For the most part, Brendan was a kind and attentive husband, the sort of man who might surprise me with an unexpected dinner out or a weekend away. He chose birthday and Christmas presents with care—I never woke up to a food blender, unwrapped and still in the Arnott's bag, with the receipt languishing at the base—and kept himself fit and well groomed, as much for my sake as his own. He only unearthed his nasty side whenever his fragile masculinity was brought into question. And I loved him, I truly did. Although, of course, as it turned out, I barely knew him at all.

Emma was the most uncomplicated baby a first-time mother could wish for. She slept well, ate whatever was put in front of her, and seemed endlessly fascinated by the world around her. I suffered no postnatal depression and grew skeptical over the horror stories I'd heard about how difficult motherhood could be. When I took her for walks in her pram, other women stopped to comment on how beautiful she was and, as if she was aware of the compliments coming her way, she would smile and extend her arms toward them. Maybe she was trying to get away from me.

To my surprise, however, Brendan, the prime mover in our decision to become parents, was not as attentive a father as I had expected. He was disappointed not to have had a son and made no attempt to hide this. It wasn't unusual that he didn't change nappies or do any of the feeds, most men didn't in those days, so that didn't bother me, but I was baffled by his indifference toward the baby. Whatever disappointment I felt, however, was more than compensated for by the bond I was building with my daughter and, after a year passed, it was I who suggested that we have another child in order that Emma would not grow up without a playmate.

"We'll try for a boy this time," was his response, as if either of us had any say over the outcome. And, a year later, Rebecca was born.

The opposite of her sister in almost every respect, Rebecca was problematic from the moment of conception. My pregnancy left me feeling enfeebled and bilious, and while Emma had popped painlessly out of me, as if she simply wanted to get going on life without another moment's delay, Rebecca's was a long and challenging labor that required the intervention of two doctors and a fleet of nurses. When she finally appeared in a tsunami of blood, shit, and screaming, Brendan looked like he was going to throw up with the drama of it all, and when he saw that I'd been delivered of a girl, he muttered, "Ah Christ!" under his breath, loud enough for those in the room to exchange looks that suggested this would be the talk of the tearoom later.

When we brought her home, she was impossible. She would only sleep when I was awake but insisted on attention when I could scarcely keep my eyes open. She refused most foods but demanded to sample everything that came into her orbit before scrunching her face up in indignation as the flavors hit her taste buds, before spitting them back at me. She would scream for no reason, earth-shattering sounds that bore into my skull and made me feel that I was going mad. She hated being bathed, and this nightly ritual soon became so traumatic that I assigned the job to Brendan, refusing to have anything more to do with it.

"Sure what do I know about washing a baby?" he asked, as if I was asking him to scale Mount Kilimanjaro or paint an Old Master.

"You know how to wash yourself, don't you?" I shouted at him, unable to put up with his indolence any longer. "It's no different. There's just less of her."

The only thing, or rather the only person, who could soothe Rebecca was Emma, who would toddle over to her sister as she lay screaming on her mat and collapse next to her, placing a small hand upon her forehead, and, in that instant, she would calm down. Although they were different in so many ways, there was an extraordinary connection between them from the start and I was grateful that Emma did not show any signs of jealousy. She had a way with Rebecca that both Brendan and I lacked. Or maybe Rebecca simply preferred her to us.

Was I as insentient to Emma's needs even then? Was I a terrible mother from the start, driven, as I was, by status and my busy social life, viewing her as just another accessory, like my necklaces or earrings or perfumes? If I dwell on these questions too much, I will bang my head against the wall until I, like her, am dead. I failed her. And yet they are ever-present, fighting to be answered, challenging me constantly.

That sisterly bond was to grow and strengthen in the years that followed, and while they say that a parent never gets over the death of a child, I think it is Rebecca who will suffer the most in the decades to come. Emma, only two years older, was the mother she needed, and she can't forgive me her loss. It's an injustice, but I suspect she blames me more than Brendan for what happened.

The next few years were so taut that there was no more talk of babies after that, until both girls had started school, when I experienced an unexpected rush of loneliness and decided that I might like one more.

I suggested as much to Brendan, but he refused even to countenance the idea. (By now, he had decided that condoms were not such a terrible idea after all, and our sex life, while hardly as busy as it had once been, had not entirely vanished.)

"I'm surrounded by women as it is," he said, trying to make a joke of it. "I'm not going to be outnumbered even more."

"But we might have a boy this time," I protested, but he wouldn't be convinced, and, in time, I made my peace with it. A family of four, after all, was more than many had. Not quite a Gentleman's Family, but close enough.

Still, I've always felt certain that we were supposed to have a third child, and that if we had, it would have been a boy. I'm so convinced of this that I occasionally find myself mourning the son that I did not have as much as the daughter that I did.

I would have called my son Zac, a name I have always loved, but in our family, he would have been called Zaccy, until puberty hit, when he would have demanded that we revert to his given name. And, although he would have been the youngest, I believe this ghost-child would have protected us all.

5

I take Ifechi's advice and decide to make a pilgrimage to the church, standing outside for a long time before deciding whether to enter. If there is a God, I want to make it clear to Him that I'm not here for spiritual reasons, but simply to understand the island better. It's a small stone building, the right size, I suppose, for such a tiny population, and, unlike the much grander one I attended throughout my married life, it has a humility to it. The front doors are open, but from where I stand, with the sun shining before me, I can see nothing but darkness ahead. Still, something summons me inside.

It takes a few moments for my eyes to adjust to the interior gloom, and I instinctively reach out to dip my index finger into the holy-water font before touching it to my forehead. It was hot outside but it's cool in here. On a cold day, I imagine those conditions are reversed, as if the church is a place of opposites. I remain at the back for a few moments, my attention taken by a wire rack holding a collection of information booklets that look as if they're even older than the building itself. I notice the familiar figure of Padre Pio, his hands joined in prayer, on the cover of one; the Virgin Mary, her arms outstretched in supplication, on another. Beneath my feet, the ground is tiled with what appears to be a granite mosaic, sprinkled with an occasional floral design.

There are few people present. A man seated at the end of the second pew, hunched over with his head in his hands. A woman, six rows behind him, on her knees and clicking a set of rosary beads between her fingers as her lips move soundlessly. Most surprising of all is the sight of a teenage boy seated only a few feet from where I stand, next to the confession box. I glance in his direction and, at the same moment, a light flicks on above the box and the boy stands, opens the door, and makes his way inside. He can't be more than seventeen, and not only does it surprise me that he would have sins to confess, but, if he does, that he would have any interest in doing so.

Churchgoing, as I have mentioned, was more Brendan's area than mine, because Fr. Yates's friendship mattered to him, and the parishioners' recognition of him strengthened his belief in his own importance. What he never understood, however, is that religion begins in the soul, not the ego.

I'm drawn to the Stations of the Cross, seven hanging on one wall, and seven on the other. I've always been intrigued by these, for an artistic priest can use a little imagination in the commissioning of a design as there seems to be no demands on their style and they differ from church to church. Here hangs a set of fabrics, painted in black ink upon a linen background, that recall the work of Japanese calligraphers. They are very beautiful. As I cross the nave to the right-hand side and examine the tenth station, *Jesus Is Stripped of His Garments*, I am struck by the expression the artist has imposed upon His face, blending confusion, dismay, and humiliation. For once, the Son of God appears almost human.

The whole business of the Twelve Apostles has always bothered me, the hard-nosed maleness of their clique, the decision from the start to exclude women from their number. Most became saints, I think, but did that prevent them from leering at the women who served their food, or making vulgar remarks about girls they noticed on the streets? Did James lose interest during the Sermon on the Mount, his attention captured by the breasts of a young woman seated near him? Did John lure a serving girl at the Wedding at Cana into an anteroom and press himself against her, ignoring her pleas to be released? And what of Andrew, or Matthew, or Judas Iscariot? Did they take women without permission, forcing their unwashed parts into unwilling bodies whenever they felt so moved? All these men, all these fucking men. Sacred and hallowed and venerated for two thousand years. And yet it was the women, and only the women, who were there for Him at the end when the men betrayed Him, denied Him, ran from Him, pocketed their thirty pieces of silver for traducing Him. Here is Veronica wiping His face. Here are the women of Jerusalem greeting Him as He carries His burden. Here is Mary, weeping at the base of the cross. Loyal women; unfaithful and treacherous men. The former left to gather up His soiled and bloody clothes; the latter sanctified.

Oh, I feel such anger.

It's now that my mind turns to Gareth Wilson and Niamh Loomis.

Gareth, that formidable man, six foot four in height and built of pure iron, standing in the dock of the Four Courts in Dublin, focused entirely on salvaging his reputation as he spoke of the man he personally installed as director of the National Swimming Federation, and by whose side he stood for years. Swearing that he knew nothing of my husband's behavior and can still hardly believe it, for a more dedicated servant of the sport he cannot imagine. And then Niamh, his secretary of fifteen years, being questioned by Brendan's barrister, who feigned disbelief that such crimes could have taken place without her noticing any of it.

"You never had any children yourself, Miss Loomis, did you?" he asked, as if this had any relevance to the matter at hand. "Or married, for that matter. Was there a reason for that?"

Objections raised, the question left unanswered, but the implication of her nature left to settle in the minds of the jury. It is imperative to find a woman to blame for a man's crimes.

Then my own interrogation, of course, the questions approved by my husband, where the culpability was extended to me.

Did you love your husband, Mrs. Carvin?

Did you have a natural sexual relationship with your husband, Mrs. Carvin?

Were you ever unfaithful to your husband, Mrs. Carvin? You struggled to conceive your first child, didn't you, Mrs. Carvin?

Were you affectionate with your husband, Mrs. Carvin, or could you be, shall we say, prone to mood swings?

Would you call yourself a good wife, Mrs. Carvin?

From above, the chorus of hissing from a group of mothers who would have tumbled into the dock to tear my husband limb from limb if they could, turning their fury on anyone who tried to stop them, their teeth bared, their fingers curled like claws.

Next to me during all these testimonies sat Rebecca, her body rigid, her face set like stone, grinding her teeth in so annoying a fashion that I wanted to slap her.

And finally, after his conviction, after his sentencing and his disgrace, the pundit who wrote in his newspaper column that while his actions should be condemned, no one should forget just how much Brendan Carvin had done for Irish sport and that, in the end, we should be grateful for that at least. Outrage, of course. Social media up in arms. The usual half-hearted apology—*if I offended anyone*—but he meant what he had written.

The sound of someone releasing a cry of pain drags me from my reminiscences, and I look ahead and realize that the man at the end of the second pew is Tim Devlin, proprietor of the new pub, the man who always seems inclined to talk to me when he brings me my sandwich and bowl of soup, and whose eye I deliberately avoid so as not to give him false hope. His right hand has transformed into a fist, and he is lifting and dropping it onto his knee with metronomic insistence. This is a man in pain. This is a man with something on his conscience. The church turns claustrophobic, and I move away from the Stations, making my way back along the nave toward the doors. As I do so, I notice the teenage boy once again, for he has emerged from the confessional now, and is on his knees, his eyes closed, muttering his penance. I wonder what his friends would say if they could see him. They would mock him, I expect, but I find myself moved by such piety, which is rare in the young. It's rare in the old too, for that matter.

Outside, emerging into the sunlight, I inhale deeply, filling my lungs with air, and feel a sense of relief to have escaped a building that exists solely to comfort the troubled. There is birdsong in the air and a playful scurrying somewhere in the grass beneath me, which needs cutting but, in its unshorn state, provides a useful hiding place for unseen life. I sit down on a bench and am enjoying the feeling of the sunshine on my face when Fr. Onkin appears from the church and strolls toward me, smiling, as ever.

"Good morning, Willow," he says, opening his arms wide, displaying the palms of his hands. "You changed your mind, I see."

"Think of me as a tourist, Ifechi," I say, nodding toward the space next to me and inviting him to sit down. "I'm only here to gawk at the splendor of the place and see if I can grab the smell of incense."

"You are nothing as transitory as a tourist," he says, settling himself beside me. "I think there is much more to you than that."

"That's only because you don't know me. Inside, I'm completely empty."

He shakes his head. He's not going to argue with me.

"Has it ever occurred to you," I ask after an awkward silence, "that faith is little more than a matter of geography?"

"In what way?" he asks.

"Well, think about it," I say. "Ireland has long been a Catholic country. Almost everybody born here was christened Catholic but had no say in the matter. Some take to it like a duck to water and build their lives around it. Others wear it as a winter coat. Then there are those who have no interest in it whatsoever but still send their children to make their First Holy Communion or their Confirmation. But if they'd been born in Israel, say, or Tehran, or Moscow, they never would have been Catholic to begin with, would they? Even the Pope, and all his predecessors, are only Catholics because of where they came from. All those Italians for so many centuries. Would any of them have discovered Catholicism if they'd been brought up in Tokyo?"

"Some, perhaps," he says. "Faith has a way of finding you."

"And what about you?" I ask. "Were you born into it?"

"In my country," he says, "there are two tribes. Muslims in the north, some Sunni, some Shia, and Christians in the south. But most of those Christians are Protestant, not Catholic. Maybe only one in five people in Nigeria consider themselves Catholic. I myself was brought up Protestant."

"Really?" I say, surprised. "So what made you defect, if that's the right word?"

He turns his face toward the bright blue sky above us, or perhaps toward heaven, and smiles. I understand. He's not going to tell me. He too has secrets.

From the door of the church, the teenage boy emerges, pulling a cheap pair of sunglasses from the open neck of his T-shirt. He's taller than I realized, and very good-looking, with an athletic build, blond curly hair, and smooth skin. He glances in our direction and raises a hand to Ifechi, who nods back as the boy pulls his backpack on and continues on his way.

"That can't be very common," I say.

"And what is that?" he asks.

"A boy his age. Going to confession."

He says nothing. Although I witnessed it with my own eyes, the boy's business inside the church is not something he can discuss with me.

"It is true," he says, after much thought, "that I do not see as many youthful faces in my congregation on a Sunday as I would wish. But there are some. That boy, Evan, is one."

"Brought by his parents, I suppose."

"Some are interested, even if they would never dare to admit it."

"When I was his age, we all had to go," I tell him. "It would have been unheard-of not to. And I brought my own children too, even though I'm not a believer. So I suppose that makes me just as big a hypocrite."

"But something must have made you bring them," he insists. "Perhaps some part of you was hoping to receive the Spirit, even if you didn't realize it?"

"I brought them to keep my husband happy," I tell him. "I don't know how much you know about Irishwomen, Ifechi, but that's what we do. It's what we've been doing for centuries now, and look where it's got us."

"And where is that?"

"Here. To some godforsaken island in the Atlantic Ocean, where we know no one and no one knows us."

"This island is not godforsaken," he tells me quietly, placing a hand gently atop my own. "No place is."

"It was a turn of phrase, that's all," I tell him, for I don't want to offend the man, who seems kind and devoted to his calling. Although,

God knows, I'm no judge of character. "I'm sure you bring a lot of support to your congregation."

Another exit from the church. This time, it's the publican. He's walking quickly, his head bowed, unsettled by whatever interactions inside he had with the Lord. He doesn't look in our direction but makes his way toward the gate before turning left, in the direction of his place of business.

"Is he all right?" I ask, and Ifechi raises an eyebrow.

"In what sense?"

"He seemed upset. I saw him banging his fist against his leg."

"Mr. Devlin has been through much trauma," he tells me.

"Has he indeed?" I ask, intrigued now. I'm not a gossip, I never have been, not even when I lived in Terenure and counted the other mothers in the parish among my friends. But life moves slowly on the island and a little bit of scandal would liven things up. As long as it's not my scandal, that is.

"Oh yes," replied Ifechi quietly, but I can tell from his tone that he's not going to elaborate. I don't ask anything further. It would be beneath me even to try.

"Well, Ifechi," I say, rising to my feet now. "I should be on my way."

"Will I see you here again, Willow?" he asks, and I think about it.

"It's not impossible."

"If you ever want to talk, you can always knock on my door, and I will be happy to converse."

"Thank you . . . Father," I say, employing his correct title for the first time. He is a man worthy of my respect.

"Whatever has brought you here will one day be little more than a memory. Trust in the Lord, Willow. He trusts in you."

I shake my head, disappointed that he would end our conversation in such a way. "I'd never trust a man again, Ifechi," I tell him, reverting to his given name. "I'm not that stupid."

6

I wake in the night to what sounds like a large animal scrambling across the roof of the cottage. It is as dark as night gets here, which is a darkness I have never known before, and, nervous for what might be lurking outside, I turn on my bedside lamp and glance at the clock, which reads 2:35 a.m. I lie very still, hoping the noise was simply an intruder in a dream, but no, there it is again, and I have no choice but to get up and investigate.

I have felt no fear since arriving on the island, even here in the comparative isolation of the cottage, but then I've never been the type to scare easily. However, I can feel my heart beating faster inside my chest as my anxiety levels rise. It crosses my mind that, should something untoward occur, a community like this would most likely stand together to protect one of its own against any accusations levelled by an outsider.

But my mind is moving too fast toward a calamitous conclusion, and I tell myself to remain composed, that it was probably nothing more than some nocturnal animal on night patrol. I pull on a heavy jumper over my nightdress, slide my feet into my slippers, and step into the cold living room, standing silently in the center, listening, waiting.

All seems quiet now, but it is not a natural silence. It is the sound of someone trying not to make a sound, a phrase I read in a novel once and that stayed with me. I reach for my phone, which is charging in the socket by the wall, and press the home button. The screensaver is a picture of Emma and Rebecca taken on that last holiday in Wexford, the day before Emma died. They have their arms around each other, and both are smiling, wearing sunglasses because it was a fine summer's day. I don't quite know why I'm bothering—is it simply for the reassurance of seeing their faces?—for who can I call? There isn't a police station on the island. Should a crime occur, a Garda is apparently dispatched from Galway to make the necessary investigations. Still, it's in my hands now, so I open the messaging app and look at my most recent text to my surviving daughter. She's unblocked me once again and changed her picture. I press the required button to allow the image to fill the screen, then I save it to my photos. It was taken in a pub, and Rebecca is sticking her tongue out flirtatiously at the photographer. The surroundings are familiar to me, but it's not Terenure. Somewhere in the city center, I think. Is it Neary's? I think it might be. But who took the picture? Her expression suggests a certain intimacy so it's probably a boy. She'll be asleep now, I assume, so it should be safe to message without suffering the indignity of being immediately blocked.

If I'm still here in Winter, I type. I think it will be hard to tell day from night.

The message sends, a single gray tick appears. I watch it for a moment, just in case it doubles, then turns blue, but no.

Returning the phone to its charger, I move toward the front door, opening it cautiously and looking outside. It is a fine night, not a breeze in the air, and a waxing moon offers little illumination to the sweep of fields that stretch down toward the sea. I remember when one of our book club insisted on our reading *The Hours*, and I could not face it, even though it was short, so watched the film instead, and then read a little about Virginia Woolf online before our meeting, desperate to have something intelligent to say. I spoke about how she filled her pockets with stones before walking into the river, all her cares scattered behind her like confetti on the riverbank. Would I be missed if, tonight, I followed her example? Would I even be found? I read that it took three weeks for the poor woman's body to be discovered, and who knows what terrible condition it was in by then. I'd prefer mine to float away and offer sustenance to the creatures of the sea, my flesh becoming one with theirs as my bones sank to the ocean floor, settling peacefully into the sand to rest there for eternity.

When Emma's body was retrieved from the beach near Curracloe, she was taken to the mortuary at Wexford General Hospital, where Brendan and I identified her together. He broke down when the sheet was lowered to reveal her face, but I found myself unable to cry. It didn't seem real to me at the time. After only twelve hours in the water, her features hadn't grown bloated, but still, the body that lay before me did not seem like that of my daughter but rather like a poor approximation of her. Something one might see at a waxworks. The attendant asked whether this was, in fact, Emma, and I said, "I think so," an answer that did not satisfy him, and so he turned to Brendan, who was less equivocal in his response. And then she was covered once again, and we were led from the room. All the time, I felt as if I were in a television show, or a film; it seemed impossible that such a thing could happen in real life.

I step a few feet away from the cottage now, the better to see the roof, but nothing makes its presence felt until a shape darts past my ankles and charges through the open door. I'm too surprised to scream, and by the time my breath is recovered I see that it is only Bananas, out on one of his late-night hunting sessions. Relieved, and feeling a little foolish, I'm torn between reprimanding him and wanting to take him in my arms. Despite Mrs. Duggan's demands that he stay away, he has continued to be a regular visitor, but I've stopped giving him food on account of the alleged irritable bowel syndrome. I continue to offer saucers of milk, though. I don't buy the lactose intolerance for even a moment. He's a cat, after all. And cats drink milk.

Something draws me down the path that leads to the sea and I make my way along, guided by the moon and the glistening light that dances on the waves like sparks from a flint. It takes no more than ten minutes to reach the beach. I stroll along it most afternoons and could find my way there with my eyes closed. The small groups of teenagers who live on the island generally cavort around it with a mixture of excitement and tentativeness. Now that the weather is improving, the boys peacock with their shirts off, displaying scrawny chests and thin legs, while the girls tease them by removing their clothes beneath towels before magically reappearing a few moments later in two-piece swimsuits. In the sea, the young people behave chaotically, unable to control their desires and frustrations. They are masters of all they survey here, but I wonder how they will survive when adulthood takes them to Dublin, London, or further afield. They are water babies, nourished by the waves, and they will struggle when they are, by necessity, dragged to dry land.

It was through swimming, of course, that Brendan and I met, when I was twenty-one and he a decade older. I had a trip planned to Greece with two friends, to the island of Kos, and, embarrassed that I had never learned, I signed up for an intensive course of sessions in my local pool, where Brendan was assigned to be my coach. I had expected a woman to teach me and felt slightly unnerved when this tall, good-looking man approached in shorts and T-shirt, with bare legs and feet, to introduce himself. Naturally I was in my swimsuit at the time, which felt like a strange way to encounter a man for the first time. I was glad when he invited me to descend the ladder into the water, for although I was confident that I had a decent body, it was unsettling to stand in such near-nakedness before him.

He was a good teacher, calm, patient, and deliberate, and it only took about six classes before my confidence grew. His too, I suppose, because he invited me out for a drink then and, having developed a crush on him, I said yes. It was so strange to go out on that first date, when both of us were fully dressed for the first time, my hair combed and not hidden beneath a cap. Goggle-less. There was a curious sensuality to it; the opposite experience of most couples who, over time, move from clothed toward a state of undress.

I didn't keep up the swimming after we were married, only starting again when Emma was a baby, when I took to driving to Dún Laoghaire after lunch every day and taking a dip in the Forty Foot. You could always rely on two or three other young mothers with children to be there and we would entrust our offspring to each other as we dived into the icy water and felt the good of it on our skin. Part of the fun was the fury on the faces of the men, who still resented the presence of women in this once sacrosanct area. Some even continued the ancient practice of swimming naked in the hope that this would intimidate us into leaving them in peace, but it would have taken more than a bunch of fat sixty-year-olds with flabby bellies drooping over sagging cocks to frighten us away.

When he learned of these afternoon trips, Brendan accused me of keeping this from him, and he wasn't entirely wrong. I wanted something for myself, even if it did echo his activities as he ascended the ranks of the National Swimming Federation. He was one of those who believed that women had no business being at the Forty Foot and, when he asked me whether there were naked men there, I said there were, on occasion, and he went into one of his moods and wouldn't come out of it for days. Unwilling to argue, I asked would he prefer that I didn't go there anymore, and he said he would, sure wasn't there a perfectly good swimming pool in Terenure College and it had a ladies' morning every Wednesday and Friday, when both Emma and I could get into the pool together.

And to keep the peace, I did as he asked. I never returned to the Forty Foot, nor did I ever again meet the friends I had inadvertently made.

On the beach now, I remove my slippers and my toes burrow into the cold, moist sand. It has none of the pleasing, warm sensation I am accustomed to from daytime, so I step forward into the water itself, intending only to wet my ankles, then feel the tide hurl itself against me in a fury, surprised and enraged by my intrusion. It dampens the base of my nightdress as if to say, *Away you, away!* It is cold. Oh, it is so cold. *Was it as cold as this when you walked into the sea in Wexford, Emma? Did you plunge down into the water to break the shock of it, or did you step gingerly forward, one eye on the horizon, uncertain whether you really meant what you were doing? And how far out were you when you knew that there was no way back, even for a strong swimmer like you? In that moment, did you feel panic? Regret? Fury? Relief? I have so many questions for you, my darling girl, but you aren't here to answer them.*

I recall Rebecca's question of me, after it all came out.

Did you know all along and just didn't care?

I plunge down into the water now, submerging myself up to my neck, and when my body has adjusted to the temperature, I sink lower again, beneath the waterline. Immediately, the sounds change. It's a different universe under here. A song from an old Disney movie that the girls watched hundreds of times when they were children forms in my head and I open my eyes, looking for friendly lobsters and dancing prawns. But I am alone down here, except for the microscopic life forms moving around me, each one wondering why this interloper has disturbed their agreeable night. I don't feel cold anymore but know that when I raise my head into the world again, I will. I anticipate this with regret, even anger. I would rather stay down here, like Emma did, and, tomorrow, float in on the tide.

Water has been the undoing of me. It has been the undoing of my family. We swim in it in the womb. We are composed of it. We drink it. We are drawn to it throughout our lives, more than mountains, deserts, or canyons. But it is terrible. Water kills.

I can't stay down here any longer. With no stones in my pockets, my body forces me back to the surface, and I emerge, gasping. Instinctively, I put my hands to my forehead to brush the hair out of my eyes but, of course, it is gone, scalped close, not daring to grow back in case it provokes me to get the scissors out again.

I drag myself back toward the beach, weighed down by the sodden nightdress and the woolen jumper, and look up toward the sky, feeling strangely calm now, before making my way back toward the path that leads me home, if home it is.

And it is then that I feel eyes on me, like a torch pointed toward my heart. Turning my head in the direction of the Duggan farm, what light the moon offers reveals a figure in the distance, observing me. I cannot make out his face—he might be a scarecrow for all the movement he is making—but there is a moment of connection, where we are the only two people in the world. I pull off my jumper, for it is too heavy, the saturated wool weighing me down, and then, in an act of defiance, I slip out of the wet nightdress too and march naked toward my door. Why shouldn't I, after all? It is my door. It is my body.

Watch me all you like, Luke Duggan, if it makes you happy.

Back inside, I feel in desperate need of a hot bath and a cup of tea.

Bananas has left me a gift by the kitchen table, but what use have I of a dead mouse is a mystery to me.

Later, when sleep returns, I dream of the boy on the hill, but this time he is not just standing there watching, he is making his way down toward the sea too, only it is a different sea, an unfamiliar one, and he is throwing himself into the waves with the grace of an Olympian. He vanishes from sight for a moment, and when he emerges, he draws the air back into his empty lungs, but he is not empty-handed. No, he has found my daughter.

He is holding Emma in his arms.

He is carrying her back to the shore, back to safety, back to me.

7

When he knocks on my door a few days later, I realize that I've been expecting him to call. At first, I don't even know for sure that it is him, but the embarrassed look on his face, not to mention the vague resemblance to his mother, gives the game away. He's tall, with sandy hair that falls over his eyes, which I notice are two different colors, one pale blue, the other green. He's in his late twenties, I'd imagine, and carrying a not unpleasant musk of sweat about him.

"I'm sorry to bother you," he says, unable or unwilling to look me in the eye. "I'm Luke. I live in the—"

"The farm over there," I say, nodding in the direction of his family's land. "Yes, I know."

"I wondered if I could have a word."

The poor boy looks so mortified that I step out of the way and invite him in. Bananas glances up from the armchair, perhaps surprised to see a familiar face here, and jumps down onto the floor in deference.

"You may as well take it," I say, pointing toward the vacated seat. "He doesn't do that for just anyone. Will you have a cup of tea?"

"I won't," he says. "I'll not stay long." He sits. "Only I wanted to apologize to you."

"Oh yes?" I ask, taking my usual spot on the sofa. "For what?"

"A couple of nights back, I was . . . well, I was outside late. Just having a smoke above. And I saw you coming back from the beach. I didn't mean to see you, but I think you noticed me up there. It might have seemed like I was watching you, but I wasn't spying or anything like that. I'm not some . . ." He searches for the right word. "I'm not one of those types, do you know? Who'd be out in the middle of the night looking at women in that way."

"It's fine," I say, not wanting him to feel any more tortured than he already does. "I'm not surprised you stared. I imagine it's not every day you see a middle-aged woman walking back to her cottage stark naked."

"No," he admits, blushing a little, which is when his beauty shines through. He looks up at me now and offers a half smile.

"You must have thought me mad."

"Sure it takes all sorts."

"Well, I hope you enjoyed the show."

"I've had worse nights."

And now it's my turn to blush. We look at each other and something strange passes between us. An understanding of some sort.

"What were you doing up at that time of night anyway?" I ask, and he shrugs his shoulders.

"I might ask you the same thing."

"I had a nightmare. And then I woke to the sound of something on my roof. It turned out to be that wee scut there," I say, nodding toward Bananas, who has settled on the floor, preparing for one of his regular naps. It occurs to me how quickly I have adopted the language of the island, for this was exactly the way Luke's mother described the cat on our initial encounter. "Then I was awake anyway and something drew me toward the sea."

"It can be dangerous down there at that time of night," Luke tells me. "You'd want to be careful doing that sort of thing."

"I'm a strong swimmer."

"No matter. Water is dangerous."

"Oh, I know that."

"I'm not telling you what to do, but you'd be well advised only to swim when there's someone else nearby."

"Thank you," I say. For some reason, I don't feel patronized. After all, he's lived on the island his entire life so must know the dangers of the tides better than I ever could, and his tone is not condescending.

"You're right. I'll be more careful in the future. If you won't have a cup of tea, would you take something stronger?"

He thinks about this and smiles. A boyish expression on his face.

"Sure why not," he says. "If you're having one."

I stand up and make my way toward the kitchen area, where I pour two small glasses of whiskey, dropping a large ice cube into each, and hand one across. My earlier vow not to keep alcohol in the house evaporated a few weeks ago, although I've drunk very little here. But I like to know there's something on hand in case of an emergency.

"I should have introduced myself," I say when I sit down again. "I'm Willow. Willow Hale."

"Mam told me," he says. "She came to visit you, I believe."

"She did. She seemed put out that I'd been feeding her cat."

"That creature is the bane of all our existences," he says. "She roars at it from morning till night, but she'd trade any one of us in for it."

It doesn't surprise me to hear this. Despite her army of children, Mrs. Duggan didn't strike me as the maternal type. Not that I'm one to talk.

"So, are you enjoying yourself here anyway?" he asks after an awkward silence.

"It's giving me time to think," I say, recognizing that this is an answer to a different question entirely.

"You're from Dublin, I'm told?"

"Yes."

"Most people leave here to go there. Not the other way around."

"I needed a break," I say. "I had some family issues and—"

"No, stop," he says, waving a hand in the air. "It's none of my business. I wasn't prying."

"It's fine," I say. It's curious, but even though we've only just met, I feel as if I could trust him with the upsetting facts of my life and he would keep them to himself. I felt the same with Ifechi. Something in the insular nature of island life, perhaps. A tendency to respect the privacy of others.

"I rarely get to talk to people, other than Mam and Dad," he tells me. "So I'm not the best at it. Throw me out when I get boring."

"I will, but we're not there yet. I suppose people have mentioned David Bowie to you before?"

He nods and closes his eyes for a moment so I can no longer see the different colors of his pupils. He seems embarrassed by them, when, in fact, they only add to his attractiveness.

"I don't really know the lad myself," he tells me. "Some of his songs, I suppose."

"Before your time," I tell him. "I grew up with him. Metaphorically speaking."

I notice a gaping hole in the right knee of his jeans and can see the dark brown skin beneath it and a sprinkling of golden hairs. It baffles me that I feel unexpected desire for this gentle young man, who can't be more than a few years older than Rebecca. And yet I do. I can't remember the last time I felt desire for anyone. When I realize that I've gone silent, I force myself back to the conversation.

"And what about you?" I ask finally.

"What about me?"

"It must have been near three o'clock in the morning when you saw me out there. What had you up at that time?"

He reaches down to stroke Bananas, who submits to his hand, purring happily.

"I'm not the best of sleepers," he says. "I keep what you might call odd hours."

"In what sense?"

"The farm," he explains. "It's a twenty-four-seven type of job, you know? I'd been up late the night before when one of the cows was calving and then I took a nap midafternoon, woke in the early morning, and couldn't get back to sleep. So I went outside for a cigarette on account of Mam having a conniption fit if I smoke in the house. Anyway, I don't really follow the clock in the way other people do. I wake, I work, I sleep, and then I do it all over again. It's all the same to me."

"Do you enjoy it?"

He frowns, as if this is something he's never considered before.

"It's what I do, I suppose," he tells me. "Enjoyment doesn't really come into it. Do you mind if I use your bathroom?"

I'm about to tell him where it is—not that it's too hard to find—but he's already on his feet and making his way toward it. He's been here before, then. I remain where I am while he's gone and, when he reappears, less than a minute later, he smiles and sits down again.

"This isn't your first time in the cottage," I say.

"Oh no," he says. "A couple of lads had it a few years back and I used to come over at night sometimes for a game of cards and the odd drink."

"Your mother told me about them," I say. "She said there was some sort of hostility toward them from the islanders."

"It was fucking disgraceful," he says, surprising me with the forcefulness of his response. "Mam led the charge, no better woman. They were a nice pair, though. No harm in them at all. They might have stayed longer had they not been made to feel so unwelcome. A shameful set of circumstances."

"I suspect the island isn't exactly running with the times," I say.

"No."

"Have you been to Dublin?" I ask him, a non sequitur, but I'm running out of things to say and don't want him to leave just yet.

"I have."

"Do you like it there?"

"'Like' would be too strong a word," he says. "It can be fierce noisy, for one thing. I'm not used to that. But it makes for a change, and you need that once in a while. I had a girlfriend once from Dublin. Do you know Dundrum?"

"I do."

"Well, she lived there, near the Town Centre. I never saw a place like it. All the shops. You'd lose your mind buying things you don't need."

"Did she work there?"

"No, she was a teacher."

"And how did you meet?"

"She came over with a group of students in the summer months. The ones who arrive to learn the *cúpla focal*. Áine was her name."

"That can't have been easy," I say. "A long-distance relationship."

"No. It didn't work out in the end anyway. On account of that, for the most part."

"Do you miss her?"

"I do and I don't," he says with a sigh. "But sure, it's five years gone now. She might be married for all I know."

"You don't stay in touch?"

"Ah no."

He looks around the room, and something in the nostalgic expression on his face makes me think that he might have taken Áine here when they were dating, if the cottage was empty at the time, and used it for their trysts, for I can't imagine his mother would have allowed him to use the farmhouse. He might have slept with her in my bed. The idea sends an unexpected frisson through me.

"And you," says Luke, rousing me from my reverie. "Are you married yourself?"

"Divorced," I tell him.

"I'm sorry."

"I'm not."

"Right."

He strokes the cat again. I wonder is this his default move when he feels uncertain in conversation. When he looks up again, he brushes the hair out of his eyes and smiles at me and I can see that he's trying not to study my body too closely but that he can't help himself. He's lonely. It's easy to see.

"And there's just you, I'm told?" I say. "Your mother said your brothers and sisters moved away."

"Sure, they're long gone," he tells me. "Four above in Dublin, one in America, one in Canada, one in Australia. 'Twas me drew the short straw."

"Why is that?"

"I'm the youngest."

"And that means you have to stay?" I ask. I'm not here to reorganize his life, but I wonder does he realize how ridiculous this sounds.

"Someone has to."

"You must never see them."

"The eldest pair I'd have difficulty picking out of a lineup."

"It seems unfair that you're left to look after the farm, just because of when you were born."

He nods and sighs a little before picking at the tear in his jeans. He agrees, probably, but can't see a way out of it. His mother is made of tough stuff and will still be here, I imagine, in twenty years' time. When he's finally liberated, it will be too late for him.

"I can't imagine there's much of a social life on the island," I continue. "For a boy your age, I mean. How old are you anyway?"

"Twenty-four," he says. "I'll be twenty-five in a few weeks' time."

"Will you have a party?"

"A few drinks, maybe. In the pub."

"The new pub or the old pub?"

"The old pub."

"Do you know the man who runs the new pub?" I ask, recalling my visit to the church and how distraught he seemed in his pew, beating his knee with his fist.

"I do," he says. "Tim Devlin."

"Do you know much about him?"

"A bit. Why, have you taken a shine to him?"

"Oh no, it's nothing like that," I reply quickly. I don't want him to think I would be romantically interested in a man in his fifties, even though I'm of that age myself. "It's just, I have lunch there most days and he never speaks to me. But I saw him another time, in another place, I won't say where, and he was terribly upset. I don't want to pry but—"

"He has his troubles," says Luke, and I wait for him to expand on this and feel both disappointment and admiration that he chooses not to. "But then, don't we all? I have them myself." He smiles a little as he says this. Every time he smiles, I find him more beautiful. He is wasted on this lump of rock. "But I don't have the time to indulge them."

"Is that a good thing or a bad thing?" I ask.

"It's a terrible thing," he says. "My head is wrecked half the time and I can't get it cleared."

"You must have friends?"

"A few. One or two stayed on for the same reasons as me. But most are away to the mainland."

"You're lonely."

He grows more serious now as he looks at me. "This is a fierce intense conversation, Willow Hale," he says. "I wasn't expecting this at all. I only came over to apologize and so you'd know I wasn't a peeping Tom." He takes a deep breath and looks me directly in the eyes now, the first time he's done this. "And now I feel like I want to tell you all my troubles. That I could. And that you'd let me. You're not a therapist in real life, are you?"

"Real life?" I ask, frowning.

He looks around and indicates the living room around us, the cottage, the island as a whole.

"Sure this isn't real life, is it?" he says. "You're escaping that for your own reasons, I'm sure. I would too, but I don't know how."

He looks down at the floor again and I feel great sympathy for him. I reach out, seeking his hand, and he takes it. His skin is rough and masculine. When we release each other, we both finish what's left in our glasses and stand. To my surprise, he walks to the sink, rinses them out, and places them upside down on the steel counter to dry. He is so mannerly.

"I should be going so," he says, turning around to look at me but making no attempt to leave. This is not how I expected my day to turn out, but it all seems so natural. I nod, then turn my back on him and walk toward the bedroom. He remains where he is for only a few moments before following me inside and closing the door behind us.

8

Brendan worked. The girls grew. I kept busy with the trappings of being an affluent, middle-class woman in South Dublin. I arranged spa days with my friends, had regular appointments with my hairdresser, became—for a time—obsessed with Bikram yoga. I spent at least an hour every morning working on my appearance, choosing what to wear, coordinating and curating my jewelry and fragrances. I maintained an Instagram account, wanting to advertise my perfect life to the world. I forced Brendan to come to the Gate or the Abbey with me whenever there was a new show on. I made reservations for dinner in well-reviewed restaurants. I was very involved with the girls' school, participating in fundraising drives for whatever social problem grabbed our attention. I kept a small champagne fridge in our outside *seomra*, always well stocked. I thought about building a lifestyle blog and made inquiries of website designers. I was a regular visitor at the National Gallery. I did all the things I felt I was supposed to do to live the perfect life, one that could not have been more different from the one I live now.

We might have lived in Terenure, but the National Swimming Federation, which was based only a few miles from our front door, was my husband's real home. He spent six days out of seven there and, more often than not, found himself invited to some evening event that meant he wouldn't be home until late. When he finally returned, he'd ignore the meal I'd left for him in the fridge, and wander around the house into the small hours, moving between the living room, his office, and the girls' bedrooms, even though they'd be asleep by then. Sometimes

I felt as if he was avoiding me entirely, for an hour or more could pass before he came to bed.

Soon after she turned fourteen, I found Emma hovering nearby one morning and turned to look at her. She seemed nervous and jittery, unable to meet my eye. I'd been expecting this for a year or so, and, in preparation for it, had read some articles online on how best to speak to your daughter when the moment came, something my own mother had never done for me, instead simply leaving a few old towels, cut to size, on my bed and instructing me to use them every month, to wash them myself, and never to tell anyone what they were for.

"Are you all right?" I asked, and she nodded, then shook her head. I decided there was no point prevaricating. "Have you started, is that it?"

Now she looked appalled, even insulted.

"No," she said, rolling her eyes. "God, I started that last Christmas."

I was surprised to hear this, even a little wounded that she hadn't confided in me at the time.

"Oh," I said. "And it's going all right, is it?"

"It is what it is."

"You haven't asked me to buy you any tampons."

"They give them out free at school."

I nearly fell off the seat at this, but then I had gone to the nuns, and they would have no more discussed the natural functions of the body than they would have done cartwheels across the assembly hall. I'd heard they gave out free condoms to the older students too these days but had avoided telling Brendan this, knowing how he'd react.

"Can you do something for me?" she asked after a pause.

"Of course. What is it?"

"Can you put a lock on my door?"

"Why?" I asked, for it wasn't as if I didn't knock before entering her room and she and Rebecca never argued over taking each other's things, which often seemed like community property between them.

"Because I want one," she said.

"No, I don't like locks," I told her, shaking my head. "What if there was a fire?"

"Then I'd unlock it. Or jump out the window."

I thought this through. Of course, she was getting older. Perhaps she just needed the illusion of privacy, and I would be wrong to deny her that. Another idea went through my mind, a horrible idea, one that shamed me even to imagine it, and, may God forgive me, I pushed it away. I pushed it far, far away. Why did I not listen to what she was trying to tell me?

"I keep getting woken in the middle of the night," she said finally.

"By what?" I asked.

"By Dad. When he comes home late."

"He likes to say goodnight, that's all."

"But he wakes me up."

"Well, what if I ask him not to?"

"I'd prefer a lock," she said, but I still said no. In a year or two, perhaps, I told her. When she was older.

And then, not long after, Brendan returned home to announce that he'd decided to take a sabbatical from his job. He'd left in the morning at the usual time, driven the girls to school, and a few hours later, when I was preparing my lunch, there he was, standing in the kitchen demanding a sandwich. I'd never known him to take so much as a sick day in his life.

"A sabbatical?" I asked. "I thought that was only something university professors took?"

"Anyone can," he said. "I need a break from that place." He took a bottle of beer from the fridge, which was also out of character as he was never much of a drinker, let alone at lunchtime. "All the chatter and the politics, it'd drive you to distraction. I've told them I'm taking a few weeks off for myself, to clear my head."

"But the Olympics," I began, for the Games were only eighteen months off now and preparations for team selection were in full swing.

"The Olympics will still be there when I get back."

I stared at him in bewilderment. He'd never so much as suggested to me that he found work stressful. If anything, I'd always thought it was homelife that he didn't enjoy.

"I work too hard," he said, seeing how puzzled I was. "Sure don't you always say that yourself?"

"Yes, but—"

"But what? I'll still be getting paid, if that's what you're worried about."

"That's not it at all," I said, annoyed by the suggestion. "I'm just surprised, that's all."

"Am I messing up your day by being here, is that it?" he asked, growing angry now. "Would you prefer I went and sat in the library for a few hours or took myself off into town to see a film?"

"Of course not," I replied, trying to lessen the tension. "No, I'm just—"

"I've said I'll give them a shout when I'm ready to go back."

"And they won't give your job away in the meantime?"

"How could they? Sure amn't I too well known for that?"

"Are you depressed?" I asked, sitting down next to him. "Is that it? Is there anything you'd like to talk about?"

"What I'd like, Vanessa, is *not* to talk about it," he replied.

"And what will we tell the girls?"

"That I've taken some holiday time that was owing to me. Sure they're too self-involved to care anyway."

He was right about that at least. By now, Emma and Rebecca were far too involved with the drama of their respective social circles to pay the slightest attention to anything that went on at home. When they realized that their father wasn't going to work, they barely asked any questions, but despite his repeated insistences that I had nothing to worry about, I continued to find the whole thing peculiar.

My confusion was only piqued when I found myself in Dunnes Stores in Cornelscourt a week or so later and ran into Peggy Hartman, whose husband, Seán, was director of the National Athletics Foundation, a sister organization to Brendan's. I didn't know Peggy well, but our paths had crossed a few times over the years at fundraising benefits and our husbands reported to the same minister, often joining forces when it came to funding applications.

"Peggy," I said, stopping my trolley halfway along the frozen-food aisle when I saw her coming toward me. "How are you? I haven't seen you in the longest time."

I was startled by the expression that crossed her face, which blended embarrassment with anxiety. It was as if I was the very last person she wanted to encounter.

"Vanessa," she said. "There you are."

Peggy and Seán had a son with Down syndrome, and when I asked after him, she told me that he was spending a week with his grandparents in Leitrim, a place he adored.

"That'll give you a break," I said, perhaps not choosing my words as judiciously as I might have.

"I don't need a break," she said, surprisingly quick to take offense. "Why would I?"

"No, of course not," I replied. "I only meant that it's hard work, that's all. You must be glad that your parents are happy to take him for a while."

"He's not a charity case, Vanessa," she said, and I was startled by her reaction, which was, I thought, unnecessarily defensive.

"No, of course not," I said. "I'm sorry, I didn't mean any harm. You're well yourself anyway?"

"I'm fine."

"And Seán?"

"He's fine too."

She looked at me coldly, and I got the distinct impression that whatever was going on here had nothing to do with what I had just said about her son.

"Is everything all right, Peggy?" I asked. "If you don't mind me saying, you seem a bit out of sorts."

She looked around, then shook her head as if she couldn't believe that I'd even have the gall to ask.

"I just don't know what to think," she said finally.

"About what?"

"Well, there's no smoke without fire, is there?"

I stared at her in bewilderment. She might have been speaking a foreign language for all the sense she was making to me.

"What smoke?" I asked. "What fire?"

"I think it's best we don't discuss it," she said. "Seán has made it clear that I should say nothing."

"Say nothing about what?"

She shook her head and made to move on, but before she wheeled her trolley away she turned back with a look of sympathy on her face.

"Look, I know none of this is your fault," she said. "And, of course, it could be nothing more than malicious gossip. I'm just worried that, if it's not, then whatever they discover will be brushed under the carpet."

"Peggy, I don't—"

"I know from personal experience how that can happen," she continued, growing more animated now. "In our day, it didn't matter who you told, they'd just tell you to stop throwing dirt on a good man's reputation and send you away with a flea in your ear, but I thought things had changed in this country. I really did. But it's those men, Vanessa, isn't it? It's those fucking men. They still run everything and look out for each other, no matter what. I hate them. Don't you? And it's women like us who allow it to happen. Because staying quiet is easier than causing a fuss, isn't it? Sometimes I think we're just as bad as they are. Worse."

She shook her head then, and there were tears in her eyes as she moved on. I didn't follow her. As with the conversation I'd had with Emma about the lock on her door, I blocked it out. Was I being naïve, selfish, or complicit? Was I frightened of investigating this and finding an answer that would destroy us all? I don't know, is the truth, but this is what I've come to the island to ask myself. We'd had an extraordinary conversation and, rather than following Peggy down the aisle and demanding an explanation, I went in search of the Green Isle frozen chips I liked. That seemed more important to me.

Later, I recounted the conversation to Brendan, who listened carefully and remained silent as he considered it, before finally asking at what time of day this had occurred.

"Around half past two," I told him.

"She's getting earlier, then."

"Getting earlier at what?"

"Sure, she drinks, that one," he said. "Did you not know that?"

"Peggy Hartman?"

"Oh yes. The poor woman has an alcohol problem. Seán told me all about it. I didn't say anything to you because I know you don't like gossip. Apparently she opens her first bottle of wine around four o'clock and that's it, she's on it for the night. But it must be getting worse if she was incoherent after lunch."

"I never said she was incoherent," I said. "She was perfectly articulate. And she certainly wasn't drunk, if that's what you're implying."

"She knows how to hide it, then," he replied. "The alcos are great at hiding it. Trust me, she won't have had the first clue what she was even talking about. She'll have had five stories in her head and been mixing them all up. She'll be lying on her sofa now, sleeping it off. This time tomorrow, she won't even remember having run into you."

I accepted this and asked no further questions. And when, later that evening, he suggested that the four of us take a trip down to Wexford for a week's holiday since the girls were on half term anyway, I said yes, great idea, and off we went, swimming in the sea every day because it was a fine spring week. I put Peggy Hartman, her smoke, her fire, and her supposed drink problem, out of my head.

It was while we were in White's that the phone call came. Brendan and I were having a drink in the hotel bar when one of the waiters said he had a call at reception. I wondered who might be calling him there, who even knew what hotel we had come to, and before he stood up, Brendan did something uncharacteristic. Looking like a man about to face his executioner, he placed a hand on top of my own and held it there for a moment, as if we were courting for the first time all over again, and offered a sad smile before leaving the bar and making his way into the lobby.

I sat still, telling myself not to worry, that whatever it was would be something trivial. The call seemed to take an eternity, but it couldn't have been more than a few minutes until he returned, looking excited and relieved.

"What was that all about?" I asked as he sat down, ordering us another round.

"The credit card company, that's all," he told me. "They wanted to check it was really me spending money here."

"Right," I said, wondering how they would have tracked him down if that was the case. Wouldn't they have rung his mobile? We remained silent for a few minutes before Brendan spoke again.

"Is it just me?" he asked. "Or are holidays overrated?"

"I wouldn't know," I said. "We rarely take any."

"Sure haven't we had five days here already?" he asked. "Maybe we'll skip the last two, will we? Head back up to Dublin tomorrow morning? I might drop into work in the afternoon."

"You're going back?"

"It's time, I think. We'll tell the girls later, will we? Get them to pack their things tonight? If we set off after breakfast, we could be home by one."

"All right," I said.

Could I not have asked him then? Could I not have insisted on knowing the truth about that phone call and why he'd taken this sabbatical so unexpectedly, and then ended it without warning? Could I not have said, *Brendan, I know there's something you're not telling me, and you'll say it now or I will ring the National Swimming Federation myself and find out?* Could I not have done that?

I could have, of course, but I didn't.

Why didn't I? What was wrong with me? Willow would have demanded answers; Vanessa couldn't even form the questions.

In the end, he didn't go back to work the next day, or, indeed, for the next two weeks, because we woke the following morning to the sound of Rebecca knocking on our door to tell us that Emma wasn't in her bed, that she'd been searching the hotel for her and could find her nowhere. Neither Brendan nor I were particularly concerned—she was always taking herself off somewhere, and we assumed she'd just gone for a walk in Wexford town—but by the time I was dressed and downstairs, Rebecca was conspicuously anxious and, to alleviate her concerns, I said that we'd go look for her.

And that was when two Gardaí came through the door and made their way to reception to ask whether there was a Mr. and Mrs. Carvin in residence. The woman behind the desk pointed us out, and the younger of the Gardaí, who didn't look like he was long out of short trousers, turned around with an expression on his face that suggested the conversation ahead was not going to be a happy one. When he caught my eye, he knew in that moment that I was the mother, and I knew exactly what he was going to tell me.

And even after that, I still asked no questions.

It's women like us who allow it to happen. That's what Peggy Hartman had said. *Because staying quiet is easier than causing a fuss, isn't it?*

9

I'm in the old pub, reading a novel, when Tim Devlin walks in. He stops and looks me up and down, as if I'm a car or a piece of livestock that he's considering putting in an offer on, and I stare back, challenging his gaze, but neither of us says a word. Instead, he makes his way toward the bar and orders a pint of Guinness before walking back toward me.

"Do you mind if I join you?" he asks.

I haven't spoken to anyone in almost a week, and realize that I'm in need of human contact, so I put my bookmark in its place and indicate the seat next to me.

"I thought you and I were never going to talk," I tell him.

"Well, one of us needs to make the first move, I suppose," he replies, a phrase that bothers me. Does he think we've been dancing around each other all this time, waiting for the right moment? If he does, he would be wrong. "Let me get you another drink first," he adds, seeing my almost empty glass. "What's that, a white wine?"

"Yes," I say, and he puts his pint down, then returns to the bar, where he chats briefly with the publican. I wonder what sort of relationship they have, these two men supposedly in competition with each other. It's a small island of only four hundred people, but perhaps those four hundred have a rare thirst on them so there's enough business to go around.

"Now then," he says when he returns, taking the stool opposite me rather than joining me on the banquette. "I don't think I've introduced myself, have I? Tim Devlin."

"Willow Hale," I say. "So, what made you decide to talk to me today?"

"I've been serving you soups and sandwiches for months now," he replies, "and we never exchange more than a hello and a goodbye. It's got a little awkward, don't you think?"

"A little," I agree, finishing my first glass of wine and starting on the second.

"I had the impression from the start that you wanted to be left alone."

"I did, for the most part. You probably thought I was the rudest woman in Ireland."

"Oh no," he replies, shaking his head. "I already met her. Sure I was married to her daughter for years."

I laugh, despite myself. A mother-in-law joke. I thought they'd gone out with the ark.

"This island seems to draw us in, doesn't it?" I say.

"Us?"

"The forlorn."

"What makes you think I'm forlorn?" he asks.

"You wear your loneliness like an overcoat," I tell him. "It's one of the reasons I haven't talked to you either. I always assume you just want to get on with your work without any fuss."

"That's true enough."

"Can I guess?"

"Can you guess what?"

"What you're struggling with."

He shrugs.

"If you want," he says.

"You were a bad husband," I say. "You drank or you gambled. Maybe you cheated. In the end, your wife divorced you and it was only then that you realized what you'd thrown away. You've regretted your actions ever since, but she met someone else in the meantime and wouldn't return to you, so you came here, to the island, to disappear."

"Not bad," he tells me, nodding his head. "Although my wife didn't divorce me. She died."

I have the good grace to look ashamed of myself.

"I'm sorry," I say. "That was flippant of me."

"You don't need to apologize," he replies, waving this away.

I wonder whether I'm supposed to ask how his wife died but, before I can, he changes the subject.

"And you," he says. "How are you enjoying life on the island?"

"The first few months weren't easy," I tell him. "I found the isolation strange. But now, well, I'm worried that I'm becoming institutionalized. Although I feel quite content most days. So maybe that's not such a bad thing."

"Content enough to stay?"

"Not forever, no. But for a time. When I arrived, my head was quite . . . how shall I put this? Messy."

"And now it's clean?"

"Cleaner than it was anyway. There's something about long walks, little social interaction, and no Wi-Fi that does wonders for the soul."

"It's why I have no router in the new pub," he tells me. "I don't want people sitting on their phones, Twittering away or checking their Face-books or any of that shite."

"I never understood the appeal of all that," I tell him. "Sharing every random thought or interaction we have with the world. Don't most people prefer privacy?"

"You're better off not being on it," he says, leaning forward and low-ering his voice. "When you come under the kind of scrutiny you came under, it must be corrosive to the soul. All those strangers attacking you, calling you names, thinking they know you when they don't have the first clue. Using you to alleviate their personal misery and sense of failure."

I turn my head to my right, toward the wall, and close my eyes for a moment. When I open them again, I find that I'm looking directly at a framed poster of *Man of Aran*, the Robert Flaherty documentary, that looks as if it's been hanging there since the dawn of time. A confident man with a hoop of rope is staring at the camera, penetrating the lens with his masculinity. To his right, a little behind him, visibly subservient, stands his wife, strands of hair blowing into her eyes. She has no expectations of life.

"You know who I am, then," I say finally, turning back to him, resigned to my unmasking.

"I've known who you were since the first moment you walked through my door," he says. "But I didn't like to say anything. I didn't want to frighten you off, for one thing. And it was none of my business."

"Have you told anyone?" I ask.

"I haven't, no. I would never do something like that." A silence descends upon us. Part of me wants to leave; another part wants to unburden myself of my secrets, for who else do I have to confide in, after all? Rebecca refuses to answer any of my messages. *I'm not cutting you off forever,* her actions tell me. *But I will only talk to you when I'm ready, and then it will be on my own terms.*

"The first thing I did when I arrived on the island was change my name and cut my hair," I tell Tim, deciding to let some of my horrible story escape into the world. "I scalped it right down, as you can see. It doesn't seem to be growing back either, which both worries me and doesn't bother me in the slightest, if that makes any sense."

"Why your hair?" he asks.

"I didn't want anyone to recognize me. I've been in the papers so much over the last year and I wanted to be anonymous. Believe me, when you achieve a certain amount of fame or notoriety in this country, there are days when you long to have a different face or be a different person entirely. Just to keep the jackals away. A stranger arriving on the island would inevitably attract interest, and I didn't want to give myself away too easily, so I had to make some changes."

"Most people don't read the papers here," he tells me. "You've probably noticed that Con Dwyer only gets in a dozen or so copies of the *Irish Times* and the *Indo* every day. And even those are always a day late. No, we have enough problems of our own to worry about here without bothering about what goes on over there." He nods in the vague direction of the mainland.

"Perhaps I'm overestimating my celebrity," I say.

"Well, they're not ignorant," he adds. "They'd know the story, the islanders, if you asked them. Sure it was all over the news. They just might not recognize the players."

"'They,' not 'we'?" I ask.

He shrugs, perhaps uncertain if he's ready to fully align himself with this community. Is he an outsider too, then?

"I wasn't sure it would be enough," I tell him. "The haircut, I mean. But I seem to have got away with it. At least I thought I had. Until now."

"I've always been a great man for the sport," he tells me. "So, a story like yours—"

"Not mine, my husband's."

"When it rears its ugly head, I pay attention. Twelve years, wasn't it? That's what he got?"

I drink half my glass of wine in one gulp. I don't get the sense that he's being unkind, or that he's prying. He's simply talking to me.

"That's right," I say.

"So, what, he'll be in his mid-seventies when he gets out?"

"He won't serve the full term if he behaves well."

"Does he have a history of behaving well?"

The look I give him probably says it all.

"Are you worried that the other prisoners will hurt him? They don't take kindly to people who do what he did."

He's right about this, and it bothers me that yes, I am. It does concern me. I've known Brendan more than half my life, after all, and I know how vulnerable he must be in prison. He's not a strong man. He likes power, and authority, and fame, but he's weak at heart. I don't love him, I don't even like him, but he's part of me. We created a family together and destroyed it together. Despite the terrible things he's done, it's very difficult to abandon those feelings entirely. I know he will be constantly frightened. But then, those eight little girls—the eight that we know of, anyway; I have no doubt that there were many more—he has caused unspeakable damage in their lives. If he were killed in prison, that would be celebrated by most. How can I explain, to myself, to anyone, the fact that I would weep?

"I'm sure the wardens will keep charge," I say weakly.

"You don't understand the prison ecosystem," he tells me. "There's not much difference between the wardens and the prisoners. It's just hundreds of men all stuck together inside a big stone building, some getting paid for the privilege, some not. Some sleeping in cells, some going home of an evening."

I catch the barman's eye and raise my eyebrows to indicate that I'd like to order another round. When it arrives, Tim downs the final quarter of his Guinness, before standing up and carrying our empty glasses to the bar. I like the fact that he'd never make another barman clear up after him.

"You've been to prison, haven't you?" I ask when he returns. I'm determined to keep my voice steady, even if his crime was something heinous. I don't want him to think that I'm frightened of him. I refuse to be frightened of men anymore.

"I spent six years in Mountjoy," he admits. "I came here the day after my release."

"Do you mind if I ask what you did?"

"No. Most people on the island know anyway. I'm surprised no one's told you, to be honest."

"I find that people here are very discreet."

"True enough. Drink-driving." He looks down at the table that separates us and scratches the woodwork with the nail of his thumb. "My wife and I had been out for the night and I was supposed to leave the car behind and collect it the next day, but we'd had a row about something stupid and when she tried to take the keys off me, I got lairy with her and insisted on driving us home. She should have refused to come with me and took a taxi home instead, but no. I don't remember anything after that. All I know is I woke up in St. James's Hospital the next day to be told that I'd escaped the crash with barely a scratch but that my wife was dead. Which explained why my left wrist was handcuffed to the bedframe and a young Garda was sitting next to the bed reading *The Da Vinci Code*."

I wonder should I offer condolences but decide not to. He is the author of his own misfortune, after all. Is it any wonder he looked so distressed in the church that day?

"And you loved her," I say, uncertain whether I mean this as a question or a statement.

"I did," he replies.

"Did you have children?"

"A young lad, yeah. Well, not so young anymore. He lives with his aunt. My wife's sister. He won't see me. I don't blame him. You lost a daughter too, am I right?"

This unsettles me. An estranged son and a dead daughter are not the same thing. Also, it's starting to grate on me that he knows so much about my life.

"My daughter took her own life," I tell him. "I have another, Rebecca. But right now, she's not talking to me either."

"I'm sorry," he says.

"I hoped this time apart would be good for us," I continue. "That she would miss me. Worry about me, even. But I don't think she does. I think she'd prefer that I never return."

"Does she talk to your husband?"

"Ex-husband. And no, she doesn't. And whether or not she ever reconciles with me, I know she'll never speak to him again. I know that with absolute certainty."

"She blames him, then."

"For abusing all those children? Of course she does. Why wouldn't she?"

"No, I mean she blames him for her sister's suicide."

I'm surprised to find myself having such a personal conversation with a relative stranger. I've never had such a conversation before. And yet, I keep going. At this point, I have nothing to lose. And it feels good to speak about something that I've been hiding since boarding the ferry in Galway all those months ago.

"Yes," I say.

"She thinks he did it to her too."

"Yes."

"And do you?"

"Yes."

"So she blames you for that?"

"Yes."

He breathes heavily through his nose, as if all the pain of the world is bottled up inside him, desperate for release, then stands up and goes to the bar, where he orders more drinks without bothering to ask whether I want one. I still have almost a full glass of wine before me, but I drink it down, enjoying how it numbs me from the inside. I don't want him to outpace me.

"It's a terrible thing, guilt," he says, when he sets the drinks down before us. "I have nightmares sometimes. Do you?"

"No," I lie.

"I thought everyone who suffered a trauma did."

"Not me."

We remain silent for a few moments.

"What was it like?" I ask eventually.

"What was what like?"

"When you woke up in the hospital and they told you what you'd done. How did you feel?"

He looks out into the center of the bar and considers it. A few more people have come in by now. Some I recognize from my wanderings around the village. Some are strangers to me. Two, I think, are tourists, for the summer season has just begun. They are, without question, American, and seem to think they've walked onto a film set. The woman immediately takes her camera out and starts snapping photographs. When she turns and aims it in our direction, I tell her, in no uncertain terms, not to press that button.

"How did I feel?" says Tim, when the Americans have scattered to the other end of the pub in fright. "I felt as if my entire life had been leading toward that moment. The truth is, I was always what might be called a dissolute youth. I drank. I took drugs. I womanized. I was not always kind to people. I was certainly not kind to my parents, God rest them. I stole from my employer and got away with it. Just small amounts, but they added up over time. I cheated on my wife for no other reason than I could and because I believed I was entitled to as much sex as I could get, with as many people as would have me. When I was in my late twenties, I was rougher with a girl in this regard than I should have been. She lodged no complaint with the Gardaí, but I remember what I did, and I think about it often. And the party we were at, the night of the accident, was a birthday party for the wife of a good friend, and I'd been seeing that woman secretly for months. My problem is, I don't think I ever understood how to be an adult. In my heart, I still feel like a teenage boy. So you ask how did I feel? I feel that there was an inevitability to it all. The moment I was told what I had done, I made my peace with the fact that I would be going to prison and, even then, lying in that hospital bed, I began to think about the changes I would make when I was eventually released. I resolved to be a better man."

He returns to his pint now and glances up at me cautiously as if he expects me to reach across and place my hand atop his, to commend him for his honesty and tell him that he must forgive himself, that his wife would not want him to live with such guilt, and that he must learn to live again. I can see this in his face and wonder whether he has told this same story to other women, and they have comforted him in this way. But I refuse, I absolutely refuse, to comply. He can anticipate his cathartic moment all he likes, but I won't be providing it.

"I don't think I ever understood how to be an adult," I say, mimicking him. *"In my heart, I still feel like a teenage boy.* But that's the problem with men like you, isn't it? You refuse to accept that you're not, in fact, a teenage boy, any more than you're a cow or a sheep. You're nearly sixty, for God's sake. You think the world has treated you cruelly by forcing you to age. But the women, we're not allowed to act like teenage girls, are we? No, we become wives and mothers and we try to keep our families together and we make excuses for these infantilized beings we call husbands. Have you listened to yourself? Your first thought when you woke up in that hospital was to fast-forward to years after your trial, years after your imprisonment, all the way to your release, and who you would be then and what you would do. Not a thought in your head for the poor woman you'd killed and to whom you'd, presumably, once offered words of love and a lifetime of fidelity. Just the endless selfishness of the middle-aged man who does whatever he wants and leaves his wife to pick up the pieces. I don't doubt your grief, Tim, or your guilt. But God Almighty, will men like you ever stop telling stories like this and asking the world to excuse you, because you still feel like a teenage boy and, somehow, you can't help yourself? You *could* help yourself if you just grew the fuck up and behaved like an adult, which is what you are. But you choose not to. Do you hear what I'm telling you? Tim? Are you listening to me? Do you hear what I'm saying?"

10

There's a flurry of activity on the beach, and I make my way along the path toward the spot where a group of islanders has gathered. In among them is Luke's mother, concealed beneath so many layers that it might be the dead of winter and not a clear summer's evening. I wonder if she knows that her son and I had sex, and that we continue to, whenever the mood takes us. I don't for a moment imagine that he would have confided in her, but mothers, some mothers anyway, have a way of intuiting these things.

"Mrs. Duggan," I say, and she looks me up and down as if there is so much wrong with me that she wouldn't even know where to begin. "What's going on?"

"Evan Keogh," she replies. "He took off early for Galway and hasn't been seen since."

The name rings a bell, but I can't quite place it until, at last, I remember her mentioning him to me when she first came to remonstrate with me for feeding Bananas. A talented footballer, if I remember correctly. Didn't his father want him to go to England for a trial with one of the clubs there?

"Took off in what way?" I ask. "Not swimming, I presume?" If the boy's been out swimming since morning, I'm not surprised there's concern. I've read of charity swims between the island and Doolin, so I suppose a distance like that is possible. But Doolin is only ten miles from here, while Galway is twenty-four. Only a fool would attempt such a thing without a vessel following in case of an emergency.

"Ah, no," she says. "He took Charlie's boat out, and he's never done that before. Not on his own anyway. And neither sight nor sound of him since."

I look out across the waves, as if I will see the missing boy surfing toward me on the horizon.

"He couldn't have got into difficulty, surely," I say. "It's been such a fine day. No wind at all."

"Accidents happen," she replies with all the pessimism that women like her revel in. "Better things have happened to worse men."

A little further along, within a circle of protective friends, stands a middle-aged woman looking pale and frightened, even annoyed. I take her to be Mrs. Keogh, who I recognize from the knit shop in the village. I bought a scarf from her a few weeks after I arrived and it's a thing of beauty, made from Merino wool, with intersecting threads of turquoise and tangerine. I wear it on cold evenings if I'm going to the old pub for a meal. One of the women tries to place a consolatory arm around her shoulder, but she shrugs it off and marches down toward the shore, fierce in her stride, to where the tide rolls in. She's beseeching the water to go against its nature, to show compassion for once, but, like King Canute demanding that the tides fall still, she's asking in vain, for water is the cruelest of all the elements and will swallow up anyone who challenges it.

"Has someone gone looking for him?" I ask.

"Charlie's gone, of course. And my Luke, along with two of his pals. They're away an hour since. We'll stay here now till they all get back safe, God willing."

A part of me wants to return to the cottage and hide under the bed-sheets. I cannot be here if the men return with bad news, as those two Gardaí did for me on that long-ago holiday in Wexford. I cannot witness any mirroring of my grief.

I remember a small van that, since the arrival of the summer tour-ists, is usually parked at the top of the dunes, selling teas and coffees, ice creams, and soft drinks from a window hatch, and I make my way back up to the road and walk in its direction, hoping it will still be there, despite the hour. Sure enough, it is, although when I reach it, the girl inside is packing up for the night.

"Are you still serving?" I ask, and she glances toward the hot-water urn, pressing a hand briefly against its steel surface, before nodding.

"You just caught me," she says. "And it's still hot. What will you have?"

"A large tea," I tell her. "Strong and sweet."

She takes the largest of the Styrofoam cups from a shelf behind her and drops in a tea bag before filling it with steaming water and reaching for the bag of sugar.

"How many?" she asks.

"Two," I say, handing across a couple of euros and taking the cup from her, pressing the lid in place, and walking back toward the beach. To my surprise, Mrs. Keogh has separated herself from the ghoulish gathering and is now alone in the dunes, her arms folded before her. I approach cautiously and clear my throat so as not to surprise her. When she turns to look at me, she blinks a little, as if she's just woken from a dream.

"I brought you some tea," I say, handing it across. "I put some sugar in it. I'd have put whiskey in if I'd any to hand."

"That's kind of you," she says, taking it and warming her hands on the cup's surround.

"Would you like me to leave you alone?" I ask, conscious that she might have changed position for privacy's sake, but she shakes her head.

"Stay if you like," she says. "This is all a lot of fuss over nothing. Evan's a good sailor. No harm could come to him on a day like this. He'll have docked on a beach somewhere and gone into the town for the afternoon."

"I don't doubt it," I say, wanting to reassure her.

"He'll come sailing back any minute now and throw a fit over why we're all acting like he's drowned."

I bristle a little at the casual use of the word but decide not to pick her up on it. I don't know if she's trying to persuade herself or me.

"We haven't met, have we?" she says eventually, sipping on the tea.

"Not really," I say. "Although I've been in your shop. I'm Willow Hale."

"Maggie Keogh. You're famous, you know." I frown, unsettled by this remark.

"Sure everybody was talking about you when you first arrived," she explains. "The Pope himself wouldn't have garnered so much interest. A woman from Dublin and not a husband in sight!" She indicates the men and women gathered on the shore before us, who seem to have forgotten about her and are locked in chat as they wait to see how this drama will play out. "That's what they were all saying anyway. Gossips, the lot of them. They drive me around the bend with their nonsense."

Something in her voice makes me realize that she is not a native islander.

"Where are you from?" I ask.

"Wicklow," she tells me. "I met Charlie when I was too young to know any better and allowed him to drag me here."

There's so much bitterness in her tone that it shocks me. It makes me think that she is already anticipating the worst and has adopted the persona of the grieving mother earlier than necessary. Each of us does it differently, of course.

She takes her phone from her pocket and taps a couple of numbers on the screen before lifting it to her ear, waiting a moment, then sighing in frustration as she returns it to her pocket.

"This is what I don't understand," she says, looking to me as if I can offer an explanation. "He never turns his phone off. Evan, I mean. He has it on him all day long and he always answers. And now it's just going to voicemail. What does that mean, do you think? Might it have been stolen from him?"

Until now, I have assumed that the islanders are merely creating a commotion to give their day a bit of excitement, but this makes me wonder. Perhaps the boy has come to mischief, after all. I take my own phone from my pocket, open the messaging service, and there is Rebecca's photograph, only it's changed again. Now it is a picture taken from behind, and she is standing much like I am, on a dune somewhere, looking out to sea. Which sea is this, I wonder? And what is she doing there? I check when she was last online. An hour ago. I type a message.

I miss you. I am well.

I wait to see that she has received and read it before returning the phone to my pocket, hoping for the sound of a reply but anticipating none. Maggie Keogh looks at me.

"Who were you texting?" she asks.

"My daughter," I say.

"Do you have just the one?"

I find this a complicated question to answer. The intimacy of the truth would be too much in the present moment.

"Yes," I tell her. "Rebecca."

"She didn't come here with you?"

"Oh no," I say. "She'd go out of her mind in a place like this."

"Sure we all do that," says Maggie. "Most of us lost our minds long ago. Would it surprise you to know that I haven't set foot on the mainland in eight years?"

"Why not?" I ask her.

"He won't let me," she says.

"Who won't?"

"Charlie."

"I don't understand."

She shrugs her shoulders, as if she's long since stopped thinking about it. "Neither do I," she says.

What a strange existence, I think, to spend so much of one's life in a place like this, ruled by the whims of a man, and to know so little of the world. Never to have climbed the Eiffel Tower, or walked across the Sydney Harbour Bridge, or stared into the depths of the Grand Canyon. To settle for a barren rock in the Atlantic Ocean where you could probably spend a lifetime and encounter only a few hundred different faces. I think of those Japanese soldiers who lasted for decades on small islands in the Pacific, still believing the war was going on.

"So he's run away," I say. "Your son, I mean. He's escaping his father."

"He's frightened."

"Of your husband?"

She looks at me with an expression on her face that's difficult to read. This is a woman who needs to unburden herself of something. "Partly," she says.

"You don't have to tell me," I say, stating the obvious. "It's your business. Did I hear that he wants to be a professional footballer?"

Maggie laughs bitterly. "He has the talent, that's for sure," she tells me. "You've never seen such skill with a ball. But he doesn't want it. He has no interest in the game. His father is all for it, though. He likes the idea of Evan lining up in Lansdowne Road, singing 'Amhrán na bhFiann' at the top of his voice as the television cameras pass by."

"And what does Evan want?"

"To paint, apparently."

"Is he good?"

"I don't know," she says, her face filled with emotion.

"But you've seen his paintings, I presume?"

"Oh. You meant his art."

"What else would I mean?"

She smiles now and shakes her head. "That's the problem," she says. "I don't think he is. He doesn't have the talent to do what he wants, but he has the talent to do what he doesn't want. So there's a conundrum for you."

I nod. "Yes," I say.

"They all think he's drowned," she continues, nodding toward our neighbors. "But he hasn't. He's run away, that's all. He's frightened. He's hiding. I hope they don't catch him. Let him go to Dublin or London or somewhere further afield and escape all this." She waves her hand around, as if conjuring a spell. "I should have done it myself long ago."

She closes her eyes, breathing in the cool evening air as if desperate to cleanse her lungs. I consider placing my hand on her arm to comfort her when a roar rises from the beach and we both startle, looking out toward the horizon, where the sun is starting to set.

"It's them," she says, and, sure enough, a small boat can be seen in the distance making its way toward the shore. She drops the cup in the marram grass that protrudes from the sand, and the lid falls off, tea spilling out and darkening the sand like a spreading sin, before making her way hurriedly in the direction of the water. I reach down to pick the cup up, unable to litter a beach, and follow her. Like the neighbors that I'm so quick to condemn, I'm eager to know how this evening's story ends.

There's a sharp buzz among them as the boat draws closer, and I can see the large handsome shape of my lover, Luke, on board. We have formed an easy friendship, based on conversation, intimacy, sex, and a mutual understanding that neither of us wants anything more from the other than what we are willing to give. It is uncomplicated and it is welcome.

Behind Luke, I can make out his two friends, and an older man, sitting near the stern, with a cap pulled down over his forehead. I take him to be Charlie Keogh, and he does not look like a brute, but, of course, appearances can be deceptive. I blink, thinking I must have missed someone, and look at each again in turn. I want to tell someone, to shout that the boy is missing, drowned, dead, but who am I to spread such a terrible alarm? If the worst has happened, then let Maggie Keogh enjoy what time is left to her before she is forced to become a—what? There are widows. And widowers. And orphans. But there is no word to define a parent who loses a child. The language is missing a noun. Perhaps because it is so unnatural.

The babble dies down when the boat pulls into the shore, and no one moves as they see what I have seen and make their own calculations. I catch Luke's eye and offer him an expression of support. I admire this heroic side to his character, the young man who will take to the water to search for a missing islander. His friends rise and then, behind them, hidden from view until now, I see the boy. The crowd howls in relief as he pulls himself to his feet, looking around in fury and humiliation. Even from here, I can see the black eye that is blossoming on his face, no doubt the result of his father's violence. He waits until only Luke is left on board before stepping onto land, and I wonder where his boat is, the one on which he tried to make his escape. In Galway? Or sunk? How has he left in one vessel and returned in another?

And I see his face even more clearly as he turns and looks in my direction, unwilling to accept the embraces of those who have known him since birth. Our eyes meet and I realize that he is the boy I saw in the church that day. The boy who went to confession in the certainty that he had sinned.

His mother runs toward him, her arms outstretched, but he will not allow her to enfold him. Instead, he charges up the dunes, his runners finding quick purchase in the sand, and disappears over the top, to a place where he can be neither seen nor hurt.

11

A general election is taking place, and a politician visits to address the voters he hasn't laid eyes on in almost five years. His appearance offers a timely interruption to the repetitive nature of our lives, so most of us gather in the church to hear him speak, where the sense of excitement is completely out of proportion to the identity of our visitor.

I showed up under the impression that we were to be addressed by a young woman standing for one of the five Galway West seats for the first time, but, when the doors are closed and the welcoming party ascends the altar steps, I'm horrified to see that she has been replaced by a more senior member of her party, a fellow named Jack Sharkey, the current minister for tourism, culture, arts, the gaeltacht, sport, and media. I've known Jack for many years, since long before his elevation to the cabinet. In fact, it was while he was a humble TD in a previous administration that he, along with Gareth Wilson, pushed for Brendan to be created director of the National Swimming Federation. Many human dominoes toppled after my husband's disgrace, but somehow Jack has remained standing.

Ifechi may have loaned his church to accommodate the speech, but naturally he cannot be seen to have any involvement in party politics, so he is perhaps the only islander to be absent, and his place is taken by Larry Mulshay, proprietor of the old pub and the unofficial mayor of the island. Leaning too close to the microphone, Larry welcomes us before announcing that the young woman we had been expecting was unable to make it, but we should be honored that Mr. Sharkey has come instead. I can tell this is a lie. Jack probably heard about this evening and, knowing the constituency to be finely balanced, decided that the votes of four hundred people could make the difference between election and unemployment, so used his influence to keep his colleague on the mainland. Either that, or he tipped her into the water on the ferry over. We are also informed that, while we're all entitled to our own political viewpoints, Larry is certain that we will listen to Mr. Sharkey—Jack—politely and be respectful in our questions afterward.

It is as if we are children gathered in an assembly hall, being instructed by the head teacher that any transgression will land us in trouble. I half expect him to remove a cane from his sleeve and patrol the pews, watchful for any gum-chewing or illicit texting.

I am in the sixth row, two places removed from the aisle, and I sink down in my seat, hoping that Jack will not catch my eye. I'm not certain that he would recognize me, but it's not impossible. Over the years, we've been in each other's company on perhaps half a dozen occasions, and he was the subject of multiple inquiries from the media during Brendan's trial, so no doubt observed it closely, lest he be dragged before an Oireachtas committee to explain his early support for my husband. Still, my current appearance is far removed from the glamorous wife he might remember, if he remembers me at all, so my newfound invisibility to the male gaze is an asset.

He takes to the microphone now in a more professional manner and thanks us all for coming. He tells a few politician-mocking jokes that sound as if they've been trotted out multiple times over the years. He's from Galway himself, of course, Oughterard, and speaks of his abiding love for these islands and for this island in particular. His voice cracks when he recounts stories of summer holidays he spent here as a boy with his sainted parents, now gone to their eternal reward, then looks down at the floor as if he's not sure that he can go on, but then, somehow, like Beckett, he goes on.

He talks of agriculture. He talks of emigration. He talks of civil war politics. He talks of NATO. He talks of the Gardaí. He talks of hospital beds. He talks of the elite up there in Dublin. He talks of farmers. He talks of bricklayers. He talks of class sizes. He talks of carbon emissions. He talks of the British prime minister. He talks of Brexit. He talks of the pandemic. He talks of his father, who represented this constituency before him. He talks of a close friend who is black. He talks of a niece who is embracing a male identity. He talks of young people and of why they are our greatest natural resource. He talks of solar power. He talks of the GAA. He talks of Bono and Sinéad O'Connor. He talks of fishing quotas. He talks, in English, of his love for the Irish language. He talks, in Irish, of his love for Manchester United. He talks of his admiration for women. He talks of the EU. He talks of Emmanuel Macron. He talks of his cabinet colleagues. He talks of RTÉ bias. He talks of *Ulysses*, and *The Commitments*, and *Normal People*, and of how Irish writers have given so much to the world. He talks of Michael D. He talks of the Eurovision Song Contest. He talks of the rise of populism across Europe. He talks of Ukraine. He talks of his hernia operation.

And just when I think he will talk forever, that we will all grow old and die here, that our bodies will decompose and slowly turn to dust while he continues to talk and talk and talk, he stops, and his audience delivers a loud round of applause, as if to say that, whatever he might have planned next, he can forget it, because we consider this the end of his talk.

He appears to accept this and takes his place on a high stool that I recognize from the old pub and sips a glass of water while a roving mic is brought around the audience. Anxiously, we await the brave soul who might accept it first.

When a question comes, it is from the mother of an autistic son who asks when more resources will be provided for boys like her Tomás. His teacher, she says, is a wonderful man but he simply cannot cope with her son's special needs. It's not his fault; he doesn't have the training. What can be done, she wants to know? And when will it be done? Jack asks the appropriate questions in reply, pretending to care, before saying that this is a question for his good friend, the minister for education, and that if she gives her details to his assistant later, he will make sure that someone from that department is in touch soon.

Before the woman can speak again, the microphone is ripped from her hands and given to an elderly man who I have seen sinking pint after pint of Guinness in the new pub and who wants to know how Jack voted in the Equal Rights Marriage Referendum of 2015.

"Sure that was years ago now, wasn't it?" says Jack, laughing a little, and an uncomfortable frisson passes through the room. "I can barely remember what I had for my dinner last night." Whatever it was, I think, he went back for seconds.

The man insists on an answer. He says that he grew up in a Catholic country, but politicians have turned it into Sodom and Gomorrah, and that John Charles McQuaid would turn in his grave if he saw what a den of iniquity this once holy land has turned into. Fellas kissing fellas, he says. And girls kissing girls. In public! On the street! Without an ounce of shame! And half of them don't even know if they're a fella or a girl! Was it for this that the men of 1916 fought and died, he blathers on, and I take a moment to examine my nails and notice they need cutting.

Jack hears him out but takes his time to formulate a reply.

"I voted no," he tells us eventually. "At the time, I considered marriage to be a sacred institution between a man and woman. And while I am proud to have voted with my conscience, I'm not convinced that I would vote the same way again, although perhaps I would. Or maybe not. Yes, men are now free to marry men, and women are free to marry women, but the world does not seem to have fallen off its axis since the legislation was passed. The fact is, we need to move with the times while recognizing that, sometimes, the old ways are best."

In his search for an answer that will satisfy no one and everyone in equal parts, I have to concede that Jack has succeeded admirably. He is a politician down to his fingernails.

A third question emerges, this one an obvious plant from a supporter. The man wants to know: If Jack is minister for tourism, culture, arts, the gaeltacht, sport, and media, then what in God's name does he do on the seventh day? The audience laughs appreciatively, pleased to have moved on to a less contentious topic, and Jack tells us that even the good Lord rested on Sunday and that surely no one, not even his political opponents, would begrudge him a day off.

More questions follow, some anodyne, some pugnacious, until finally a young woman who serves behind the counter in Con Dwyer's newsagent's rises to her feet and takes the microphone, holding it nervously but defiantly in her hands, like a contestant on a television singing competition.

"My name is Lucy Wood," she says, "and I'll be a first-time voter in this election."

There's a predictable round of applause for this, and Lucy blushes a little, but, I notice, she does not smile. She does, however, wear a determined expression on her face.

"Many people in this country know what it is to face sexual abuse," she begins.

From behind me, a man mutters, "Ah, for God's sake."

"I've faced it myself," she continues into the disapproving silence. "So I want to ask you a question in relation to your support of Brendan Carvin. You appointed him as director of the National Swimming Federation in 2004, isn't that right?"

I feel my heart begin to pound faster in my chest. I have studiously avoided catching Jack's eye since he appeared on the altar steps and have no intention of looking up now.

"No, that decision did not fall to me," replies Jack after a pause. "Although I was party to it, as I have admitted on many occasions over the last year. It is to my eternal regret that I was. It is a cross that I have to bear."

It's interesting to me that he immediately casts himself in the role of the victim. Also, this is the second time he has compared himself to a member of the Holy Trinity. Messianic complexes, I'm sure, are rife in his line of work.

"So, that being the case," continues Lucy, ignoring his last comment, "do you have anything to say to those eight little girls who that man abused?"

"Leave it alone, sure what's done is done!" cries a voice from a few rows behind me that I recognize immediately as belonging to Mrs. Duggan. She is not alone in her desire for this subject to be dropped; several others chime in too. And inside, silently, so do I.

"Naturally, my heart goes out to those young women—"

"No, they weren't young women," insists Lucy with a lawyer's need for precision. "They were children."

"Yes, indeed. Children," agrees Jack. "And I hope they find the healing they need in the years ahead. With God's help—"

"Oh, fuck off," says another voice, one I do not recognize, from the rear of the church, but it is a youthful, male voice. I have nothing to base this on, but somehow I think it might be the voice of Evan Keogh.

"With God's help, they will get past whatever might have happened to them."

"*Might* have happened to them?" asks Lucy, growing angry now.

"*Did* happen to them, according to the courts," says Jack, correcting himself, and I marvel at how he can make an entirely accurate remark sound as if he's casting doubt upon the verdict.

"But at his trial," continues Lucy, and, finally looking up, I see the growing indignation on Jack's face. He didn't come here to be challenged by an eighteen-year-old girl. He came to trot out his stump speech and drink a few pints of Guinness later with people he thought could ensure his reelection. "At his trial, you said, and I quote"—and here she unfolds a newspaper clipping she has brought with her—"*Brendan Carvin was a great gift to Irish swimming. Fiercely proud of his young swimmers, dedicated to their advancement, and relentless in his pursuit of funding. His track record at the Olympics alone shows that we were right to appoint him to the job.*"

"What I meant by that," says Jack, raising a hand in the air as if she's a buzzing fly that needs swatting away, "was that on a purely professional level, if you look solely at the results he achieved, we appointed the right man."

A murmur of dismay emerges across the aisles—even those who are, by their nature, supportive of middle-aged men and dismissive of young women find this remark problematic—and he raises his voice to be heard. "No, listen now," he says, waving a pudgy hand in the air. "Yes, we got it badly wrong in some ways. We believed Mr. Carvin to be a man of honor. Sure, there was nothing to suggest otherwise. But if you take the emotion out of the story and just separate the man and the job from what we subsequently learned, there's no one can deny his success in the role."

"True enough," says a man in the second row.

"How many medals did we win, after all, at the Olympics during his tenure? The world is a complicated place, Missy," he continues, pointing his finger at his inquisitor. "You'll find that out as you get a bit older and—"

"Don't patronize the girl!" shouts a woman from the back of the church, and half the audience bursts into applause while the other half, the male half, folds its arms. What is it, I wonder, about sporting success that seems more important to these men than basic decency?

"Look, I don't think any of us want to get bogged down in talking about Brendan Carvin," says Jack, clearly eager for us to leave this conversation behind us. "The man is where he ought to be, in the Midlands Prison, and there he will stay for the foreseeable future. And rest assured there will be more stringent safeguards put in place in the future to prevent something like this from ever happening again. If reelected to Dáil Éireann, I will make it my personal responsibility to—"

And then, abruptly, he stops talking. I look up and realize that he is staring directly at me. In the moment, he's not entirely sure that I am who he thinks I am. My eyes meet his and I shake my head almost imperceptibly, beseeching him not to identify me. He continues to look, perhaps trying to understand what's happening here—is it me? If it is, where have I come from? And what do I want?—then, troubled, uncertain what to do, returns to what he was saying.

"I will make it my personal responsibility to make sure that nothing like that ever happens again," he continues, quieter now, his confidence and bonhomie noticeably diminished. "This country has a long and shameful history of people using their authority to destroy the lives of young people, and we cannot allow that to continue. My colleagues and I will put an end to the Brendan Carvins of this world." He pauses and looks at me, as if to suggest that I am the villain of this story. "And we will put an end to their enablers too. Those people who knew what was going on and looked away. In my book, complicity is just as bad as the crime itself."

This goes down well and there's a sustained round of applause. I can't imagine that Lucy is satisfied with the response, for, after all, he is disassociating himself from the very crimes that he helped facilitate, while claiming credit for the medals that Ireland won. But the meeting is called to an end now and the audience rises to its feet, eager for their pints. I brush past the other people in my row, determined to get out quickly, and make my way down the nave toward the front doors. Pushing them open, I can't help myself. I glance back for a moment, and I see Jack taking selfies with some of the voters, a broad smile on his face. Perhaps he knows I'm watching, because he looks down at me and the expression on his face changes immediately.

Don't you fucking judge me, it says. *Not you, of all people.*

12

On the day the police showed up at our front door, I was awake and dressed early, ready for a hair appointment booked for nine o'clock. The doorbell rang shortly before eight and, when I answered it, I was confronted by two Gardaí, one in plain clothes, who introduced herself as Sergeant Kilmartin, and the other in uniform. I froze when I saw them—it brought me immediately back to the day two of their colleagues had shown up at the hotel in Wexford—and my thoughts immediately turned to Rebecca, who had already left for college.

"What?" I said immediately, desperate for an answer to a question I hadn't even asked yet. "Is it my daughter?"

"No, it's nothing like that," said Sergeant Kilmartin, shaking her head quickly. "Please don't worry, we're not here to deliver bad news."

"Oh, thank God," I replied, allowing myself to breathe again, but it only took a moment for me to wonder why, if that was not their purpose, then what was it?

"It's Mrs. Carvin, isn't it?" she asked, and I nodded.

"That's right, yes."

"Is your husband at home?"

"He's upstairs," I said. "Getting ready for work. Can I help you with something?"

"I'm afraid not, no. We need to speak to him. Do you mind if we come in?"

It was framed as a question, but in the moment I understood that I was not being given the option to refuse, and so I stood out of the way to allow them into the hallway. The senior officer looked tough and determined, while the junior appeared more apprehensive. From the kitchen, I heard the kettle turning off as it came to a boil and, a moment later, the toaster popping. Pointlessly, my mind drifted to a pot of jam I'd bought at a farmers' market a few days earlier that I'd intended on opening with my breakfast. Anything, perhaps, to stop myself from questioning why two officers might be standing before me. Stepping around them, I closed the front door and we stared at each other awkwardly until Garda Chen—his name was printed on his lapel—piped up.

"Perhaps you could call your husband down, Mrs. Carvin," he suggested, and I nodded before shouting up to Brendan, telling him there were some people here to see him. I heard him emerge from the bedroom, no doubt surprised that someone might be calling at such an hour, but he only made it halfway down the stairs before stopping. The moment he saw the Garda uniform, he visibly slumped against the bannister. That phrase one reads in books suggesting that the blood drains from a person's face when confronted by something horrific was proved wrong, for in Brendan's case, the opposite happened. Rather than paling, his cheeks grew inflamed, as if he had been surprised while committing some vulgar act and was mortified by his exposure.

"Mr. Carvin," said DS Kilmartin, looking up and introducing herself and her colleague, just as she had done to me. "Could you come downstairs, please?"

Brendan took the rest of the stairs slowly, his head bowed.

"Mr. Carvin," she repeated when he was facing her, and she glanced quickly at her watch. "It's 8:04 on the morning of March twenty-third and I am placing you under arrest on the suspicion of sexually abusing a minor. You are not obliged to say anything unless you wish to do so, but whatever you say will be taken down in writing and may be given in evidence. Do you understand what I've just said?"

I looked, open-mouthed, from the two Gardaí to my husband and back again, before emitting something that sounded like an inappropriate laugh. I felt as if I was in a television drama, the words she had used being so familiar to me. Somehow, it surprised me that people actually employed them in real life.

"Brendan," I said, turning to him now, but he wouldn't catch my eye. Instead, he continued to stare at the carpet, no doubt understanding immediately that, as of two minutes ago, the life that he had previously led had come to an end and that only ignominy and public disgrace lay before him. Before all of us.

DS Kilmartin turned to Garda Chen, nodded at him, and the young man stepped forward, producing a set of handcuffs, which he attached to Brendan's wrists, and my husband accepted them without a word of protest.

"Brendan," I repeated, my voice rising now. "Brendan, what's going on? What's happening here?"

"It's a mistake, Vanessa," he muttered, shaking his head. "A misunderstanding, that's all."

And yet I knew that it wasn't, because if it was, he would be behaving with more outrage and surprise, rather than submitting himself in such a docile fashion.

"What is it you think he's done?" I asked, turning to DS Kilmartin, even though I had heard her words perfectly. "Sexually abusing a minor? What minor? Who?"

"Mrs. Carvin, I'm sorry, but I'm not at liberty to reveal that information to you," she replied, not sounding sorry in the slightest.

"But you can't just—"

"We need to take your husband to the station now for questioning. You're welcome to follow if you wish, but I'm afraid you'll have to remain in reception, which doesn't have many facilities, and I expect your wait will be rather a long one, so I'd advise against. I imagine that Mr. Carvin will be detained for most of today as we continue our inquiries." She nodded toward Garda Chen once more, and he promptly opened the front door and walked out, preceding Brendan, who trailed him like a dog, content to be led on his walk. The detective sergeant followed, while I stood in the doorway, blinking in the early-morning sunlight, bewildered by what had just taken place. As they put my husband into the back seat of their car, the postman wandered up the drive and handed me a letter, looking from me to the departing vehicle in curiosity. I glanced down at the envelope in my hand and could feel through the paper that it contained my new debit card, which I'd been expecting for the last few days. Uncertain what else to do, I returned inside, removed my old one from my purse, cut it up with the kitchen scissors, and replaced it with the new before sitting down and replaying the entire scene in my head.

I'm not sure how long I sat there, trying to process it all, but I suspect it was quite some time. I only snapped out of my daze when my mobile phone, which was sitting on the table before me, rang. I picked it up and looked at the screen. An unfamiliar number came up but no name, and thinking that it might be someone from the Garda station apologizing for what they'd done and inviting me to collect my husband and bring him home, I answered it.

"Mrs. Carvin?" said a voice on the other end.

"Yes?"

"Richie Howling here, sports correspondent from the *Irish Times*. Do you have a moment to talk?"

I frowned. Why on earth was a reporter from the *Irish Times* calling me? How had he even got my number?

"Not really," I said. "What is it you want?"

"We've received a report that Brendan's been arrested on suspicion of abusing some of the young girls in his care at the National Swimming Federation. Do you have any comment to make?"

I held the phone away from my face and stared at it as if it was my mortal enemy, before trying to locate the button to end the call, but my vision had grown blurry now, and I couldn't seem to find it.

"Mrs. Carvin?" he continued, his voice echoing through the empty room. "Mrs. Carvin, are you there? This is obviously going to be a major news story and I thought it might be helpful for you to get out front of it all and—"

I managed to hang up then, before throwing the phone away from me, like a hot coal or a grenade.

The rest of the day went by in free fall. Feeling that it would be a mistake to drive, I walked to the Garda station on Terenure Road West, where, as promised, I was left sitting in a stark waiting room with posters on the wall relating to domestic violence, cybersecurity, and lost dogs.

To their credit, the Gardaí on duty, recognizing my confusion and distress, displayed some sympathy toward me, keeping me going with mugs of hot tea while expressing regret that they couldn't answer any of my questions. Finally, almost eight hours since she'd shown up at my front door, DS Kilmartin appeared to inform me that Brendan would not be permitted to return home that evening but would be held in the cells overnight before further questioning the following morning.

"But it can't be true," I said, beseeching her to explain to me how something like this could happen. "Brendan would never . . ." I found the words were lost in my throat. "Who would say such a terrible thing about him?"

"I'm sorry, but I can't tell you that."

"Well, whoever it is must be mad in the head."

"We're investigating, Mrs. Carvin. That's our job."

"But you can't keep him here on the word of a disturbed child!" I protested.

"Actually, over the course of the day, more than one complainant has come forward," she told me in a tone that seemed rather pleased to be able to pass on this information.

"How many?" I asked, disbelieving.

"Two more. So far."

It would be eight, of course, by the time the case came to court, and these were only the eight who chose to make their voices heard.

"But that's not my husband," I protested. "It's not. He's . . . he's a father . . . he's—"

"That's what we need to determine," she interrupted, glancing at her watch, and I hated her for the contempt she was showing me. She seemed tired and, unlike her colleagues, unwilling to dispense any compassion toward me. She didn't accept my incredulity, and this was a sensation I would grow accustomed to over the year ahead. The feeling so many people had that if he was guilty, then I must have known about it all along.

"Has he admitted anything?" I asked.

"Not at all," she replied, with a snort of a laugh. "He claims he's innocent."

"Well, then," I said, as if that brought the matter to a close. "What more do you need?"

"I'd advise you to go home," she said. "I won't have any more information for you tonight."

I tried to protest, but she wouldn't be persuaded and, eventually, I had no choice but to leave. When I opened the doors of the station and stepped out onto the street, I was astonished to see a scrum of news reporters and photographers standing there. I glanced behind me, wondering who they were waiting for, but then the flashbulbs went off. When they started shouting my name, I realized they were waiting for me. I couldn't reply to their questions because the whole scene was simply too brutal and terrifying for any words. Instead, I threw myself into their center, pushing forward and forcing them to make way for me, before practically flinging myself into the road in front of a passing taxi that had its lights on, and, fortunately, it stopped for me.

When I arrived home, Rebecca was sitting in the dark in the living room. I turned the lights on, and we stared at each other for a long time. Her expression was entirely unsympathetic.

"Did you know?" she asked, and I shook my head.

"Of course not," I said. "How could I have? It's not true anyway. It can't be true. And who told you?"

"It's all over the fucking news!" she roared, frightening me with her anger. "A friend pulled me out of a lecture to show me what people were saying on Twitter."

And then she stood up and approached me and, for the first time, I realized that she had grown to a height where we could look each other directly in the eye.

"Emma," she said.

I frowned, wondering why she was changing the subject.

"What about Emma?" I asked.

"Emma," she repeated, and, finally, I lost my composure for the first time that day.

"What?" I screamed, spittle flying in my daughter's face. "What about Emma? What are you talking about, you silly girl?"

And now I felt the room begin to swim, and I might have collapsed had Rebecca not reached out to steady me. It had been half a day since the doorbell had rung, and this had never crossed my mind.

"No," I said, my voice low as I shook my head, unwilling to concede for even a moment that what she was suggesting might be possible. "No, he didn't. He wouldn't. He couldn't. No, you're wrong. He'd never do such a thing to his own daughter. He loved her. Why would you say such a thing? What's wrong with you? What in God's name is wrong with you?"

13

When the storm comes, I am frightened. It streaks across the island like a banshee, and Bananas raises himself in the armchair, his claws gripping the frayed wool, turning to glare at me as if he holds me responsible for the weather. I cannot get out for two days because the rain and wind are so strong that there's a chance I might not even make it to the village in one piece, although I long to be in the warmth of either pub with the consolation of other voices around me. I am careful with the food in the fridge, rationing my provisions as people must have done in Famine days.

When the squall hurls itself against the windows, I wonder how they don't concede defeat and shatter inward, shredding me in the process. Even the roof seems as if it's only clinging onto the masonry out of good manners. But who was it who told me that Peader Dooley's cottage had been built from good bricks? Whoever it was, he was right.

Bananas is mewling at the door now, scraping his nails against it, and although I caution him that there is nothing but danger outside, he seems desperate to leave. As comfortable as he is here, it seems that he would, inexplicably, prefer to be with that scourge Mrs. Duggan. When I open the door, he flings himself outside, where the rain falls in sheets, and, in a moment, he has vanished from sight altogether. I call his name, beseeching him to return, but he's a braver soul than I and is surely running as fast as he can toward home. Perhaps he would like to be wrapped up safely in Luke's arms, a sentiment to which I can relate.

I remain in the doorway for a few moments, taking in the extraordinary sights and sounds that greet me, warning me from going any further. This is how I had imagined the island would be when I first studied it on a map and considered it for my exile. Torrential rain. Inhabitants crouched in their houses, waiting for the eternal tempest to soften. The fear of what might be happening to those on the water. I shout into the wind, eager to hear my voice, to confirm that I still have one, but it's lost in the gale, which howls back at me, impressed by my fortitude but demanding that I return inside. I draw the latch across the woodwork, throw some more logs on the fire, and collapse on the sofa, laughing a little. We never had weather like this in Dublin. It's an experience, if nothing else.

My phone rings and I'm greeted by an unfamiliar number. My first instinct is that someone from the village is calling to check on me. Ifechi, perhaps. I want to be rescued but I'm loath to have my solitude disturbed and am uncertain whether to answer. Curiosity takes hold of me, however, and, before it can ring out, I answer.

An automated voice tells me that a call has been placed to me from Midlands Prison. If I am willing to accept it, I should press "star" now. If I am not, I can simply hang up. Despite myself, I search for the "star" and do as instructed.

He says my name. My real name. Vanessa.

"Brendan," I reply, uncertain how to react. "Is it you?"

"Who else would it be?"

"But how are you calling me?"

"We're allowed calls," he tells me. "I wanted to talk."

I say nothing. In my head, I summon up images from American prison movies. Brendan standing at a pay phone, one arm locked around it for privacy, while a group of impatient men stand behind him, ready to drag him away if he stays any longer than necessary. I wonder is what we see in films anything like real life. Probably not.

"Talk about what?" I ask, and I wish I had received some warning of this call, that he had not ambushed me in this way. There's been so many times when I've imagined the things I would say if I was confronted by him—I've paced the cottage holding make-believe conversations aloud—but they're all lost to me now with the surprise.

The last time we spoke was on the morning of his sentencing, when Rebecca and I arrived at the Four Courts and spotted him standing in a corner with his barrister. He came toward us both, and while Rebecca turned on her heel and made her way quickly into the courtroom, I stood my ground while he told me that he was innocent, that the jury had made a mistake, that the whole thing was a kangaroo court, that the media had played a part in his conviction, that the girls who had accused him were filthy little things who'd shown an interest in him but he hadn't reciprocated, that nothing was more important to him than our marriage, that he loved me, that he needed me to tell the reporters outside what a sham all this was, that he'd never survive in prison, that the judge would surely overturn the verdict, that he might have to sue his barrister, that he'd take this to the European Court of Human Rights if he had to, that—

He said more, I daresay, but it was all to my back.

Now, however, he is silent. Even though he's the one who called me, he doesn't seem to know what he wants to say. I can't help myself I fall into old ways and act the part of the dutiful wife.

"How are you getting on in there?" I ask, and I hear a deep sigh, followed by what sounds like a sob.

"It's not easy, love," he says.

"It's not supposed to be."

"I can't do twelve years of it."

"You probably won't have to."

Another long silence before he speaks again.

"How are things at home?" he asks, and I decide not to tell him that I have left Terenure, that our house is locked up for now.

"Quiet," I tell him.

"Are the neighbors giving you a hard time?"

"Not too bad," I say, even though most of them ignored me from the moment Brendan's actions made the papers. People I'd known for decades. People I considered friends. "I'm thinking of taking a holiday," I say, inventing this out of thin air.

"What?" he asks, surprised. "Where to?"

I search my brain for destinations far away. "Sydney, Australia," I tell him. "I've never been."

"And how will you pay for that?"

I frown. It can't be that big a mystery to him. "From our savings," I say.

"Don't be digging into that too much," he says. "I'll need that for the appeal."

"You can't waste money on that," I say.

"Why not?"

"Because it won't change the verdict."

I feel rather brave speaking to him in this way. I'm not sure I would have the courage if he was standing in front of me.

"The truth will out," he insists.

"It already did."

"No, it didn't," he snaps. "They've put me in here to cover their own backs. It's a conspiracy, sure a blind man could see that."

I sigh. I really don't want to hear any more of his self-justifications or his lies.

"Have you made any friends at least?" I ask.

"You're joking, aren't you? Sure there's rapists and murderers and all sorts in here."

"But you're a rapist," I say calmly. "And you have blood on your hands."

"I can't make friends with the likes of them," he continues, ignoring this. "I don't have a fair shake of it on account of what they all think I did."

"But you did do those things, Brendan," I point out. "And more besides, I daresay."

"I didn't," he insists, raising his voice. "Sure what do you take me for?"

"But you did," I repeat. "And at some point you'll have to face up to it and admit what you did. You're a guilty man."

A pause.

"You always thought the worst of me."

"Brendan," I say, and again my tone remains composed, despite the words that tumble from my mouth. "It's not just about the eight girls you abused, the eight that came forward, I mean. It's also about Emma. You abused her, you terrible man. You violated her. I don't know how long it went on for. I don't know how many times you did it. She tried to tell me once, you know, and I didn't listen. I should be in that prison alongside you for not listening. I am, in a sense, although there are no locked doors." I recognize the irony of my words, for all Emma ever asked of me was for a locked door and I denied her it. "You raped our daughter, Brendan. You raped her. Don't you see that? Will you not acknowledge it at least, out of respect for her memory? And she killed herself because of it. She swam out as far as she could one dark night on Curracloe Beach, to a point where she knew there would be no way back. Do you ever wonder what went through her mind at that moment, when all was lost? Did she panic? Did she feel regret? Or was it relief, because she knew you couldn't get your filthy hands on her ever again. Does that not keep you awake at night, Brendan? Because it does me. Our job was to protect her, to protect both of them. Nothing else. But what I didn't know when I married you was that you were a man of no conscience or moral character. Quite honestly, my preference would be that you die in prison. That's the call I want to receive from Midlands Prison. From the governor. Telling me that you're in a box. Not this nonsense from you, pleading innocence and talking about appeals."

I almost can't believe that I've managed to say all this without stumbling over my words or having him interrupt, but there's so much relief in having said them at last. When he eventually replies, his tone is hard and vicious.

"You're as brainwashed as the rest of them," he tells me. "You lived off for me for thirty years, you filthy bitch, and when I'm laid low, when I need you more than—"

I don't hear the end of that sentence as I've already hung up. I'm trembling. I stare at the phone in my hand, as if it has betrayed me in some way. I picture my husband shouting "Hello? hello?" into the receiver and someone behind him telling him that his time's up and to fuck off out of it, and Brendan simpering before him like the coward he is before running back to his cell with his head down. Should this image satisfy me? Because it doesn't. I can take no pleasure in it whatsoever.

I open one of the cupboards and extract the bottle of whiskey, pour myself a healthy glass, and drink it down in one go. The phone sits on the counter now, and I pick it up, opening the text application to see the face of my remaining child.

She has changed her picture again. Now it shows her and Emma in their teenage years, arms around each other, laughing uproariously. I've never seen this one before, so I take a screenshot and save it to my gallery before she can change it again.

Your father phoned me, I write and, a few moments later, to my astonishment, a reply appears.

There is no such person.

I nod and put the phone away.

Outside, the storm is worse than ever. How can the island even retain its foundation in the earth? How is it not dragged from its mooring and hurtled into the sky, spinning away into the clouds like Dorothy's house? I pull on my raincoat. I need fresh air. I need to feel the wind and the rain on my face in order to wash away the obscenity of that call. I open the latch, then the door, and it bursts outward in ecstasy, like a body emerging from a near-drowning, reaching the surface and gasping for air.

I don't quite know where I'm going, and it's difficult to see anyway, but I make my way in the general direction of the seafront and start singing at the top of my voice. An old song. "The Shoals of Herring." I'm no great singer, but it doesn't matter. These are shouts more than anything else. I'm roaring into the wind about fishing the Swarth and the Broken Bank, sailing toward Canny Shiels with a hundred cran of silver darlings, and oh, if anyone was to hear me now, they would think Willow Hale, the woman who came from Dublin without a husband and took up residence in Peader Dooley's cottage, and talked to islanders, and had her lunch every day in the old pub, and slept with Luke Duggan, has gone off her mind from loneliness and will now be known as the Madwoman of the Upper Hills. But no one can hear me, for I am as alone here as I have ever been in my life. I stretch my arms wide and throw my head back, opening my mouth to capture the rainwater, and how is it possible, I ask myself, to feel so at peace in such chaos?

In the distance, on the Duggan farm, I think I see Luke staring down at me, as he did the first time I saw him, but he would be as foolish as me to venture out into this bedlam, so perhaps I'm imagining things. I daresay that mother of his would drag him back in by the scruff of the neck anyway, promising him pneumonia if he stays outside another minute. I blink, my eyes finding it difficult to focus, and maybe he is there and maybe he isn't, and what matter either way, because I can't get that line out of my head, it's repeating over and over—

You lived off for me for thirty years, you filthy bitch, and when I'm laid low . . . You lived off for me for thirty years, you filthy bitch, and when I'm laid low . . . You lived off for me for thirty years, you filthy bitch, and when I'm laid low . . .

Before struggling back toward the cottage, I weep at the loss of everything that was once mine. The loss of Emma. The loss of Rebecca. And, may God forgive me, the loss of Brendan too, who I loved once. The wind is against me and every step takes effort and there is a part of me that wants to lie down on the grass and let it do its worst. How long would I survive? An hour, perhaps? A little more? The elements—water, earth, fire, air—are our greatest friends, our animators. They feed us, warm us, give us life, and yet conspire to kill us at every juncture. But I don't need their permission to take me away. If I could simply clap my hands and fall into a deep sleep out here, never to wake again, I would clap them. I would clap them again and again and again until I was gone from this world and reborn or forgotten, whatever the universe decided.

The door is in sight now, and I trip over what I think might be a rock, and fall to the ground, my hands splayed out before me. Grizzly pebbles crush into my palms, tearing at them, drawing blood, stigmata on my skin, and I lie there, sodden, the storm doing its best to finish me off. I am howling at the pain and misfortune of my life, and when I turn to curse the stone that felled me, I see that it was no stone at all, it was Bananas the cat, for he would not take my advice and stay indoors, and the weather has done for him. In that moment, I weep for this miserable, aggressive feline who somehow came to be my companion, but I envy him too.

"You're better off out of it, my love," I say, but the wind lifts my words away, and what does it matter anyway when he's past hearing them.

14

And now, here she is.

In my cottage. Unannounced. Unexpected. Uninvited. But welcome, always welcome.

My child. My daughter. My survivor.

Rebecca.

"How did you find me?" I ask her, sitting down on the sofa and placing my hands between my knees, for they are noticeably trembling. I feel that I should maintain some distance between us in case I suffocate her with too much affection and she takes fright and runs away. It's the afternoon before wash day and I'm in my rags. I don't know if this will count for or against me. Maybe she'll think I've let myself go since leaving Dublin. I don't want her to think that Brendan has somehow weakened me; he hasn't. If anything, after all this time, I've found strength here. Without him.

"You told me where you were," she replies, and I shake my head.

"No, I meant the cottage," I say. "Not the island."

"Oh, I went into the pub when I got off the boat," she tells me. "I asked about you there."

"And they told you?"

"Yes."

I frown. How is this possible? Everyone here knows me as Willow Hale. But Rebecca knows me as Vanessa Carvin.

"It was weird," she continues, glancing around, taking the place in. "All I had to say was, I'm looking for my mother, and the man behind the bar knew who I was immediately. He said I was the spit of you."

I smile. People always said that Emma was the one who took after me; it's nice to know that I might have passed on something to Rebecca too.

"I don't think we're anything alike, though," she adds, bursting my bubble.

"Why didn't you let me know that you were coming?" I ask.

"I wasn't sure if I was really going to or not and didn't want to say I would and then disappoint you. Even when I arrived on the island, I thought about turning back."

"Why?"

In reply, she simply sniffs the air, as if she's caught a scent of something distasteful.

"Do you have a dog?" she asks. "Is there a dog here somewhere?"

"A cat," I tell her. "Well, it wasn't mine. It just liked to visit. It used to sit where you're sitting, that's probably the scent you're getting. Then it went out in a storm and didn't make it home. I miss it, even though neither of us ever showed the slightest affection for the other."

"You miss the cat," she says, and I can't tell whether this is a question or a statement of fact. Perhaps she's thinking it through in her mind. Her mother is here alone, she's lost a daughter, her husband is in prison, her other daughter barely speaks to her. And she misses a cat.

"It's good to see you," I tell her.

"And you," she says, relenting a little. "I've missed you."

I nod but don't repeat the words back to her. I have to play this very carefully if I'm not to scare her away.

"And how are you?" I ask, thinking that small talk is a good place to start.

"Better than I was. But not as good as I could be. And you?"

"The same, I think."

"You like it here?"

"I don't dislike it."

"You never told me why."

"Why what?"

"Why this island?"

"Oh," I say, laughing. "I probably never told you this, but I came here once before. Years ago, when I was just a girl. Fifteen years old, I think. It's a Gaeltacht area during the summer and six of us from school arrived for three weeks after our Inter Cert, supposedly to improve our Irish. It's so long ago I can't remember much about the place other than the fact that I enjoyed it. It was the first time I got away from your grandparents, you see, so it was a chance for a bit of independence. After the trial, when I knew I needed to escape Dublin, I considered London, but thought that would have been too busy. Then I wondered whether I might go to America. But the States would have been too far."

"From home?"

"No, sweetheart, from you. So then I thought . . . here."

Rebecca smiles. "First kiss?" she asks, and I laugh, delighted that she wants to tease me. This is the relationship I want to have with my daughter. One where we can laugh and share, like adults.

"It was, actually," I say. "Everyone back then had their first kiss in the Gaeltacht."

"What was his name?"

"Oh, for heaven's sake, I can't remember! It was so long ago. Although I remember he had a mullet and looked like one of Echo and the Bunnymen."

"Who?"

"They were a band. Colin liked them."

"Who's Colin?"

"The boy I kissed."

"You said you couldn't remember his name."

I laugh and find my face bursting into a scarlet blush, which makes us both laugh. This is delightful. "Fine," I say. "His name was Colin Marley and I was obsessed from the minute I laid eyes on him. He wore a leather jacket and, along with the mullet, he had beautiful blue eyes that looked at you as if he was a little confused why you, or he, were even alive in the world. He was from Westmeath, and when I got back home we wrote to each other for a couple of months, and swore that we'd meet up at Hallowe'en in Dublin, but then he wrote to tell me that he'd found a girlfriend in Athlone, and I cried for days."

Rebecca looks overjoyed by this story. My mind drifts for a moment back to that boy, back to Colin. He sat next to me in Irish class on the island and sometimes I thought he was too beautiful even to turn my head to look at. As if he was some gorgeous Medusa who might turn me to stone if I so much as glanced in his direction.

"Your hair," she says.

"Yes, I know."

"It's so short."

"It's convenient."

"Actually, it looks good."

"Do you think so?" I ask her. "I did it myself with a pair of scissors. There's a woman below in the village who cuts hair in her kitchen, but I didn't want to bother her. She'd only end up yapping at me and asking me questions. Anyway, it was the first thing I did when I came to the island. No, the second."

"What was the first?"

"It doesn't matter."

I don't want to tell her that I've changed my name. She's still a Carvin, after all, and I don't want her to feel that I've placed more than just a geographical distance between us.

"Have you come to bring me home?" I ask after a lengthy pause, and she shakes her head.

"No," she tells me. "It's up to you where you live. And you've been here, how long is it now? Seven months?"

"Eight."

"And you're not bored?"

"You'd be surprised how busy a person can keep when there's nothing to do. Every night, I make a full plan for the next day before I go to bed. I go for long walks. I talk to people in the village. And there's always a bit of drama to keep me occupied." I hesitate for a moment, then decide to throw caution to the wind. "Also, I have sex quite frequently, and that's been a godsend. I'd forgotten how good it can be if you're doing it with someone who knows what he's doing and wants you to enjoy it as much as he does."

Her eyes open wide, and I can tell that she's not entirely sure she heard me correctly. I rather enjoy the fact that I've shocked her.

"What did you say?" she asks.

"I said I have sex quite frequently," I repeat. "It's nothing long term. A younger man."

"What? How young?"

"Well, I was at his twenty-fifth birthday party in the old pub a few months back."

"Twenty-five?" She looks astonished.

"Yes. A gentle soul. He was interested, so was I, so we both just went with it."

"I see," she says, and it's clear from her expression that she thinks I have taken leave of my senses. "And is this a . . . is he a boyfriend now? Are you, like, dating?"

"Oh no," I reply quickly. "Not at all. But we've become good friends, and the reason it works is that neither of us places any demands upon the other. Sometimes, if I'm in the mood, I text him. Sometimes, if he's in the mood, he texts me. Then he comes over, we have a drink and a chat and when we've exhausted all our conversation we go to bed together. He doesn't stay over. It's something we both take pleasure in. I like him, I think he likes me too. But if either of us ended it tomorrow, I'm sure that neither of us would give it another thought, and our lives would go on as before."

"Right," she says, and I can tell that she doesn't know how to process any of this. This is a conversation she never imagined having with me. I suspect she wants to place it somewhere in the corner of her mind and think about it, or not think about it, later.

"What's his name?" she asks.

"Luke."

She nods.

"Luke what?"

"Luke Duggan."

A silence.

"And what about you?" I ask. "Are you seeing anyone?"

"No one special," she says, as secretive as ever. "So, is this it? Do you live here now? Are you never coming back to Dublin?"

"I will, sooner or later," I tell her. "Right now, I'm still taking it day by day."

"What about the house?"

"What about it?"

"Are you going to sell it?"

"I hadn't given it any thought. Why, would you like it?"

"No," she says quickly. "No, I don't ever want to set foot in it again. But if you sold it—"

"If I sold it, I would give you half," I say, and, making my mind up suddenly, I add: "In fact, let's do that. I don't want to go back there either, so I'll get in touch with someone tomorrow and put it on the market and we'll split the proceeds fifty-fifty. How does that sound?"

She stares at me, as if she's uncertain whether she can allow herself to believe this spontaneous offer.

"Really?" she asks. "You'd do that?"

"Of course I would. I've plenty of savings. And adding my half of the house into that will give me security for life. And your half will set you up nicely, won't it?"

"It will," she says. "But you should think about it. It's a lot of—"

"I have thought about it. I thought about it just now. The plan is made. There now."

"And what about . . . him?" she asks. "Won't he have some say in it?"

"Not a thing," I tell her. "Your grandad gave us the deposit for a wedding present but insisted on putting my name on the deeds. We always meant to change them but never got around to it. So I can do whatever the hell I want. I'll empty the joint account too and split that between the pair of us."

"Then what will he do for money when he gets out?"

"He can live on the streets, for all I care. Do you care? If you do, tell me now, and I'll split it three ways."

She thinks about it. "No," she says. "No, I don't. But maybe we could take his third and—"

She makes a suggestion for what to do with Brendan's share and it tells me what a marvelous young woman she is. She wants to help others. Girls like those who my husband, her father, has destroyed. I agree immediately.

"Thank you," she says. "I wasn't asking so you'd say something like that. But my share will give me options."

"Just use it wisely, that's all I ask."

Always the mother.

She smiles.

I feel I have done something good for her at last.

Another lengthy pause. I can sense this question is coming. He's still her father, after all.

"Have you spoken to him?" she asks.

"Just the once," I tell her. "But we didn't talk for long."

"What did he want?"

"To tell me how miserable he was. And how innocent he was. And what a terrible wife I was."

"Fuck him," she says, and it shocks me a little to hear my daughter use this language. It would never have been allowed when she was growing up. But:

"I couldn't agree more," I tell her.

"I hate him."

"I know."

"Sometimes, I've hated you too."

"There'd be something wrong with you if you hadn't."

"Why did you let it happen?"

"I didn't," I protest. "If I had known—"

"If you had known what?"

"About those poor girls."

"And Emma?"

Mentioning her name is like pressing a sharp knife deep into my heart. The pain of it.

"I don't know," I whisper, looking down at the floor, for I cannot look her in the eyes. "I came here to find out whether I was—"

"What?"

"Complicit," I say.

"And?"

"I don't know," I tell her truthfully. "Maybe I'll never be able to answer that question. I've tried, God knows I've tried, but I think I'm condemned to ask it of myself every hour of every day until I breathe my last. I tried to be a good mother." To my surprise, I realize that tears are running down my cheeks. I wipe them away—both hands, it takes—but they continue to fall. "Truly, I did. Perhaps I wasn't cut out for it, but I did my best. I loved you both. You were my daughters. Nothing mattered more."

"I know," she says.

"I would die for you, Rebecca, do you realize that? I would throw myself under a speeding train if it kept you safe. And I would die to bring Emma back to life."

"She never told you? What he did to her? You promise me?"

"I swear it on my life," I say.

A lengthy pause. She waits. I bow my head. I feel my body collapse into itself. I must be honest. If I'm not, then how can we ever be what we should be to each other?

"Once, she asked me to put a lock on her bedroom door," I tell her. "I didn't like the idea of it, so I said no. It was . . . it was a mistake."

"Did you know why she was asking?"

I want to throw my head back and scream at the moon.

"I don't know," I tell her. "I can't put myself back in that moment."

And now I am weeping.

"I don't know if I guessed and chose to do nothing, or if it didn't cross my mind at all. I don't know. I don't, I swear it. If she had told me and I'd accused her of lying, or just ignored it, then I would have been a monster. But never even to notice? Never even to suspect? That's what shames me the most. That's what makes me question myself. Was I blind, or just stupid?"

She's crying now too but she shakes her head. She cannot answer this question for me. Neither of us can.

I stand up and make my way toward the sink for some paper towels to wipe my eyes dry. "That is what haunts me more than anything else," I tell her. "I don't know if I knew or not. I don't know. One makes me blind, but the other makes me inhuman. Either way, I don't come out of it well."

I stare at her. She is looking down at the floor. I've never known her to cry so much, for she's never been an emotional person, not even when she was a child. Even when Emma died, she was more brittle than demonstrative in her grief. At the funeral, she simply stared ahead and refused to speak to anyone.

"What?" I ask her. "What's wrong?"

"You can't guess?" she asks, looking up at me.

"No. What is it?"

She breathes heavily, as if she has just finished running a race, before putting her head in her hands.

"She told me," she says in a low voice. "The night before she died, she told me. We were on holiday, remember?"

I nod but say nothing. Of course I remember.

"She told me that night in the hotel bedroom. She told me what he did to her. What he'd been doing to her for years. She told me because she didn't want him to do it to me. And I called her a liar. I said it wasn't true, that she was only saying it for attention, because he never touched me. I said some terrible things to her. She begged me to believe her, but I wouldn't. I threw her out of the room. I told her that I didn't care where she slept, but that she wasn't sharing that room with me. I locked the door. I went to bed. And, in the morning, she was gone. So, you see, I blame you but it's really my fault. If I had just listened to her, if I had believed her . . ."

I'm in shock. There's a part of me that wants to slap her across the face, to drag her to the floor and kick her until she curls up into a ball. And there's another part that wants to wrap her up in my arms and tell her that we are none of us innocent and none of us guilty, and we all have to live with what we've done for the rest of our lives, and that the only way through this terrible thing, if we are to survive it at all, is to be kind to each other and to love one another.

Instead, I tell her that I need a moment on my own and retire to the bathroom, locking the door behind me, and stare at myself in the mirror.

"My life," I whisper under my breath. "What has become of my life?"

When I finally emerge, she is standing by the window, and, to my astonishment, she has taken the kitchen scissors and cut her hair to match my own. Her long tendrils are on the floor around her feet.

"We're the same now," she says. "As bad as each other."

"The Carvin women," I say, shaking my head sadly.

"No," she replies. "Not me. Not anymore." I frown, uncertain what she means.

"I changed my name. Well, my surname, at least."

"When?"

"The day you left. Well, later that day, actually. Probably when you arrived here."

I remain silent for a moment.

"To what?" I ask.

"I didn't have many options. I could invent a new one or choose yours. Your maiden name, I mean. So that's what I did."

"Hale," I say.

"Hale," she agrees.

I feel a flood of love wash over me. I don't bother to tell her that I did the same thing at the same time. I will, some day. But not just yet. It is wonderful. It is right. We are no longer Carvins, either of us. We are no longer his.

I step toward her. I place my hands on her shoulders and lean forward, and she does the same. Our foreheads meet and we close our eyes. If it were possible, I would stay in this position forever. Between us lingers the presence of another. It is Emma. We three are here together, a mother and her daughters. He, that man, is absent. He is no longer part of us. He is a demon, exorcized. Emma pulls us together, restful, serene, wrapping her arms around us, happy to see the two people she loved the most are at peace with each other.

Or are at the beginnings of a peace anyway, which is almost the same thing.

15

Today, I leave the island.

I pack my suitcase and, although I've bought no new clothes or souvenirs during my stay here, it seems fuller than when I arrived. Walking around the few small rooms that have been my home this last year, I make sure that I have left nothing behind me, before writing a note for Peader Dooley, whoever he might be, thanking him for allowing me to rent his cottage, and placing it on the table. As I stand in the center of the living room, I wonder how much I have changed in the time that I've spent here. I feel more at peace, certainly. When I first took the train from Dublin to Galway, and then the ferry across to the island, I was frightened of discovery; now, I'm less concerned, as the media has inevitably moved on since Brendan is more than a year into his sentence. I daresay there have been other scandals in the meantime, scandals to which I am oblivious. Other women fleeing the misdeeds of the men they trusted.

When I hear the sound of a car pulling up outside, I assume it is Mícheál Óg Ó'Ceallaigh, who I have asked to collect me, and I feel only a small sentimental sadness as I lock the door behind me, placing the key under the flowerpot as instructed, and make my way toward him. Only, to my surprise, it is not Mícheál Óg sitting behind the wheel, it is Luke.

"I canceled your taxi," he tells me when I open the door. "You don't mind, do you? I thought you might prefer a friendlier face on your last morning. Mícheál Óg's would curdle milk."

I smile and feel an enormous sense of gratitude toward him. We said our goodbyes already, two nights ago, but what harm to say them again.

"Thank you," I say, settling into the passenger seat and buckling the belt as he drives over the gravel and down the makeshift road. "This is very good of you."

How lucky I was to have met him! We were a mutual convenience that worked out splendidly. We never bothered to discuss what our relationship is, or was, or might have been. We just enjoyed every minute of it.

"I hear he's already got it rented again," says Luke as we drive along. "Peader, I mean."

"The cottage?"

"Sure enough. The rumor is that it's some actress escaping Hollywood after a breakup with her fella."

"Good Lord. And I suppose you'll head over to say hello?" I ask, teasing him, and he laughs, even blushes a little.

"Well, it's good to be neighborly, isn't it?" He turns to smile at me, then we both dissolve in silly giggles. I adore him and want nothing from him. We want nothing from each other. Which was why what we shared was perfect. "So, what's next for you?" he asks, and I shrug my shoulders, for I've been asking myself the same question over the last two weeks, since I decided it was time to leave, and I still haven't arrived at a satisfactory answer.

"I have to pack up the house," I tell him. "It went sale agreed a few days ago so I'll box up the things I want to hold on to and get a man with a van to take what's left to the charity shop. After that, I need to find somewhere to live. And, I thought, get a job."

"What sort of a job?"

"Whatever will keep me busy. The thing is, Luke, I've never worked. And I'm only fifty-three. I want to be out and among people. To have some fun. I haven't had much fun in my life. It never seemed like a priority. I feel ready to change that. We had fun, didn't we?"

"Plenty of it."

"And I'd like some more."

"So you'll stay in Dublin?"

"Probably," I tell him. "But who knows? You're welcome to visit if you want," I add tentatively, and he turns to me and smiles, as if to suggest that he's grateful for the offer but no, that's not something he'll be doing. I'm not sure that I'd even want him to. He wouldn't belong there any more than I ever belonged here.

"You'll be fine," he says, and, as on the first night we met, when he first advised me to be careful of the water, there's nothing patronizing in his tone.

"And you?" I ask. "You'll stay here?"

"I will," he admits. "Sure, I'm too old to move now."

"Luke, you're twenty-five," I say, rolling my eyes at such defeatism. "You have your entire life in front of you."

"I know, but, well, I'm happy enough here. I fit in." He nods in the general direction of the bigger island that gives us our identity. "I'd be a fish out of water beyond."

We pull into the dock and he places the car in neutral, pulls up the handbrake, and takes my right hand in his left, before lifting it to his mouth, kissing it gently, and releasing it.

"Right then, Willow Hale," he says. "Shall we get moving?"

We climb out of the car and, as he retrieves my suitcase from the boot, I notice Ifechi standing by the platform that leads to the waiting boat. It's not the regular ferry, but a smaller one that can be specially booked when you need to travel outside of the scheduled hours. I smile in his direction. I'm glad he came to see me off.

"I didn't make a convert out of you," he says when I approach him, and we shake hands, somehow nervous of hugging.

"I'm afraid not," I reply. "But you did your best and that's what counts."

"Will you come back to see us again?"

Luke places the suitcase on the ground next to me and looks up, interested in the answer to this question.

"I don't think so," I say. "I must put all of this behind me now."

"But you won't forget us?"

"Oh no," I say, extending the handle of the suitcase and shaking my head. "No, I won't forget you. Any of you. Goodbye, Ifechi."

Two kisses, one for him and one for Luke, and that's it. I make my way along the platform and a man I don't recognize helps me on board, taking my suitcase and placing it in the rear, in the center, for balance. Then, as I am the only passenger, he starts the engine, but, before he can leave, a voice from the dock stops him. I look around, and it's Evan Keogh, the boy who took his father's boat out and almost didn't come back. He's running toward us, his mother a few steps behind, a rucksack slung over his shoulder.

"Are you joining us, Maggie?" shouts the sailor, and she shakes her head.

"Not me," she calls back. "Just Evan."

Mother and son are locked in conversation now, and I see her putting a bundle of banknotes into his hand, folding his fingers around them. She pulls him toward her, tight, as if she might never see him again, then pushes him away.

"Go on now," she says, her voice filled with urgency, as if they're being chased. "Go on now, you, and don't look back."

And he follows her instructions, throwing his bag into the boat and leaping in.

"Right so," says our captain, and, a moment later, the boat pulls away, its stern pointed in the direction of Galway. I watch Maggie Keogh—her expression blends sorrow and relief—until she has disappeared from view.

"You're leaving, then?" I ask, turning to Evan, who startles a little, as if surprised to be spoken to.

"I am," he tells me.

"Tell me to mind my own business if you want, but am I right in thinking you're a great footballer?"

"That's what they tell me," he says. "But I have no more interest in it than I do in the man in the moon."

I'm surprised by his response. I understood that most teenage boys longed for a life in sport. Clearly, he's different.

"And where are you going?" I ask.

He smiles. The weather is perfect for this voyage, and we make easy companions.

"England, to begin with," he tells me.

"And what's in England?" I ask.

"My future. And you?"

"Dublin."

"And what's in Dublin?"

"My past."

"Then leave it there," he says, and I'm surprised to hear such sensible advice from a boy who can't be more than seventeen.

"What do you suggest?" I ask.

"Go somewhere no one knows you. Start again. I know who you are, by the way. And who your husband was. I never told anyone, but I always knew. I've seen you around."

"And I've seen you around."

"I was a bit intrigued."

I laugh. It's an unusual phrase for a boy his age.

"Were you indeed?" I say.

"Yes," he replies.

"Well, thank you for keeping it to yourself."

He nods and looks out at the water. We are safe from it in this sturdy little boat, but I will be happier when we reach Galway.

"Did the island give you whatever you needed?" he asks me after a while, and I have to think about this, because I want to give him an honest answer.

"I think it did," I tell him. "Now, I just have to figure out how to use its gifts."

"Don't go to Dublin," he says.

"Why not?"

"Because it's small. And the world is big. Fuck Dublin," he adds. He seems so excited to be on this boat. He is breathless for the life he's entering into, and I hope that he will not know pain or betrayal or disappointment, but of course he will, because he's alive and that's the price we pay.

We say nothing for a while, occasionally looking across at each other and smiling, but feeling no need to continue with our conversation. Might you have been Zac, I wonder, imagining my ghost-child, the one who might have saved us all, since the living proved so hopeless.

"Do you know anyone in England?" I ask him in time.

"Not a soul."

"And you're not frightened?"

When he smiles, his whole face lights up. He is the very sunshine.

"Not a bit of it," he says. "I'm excited. Do you know the first thing I'm going to do when I get there?"

"What?" I ask.

"Change my name."

The three of us—the sailor, the boy, and I—remain silent for the final part of our voyage. The sailor is probably thinking about what he'll have for his dinner when he turns around, having dropped us off and made his way home. The boy is looking toward the mainland, anticipating everything to come. And me, well, I intend to get riotously drunk in the pubs around Eyre Square tonight, on my own, and I will call this the end of the first half of my life. Tomorrow, I will wake up and begin again.

Soon, lights start to twinkle in the distance, through the mist, and I can hear the sounds of life on the approaching shore. It's only another island that I'm approaching, of course, a larger one than the one on which I've spent this last year, but it holds the body of my elder daughter in its earth, the worthless bones of my husband in one of its prisons, and the beautiful spirit of my younger daughter in its capital. And, in a few minutes, it will reclaim me.

Willow Hale.

Vanessa Carvin.

Whatever name I choose.

I can be any woman in Ireland.

The engine dies, and the boat drifts toward the shore.

The sailor throws out a rope to a man waiting on the dock, and he ties it quickly around a mooring post. I'm gathering my things together as Evan makes his way nimbly off the boat, puts his rucksack down, and, a gentleman to his core, reaches out a hand to take my suitcase from me, but I wave it away.

"No, you're grand," I tell him. "I can do it myself."

EARTH

1

I dreamed that I dreamed about the musty gray soil of the island and the sweet perfume it emits after rainfall, a double remove from a place I will never visit again. My mother explained to me once that the fragrance comes from a combination of chemicals and bacteria in the earth which form filaments when wet, sending spores of aromatic vapor into the air. We find the scent comforting, she told me, because we want to believe there'll be a welcoming place for us one day, when we're buried deep inside it.

I've been awake for almost an hour when my phone lights up with a message. I ignore it until another arrives a few moments later. Lifting it from its charger, I see that it's from Robbie, as I knew it would be. I read the first one:

Counting on you today, bro. Don't let me down.

And then the second:

Delete that, yeah?

I wonder how he can be so stupid as to text me at all. Messages like this have contributed to the trouble we're in. The WhatsApp group chat where he had to brag about that night, and the replies, all made public, that made us look like a bunch of animals. He thinks that boasting is proof of our innocence, that if we'd actually committed a crime, then the last thing either of us would have done is brag about it. That might be true, but doesn't he know that deleting them means nothing? Everything is saved in the phone's internal hardware, or in the cloud, or on some anonymous server in a vast warehouse located under the Mojave Desert.

Nothing disappears. Nothing is forgotten. Everything we say or do these days clings to us forever.

I climb out of bed and place my feet on the carpet. These feet that can do things that other boys' feet cannot. Run down a pitch, evading human obstacles, with the grace of Rudolf Nureyev. Pick up a ball and bounce it effortlessly on strong toes. Curve it from the corner spot in a perfect arc, landing on the head of a chosen forward, or send it soaring over the leaping bodies of crotch-guarding defenders into the top-right corner of a net. How many times have they carried me to the sidelines, where I drop to my knees before our army of fans, arms outstretched, pretending that I care about the adulation coming my way? They've been able to do this from as far back as I can recall, in the same way that some children are able to draw, or sing, or do impressions. Unfortunately, whatever magic I was granted found its way to the wrong limbs, for I did not want to be a footballer. I wanted to be a painter, but my eyes and hands did not have the gifts granted to my feet.

I walk over to the curtains and pull them apart, looking down toward the residents' parking spaces below. My bright yellow Audi R8 glistens in the sunshine. I spent a fortune on it a year ago, eight weeks' wages at the time, I calculated, and I only ever drive it to the training ground and back. It would have been cheaper to use taxis.

The fourteen-story building I live in is located on the outskirts of the city, near the river. Each floor contains only a single apartment of 2,500 square feet, and I live on the twelfth. Facing it, on the other side of a perfectly manicured circle of flower beds with a fountain at its center, stands an identical building, where Robbie lives in a penthouse duplex. On the floors below me live two well-known actors, a moderately successful pop-star, and a former home secretary. In Robbie's, there are three other footballers and a disgraced tennis coach. Our homes have more space than any of us need. There are home pods in every room, and if I want to hear a song, I say its name out loud and it plays. My voice controls the temperature, the water flow, the underfloor heating. There are six televisions, one in the living room, one in each of the three bedrooms, one in the kitchen, and one facing the bath. I'd have preferred something simpler, but the club insisted, because they like to send the glossies over occasionally to photograph us relaxing with our girlfriends and this is the kind of place that the fans expect. Not that I have a girlfriend. Although they arranged one for me a few weeks after I moved in, when *Hello!* came to call. She seemed friendly enough, even suggested going for drinks afterward, but I said no, blaming the following morning's training session.

"I'm not looking for anything," she told me. "It's just a drink. I've been living with a woman for the last three years."

I still said no.

"Then I guess we're breaking up," she said, kissing me on the cheek as she left. "It's been fun, Evan."

As I head toward the en suite, my phone rings and I sigh, assuming it's Robbie again, but no, when I look at the screen, I see that it's Dad calling. He and Mam arrived four days ago and are staying in a hotel in the city center. I wish they hadn't come over at all, but there was nothing I could do to keep them away. I consider rejecting the call, but I know what he's like. He'll keep phoning until I answer.

"Hi," I say, lifting it to my ear.

"You're up, then."

"Of course I'm up."

I can hear him breathing heavily. This life, this terrible life that I have, was his dream, not mine. I've become everything he wanted me to be since I left the island four years ago, but he's still controlling me.

"Watch your tone," he says quietly, and my nostrils fill with the smell of the loam, as they always do when I'm frightened or when I remember what I did that made me run away in the first place.

"Sorry," I say.

"You're getting a taxi?"

"Yes."

"Did the club organize it?"

"No. They can't get involved."

"Do you want me to have a word with them?"

I stifle a laugh. He actually thinks the club would listen to him. Its owner, directors, and assets are worth somewhere between three and four hundred million pounds. He might be a big man on the island with his farm and his third share of a grocery store and his fifth share of a boat, but he's nothing here. He wouldn't even get through the front door.

"Best to leave it," I say. "I'll use an app, it's easier."

"Right." There's a lengthy pause. I wonder whether I can hang up, but the choice is taken away from me when he does so first. I throw the phone onto the bed and take a long, hot shower, shaving carefully, then use the hair-dryer to plump up my blond curls. I know how innocent they make me look, and I might as well take advantage of that. My face has a childlike aspect to it, making me appear younger than my twenty-two years. More innocent. If I wasn't so well known in the city, I'd have trouble getting served in bars. As it is, the only difficulty I have is paying for my own drinks. When I go out, girls want to get close to me and boys want to be my best friend. When I went out, I mean. I don't anymore, for obvious reasons. The only person I see regularly is Wojciech, and even he seems to be reconsidering our relationship. We go to a local pub sometimes, one where the regulars have no interest in football, and I keep my back to the room and pull a baseball cap down over my fore-head. More often than not, though, he just comes here, and we watch a movie together, my head in his lap. I like how he strokes my hair. Mam used to do that when I was a boy, lying on the sofa watching *Toy Story* over and over. Cormac and I knew every line of that film, and when we were children we would go to each other's houses and act out scenes for our parents, who howled with laughter, even Dad, who only allows himself a handful of smiles a year, as if each one costs him something he can't afford. We were so close, Cormac and I, united as much by having known each other since we were babies as by the fact that I had no sib-lings, while his only brother, his senior by only a year, had been killed in an accident when we were seven. He'd never quite got over Ronan's death, traumatized at an age when he would either move past it quickly or not recover at all, and he clung to me in his grief.

I open one of my many wardrobes and stare at the suits within, most of which I don't recognize, since I don't buy my own clothes. The club employs a woman, Lucy, who takes care of all that for us. She stores all the players' measurements—shirt size, shoe size, trouser length—on her laptop and seems to understand instinctively what will look best on each of us. Every month two boxes arrive, one from Nike, because they're my sponsor—were my sponsor—and the other from one of the big luxury brands. If I'm photographed in them, and those pictures subsequently appear in the papers, my account is credited with 30–50 percent of their value, depending on the publication. I don't wash my boxers or socks; they go straight in the bin after a single use. There's always dozens more waiting in my underwear drawer. I've been given clear instructions on how to dress today: relatable but aspirational. It's important that I look like I care enough about, or at least respect, what's happening to make an effort, but that I'm too distressed by the injustice of it all to try too hard. In the end, I select a dark blue Armani suit with a white Balenciaga shirt and a navy Tom Ford tie. A pair of dark brown Ted Baker shoes that feel uncomfortable on my precious feet. Maybe if I wear them long enough, I can cause some permanent damage and be set free.

Before I dress, however, I examine my body in the bedroom's full-length mirror. My left arm is a little stiff this morning, which it occasionally is when I feel stressed. I broke it a few years ago—or rather, I had it broken for me—and it's never been quite the same since. But I'm still toned, since I use the building's gym and private pool most days, although the definition of my abdominals has diminished a little. Neither Robbie nor I are allowed anywhere near the club right now, so I can't eat in the players' canteen, where the food is carefully prepared and nutritionally balanced, so my diet has slipped. A private trainer shows up three times a week, supplied by the club, and this is something we're not allowed to tell anyone. Robbie's worth more than ten million pounds, and I'm valued at just over half that amount, so it needs to protect its assets. When this is over, if it goes our way, we'll be expected back on the pitch as soon as possible. If it ends badly, they'll never speak of us again. We'll be erased from their records as if we never existed and, I imagine, the insurance will kick in.

By nine fifteen, I'm dressed, and I return to the window, waiting for Robbie to leave. I'm only there a few minutes when a taxi pulls up and he emerges from the front entrance. Only when it drives away do I open the app and order one for myself. I could have traveled with him, of course, but Catherine, our barrister, said it would look better if we arrived separately.

When the driver pulls up, I'm standing by the small area of overgrown grass which houses the development's performative commitment to the environment, a wild sanctuary that allows insects and birds to land or nest without disturbance. It has a rough beauty to it, but it contains a secret in its depths, and I become so lost in thought that the driver has to sound his horn to snap me out of it. I turn away, open the back door, and step inside. I've entered my destination already, so there should be no need for conversation. I keep my head low, pretending to scroll through my phone, and it's only when we're halfway there that I notice how he keeps glancing at me in the rearview mirror.

"I know who you are," he says.

I don't reply.

"It starts today, doesn't it?"

I nod.

"I'm a fan," he tells me, his face breaking into a wide smile. "That goal you scored against—"

"Thanks," I say. I have no interest in reliving the highlights of my brief career.

"So how long will it go on?" he asks.

"A couple of weeks, I'm told."

"If you like," he says, "I could pick you up every morning. And then, when you're done for the day, I could be waiting outside. Might make life easier for you."

He's not wrong. It would be more convenient to use the same taxi and driver throughout this whole ordeal. After a day or two, he'll grow tired of interrogating me.

"All right," I say.

"What time should I come back for you today?"

"Four."

"And pickup tomorrow at nine thirty?"

"Yes."

"I'll bill you when it's all over."

"Fine."

"So don't go to jail."

My teeth grind against each other.

"And do I call you Evan or Mr. Keogh?"

"Evan's fine," I tell him.

"Then I'm Max," he says, reaching into a pocket between the two front seats and extracting a pack of business cards before passing one back. "All my details are on there. But you don't need to worry. I'll be where I'm supposed to be."

"Thanks," I say.

As he turns a corner, the courthouse appears in sight, and I see the media scrum outside. I realize now that I should have left before Robbie. Then I could have been inside when he pulled up, and they would have turned their attention toward him. He's the bigger star, after all. Now they'll focus on me.

We pull up, and I reach for the door handle.

"Give 'em hell, lad," says Max, turning around and grinning. His teeth are yellow and his lips badly chapped.

Hair springs from beneath the collar of his shirt, his eyebrows, his ears, his nose. He's an unkempt forest of a man. "Remember, any girl who takes on two lads like that is nothing more than a cheap little whore, and the jury will see that. You think I've never been there? Some girl saying no when you know they mean yes? More times than I can count."

I imagine how it would feel to pull his head toward me and smash it into the gap between the seats, to keep pounding it against the cheap interior until I've ended him. But I do nothing. Instead, I simply nod, open the door and step outside, the flash of the cameras and the shouting of the reporters overwhelming me, like I'm arriving for a film premiere and not a rape trial. I wonder, as Max drives away, does he notice me crush his business card within my fist and toss it away, flicking it with my index finger so it lands in the dark soil of the bushes outside the building. He can come back at four if he wants, but I won't be waiting for him.

A policeman approaches. I think he's going to guide me into the courthouse, but no, he reprimands me for littering, making me pick up the card while the photographers snap away and the journalists roar my name. It's dirty now, covered with moist earth, and muddies the fingers of my left hand, but I don't want to wipe them against my suit, so I wait until I enter the building, where the people standing in the lobby turn to look at me, then discard it in the nearest bin and run my hand under a sanitizing tap, a holdover from the days of the pandemic, when we could all stay inside, alone, and avoid the world entirely.

2

Twelve hours after leaving the island, I boarded a ferry from Dublin to Holyhead, before hitching a ride to South Wales, where I found work on a farm cultivating a mixture of wheat and barley. I'd worked with crops before so fitted in well, being suited to early starts and long days. Eight of us lived in a house on the northeast corner of the land, two in each of the four bedrooms. My roommate was a boy named Buddha, a nickname he'd earned because he was fat and bald, despite being only a few years older than me. He was involved in an on-off relationship with a Canadian girl, Joanna, who slept in the room opposite ours. Buddha and I didn't get on well. He'd had the room to himself for two months before my arrival and objected to my intrusion. He was vulgar in his habits and spoke of women in ways that made me uncomfortable. When he and Joanna wanted to have sex, he'd send me to sleep on the sofa downstairs, where the springs pressed into my back. I protested once and a threat of violence followed, so I backed down.

I asked Joanna's roommate whether I could use the spare bed in her room when it was empty, and she said no. I told her I was gay, so she didn't have to worry about me making a pass at her, but she said she didn't care about my sexuality, she just didn't want to share with a boy.

"Don't you like boys?" I asked her, and she said that was the problem, she liked boys too much, and that I wouldn't be safe around her. I must have looked bewildered, as she burst out laughing and told me not to flatter myself.

Once I was settled, I wrote to Mam and Dad to reassure them that I was safe and had a job, but didn't give them my address. I did, however, share my new mobile number, and a few days later, the phone rang. It was Dad, calling to tell me what a useless cunt I was, that I had it in me to be one of the great footballers of all time—better than Pelé, he said; better than Georgie Best—and that I was throwing it all away.

"But I don't want to be a footballer," I told him, for what must have been the thousandth time since I was a child. "I'm not even interested in watching it, let alone playing it."

"What's that got to do with anything?" he roared. "You have a God-given talent that I would have killed for. Do you know how many trials I had when I was your age?"

"I know," I said, for he'd told me often enough. Manchester, Liverpool, Leeds, Birmingham, Newcastle. A long list of cities and towns he'd traveled to when he was a teenager in the hope of escaping his own father. But he didn't have the skill that I did.

"I'd have given my left foot to have your talent," he said.

"Wouldn't have made you much of a footballer then, would it?" I replied, and he swore at me and demanded my address, which I refused.

"But a farm," he said, exasperated. "If you wanted to work on a fuckin' farm, you could have stayed here."

"I don't want to work on a farm," I said. "It's just somewhere to make money, that's all. I want to be a painter."

"You're not going to be a fuckin' painter!" he shouted.

"I am," I said.

"Like a fuckin' . . ." like a fuckin' queer," he said.

I fell silent then. I wasn't sure what the connection between art and homosexuality was in his mind, but they seemed to be closely aligned. Of course, he'd never read a book in his life. Or gone to the theater. Or watched a film that didn't have explosions in it. He would have thought it effete. He would have thought my using the word *effete* was effete, for that matter. I felt like telling him the truth about me, just to make him even angrier, but worried that if he knew, he might march down the road to take out his fury on Cormac. And I couldn't risk Cormac telling him why I ran away the first time. Or why I left forever a few months after that.

He started ranting then, so I ended the call and blocked his number. When I looked up, Buddha was standing in the doorway, staring at me.

"What's wrong?" he asked.

"Nothing," I said.

"You're crying," he said, and I put my hands to my face. To my surprise, my cheeks were wet with tears.

"My dad," I told him. "He scares me."

He nodded and sat down on the bed next to me and I placed my head on his shoulder and he allowed it. He put an arm around me and asked did I think he was working on this farm because he wanted to? I'm running away from something too, he told me. Not getting into it. Too long a story. Too fucked up. But you're not alone. So no more crying, all right? You're a bit of a twat, Evan, but you don't get to cry around me. If I have to, I'll tickle you to make you smile again. I couldn't imagine anything more uncomfortable, so I dried my eyes, not wanting to test his resolve. We grew friendlier after that.

One Sunday afternoon, a game of football was arranged in the southwest field, five-a-side, temporary workers versus the farmer and his four sons. The second-to-youngest son's name was Harry, he was my age and had spent the summer working alongside us. He talked relentlessly about the girlfriend he had in university, how beautiful she was and how they did it every night. He was obsessive on the subject, making sure everyone knew. I kissed him by the side of a barn one evening and he kissed me back, and the next day he pretended that I didn't exist. I didn't know any other way to play football than well, so we won 18–2 and I scored fourteen of those goals. Harry was their goalkeeper, and he looked humiliated by the end of it. The farmer took me aside afterward and asked me why I was working there and not as a professional footballer.

"It's not for me," I told him. "I don't mind the odd game, but I don't want to play for a living."

"But you could make millions."

I shrugged. I was fond of the farmer, but he was beginning to sound like my father.

Later that night, I glanced out my bedroom window and saw Harry standing by a tree, smoking a cigarette, looking up at me. I put my shoes on and went outside to join him and we made our way into one of the far fields where we were hidden by the trees.

The next day, he ignored me again. I didn't much care.

I used my wages to buy canvases, brushes, and paint supplies online and set myself up in a small, empty storehouse that the farmer wasn't using and, over the course of about seven months, during the evenings, created a portfolio of work, more than two dozen paintings that I was proud of. Some of the laborers came to look at them and made complimentary remarks, but I could tell they were baffled by what I was doing. I didn't paint landscapes or seascapes or people or animals. My work was abstract. I liked geometric shapes. I admired Kandinsky. And Mondrian. And Paul Klee. The only thing that reappeared time and again in my work were images of soil, not the smooth, tilled land of the farm I was working on, but the rough, unplowed hills that led from the island port to my parents' house. I was reared in the mud and the dirt, and it showed up repeatedly on my canvases, even when I didn't want it to. But the earth is a part of me. The feel of it on my skin. The taste of it in my mouth.

When the season was over and it was time to leave the farm, I made my way to London, naively intending to live as an artist. I thought that if I could sell some of my work, then perhaps I could rent a studio in one of the cheaper parts of the city. Somewhere I could shake the land out of my system and replace its ugliness with color, beauty, fine lines, and the wild ideas that roared through my head and often made no sense, not even to me.

Over time, I approached every gallery I could find and was rejected by all of them. Each one said the same thing, that I was not untalented but that there was no originality in what I had produced.

"You like Kandinsky, don't you?" one gallerist asked, carefully examining the three canvases that I considered my best, stepping very close to them to study my brushwork and the places where the lines intersected.

"I do," I said.

"And Mondrian."

"Yes."

"And Paul Klee."

I nodded.

"I can tell," he said, sounding half regretful, for he was kind and didn't want to hurt me unnecessarily. He put a hand on my shoulder and gently massaged the muscle there. "And that's the problem."

"Should I go to college," I asked, knowing I couldn't afford it anyway, and he shook his head, telling me that I would be wasting my time.

"You must be born with the gift," he said. "And I'm sorry, but you haven't been. You're young, Evan. You must find something else to do with your life. Trying to achieve the impossible will only bring you misery. And you will grow to hate art, as if it is your enemy."

This broke my heart. But when I stood before the paintings that hung in the museums and galleries around London and compared them to my own, I knew that he was right. I was no artist. I was just good at painting. In the same way that my father was good at football but was no footballer.

I couldn't allow myself to return to the island. Not because I was afraid to admit failure, but because I didn't want to grow old with the eternal mud beneath my fingernails, dirt that would remain there stubbornly, no matter how hard I tried to wash it away.

But my money was running out. I wrote to the farmer, asking for my job back, and he said he was sorry, but he'd hired someone in my place. I moved into a rented room in Dagenham, in a house that contained twelve decrepit bedrooms and a shared kitchen where the mice lived for free. The other residents were mostly off their heads on drink and drugs. My room had a single bed and a sink and there were only two showers on the third floor, which you came out of feeling dirtier than when you went in.

A woman older than my mother knocked on my door late one night demanding sex, saying I was the most beautiful boy she'd ever seen in her life. I refused and she called me a faggot. She said if I didn't fuck her, then she'd tell everyone in the house that I liked boys, and I told her she could do what she liked, what did I care, so she asked me whether I could lend her a cigarette instead, but I said I didn't smoke, and she told me I was fucking useless and I should fuck off back to Ireland like the Fenian bastard I was.

And then one night, with only sixty pounds left to my name, I took the Tube to Walthamstow, to a pub I'd heard about but never visited before, hoping to find a boy my own age to talk to, someone who might take me home with him. For a warm body. For arms around me. For a hot shower.

But I was the youngest there by far. The old men who sat on stools by the bar, nursing tired gin and tonics, perked up briefly when I walked in. I could have left but had nowhere else to go. I ordered a beer and sat in a dark corner, underneath a poster for a film called *La Cage aux Folles*, sipping my drink while I tried to figure out what to do next with my life.

That's when he approached me.

I could sense him as he made his way across the floor but didn't look up, even as his footsteps grew louder, brogues tapping on the woodwork. He didn't look like the dinosaurs at the bar, although he was a good twenty-five years older than me. His clothes were smart, and he had short graying hair and pale blue eyes. Handsome, for his age. For any age. Sitting down opposite me, he lit a cigarette. I glanced toward the barman, expecting him to intervene, to tell him that he couldn't smoke in here, but he didn't seem to care. The man studied me carefully as he drew on it.

"I'm Rafe," he said, reaching a hand across, and I shook it. He wore a gold signet ring on the little finger of his left hand.

"Evan," I replied.

He raised my chin until I was looking him directly in the eye. We held each other's gaze.

"Have you ever heard of Luchino Visconti?" he asked. I shook my head.

"You're probably too young," he said. "He made a very famous film—well, he made quite a few of them—but in one, there's a boy. A boy who becomes the obsession of an older man. In the film, the part was played by a young actor who you won't have heard of either, but for a time he was known as the most beautiful boy in the world."

I stared at him. I waited for him to continue, although I knew exactly what he was going to say.

"You could be his twin," he told me.

3

I'm escorted up a staircase by my barrister, Catherine, who explains how the day will unravel, but I'm so conscious of the contemptuous way people are staring at me that I find it difficult to focus on her words. There's the click of an iPhone camera from somewhere behind me, and she spins around, making it clear to whoever took the shot that photography is not permitted within the court building, before taking me by the arm and leading me along the corridor toward a large oak door. Stepping inside, I'm surprised by the brightness of the room. Enormous windows flood the space with light while the walls are covered in artworks, all reproductions, of course, but they're where my eyes go first. Traditional British landscapes. Portraits of people I don't recognize. A long table dominates the center, and at one end sits Robbie. He glances up when I enter, and our eyes meet; there's a warning in his expression, a successor to his messages from a few hours earlier. I'm sure he's checking social media to see whether we're trending.

In his suit, he looks handsome, and the unexpected longing I've felt for him since our first meeting rears up inside me. He's still one of only two boys I've ever truly desired, and he knows this. It's how he's kept his hold over me.

Near him, standing by a bookcase, are his parents. His mother looks me up and down with obvious disdain, as if she can't quite accept that her life, for now, is intertwined with the life of someone like me.

"I'll leave you here," says Catherine, looking around and probably as anxious to escape this room as I am. "We'll be called in about twenty minutes. I'll come back for you all then."

She disappears, and now there's just me, the Wolvertons, and my parents, who followed me upstairs. We stare at each other awkwardly, four adults, two young men, none of us quite knowing what to say. Finally, Lady Wolverton strides down the room as if she's walking a runway, which, of course, she often did in her youth, before extending her hand to Mam.

"Grace Wolverton," she says. "Robert's mother."

"Margaret Keogh," says Mam, using her full name for once. Everyone on the island knows her as Maggie. "And this is my husband, Charles."

"Charlie," says Dad, eyeing Lord Wolverton warily as he approaches. Robbie's father is studying my parents in the way that wealthy, privileged English people often do whenever they're confronted by Irish people with accents as thick as ours. They assume that we're barely literate and will be astonished by the fact that the room is illuminated by electric lightbulbs. He introduces himself to my parents, extending a hand somewhat reluctantly.

"Well, this is a fine state of affairs, isn't it?" he says, glancing toward his son, who's leaning back in his chair, watching the drama play out. "Not a situation I ever thought I'd find myself in, I must admit."

"Us either," says Mam, then corrects herself. "Us neither, I mean. Is it either or neither?"

I'm embarrassed by her obsequiousness and worry that she might drop a curtsy before them. The majesty of the building and the aura of affluence that surrounds the Wolvertons are simply too much for her, a woman who's never known life outside the island since she was brought there as a young bride. My father visibly wilts inside his cheap suit, the tie loosened at the neck and the top button undone, his chin being too fat to keep it closed.

"It's such a nonsense," continues Lord Wolverton. "The CPS is obviously trying to scapegoat Robert and . . ." He glances in my direction; apparently, I'm not important enough even to have a name. "Your son. If they weren't who they are, I doubt it would have even got this far. The girl at the center of all this seems a rather cheap person, don't you agree? She comes from a broken home, but I assume you know that."

"Darling," says Lady Wolverton, placing a hand on his forearm.

"I'm simply stating the facts," he says with the tone of someone who

[136]

is unaccustomed to being interrupted or corrected. "I know we live in supposedly progressive times"—and here he makes inverted comma symbols with his fingers in the air—"but more often than not, that means we must believe the victim, however absurd the allegation, without any consideration for due process."

"She's not a victim," says Robbie from the other end of the room, and we all turn to look at him. "Don't use that word."

"You're quite right," replies Lord Wolverton, nodding emphatically. "If anyone is the victim here, it's you." He pauses, and we all wait for the obvious addendum. Finally, grudgingly, he deigns to offer it. "And your son, of course."

"Evan," says Mam.

More silence. I wonder whether, if I flung myself toward one of the enormous windows, would it break upon impact, letting me plunge to the street below. The staircase outside was highly elevated; we must be at a significant distance from the ground. I'd probably die. That would be nice.

"Are you a football man yourself, Lord Wolverton?" asks Dad, and I make my way around the table, taking a seat opposite Robbie. I glance down toward the carpet. He's wearing invisible socks, and his trousers, as he sits, rise to expose his ankles.

"I was brought up an Arsenal fan," he replies, speaking as if he's addressing an audience at the Guildhall. "Or 'The Gunners,' as we call them over here."

"I know who the Gunners are," says Dad, who's willing to be subservient but won't be patronized when it comes to the subject of football.

"Although I rarely have the time to go to matches," he continues. "Busy with work and social commitments and what have you."

"You were a politician, weren't you?" asks Mam. "That must have been very interesting."

"I still am, in a sense," he replies. "But I maintain many diverse business interests."

"You came to the Birmingham match last year," I point out, and he turns to look at me now, a nerve in his cheek twitching slightly.

"We go when we can," says Lady Wolverton. "Quite honestly, it's not what we ever expected of Robert. I had always hoped he might go into medicine or the law. But from the time he was a child, it was just football, football, football. I don't know where he got it from."

Lord Wolverton is still looking at me and, to my frustration, I'm the first to look away.

"I have to admit that I find the atmosphere at football matches very hostile," continues Robbie's mother. "All that shouting and cursing. And the . . ." She hesitates. "Well, one doesn't mind the homophobia so much, I suppose the fans have to let off steam, but the racist chanting every time one of the colored players has the ball—"

"Jesus, Mum," says Robbie, bursting into laughter. "*Colored* players! We don't use that word anymore."

"It's difficult for us too," says Mam, ignoring this. "Given where we live, I mean. We have to take a ferry across to Galway, and then it's a flight from either Shannon or Dublin. But we've been over a few times. We went to the FA Cup semifinal last year, didn't we, Charlie?"

"We did," says Dad. "Nearly eight hundred euros that trip cost me, and I'd have been better off pissing the money up against a wall."

"We've gone to some of the international matches in Dublin too," she continues. "Actually, Charlie goes to all of them."

"That was always my dream," says Dad. "To line up for my country. Did you see the final group match for the Euros a couple of years back, no?"

The Wolvertons stare at him as if he's speaking a foreign language.

"We were playing Greece," he says, holding his hands far apart, as if a hologram of the game might appear between them, allowing us to relive the moment. "And all we needed was a draw to get through. It's 2–1 to the Greeks in injury time. And we get a penalty. And who steps up to the spot? This cunt." He nods in my direction. I'm that cunt. "And sends it well over the bar. It's still up there, somewhere, I'd say, shooting across the Milky Way. It'll fall back to earth one of these days soon."

Lord Wolverton considers this and has enough self-awareness to recognize that, even though my father has denigrated me, he's also initiated a competition in which he has no choice but to participate.

"Of course, it's harder for Robert to make the national team," he counters. "We have so many extraordinary players here in England.

Easier for your son, I imagine. Ireland needs to take players from the Second Division."

"The Championship," says Robbie, looking up from his phone, his tone filled with exasperation. "It hasn't been called the Second Division for decades."

"In England," continues his father, ignoring this, "the players would have to be Premier League."

The room grows quiet again. We're not here to talk about football, after all. We're here because Robbie and I are being tried for rape and accessory to rape respectively.

"We've never had anything like this in our family before," says Lady Wolverton eventually, laughing nervously, as if this is a tremendous joke.

"Neither have we," says Mam.

"I do wonder about the part these football clubs have to play in it all," she continues. "From what I hear, the atmosphere there is drenched in the most despicable misogyny. All these young men given fame and fortune, but that just makes them targets for cheap tarts in nightclubs wearing next to nothing. WAGs, that's what they call them, isn't it?" She pauses and shakes her head. "WAGs! Such a term! Always in the papers too, these girls. Mutton dressed as lamb. Remember those two who ended up in court over some ludicrous Twitter argument?"

"Instagram," says Robbie.

"Two privileged fools wasting millions arguing over something of absolutely no consequence to anyone," she says, shaking her head. "Utterly ridiculous. When there are people in the world with actual problems."

I wonder what she knows about people with actual problems. Very little, I imagine.

"And you, young man," says Lord Wolverton, turning to me. "You're very quiet. What do you have to say for yourself?"

"Not guilty, Your Honor," I say, resisting the urge to punch the smug bastard in the face.

"Not guilty indeed," he replies. "You look like butter wouldn't melt, don't you?"

"Now hold on," says Dad, raising himself up to his full height. "Let's not forget that my son is not the one accused of rape here. That's your lad. Mine was just in the room."

"And recording it on his smartphone," says Lord Wolverton. "An uncontested fact, I might remind you. What kind of animal does such a thing? My son and that girl engaged in a consensual sexual encounter. But it was your son, Mr. Keogh, your son, who filmed them like some sort of pervert, no doubt getting his jollies from watching it back later on. Isn't that right?" he asks, turning back to me. "Evan," he adds, with emphasis.

I remain silent.

"And as for those WhatsApp messages," he continues.

"My son didn't say anything in them," says Dad, which isn't true, because I did. I said a lot; none of it good. "Yours, on the other hand—"

"Locker-room talk," insists Lord Wolverton, waving this away.

"So it's locker-room talk for your son," says Mam. "But ours should be shamed for it, is that what you're saying?"

"I know that our son wasn't brought up to use the sort of language that yours did."

"Jesus, Dad," says Robbie, throwing his phone down on the table. "Leave it, will you? This isn't helping anyone."

"I simply think it would be better for all parties involved," says Lord Wolverton, retaining his composure, "if we acknowledged the truth. We might not need to go through this sham of a trial if your boy simply owned up to what he did. He filmed a sexual encounter between two consenting adults, which is a disgusting thing to do. Grounds for a charge of voyeurism contrary to the Sexual Offences Act, as I understand it. If he accepted that, and took his punishment, then maybe this girl would be happy to let the rest of the matter go. Everyone could claim victory and we could all get on with our lives."

"You mean our son should take the blame while yours gets off scot-free?" asks Mam, rearing up now. "Let's not forget that your son is the sicko who forced himself on that poor girl."

Lady Wolverton laughs and shakes her head. "No offense, Mrs. . . . Keogh, is it? But look at Robert. Does he look like someone who would need to force himself on any girl? He's never had any difficulties in that area. Quite the contrary."

"This is a mess of both their making," says Dad. "So the pair of them can stand together to face the jury. And if things go badly, well, it won't be our son who'll be serving the longer stretch or listed on the sex offenders register for the rest of his life. It'll be yours."

Lord Wolverton takes a slow step toward my father now. He's taller. He's fitter. He's stronger. And Dad retreats. I can't help myself. I smile. Let him feel what it's like to be frightened for a change.

"I'm just trying to bring this obscenity to an end," says Lord Wolverton. "I don't know what kind of upbringing boys have on that little island of yours, but here on the mainland—"

"The *mainland*?" roars Mam, because there is no word that is more of a red rag to an Irish person than that. "What mainland is that, would you mind telling me?"

"Here on the mainland," continues Lord Wolverton, not even deigning to look at her, "we instill certain standards in our children."

"And we don't?" she asks, and I think she might be close to physically attacking him. "Do you think we told Evan it was all right to attack any girl he sees on the street?"

"As far as I understand it," says Lord Wolverton, remaining so calm that it's chilling to observe, "it's not girls who are at jeopardy around your son."

I feel a stab in my stomach and glance toward Robbie, who looks away, unwilling to meet my eye.

"And what in God's name is that supposed to mean?" begins Dad, but before he can get any further, the door opens, and Catherine returns.

"For pity's sake, I can hear the lot of you out in the corridor," she says, glaring at all of us like a furious mother scolding her children. "And so can everyone else. It's not a good way to begin proceedings when we're trying to convince a jury that your sons are innocent men."

The four parents each have the good grace to look a little shamefaced.

Catherine shakes her head in disgust before turning to Robbie and me and saying the words that I've dreaded for months.

"It's time."

4

I looked up Luchino Visconti when I was next online and it wasn't difficult to track down the film that Rafe had mentioned, or the young actor to whom he'd compared me. I couldn't see the resemblance myself, other than the fact that we were both young and blond, for the boy's hair was long and feminine, in that heavy 1970s style, while I had a tight mop of curls. His face had a gauntness to it too that mine lacked. But Rafe had insisted upon the likeness.

He was quite up-front in the bar in Walthamstow, telling me exactly what he wanted to do to me, what he expected me to do to him in return, and for how long he would require my services. His offer was three hundred pounds, five times more than remained in my bank account. I didn't even think about saying no.

Rafe had an apartment close to London City Airport, with a view over the Thames near Woolwich Ferry. The hallway was lined with books. I'd been fond of reading when I was growing up but hadn't devoted much time to it since leaving the island. Books were expensive, after all, and most of my money had been spent on canvases, paint, and brushes.

"Nice place," I told him, meaning it. This was the type of apartment I had imagined myself living in when my artistic dreams still seemed achievable.

"It serves its purpose," he said. "It's just my bolt-hole, really."

He could tell from the expression on my face that I didn't know what that meant.

"A place to stay when I'm in London," he explained. "The family home is elsewhere."

"You're married?" I asked.

"Of course," he said. I glanced around and saw some framed photographs and walked toward them. One showed him and his wife with their arms around each other in a place that I thought was St. Mark's Square in Venice, smiling for the camera. He had children too. Some daughters in tennis whites. A son in a football strip.

"More of a squash man, myself," he said, noticing where I was looking. "You?"

"Me what?"

"Are you interested in sport?"

I shook my head and continued to study the room. An entire wall was filled with vinyl records, and I gravitated toward them, scanning them like objects in a museum. I had never held an actual record in my hands before but liked the feel of one when I took it down.

"Do you enjoy music?" asked Rafe, pouring us both a whiskey, and I took mine and sipped it slowly. The glass was remarkably heavy. The difference between the rich and the poor, it occurred to me, was that, for the former, their glassware was just as expensive as the liquor they poured into it, while people like me were happy to drink out of cans, bottles, or plastic cups. As the alcohol entered my bloodstream and mixed with the beer from earlier, I began to feel more relaxed, which I hadn't in the taxi. Traveling the twelve miles across London, I'd started to worry that I was making a mistake. Maybe he would try to kill me when he got me home. When we stopped at a traffic light, I'd even considered opening the door and jumping out, but the money was too alluring.

"Doesn't everyone?" I asked, examining an old Prince album I'd plucked out.

"Tell me an artist you like," he said, kicking off his shoes, and I noticed that he wore garish Kermit the Frog socks, the type that a man his age might think made him appear youthful and unconventional but just made him seem a little ridiculous. I listed a few bands and singers that I listened to regularly, assuming he wouldn't have heard of any of them, but, to my surprise, he strolled toward his collection and removed an album by the first group I had named, whose members were only a year or two older than me.

"I like this song particularly," he said, removing the record from its sleeve and placing it on the turntable. He dusted the black grooves with a small cloth before examining the needle and placing it gently upon the vinyl. I liked the ceremony with which he did this, I respected it, and understood why a person might prefer to engage in such theater before the music began. It was so much more civilized than the haphazard way in which I scrolled through songs on my phone, cutting each one off to switch to another whenever I grew bored. By chance, he'd chosen a song that happened to be one of my favorites, and he smiled when he saw me move my head in time with the music. As he watched me for a few moments, I experienced a sudden fear that he would ask me to dance for him, but thankfully this humiliation did not come to pass. Instead, he simply placed his glass down on a side table and leaned forward to kiss me.

I had never kissed anyone as old as him before, nor had I ever wanted to, and found it a strange but not entirely disagreeable experience, although I didn't care for the roughness of his skin. When he placed his left hand on the back of my head and slipped his tongue into my mouth I wasn't sure whether this was because he was worried that I might change my mind or because he liked the idea of being in control. Despite not being particularly attracted to him, I found my body responding to his embrace. It was arousing to know that he wanted me. And there was a part of me that wanted to be here, to stay here, to be someone like him or someone with him.

"First things first," I said, settling into my new role as I pulled away, and he nodded and reached for his wallet.

"Quite right," he said, handing across six fifty-pound notes, which I counted quickly before slipping them into the back pocket of my jeans. The moment I did so, the atmosphere changed. He owned me now, for the agreed amount of time anyway, and wanted me to know it. "Take your clothes off," he said in a matter-of-fact voice as he dimmed the lights.

"The curtains," I said, for the windows of his apartment looked out onto the river beyond, but also toward the windows of other buildings nearby. There was a strange, inconsistent blaze of lights reflecting above the water. I would have liked to have painted it.

"Don't be disobedient, Evan," he replied, frowning. "I said take your clothes off. Please do as you're told."

I glanced toward the hallway and wondered what he would do if I tried to leave. But I didn't test him. Whatever this was, whatever I was doing, I was content to see it through. I had never known any power in my life before, but in this moment my youth and beauty had given me both and I had enough self-awareness to understand that neither would last forever. I kicked off my trainers, pulled my T-shirt over my head, unbuckled my belt, and removed my jeans.

"Socks," he said.

I took them off, and Rafe ordered me to sit on the sofa, where he took my feet in his hands, one by one, and examined them carefully, his fingers moving softly across my toes. It felt absurd to me, vaguely embarrassing. Of course, he had no idea of the things I could do with those feet. When he released them, he instructed me to stand, and I closed my eyes as he removed my boxer shorts. In that moment, I knew that the only way to go through with this was to separate my mind from its present location and allow it to remove itself to a different world entirely. Rafe did the things he had said he would do, nothing more and nothing less. He asked me to do the things that I had agreed to do, nothing more and nothing less.

And while we both performed our roles, buyer and seller, my mind returned to the island, where I walked the path through the village toward the school, greeting friends along the way and stopping to chat with one of my more considerate teachers, a man who had encouraged me in my artwork. I knelt down to tie my laces outside the old pub, where Larry Mulshay asked after my mother. I sat on the bench outside the new pub, where Tim Devlin told me he'd give me ten euros to clear all the leaves from the courtyard out the back. I made my way up the hill toward the house in which I'd been reared and the farm I would reluctantly inherit someday.

I felt the earth beneath my fingernails, the fine dust secreted into the lines of my hands, as he pressed me against the window and muttered obscenities into my ears. Perhaps he found this a turn-on, to speak in such a coarse way, but it did nothing for me. If anything, I felt disappointed in him. He had appeared so refined before, but now he just seemed like any other middle-aged man getting his kicks by trying to humiliate a boy. I wanted to tell him that nothing he could say could have any emotional effect on me whatsoever. I'd spent my life being humiliated by someone who was far better at it than him.

And still, despite all this, I didn't regret being there. I wanted him too.

He leaned into me and covered my face with his left hand, and I inhaled the smell of him. He must have sprayed cologne on his wrists before going out for the evening, something I'd never heard of anyone doing before. I thought of Cormac, who'd been given a bottle of CK One the Christmas before I left, and how he'd worn it every day and I'd teased him for it even though I found the scent dizzying. I thought of Harry, the farmer's son in South Wales, and the way he'd spun me around against an old oak tree, pushing me into the bark, and the exquisite pain of the wood as it imprinted itself on the pale, hairless skin of my stomach when he fucked me. When he finished, my knees had given out from beneath me and I'd collapsed onto the earth, content to fall asleep right there, with the dirt in my ears and the worms crawling over my face. Bury me here, I had thought at the time. Just bury me here. How many laborers had he fucked? I wondered. How many had he told that, if they revealed his secret, they would lose their job. *I'm not like you,* he'd insisted. *I'm not a queer.*

When it was over, when Rafe was finished, I asked whether I could use his shower and he looked at me as if I'd asked to borrow his car for the weekend.

"I'd prefer that you didn't," he said, glancing toward my clothes, which were scattered across the floor. He was done with me now and wanted me gone. *Well, fuck this for a game of soldiers,* I thought.

"Where is it?" I asked, turning around and walking toward the corridor, not waiting for an answer. "Down here?"

I found the bathroom without difficulty and enjoyed a long, hot shower, lathering myself with as much of his expensive shower gel as I could and exfoliating my face with a scrub that sat on the shower shelf. Even the packaging looked like it cost more than he'd spent on me. I hadn't felt so dirty in a long time and wanted to scour my body of everything he'd left upon me. Afterward, wrapping a towel around my waist, I examined myself in the mirror. I was eighteen years old and perfect. I might not be able to sell my paintings, but I could sell myself.

When I returned to the living room, Rafe was fully dressed, and my clothes were gathered neatly in a pile.

"Feel better?" he asked.

"Much," I said, stripping the towel away and dressing before him without an ounce of self-consciousness. In my absence, he'd turned the television on, and it was showing an old black-and-white movie, although he'd muted the volume. I recognized Cary Grant and Katharine Hepburn. These were the kind of films Mam had always enjoyed, and I wanted him to invite me to stay, to suggest that we watch the rest of the film together, for him to run his hands through my hair and put me to bed afterward in the spare room, to tuck me in. To be my father, to be my kind father. For me to be his obedient son.

When I was dressed, I checked my back pocket to make sure that he hadn't taken the money back while I was in the shower. He looked a little disappointed when he saw me do this.

"Now that's beneath you," he said, and, strangely, this was the first time all evening that I'd felt any sense of shame.

"Sorry," I said. "I have low expectations of people."

He shrugged, as if he shared my cynicism about human nature.

"There's a pad of paper over there, by the occasional table," he said, nodding toward the left corner of the room.

I glanced around. I had no clue what that phrase meant but walked toward a round marble table on a narrow stem, assuming this was what he was referring to.

"Write your phone number down," he said.

"Why?" I asked.

He picked up the Prince album that I'd left on an armchair and returned it to the shelf before taking the record he'd been playing from the turntable, holding it at eye level and gently blowing a speck of dust from it, then slid it carefully back inside its sleeve.

"You need money, I assume?" he asked.

"Yes."

"Then write your number down."

"You want me to come back another night?"

"Oh no," he said, shaking his head. "No, I never draw water from the same well twice. This was just . . . how shall I put it? . . . an audition."

"An audition for what?"

"Just write your number down, Evan. Or don't. It's entirely up to you."

I thought about it, then lifted the pen and pad of paper and did as he asked. *Why not?* I reasoned. I was foolish enough to think that I could remain in control.

"Good boy," he said, smiling.

"How do I get home from here?" I asked as I made my way toward the door. "I don't really know where I am."

"Where do you live?" he asked, and I told him the general area. "The DLR to Canning Town," he told me. "Then, I think, the District Line the rest of the way. Although you might want to check the map to be sure."

"It's late," I said. "Dangerous out there. Bad men everywhere. All trying to take advantage of innocent young lads like me."

He couldn't help himself. He laughed.

"Quite the little operator, aren't you?" he said, reaching for his wallet again and removing some notes before handing them to me. "Here. This should be enough for a taxi."

"Thanks," I said. We both knew I'd keep the money and just take the Tube. And it wasn't the District Line the rest of the way, I had to change at West Ham. He obviously didn't spend a lot of time on public transport.

5

The courtroom, unsurprisingly, is packed. Reporters sit in an elevated row with their backs to the wall, while about one hundred strangers have packed into the public gallery. All they're lacking is popcorn. Some, to my horror, are wearing club T-shirts, and they raise their arms in solidarity with Robbie and me when we enter the dock, then pound their fists against the club crest positioned above their hearts. They don't care whether we're guilty or not; all they want is to see us back on the pitch. Mam and Dad settle into a pew among them. Further along, I notice a man and woman in their mid-forties staring at me with such loathing on their faces that they can only be the girl's parents.

The girl.

I have to stop calling her that. She has a name: Lauren Mackintosh. She's nineteen years old and reading history at the local university. I had never met her before that night and have never met her since. But I've talked about her endlessly with the police officers investigating the case, when I've insisted that she's lying about what took place. She'd been flirting with Robbie all evening, I've told them, and it was she who took him by the hand and led him upstairs, not the other way around. I don't mention that Robbie turned to me as he followed her, giving me a grin, a wink, and the thumbs-up sign.

As for what happened after that, I have been consistent in my account of what took place.

Yes, I waited a few minutes before following them. Yes, I was jealous of her. Yes, I wanted it to be me who Robbie went upstairs with. No, I'm not ashamed of that; why should I be? Yes, most of the lads know I'm gay, but no one cares. No, the press doesn't know. Because it's private, that's why, and it would only get in the way of the football. No, I don't see any contradiction there, I'm entitled to a private life, amn't I? No, I didn't knock, the door was ajar. Yes, they both saw me enter the room. No, neither of them protested. Yes, I watched them. No, I don't think that's a strange thing to do. Yes, she was totally into it. No, she never protested. No, she never asked him to stop. Yes, if she had, I would have made sure that he did. Yes, I filmed the encounter on my phone. No, I didn't touch myself. No, just because you think that's a perverse thing to do doesn't mean it is. Yes, I enjoyed it. No, Robbie never invited me to have sex with her. No, I can't find the phone. Yes, I've looked for it, but it's vanished. Yes, I know how that looks, but remember, the truth is on that phone, so I wish I hadn't lost it, because then we wouldn't even be having this conversation, would we? Yes, you can search my apartment; feel free, I have nothing to hide. Yes, I bought a new phone the following morning. Because I needed one; why do you think? No, I didn't bother reclaiming on the insurance. It only cost a grand, that's why, and that kind of money means nothing to me. Yes, I was part of the WhatsApp group. No, that's not the way I normally speak about women. No, I don't have a sister. Yes, I accept they were disgusting things to say, but they're not illegal things to say. No, I wouldn't lie to protect my teammates, not even Robbie. Yes, I'm telling you the truth.

I've stuck by every word of that for months now.

And I'll stick by it when I'm on the stand.

Counting on you today, bro. Don't let me down.

Listening to the opening statements makes me feel like an actor in a television show. The barristers are ruthlessly polite to the judge, Dame Edith Kerrey KC, who everyone refers to as My Lady. When the King's Counsel, Mr. Armstrong, rises to address the jury of seven men and five women, he wears an expression of profound sadness. He tells them that he needs to be honest with them from the start. The club, our club, has been his club since he was a child, he says. It was his father's club before that, and his grandfather's before that. He's a season-ticket holder, he tells us, and tries never to miss a home game. His own son, only ten years old, sleeps in club pajamas and is devoted to the club. His bedroom walls are papered with posters of the club's players.

"All the players," he adds. "Including Robert Wolverton and Evan Keogh. At least, he did have their images on his walls until recently when, I'm proud to say, with no encouragement on my part, he chose to remove them."

He looks down then. His voice catches as he plays the part of Proud Father. "The credit for my son's decency must go to his mother," he continues, "who has been a far better parent than I. Always there for him, while I, for my sins, have spent rather too much of my life within the walls of this fine building, where justice is dispensed without fear or favor, to rich and poor, famous and unknown, alike."

He pauses now and shakes his head. He seems disappointed by the world.

"What do we do when our heroes let us down?" he muses, as if this question has come to him spontaneously and isn't one that he's spent weeks refining. "What will my son do? Be a better man than those he idolized, I hope, for after all, while he's too young to understand what this case is about, it's actually rather simple."

He smiles now, as if he hopes this might encourage the jury to deliver a guilty verdict before they've even heard any of the evidence, thus saving us all the bother of showing up every day for the next two weeks.

I notice Juror no. 6, a woman in her late twenties, looking directly at me, but she turns away when I catch her eye.

"On a drunken evening, a young woman was seduced by a famous footballer," continues Mr. Armstrong. "Someone that each of us might have read about in the tabloid newspapers. I must admit, I occasionally buy those papers myself," he adds, performing Man of the People now, disassociating himself from Wealthy Advocate in a Gown and Wig. "And I read the gossip. I can't help myself. How the other half live, am I right?"

Some of the jury smile and nod. They like him. He is one of them.

He understands their guilty pleasures because they're his pleasures too. "Miss Mackintosh, the complainant, entered a bedroom with Robert Wolverton, and engaged in what, in my day, used to be called a little slap and tickle. Some kissing, some touching. Nothing unusual there, and nothing to be ashamed of. Young people, young women particularly, have agency over their own bodies these days, and this, I think we can all agree, is a good thing. But when Mr. Wolverton decided that he wanted to go further, that he was not prepared to stop at a little harmless fun"—he raises his voice now, sharply; he's suddenly incensed—"he refused to take no for an answer! And ladies and gentlemen of the jury, he did what so many entitled men before him have done. He didn't listen. He chose to ignore her when she said that she did not want to have sex with him because he did not believe that was a choice that she had any right to make. So he pinned her down. As you can see, Mr. Wolverton is a strong, athletic man, and Miss Mackintosh, as you will discover, is a rather petite young woman. But before this even began, his friend, his teammate Mr. Evan Keogh, an Irishman, who had followed them upstairs, looked inside and, rather than stopping Mr. Wolverton from committing this heinous crime, he chose to film the encounter. Mr. Wolverton even invited him to have sex with his victim afterward! No, excuse me, I misspoke. Not to have sex with her. Because Mr. Wolverton did not, in fact, have sex with Miss Mackintosh. He raped her. And these are two very different things. What is it with these footballers that makes them apparently unable to perform sexually unless one of their teammates is there, watching them, cheering them on like the fans in the terraces as they, metaphorically speaking, score? They share young women in the way you or I might share a bag of toffees. We've all seen the videos leaked online as they've been publicly shamed, suspended briefly from their clubs before being taken back again. What is that all about, would someone please explain to me? It's something I simply do not understand. But these young men, sadly, do not see women as human beings but as physical objects to be used, exploited, and then tossed aside. Now, you will hear Mr. Wolverton and Mr. Keogh deny their parts in this grotesquerie, and you might ask why the police and forensic investigators have not searched Mr. Keogh's phone for evidence. Well, they would have, had Mr. Keogh not, by the most extraordinary piece of misfortune on his part, lost his phone later that same night. A phone, I might add, that he had owned for two years and that had gone everywhere with him. But on this particular night, when the footage would have given us the truth of the matter, Mr. Keogh . . . somehow misplaced it! And bought a brand-new one the next morning! Do you find this credible? I don't. He didn't bother to call Mr. Wolverton to see whether he'd left it behind in his apartment, as any normal person might do. Nor did he ask the concierge of his building whether it had been handed in. No, instead, he went directly into town and purchased a new one. The fact is, he knew that the old one would never be held by human hands again. It's terribly inconvenient for the defendants, isn't it, this distressing and inconvenient loss? Because, if what they say is true, and Miss Mackintosh was a willing participant in their swordplay, then the footage would presumably have exonerated them and none of us would be here today. But no, the phone just vanished into thin air, which allows the defendants to paint my client as a liar. The Crown will prove that these two privileged young men, blessed with sporting talent and good looks, their moral compasses destroyed by financial success and the adoration of honest football fans, simply took what they wanted, caring nothing for the pain inflicted upon their victim. Their vile WhatsApp messages will show how little remorse they felt afterward. Some of the most disgusting pieces of conversation I have ever had the misfortune to read and which I do not look forward to presenting to you. Those messages left fans throughout this city reeling. In fact, they have disgusted people across the country, and also in Ireland, where they caused shock waves, for Mr. Keogh was a vital and much-admired presence in that country's national team, a hero to children, teenagers, and adults alike from Dublin to Skibbereen to Donegal. But, worst of all, they left a young woman, just entering adulthood, traumatized and ashamed, unable to go out and enjoy her life as any young woman should be able to do."

He shakes his head now and looks as if he is about to sit down, but a final thought occurs to him. "The whole thing is sickening, is it not?" he asks, his voice lower now. "We cannot allow society to be infected by such brutality. But how do we stop it?"

He considers this, as if he's not quite sure of the answer, but then it comes to him, as if out of nowhere. "*You* can stop it," he says, his eyes panning across each of the jury members, who are captivated by him now. "I can't. My learned friend Miss Brenton can't. Judge Kerrey can't. The police, the press, the agents, the coaches, the club managers—they can't. The prosecution will prove the defendants' guilt beyond a reasonable doubt, which means that you can stop it, each of you, individually and as a collective. If you choose to." A pause. "And I hope you will," he adds, sitting down and pulling his gown around him as he turns his gaze to the floor, his face lost in a frown, as if there's nothing left for him in life but to contemplate the evils of the universe.

Although I've been told not to look at him, I find myself glancing toward Robbie, whose face is rigid, contemptuous, and angry. I turn to the press pew and note the presence of a writer known for both his fiction and for his sports columns in Irish newspapers. We've met a few times, sharing drinks in a hotel bar in Budapest during the Euros qualification campaign, when I scored a goal that put us second in the group. I don't like many people, but I always liked him. Perhaps he feels my eyes on him because he turns and looks directly at me. His expression forces me to turn away. No matter the result of the trial, I know he will never drink with me again.

I search the room for other faces I might recognize and feel that familiar twinge in my left arm where the bones didn't knit together correctly after it was broken. Naturally, no players from the club are present. They're under strict instructions not to say or do anything which might either jeopardize the case or damage the reputation of the club any more than it already has been. Several participated in the notorious WhatsApp messages anyway, so they've been keeping their heads down for months, knowing their reputations are already balancing on a pinhead.

When it's Catherine's turn to rise, she sighs a little before looking at the jury.

"This might surprise you," she begins, after introducing herself, "but I actually agree with a lot of what my learned friend Mr. Armstrong has said. We live in strange times, where young men are placed on podiums for nothing more complicated than dribbling a ball down a pitch and kicking it into the back of a net. I'm a football fan myself. I always have been." Of course she is. Like Mr. Armstrong, she must not be seen to be elitist. I notice that her accent, which had been quite refined in all our conversations to date, has suddenly taken on a more Yorkshire twang— she is from Halifax—and somehow, this doesn't surprise me. "When I was twenty, I ran into Gary Lineker in a nightclub in Leicester," she continues, "and embarrassed myself so badly that my closest friends joke about it to this day. And I won't even tell you about the time I found myself in conversation with Gary Neville at a wedding. Maybe it's the name Gary, maybe that does something for me?"

A cough from the bench, and despite the laughter of the jury, Judge Kerrey is clearing her throat for a reason. Catherine looks at her and offers an apologetic nod.

"My Lady," she says, before turning back to the twelve. "My learned friend has spoken at some length. But, of course, it takes a lot of words to persuade people of a lie. The truth, happily, requires less energy, and the defense intends to let the evidence in this case speak for itself. All I ask of you, ladies and gentlemen of the jury, is that you base your judgment on the evidence, and on the evidence alone. Evidence that will show that Mr. Wolverton and Mr. Keogh are innocent of the charges laid against them. That said, please remember that Miss Mackintosh is not on trial here, nor will I put her on trial. That level of misogyny is beneath me, beneath this court, and beneath all of you. However, it will be important that you understand that Miss Mackintosh has a history of troubling behavior when it comes to relationships. I am cognizant of the Youth Justice and Criminal Evidence Act 1999, which places restrictions on the extent to which a complainant in a sexual offense can be examined over his or her sexual history, but, before my learned friend cites this as a reason not to discuss such matters, I would remind him of Section 2 of that act, which allows such history to be examined if it has taken place in close proximity of time to the alleged offense, and the defense will prove that it has. And yes, while it might seem strange that Evan's mobile phone was lost, that is the simple fact of the matter—which of us has not lost a phone?—so we cannot surmise what may or may not have been on it and it cannot be part of this trial. Miss Mackintosh engaged in a mutually consenting sexual experience that she regretted the next day. We all make mistakes. I believe it's called being human. Under no circumstances should we condemn Miss Mackintosh for her mistake, but nor should we destroy the lives of two innocent young men over that same error. Is that what you would want if Robbie and Evan were your sons? Or would you want proof, demand proof, incontestable proof, that a crime had actually taken place? I know I would."

She retakes her seat, and the same twelve faces that were looking at us with contempt ten minutes ago now appear more sympathetic. I glance back at Juror no. 6, who has been listening carefully to everything Catherine has said. Like the sportswriter, she senses me looking at her and turns in my direction, but her expression is inscrutable.

It's hard not to wonder whether all of this will simply come down to who speaks last.

6

Following my successful audition, Rafe put me to work.

I had a very particular clientele; or, rather, he did. Mostly men in late middle age. Thriving in financially successful jobs. Some in the public eye. Occasionally married. I was professional in my dealings with them but clear from the start about what I was willing to do and what I was not. If a client ignored my rules, then I would leave, and Rafe never reproached me for this. On the contrary, I knew he could be unforgiving with anyone who demanded more than was on offer. Payments were made directly to him. He took a one-third share, and I took the rest. Despite the nature of our first meeting, I grew strangely fond of him, and wanted to impress, feeling a curious sense of pleasure whenever he reported positive remarks from clients back to me.

Some men wanted to book me on a regular basis, but I limited myself to a maximum of four encounters with each. Any more than that and they would start to believe that we were something we were not. I once spent a half hour studying Constable's *Salisbury Cathedral from the Bishop's Grounds* at the V&A while waiting for a client who was taking me as his guest to a party at the Natural History Museum. Often, when I was hired as a piece of human jewelry at some lavish engagement, the client preferred to connect somewhere nearby first to ensure that I was appropriately dressed and could adhere to basic social niceties. As it turned out, he liked me, and I didn't entirely loathe him, so we saw each other a few times afterward. He was entirely vanilla in his tastes, which was a bonus, and it probably could have lasted longer, for he was wealthy, and generous with his cash, but I ended it when he invited me to move in with him, promising that I'd never have to pay for anything again for as long as I lived. Men like him never understood what a turn-off a line like that could be.

I learned this lesson a second time with Samuel, who ran a luxury real estate company and lived in an exquisite apartment near Hyde Park. Our routine was that I would visit him on the last Friday of every month when his wife went to Cornwall to visit her parents. His needs were simple, and I was relaxed in his company, but after our fourth meeting he asked me to join him for a drink in a Soho wine bar and, as he would be paying for both my time and my margaritas, I agreed. We'd never met in the wild before, so the evening started with some awkward small talk, but it grew even worse when he announced that he had fallen in love with me and, to my intense embarrassment, seemed convinced that I had developed similar feelings toward him. He talked of leaving his wife and of our setting up home together, expressing the hope that, in time, his son would come to accept our relationship.

"What relationship?" I asked.

"This relationship," he said, reaching across to take my hand. I allowed this. He was the client, after all. "The one we've built. It's gone past just a commercial transaction, Evan, don't you think? I know you feel the same way."

"I'm sorry, but I don't," I told him. "I'm sure you're a nice enough person, if we disregard your marital infidelities and your willingness to exploit a young man in financial difficulties, but I have no interest in pursuing anything long term with you. You employed me to do a job, that's all. Outside of that, I have no feelings for you whatsoever. I do what I do simply to avoid returning to the island."

"The island?" he asked, looking puzzled.

"It doesn't matter," I said, shaking my head, annoyed that I had revealed any part of my previous life to him. "The point is, you mean nothing to me, Samuel. Nothing at all. I say this to be kind. So you won't deceive yourself."

He was clearly shocked by the brutality of my words and began to cry, which was excruciating. I grew nauseous. People were looking at us. It was too much.

"You're lying," he said, wiping away his tears. "I know you feel something."

"No."

"I don't believe you."

"Try."

"But I can give you everything you—"

I excused myself then, saying I needed the bathroom, before leaving the bar and blocking his number on my phone. That was the moment I decided I would never see any man more than four times.

Until Sir arrived, that is. With Sir, I had no choice. The decisions were all his.

That experience, my final as human chattel, began a few months after the Samuel debacle when Rafe phoned to say that he had a very special client who was interested in meeting me.

"Fine," I said. "Send me his details."

"No, I don't want to put anything in text," he told me.

"Why not?"

"Because nothing disappears. Nothing is forgotten. Everything we say or do these days clings to us forever. Meet me for a coffee and I'll explain."

We met in the Reform Club on Pall Mall, where he was a member, and he handed me an A4 envelope containing a document that he instructed me to sign. It was a nondisclosure agreement, he explained. The previous boys with whom his client had spent time had all done so, he told me, so I shouldn't worry about its contents. It simply said that I could never reveal any details about our encounters or I would be subject to criminal proceedings. I never spoke about what I did anyway, nor did I have anyone with whom I might speak about it, so was content to do as he asked. The payment, to my surprise, was more than twice my regular rate, which could change things considerably for me.

"Excellent," he said, returning the document to the envelope. "What's most important here, of course, is discretion. Are you discreet, Evan?"

"You know I am," I told him.

"I think I do, yes. But in this particular case, it's important for you to understand that, if you were to be reckless, there would be consequences."

"What kind of consequences?" I asked.

"Severe consequences."

He removed another envelope from his bag and told me that it contained a picture of his client. If I opened the envelope, he said, that would be taken as a tacit agreement on my part that I was willing to play by the rules. If I returned it to him unopened, then I could walk away now, he would find someone else, and our current arrangements would not change in any way.

"But if you say yes," he told me, "you don't get to choose when the arrangement ends. That will be his prerogative. Do you understand?"

"You wouldn't put me in danger, would you?" I asked.

"Of course not," he said, smiling at me. "You know you're my favorite boy."

I wanted to believe him but worried that I was doing what some of my clients did with me, believing that our relationship ran deeper than our professional ties. I didn't want a sexual relationship with Rafe, but sometimes, when I was with other men, I thought of him. I wanted something. Something I couldn't quite define.

I opened the second envelope and slid the picture out, recognizing the man immediately, and looked across at Rafe in disbelief.

"Obviously, now you understand the need for discretion," he said, retrieving the envelope, along with the picture, and returning both to his bag.

"Of course."

"I'll text you with details of your first engagement. A day and time, nothing more. A car will collect you at a given place and return you there afterward."

Three days later, at seven p.m., I found myself standing outside one of the lesser-frequented Tube stations in London as a black Range Rover pulled up next to me. The most enormous man I had ever seen was driving, and we both remained silent throughout the journey. It took around forty minutes until we arrived at a set of iron gates, which were immediately opened for us. We made our way up a long driveway before stopping in a central courtyard, where a second man in livery was waiting to guide me inside and upstairs. He barely acknowledged me as I exited the vehicle, simply starting to walk, and I assumed that I should follow.

"What do I call him?" I asked, and he didn't even turn as he answered.

"Sir," he said. "You call him Sir at all times."

I nodded, wishing he would slow down, for the walls of the corridors were hung with extraordinary paintings, the masterpieces of many centuries, and I wanted to pause for a moment so I could study them.

Soon, I was led into a spacious room where I recognized a chesterfield sofa and armchair, along with some handsomely upholstered chairs and a desk of Regency design. As he left the room, he instructed me to remain standing and not to touch anything. I examined the photographs that stood on the various surfaces, faces I'd seen on news programs and in magazines throughout my life. They looked like any normal family. *How had I got here?* I asked myself. I grew up on an island of four hundred people. I worked on a farm. I wanted to be a painter. After about ten minutes, a door at the other end of the room opened and he came in, walking toward me with a smile on his face. I instinctively stood as tall as I could.

"Good evening," he said. "It's Evan, have I got that right?"

"That's right, Sir," I told him.

"Splendid." He continued to smile, betraying no anxiety at how unusual this meeting was. "And where are you from exactly?"

I told him the name of the island and explained its location relative to Galway, and he nodded, looking me up and down as I talked. He seemed uninterested in my answer, even though he'd asked the question.

"Very good," he said. "And you know the rules, yes? They've been explained to you?"

"Yes, Sir," I replied. "I understand them fully."

"Excellent. Then shall we get started?" He rubbed his hands together. "Chilly tonight, isn't it?"

We engaged in no further conversation. Instead, he led me to a bedroom, where he degraded me in ways that I never knew a human being could be degraded. Behaving worse than any client ever had before, he humiliated me, physically and mentally, treating me worse than you would treat a rabid dog, while speaking to me as if I had ascended from the depths of hell to service him. *I am not here*, I told myself over and over. *I am a dead person, observing this scene from a different plane.*

When it was over, he reached for a dressing gown and left the bedroom without a word. I curled up on the floor, not wanting to move but uncertain what I was supposed to do next. There was blood. There was worse. In that, the first of our many encounters, he took something from me that would never return.

Finally, my original guide returned and seemed disgusted to find me still lying naked on a priceless rug. Instructing me to get dressed, he told me that the car was waiting outside, and within five minutes I was being driven back to the Tube station from which I had been collected.

This went on for six months, and I dreaded the encounters, barely sleeping the night before, but Rafe reiterated that I could not step away. I had made a commitment, he repeated, and there would be consequences—severe consequences—if I did anything to upset the client. Sir would let him know when he was finished with me and, until then, I had no choice but to allow him to do whatever he wanted without protest.

"You said you wouldn't put me in any danger," I whispered to Rafe on the phone after a particularly brutal session which had led me to making an appointment with a GP, who seemed appalled by the extent of my injuries and urged me to make a complaint to the police. There was a lengthy silence before the click made me realize that he was no longer there.

The sole advantage of this arrangement was that I was able to move into a small one-bedroom flat of my own. Being demeaned and physically abused every Thursday night was the price I had to pay for independence.

This might have continued for years had I not received a phone call one morning from a man who claimed to work for a tabloid newspaper and who said that he had heard certain rumors about me and Sir. He wondered whether I would be willing to meet to discuss them. He would make it worth my while, he told me. I was accustomed to being paid for my services, but this time I panicked and hung up. By chance, I was due to meet Sir that same evening. As we walked toward his bedroom, I asked whether I might speak to him for a moment. He seemed surprised, even annoyed.

"Well, what is it?" he asked, checking his watch. I explained what had taken place, and he listened carefully, a shadow crossing his face.

"And what did you tell him?" he asked.

"Nothing at all," I said. "I hung up."

He took a seat in what I was fairly sure was a George Hepplewhite chair and thought about this for a long time. When he looked up again, he nodded and told me that I had done the right thing, but it was best that I should leave now, that he wouldn't require my services that night after all. The following evening, however, I returned to my flat after a gym session to discover Rafe sitting in my living room, along with the enormous driver who always brought me to and from Sir's residence. How he got in, I did not know.

"We had an agreement, Evan, did we not?" asked Rafe, without any preamble.

"I swear I told no one," I said. And this was the truth. I had never opened my mouth about what I did or who I did it with. Should I even have wanted to confide in someone, who would I have chosen? I was alone in the world.

"I believe you," said Rafe, his tone mixing disappointment with resignation. "The truth is, in a place like that, gossip is currency. It could have been any one of his flunkies. But the fact is, he won't be requiring your services anymore and I would advise you to change your phone number tomorrow in case any other reporters try to get in touch."

"Fine," I said.

"I believe you know Dennis," he continued, nodding toward the driver.

"Yes," I said. "Although I didn't know his name was Dennis. He's never spoken to me."

Dennis allowed himself a half smile.

"You're not the only one with rules to obey," he said, and I was surprised to hear a strong Welsh accent. I don't know why, but I had always taken him for a Londoner.

"Dennis here," continued Rafe calmly, as if this was a perfectly normal conversation, "is going to break your arm. You can choose which one, the left or the right. This is not done to punish you—you've done nothing wrong—but simply to impress upon you how serious we are that you never speak about my client in the future. You will also be required to find a new source of income. I'm afraid your days of selling yourself have come to an end. If you disobey me on this, I will find out, and will assume that you are gossiping, which will be unacceptable. Do you understand?"

"I won't tell anyone," I said, shaking my head as panic settled in. "I promise. Please don't hurt me."

"As it happens, I do trust you, Evan," said Rafe. "So believe me when I tell you that I am truly sorry about what has to happen. But it's what Sir wants. Call it a shot across the bow."

For a few moments, I couldn't find any words.

"But you told me I was your favorite boy," I said at last.

"I say that to everyone," he replied, looking embarrassed for me. "Didn't you know that? You can't imagine you're anything special? I employed you to do a job, that's all. Outside of that, you mean nothing to me, Evan. Nothing at all. I say this to be kind. So you won't deceive yourself."

Somehow, in that moment, I made peace with what was to happen. There was no possibility of escape. There was no chance that I could convince him to leave me unharmed. Sir was too powerful. His secrets too important. His place in national life too significant.

Dennis walked toward me. Unlike Rafe, he seemed rather sympathetic to my situation.

"This will only take a moment," he said, "and the adrenalin rush will kick in quickly, so you won't feel much pain. Just a sort of general numbness, although you might get dizzy or nauseous. But by then, we'll be halfway to A&E, where I'll leave you."

"All right," I said, nodding. I couldn't think what else to say. "Thanks, I guess."

"So which one?" he asked, looking at me, and I raised an eyebrow, uncertain what he meant.

"Which one what?" I asked.

"Which arm?"

The thought ran through my mind that my future was now decided. There would be no further work for me in London. I couldn't sell my body anymore, and I would never be able to sell my art. But I had to live, to eat, and to clothe myself. I no longer had a choice. I would finally have to rely on the only skill I'd ever had. My beauty. I felt some relief, as if this moment had been a long time coming but had always been inevitable.

I looked at Dennis. I was right-handed, after all, so there was only one logical answer.

"Left," I said.

7

Lauren Mackintosh looks different to how I remember her, but then we've only met once. In court, she's dressed in a simple skirt-and-blouse combination, with her hair tied back in a ponytail. It's the day on which Catherine gets to cross-examine her, but I can tell that the jury has responded well to Mr. Armstrong's questions yesterday when she gave her account of what happened.

I had an unsettling experience earlier after arriving at the courthouse. Walking down a corridor to use the gents' toilets, I noticed a woman sitting by a window, bent over, her head in her hands. There was no one else nearby so I stopped to ask whether she was all right. When she looked up, however, I recognized her as Juror no. 6.

"I'm sorry," I said immediately, understanding that any conversation between us could prejudice the trial, if not invalidate it entirely. I glanced down at the notebook she held in her hands, in which I'd noticed her making notes since the opening day, and saw, scored into the cover, her name: Dr. Freya Petrus. I'm not supposed to know any of the jurors' names, but now I know hers. And her occupation. Although I suppose it's possible that she's a PhD and not a medical doctor.

"Are you all right?" I asked.

She took a long breath before replying.

"Walk on," she said. "You know we can't talk."

I continued along the corridor, looking back to make sure that no one had observed the brief encounter. When I glance toward her now, I know we have a shared moment. "Miss Mackintosh," begins Catherine, standing up and leaning forward on the desk before her. "I recognize that this is a difficult experience for you, but I want you to know that I understand the courage it takes for you to come forward and give your account of what you claim took place on the night in question. I won't keep you long, I just want to clarify a few things you said yesterday when being examined by my learned friend Mr. Armstrong. Is that all right?"

The way she phrases this implies that Lauren has some choice in the matter, when of course she doesn't. Lauren nods and reaches for a glass of water, taking a sip. Her hands, I notice, remain steady.

"You've said that you had no knowledge of either Robert Wolverton or Evan Keogh until the night of the party. Is that correct?"

"Yes."

"They are rather well-known footballers."

"I have no interest in football," she replies. "I'm not into sports at all. I know the most famous players, of course, the ones in the England squad and some of the bigger stars in the Premier League, but the defendants, well, they're not really at that level, are they?"

I feel Robbie bristle next to me. It bruises his ego that he's a Championship player, and I know it rankles with him that I play for Ireland. Played for Ireland. Whatever the outcome of the trial, I suspect those days are behind me.

"But when you went to Mr. Wolverton's apartment," continues Catherine, "you knew who he was then, yes?"

"Yes," she admits. "I'd been with my friends in the club, and they recognized him."

"And you were impressed by him."

"No, not particularly. Why would I be? He does a job like any other."

"But you went home with him."

"No, he and his friends invited a group of us back to continue partying. There were more than a dozen of us there, as you know. Saying I went home with him suggests it was just the two of us."

Lauren's unwillingness to be provoked impresses me. She is, I realize, a formidable woman.

"But you did go home with him, didn't you?" persists Catherine. "Not alone, as you correctly say, but you went back to his apartment."

"Yes."

"Even though you'd never met him before and you claim that you had no idea who he was. Is that something that you're in the habit of doing, Miss Mackintosh? Going back to the apartments of men you've never met before?"

"I've done it from time to time, yes, like most girls my age," she replies. "Particularly when there's a group of us. You meet people, you hit it off, you see where the night takes you. That's not so unusual, is it? But I don't do it regularly, if that's what you're implying."

"I didn't mean to imply anything of the sort," says Catherine. "You're entitled to go home with any man you want, even if you've just met him an hour or two earlier."

"That's not what I do," says Lauren.

"Well, as you've just clearly told us, you do it 'from time to time,' which, to most reasonable people, would mean at regular intervals. But let's leave that there for the moment. When you got to Mr. Wolverton's apartment, what did you make of it?"

Lauren frowns. "I don't understand the question," she says.

"Did you like it?"

"I suppose so, yes. It's very nice."

"Luxurious."

"Yes."

"Expensive."

"I imagine it must be."

"You live with your mother, don't you?"

"Yes."

"Why?"

"Why what?"

"Why do you live with your mother?"

Lauren stares at Catherine as if she can't believe she has to explain something so obvious. "I'm a student," she says. "I can't afford to move out."

"But you'd like to?"

"Do you mean would I like to have my own place?"

"Yes."

She thinks about it. "I suppose so, yes. But I'm happy where I am right now, to be honest. I love my mum and we have a good relationship. We get along. We always have."

This statement of filial affection goes down well with the jury, who look across at her parents approvingly.

"Miss Mackintosh, would you agree that your evidence is materially based on the jury believing that you have a good memory? That you remember exactly what you said and did on the night in question and are relating it truthfully?"

"Yes."

"And do you have a good memory?"

"I think so."

"Then you will remember the beginning of our conversation."

"I wouldn't call it a conversation," says Lauren. "But yes."

"When you explained to us that you supposed you liked Mr. Wolverton's apartment and that it was also, supposedly, luxurious."

"Yes."

"Is luxury not something that most people would, objectively, agree upon?"

"Perhaps," she says. "To a degree."

"You decide a fair deal by supposing matters after the event, don't you? Such as supposing that the apartment might have been luxurious, but only months after seeing it?"

"Something as insignificant as the design of a flat, yes."

"Am I understanding correctly that you're only guided by supposition about minor moments in life?"

"I don't know. Is that what I—"

"Including you merely 'supposing' that one day you would like to own a home and to live independently of your mother, which to most people would be a highly significant life event?"

"I obviously did not mean it that way."

"How many other apparently significant events in your life did you merely 'suppose' have happened recently, Miss Mackintosh?"

"None."

"Do you want to reflect and give a less rehearsed answer?"

"No."

"I didn't anticipate you would." Catherine shakes her head and sighs loudly. "You've admitted already that you asked your friend Jennifer whether or not Mr. Wolverton had a girlfriend."

"I asked her whether he had, yes. I don't know what you mean by 'admitted' it."

"And you asked her this question after you arrived at his apartment, not when you were in the nightclub?"

"Yes."

"So presumably you were interested in applying for the position?"

"What position?"

"The position of girlfriend."

"Oh, for heaven's sake," says Lauren, losing a little of her composure now. "It was just a question. I'd been chatting to him, he seemed nice, so I wanted to know, that's all. I mean, if he had a girlfriend, I didn't want to waste my time."

I watch Mr. Armstrong when she says this and notice a nerve twitch in his cheek. This was a mistake on her part, and Catherine immediately pounces on it.

"You didn't want to waste your time," she repeats, looking baffled, as if she barely understands English. "What do you mean by that?"

"I didn't want to . . ."

She hesitates. She knows she's slipped up.

"What? Hope that you and Mr. Wolverton might become romantically involved? That you might find yourself living in this luxurious apartment some day?"

"I wasn't thinking that far ahead," says Lauren. "Honestly, it's a standard question when you meet someone and you're having a good night out. *Does he have a girlfriend?* Guys ask me the same thing. *Do you have a boyfriend?* The difference being, I actually listen to the answer and respect it."

"So you weren't thinking of moving in with Mr. Wolverton?"

"No."

"Were you thinking as far ahead as the next day, after perhaps having spent the night with him?"

"No."

"Were you thinking as far ahead as how to get him to have sex with you?"

"No."

"Miss Mackintosh, you're not in the habit of giving much thought to matters, are you?"

"But I am clearly in the habit of saying no," says Lauren, fighting back.

"It was you who led Mr. Wolverton upstairs, wasn't it?" continues Catherine, forcing a different answer, which is given reluctantly.

"Yes."

"With the intention of having sex with him."

"We'd been talking, that's all," insists Lauren. "Having a laugh. And he asked whether I wanted to see the rest of the apartment. I said OK. The only reason I led the way was because I happened to be the one standing closer to the staircase at the time."

"Or you had positioned yourself closest to the staircase, hoping that Mr. Wolverton would issue an invitation."

"Oh, come on!" says Lauren, growing angry now. "I was just standing there, the way anyone might be. It wasn't some great Machiavellian plan."

"Still, fortunate for you," replies Catherine. "Because he took the hint."

"I'm not sure that I consider getting raped *fortunate for me*," says Lauren. "I assume it's never happened to you."

"No," admits Catherine. "But then I don't generally go back to the apartments of young, single, famous millionaires who I've only known for five minutes."

"I was waiting for that," says Lauren, offering a bitter laugh.

"Waiting for what, Miss Mackintosh?"

"Waiting for you to tell me that it was my fault."

"You misunderstand me," replies Catherine, shaking her head and looking entirely innocent of any wrongdoing. "I don't think it's your fault. After all, you can't be blamed for something that never actually happened, can you?"

Lauren looks as if she wants to climb down from the stand and strangle our barrister with her bare hands, but she has the sense to remain still and silent, even though I can see that it takes all her self-control to do so. She glances toward Mr. Armstrong, who is looking back at her. If I was seated elsewhere, I imagine I would see him urging her with his eyes to remain calm and focused.

"The thing is," continues Catherine, "I listened very carefully to your testimony yesterday. And there were a few parts that confused me. You said that when you entered Mr. Wolverton's bedroom, you had no intention of having sex with him."

"That's right."

"So what exactly did you think was going to happen in there? Were you hoping to examine his bookcases and have a conversation about his taste in literature?"

Mr. Armstrong rises, ready to object, but Catherine cuts him off.

"Apologies, My Lady. That was facetious." She turns back to the witness. "But tell me, Miss Mackintosh, exactly what did you think was going to take place?"

Lauren takes a breath before answering.

"I don't know," she says eventually. "I was having a good time. I'd had a few drinks. And I thought he was cute. I was happy just to see where things went."

"So you lay down on his bed."

"No, he pushed me onto it."

"I find that hard to imagine," says Catherine, laughing a little. "Why wouldn't you leave if he became violent?"

"Because it wasn't violent, it was playful."

"A playful push? Onto his bed?"

"Yes."

"I see. But then he joined you on the bed. No one came along to push him, I assume? In his case, it was voluntary? Or did he trip over something?"

"My Lady," says Mr. Armstrong.

"I withdraw that," says Catherine. "Please continue, Miss Mackintosh. What happened then?"

Lauren looks uncomfortable. "Well, we started kissing."

"You took your blouse off."

"No, he took it off me."

"And you allowed him to do this?"

"I thought he was going a bit quick, but yes, I let him."

"So now you're lying on Mr. Wolverton's bed in your underwear and, if I remember correctly, you testified that he took his shirt off."

"Yes."

"And still you didn't think that you were going to have sex."

"I hadn't decided yet. I wasn't uncomfortable with the . . ." She's trying to find the right word. "With what was happening. But I hadn't made up my mind yet."

"So you thought you could get Mr. Wolverton aroused to this point where you're in your underwear, he's removed his shirt, and then you might simply say no, I've changed my mind, I want to go back downstairs. Is that what you're telling me?"

"Yes."

Catherine frowns. This is not, perhaps, the answer she had expected. "I'm sorry?" she asks.

"I said yes. I assumed that if I said stop, then he would stop. I have the right to do that, don't I? Even if we were completely naked, I can still say no, can't I? Or is there a moment during foreplay where I'm legally obliged to see things through?"

Catherine looks rattled. A hint of a smile crosses Mr. Armstrong's face.

"But you didn't say stop, did you, Miss Mackintosh?"

"I did," she insists.

"Was this before or after you took your blouse off ?"

"After *he* took my blouse off."

"You said the word *stop*? Out loud?"

"Yes. I said the word *stop*. Out loud."

"When?"

"When he came in."

She nods in my direction, and the entire court turns to look at me. I can't bear to have their eyes on me and want to turn my gaze to the floor but know that will make me look guilty, so I simply stare directly ahead, toward Judge Kerrey.

"Evan Keogh, you mean," says Catherine.

"He pushed the door open, and he was just stood there, looking at us. I remember thinking—" She pauses and shakes her head.

"You remember thinking what, Miss Mackintosh?"

"How angry he looked," she says. "He wasn't even looking at me, he was looking at Robbie. At Mr. Wolverton, I mean. He looked sort of . . . jealous."

"Jealous of Mr. Wolverton?"

"No, jealous of me."

I feel a blush rise in my cheeks. I glance toward my father, who's chewing his nails with such gusto that Mam slaps his hand away from his mouth.

"And what happened then, Miss Mackintosh?"

"Robbie turned around, he saw Evan, Mr. Keogh, standing there, and he said, *You want some too?* And Evan came inside and closed the door behind him. And that's when I said no."

"No to what?"

"No to sex."

"But Mr. Wolverton hadn't offered you sex, had he?"

"Oh, come on!"

"It's a genuine question, Miss Mackintosh. Had Mr. Wolverton offered you sex?"

"Boys don't offer girls sex. It's not a Jägerbomb. They don't offer. They expect."

Mr. Armstrong's half smile again. He has a good client.

"Please just answer the question," demands Catherine. "Had Mr. Wolverton offered you sex?"

"I mean—"

"No 'I mean's. No 'suppose's. He either had or he hadn't. Had Mr. Wolverton offered you sex?"

"Well, no," admits Lauren. "Not in so many words."

"Then, I'm sorry, but I don't understand what you were saying no to? I can understand you getting off the bed, gathering your discarded clothing, and saying *I'm leaving* or *I'm going back downstairs*, but why would you say no to a question that hadn't been asked? What exactly were you saying no to?"

Lauren looks flustered now.

"Do you normally just say no to things randomly?"

"No."

"No, you do, or no, you don't?"

Mr. Armstrong rises to protest, but Judge Kerrey waves him back to his seat.

"The truth is, Miss Mackintosh," continues Catherine, "you were perfectly happy to have sex with Mr. Wolverton, weren't you? In fact, you wanted it. And it was you who asked Mr. Keogh to film your romantic encounter."

"No," insists Lauren. "And it wasn't a romantic encounter. It was the opposite of that."

"Have you ever filmed yourself having sex before?"

Lauren opens her mouth in outrage but closes it again just as quickly. Catherine looks up, pretending to be surprised. As if she's stumbled upon something unexpectedly, which, of course, she hasn't.

"I ask again, Miss Mackintosh, have you ever filmed yourself having sex before?"

"I don't see why that matters."

"You can let the court decide its importance. Have you ever filmed yourself having sex before? A simple yes or no will suffice."

"Consensually," says Lauren, her eyes moving toward where her parents are seated. "With a long-term boyfriend."

"Miss Mackintosh, with respect, you're nineteen years old. How long term could any relationship have been?"

Lauren remains silent.

"How long term are we talking?"

"Six months."

Catherine laughs and glances toward the jury, shaking her head.

"Six months is long term? I have cheese in my fridge that's been there longer than that."

Again, silence.

"You enjoy being filmed, don't you, Miss Mackintosh?"

"No."

"It turns you on, doesn't it?"

"No."

"So your previous boyfriend, I assume he forced this on you too? Did you report him to the police afterward?"

"Of course not. I agreed to it then. There's a difference."

"Is there?" Catherine keeps her focus on the jury, knowing she has them now, because the older members are looking increasingly disapproving.

"Yes," insists Lauren. "There is."

"And what did you do with the footage afterward? The pornographic video you made with this six-month, terribly long-term boyfriend of yours. Did you watch it?"

Lauren says nothing but finally nods her head.

"Can you answer in words, please, Miss Mackintosh? So the jury can hear you."

"Yes, we watched it."

"Who is we?"

"My boyfriend and me. My ex-boyfriend, I mean."

"Which one?"

"Which one what?"

"Which ex-boyfriend?"

"The one I filmed it with, of course!"

"So not with a later boyfriend."

Lauren looks incensed. "No," she says.

"So, just to be clear, you watched the video with the boy you filmed it with, but not with any later boyfriends."

"Yes."

"It was a private video," continues Catherine.

"Yes."

"Something just for you and this boy to enjoy together."

I can see Lauren visibly crumbling. She knows where this is going, even if I don't.

"It's not something you showed to anyone else," says Catherine.

Lauren is starting to cry now. I can't help myself; I look toward her parents, her loving parents. They want to comfort her, but there's nothing they can do.

"Miss Mackintosh, did you show this pornographic video you made to anyone else, other than the boy you filmed it with?"

"I was drunk," she says.

"You were drunk and . . . what?"

"I showed it to a friend. It was just a joke, that's all."

"I'm sorry. Could you repeat that?"

"I said I showed it to a friend."

Catherine waits, making sure the jury has fully taken this in. "So, just to clarify, at some point in the recent past, you got drunk, had sex with a boy you hadn't known for very long, filmed it, then shared it with others. Have I got that right?"

Lauren, reluctantly, nods.

"Again, Miss Mackintosh, I have to ask you to say your answers aloud."

"Yes," she shouts.

"But when you were in the luxury apartment of a famous footballer, lying on his bed in your underwear, and his friend walked in and started to film the encounter, this was something that conflicted horribly with your finely honed moral compass?"

"You're twisting what happened," says Lauren, tears streaming down her face.

"I'm not doing anything of the sort. I'm simply placing your evidence into context. What you complain of here is something that you have done before, and apparently enjoyed so much that you shared it with your friends. You admit to having a history of enjoying sex with virtual strangers and filming those encounters. This is not a judgment on my part, Miss Mackintosh. Simply a statement of facts."

"Yes, but—"

"And we are all here today because you had sex with Mr. Wolverton, another virtual stranger, and allowed Mr. Keogh to film it."

"This is coming out all wrong," says Lauren, looking away. Her words are almost inaudible now. "I'm tired."

"I'd be tired too, Miss Mackintosh," says Catherine, before resuming her seat. "If I'd spent the last two days lying on the stand."

8

I was six years old when I left the island for the first time, when my father and I took the boat to Galway and then a flight from Shannon Airport to England to see his favorite team play. I'd never been on a plane before, and although the stadium, when we reached it, was impressive, the crowd unsettled me, the noise of the fans so much louder than anything I had ever known. Only four hundred people lived on the island, but here I was surrounded by forty times that number. To my alarm, our seats were located in the middle of an enormous stand, where it looked as if there would be no chance of escape if a riot ensued. All I wanted was to be home again, running around familiar fields with Cormac, my fingers mucky from the earth.

I held tight to Dad's hand as we approached the stadium, but he released me as soon as we'd gone through the turnstiles.

"You're too old now for that carry-on," he said, pushing his way through the throng. I had to run to keep up with him. When we were finally seated, I looked out onto the pitch. The grass looked somehow different to the grass at home, as if the green had been painstakingly painted on, blade by blade. I wondered what the soil beneath it might feel like, whether it had the natural moistness of the island or if it might be tougher to the touch, less giving.

When the teams emerged from the tunnel and ran onto the pitch, they were greeted by deafening cheers, and I pressed myself close to Dad, but he pushed me away in annoyance. His team was playing The Enemy, and before a ball had even been kicked he let loose a string of obscenities against those players who dared to jog along the sidelines down beneath us. I'd heard him curse before—he cursed at Mam all the time—but I'd never heard anything like this. How could he have such hatred in his heart, I wondered, for people he didn't even know? One of his targets played for the Irish team and he screamed abuse at him too, even though he'd pinned a picture of him to my bedroom wall in his green-and-white strip and told me how proud the player's father must be of him.

The game was only twenty minutes in when I needed to use the toilet. I tried to hold it, knowing Dad would be angry with me if I asked to leave, but eventually it became too much. I whispered to him that I needed to find a bathroom, and he told me to wait until halftime, that he'd saved up too long to miss even a moment of this.

"But I have to go," I insisted.

"Tie a knot in it," he snapped.

"I can go myself," I told him, looking back toward the staircase that led to what I considered the peaceful Eden outside.

"I'm not letting you go alone," he said. "Sure, there's pedophiles and all sorts out there waiting for lads like you. So just sit down, shut up, and watch the fuckin' game, all right?"

I tried to do as instructed, but it was impossible. I found myself clutching at my crotch, a horrible pain building inside my kidneys as my small, valuable feet stamped on the concrete beneath me. I bit my lip and felt blood seeping into my mouth. And then, as if God had taken pity on me and decided to grant me a reprieve from unendurable discomfort, it magically eased, and I groaned in relief. It was only as I felt the warm stream of urine pass along my leg that I realized what had happened, and I looked down in horror as it traveled along the stone in the direction of Dad's shoes. His mouth fell open in disbelief. The man seated next to him saw the piss coming his way and let out a bark of anger.

"For fuck's sake," said Dad, infuriated, dragging me to my feet now and pulling me along the row, my trousers staining dark as he hauled me toward the exit. Gripping my collar, he threw me down the staircase and flung me inside. "Get in there and clean yourself up!" he roared, as one of the security guards watched us from a distance but chose not to intervene. "You filthy little animal."

I went inside and sat in a cubicle for a few minutes, sobbing helplessly, before emerging and doing my best to dry my trousers with hand towels, but there was nothing much that I could do. They were soaked. When I turned around, he was behind me.

"You're determined to shame me, aren't you, Evan?" he asked. "You can't just be a normal son. If I could only swap you for Cormac Sweeney. His parents haven't a brain cell to share between them, and yet somehow they produced him and his poor dead brother, who would have been a great hurler had he only lived. Look what I got."

"I'm sorry," I said, looking down at my runners in distress, and he waited until I dared to look up again before punching me hard in the face.

And so, when my life in London came to its untimely end, when I knew that there was only one way that I could make a living for myself, there was a part of me that wanted to offer myself to The Enemy, just to temper whatever joy he might feel at my capitulation to his plans with fury that I'd chosen the team he hated most in the world. But instead, I took a train to a city several hundred miles from London, where I walked into the reception area of the local football club and asked whether I could meet the manager.

"Mr. Hopworth?" said the middle-aged woman behind the desk, taking off her glasses. "He's not available today, I'm afraid. Can I help?"

"One of the coaches, then," I suggested. "Are any of them around?"

"Well, yes," she replied. "Some are, but they'll all be busy, my love. Did you make an appointment?"

"No," I said. "But if one had a few minutes to talk, then I'd really appreciate it."

"Talk to you about what?"

"A job."

"Oh, I see," she said, before opening a drawer and reaching for a folder. "As it happens, I think we do have a couple of openings at the moment that you could apply for. We'd need a CV, of course. Did you bring one with you? And references too. There's a job going in the canteen, I know that much, on account of a young lad from there going off to America last week—no great loss, if I'm honest—and there might be something going with the groundskeeping staff, only you'd need to—"

"No," I said, cutting her off. "Sorry. I didn't mean that type of job."

"Then what type?" she asked, looking up.

"I've decided to become a professional footballer."

A player walked past, making his way toward a staircase, and turned his head when he heard me say this, before bursting into laughter. I ignored him and kept my attention focused on the receptionist.

"I'm afraid it doesn't work that way, my love," she said in a kindly tone, throwing him a look, while speaking to me as if I was a simpleton. "You can't just walk in off the street and ask to play for us. We're a professional team, you see. A Championship club with ambitions."

"I know," I said. "But, the thing is, I'm quite talented."

"I'm sure you are, but the answer's no."

I frowned. I hadn't anticipated rejection. In my naivety I had assumed I could just show them what I could do and that would be that.

"Please," I said. "I've come a long way." I told her about the island, pretending I'd arrived directly from there. She heard me out and seemed to soften. Finally, perhaps thinking this would be the quickest way to be rid of me, she picked up a phone, dialed a number, and spoke quietly under her breath. After a few moments, she nodded and returned it to its cradle.

"You take a seat over there, my love," she said. "Someone will be down to see you in a few minutes."

I thanked her, and did as instructed. About ten minutes later a door to my right opened and a man in his late twenties emerged, sporting a man-bun and a tracksuit emblazoned with the club's colors. He glanced at the receptionist, and she pointed in my direction. He turned to me, loosening his hair now and shaking it out.

"I'm told you want to be a professional footballer," he said, extending his hand, and I stood up, shook it and introduced myself.

"That's right," I said.

"You know this isn't how we do things, right?"

"Yes, I'm sorry about that, but—"

"Where were you before this?"

"London."

"Which team? I haven't heard of you."

"No team," I said. "I've never played professionally."

"So you weren't let go from a contract?"

"No."

"Right." He looked at me, utterly baffled. "Well, which academy were you at when you were a boy?"

"I've never been to an academy," I told him. "I only played for my school. On the island."

"What island?"

"The island I grew up on," I told him, naming it and explaining where it was in relation to the west of Ireland. Then, seeing the blank expression on his face, explaining where the west of Ireland was in relation to Dublin. And then where Dublin was in relation to where we were currently standing.

Unlike the receptionist, the man, whose name was Matt, seemed to be more irritated than sympathetic.

"Look, I'm sorry," he said, glancing at his watch impatiently. "But you can't just . . . All our players have been playing since they were children."

"I've been playing since I was a child," I told him.

"I mean at grassroots level, in cages, at academies. They've been spotted by scouts. We have files on what their heart rates were when they were five years old, ten, fifteen. How they've grown, how their weight has changed. How fast they can run. I could practically tell you the date each one's balls dropped. Honestly, if you're not spotted by the age of about eight, you don't stand a chance. You can't just show up at . . . what are you now, eighteen?"

"Nineteen."

"Even worse. Sorry, but you haven't a hope."

"Just give me a chance, that's all I ask."

"There's no point."

"You don't know that until you see me play."

"Sorry," he repeated, shaking his head, trying to walk away. "And no offense, but I'm too busy for this. There's the door."

"You don't understand," I told him. "I'm good."

"If you're so good," he asked, "then why are you only getting into the game now?"

"Because I don't really like football," I said, and he rolled his eyes.

"Great," he said. "Exactly what we're looking for. A nineteen-year-old with no experience and no medical records who doesn't even like the game."

"Just because I'm good at it doesn't mean I have to enjoy it," I said.

"No, but it helps."

And it was at that moment that the door opened again and a young man emerged, making his way toward the receptionist and handing some forms to her.

"Thanks, Robbie, my love," she said. "You've filled everything in, yes? I don't need to double-check them?"

"I think I have," he said, flashing her that smile that would soon be my undoing. "But you know what I'm like, Doris. It might be worth giving them the once-over to be sure."

She slapped his arm playfully, charmed by him, as everyone always was, and he turned to look in my direction. He was taller than me, and good-looking. I stared at him.

"Hey," he said, looking from Matt to me and back again.

"Just dealing with something," said Matt.

"Who's this, then?"

"Evan Keogh," I told him. "I've decided to become a professional footballer."

Robbie was the first person not to react to this statement in a derisive way. In fact, he looked as if the only thing that he might find strange would be for someone not to hold that ambition.

"Are you any good?" he asked.

"Yes."

"Robbie's just breaking into our first team," Matt told me. "He's been with us since he was a boy."

"Just let me kick a ball around with some of the players for five minutes," I said, turning back to the coach. "That's all I ask. You can time me. Blow a whistle when the five minutes are up. If, after that, you don't think I've got what it takes, then I'll leave, and I won't bother you again."

Matt frowned, then turned to look at Robbie. "Is this a windup?" he asked, and Robbie shrugged.

"Nothing to do with me if it is," he said. "But I can give him a kick-about if you like? I'll grab a few of the lads."

Matt shrugged, then shook his head as if he'd decided that, at worst, this would make a good story for his friends in the pub later.

"Five minutes," he said, pointing a finger at me. "Not a second more. Agreed?"

"Agreed," I said. "And thank you."

Robbie led me back to the changing rooms and handed me a football strip, sitting on a bench and watching me as I changed. At first, I wondered why he was paying such close attention, but then understood from his expression that he was simply studying my body to assess whether I had the right physique for the game.

"What's your BMI?" he asked, and I shrugged.

"Haven't a clue?"

"Your body-fat percentage?"

"Don't know."

"Your resting heart rate?"

"I'm not going to know the answer to any of these questions," I said. "I can tell you my height and weight, but that's about all."

"Go on, then."

"A hundred and seventy centimeters, seventy-three kilos."

He nodded, and a few minutes later we were out on a training pitch with half a dozen other boys. They looked at me suspiciously, as if worried that I might be there to steal one of their places in the squad. On the sidelines, Matt appeared and held out a stopwatch. He'd tied up the man-bun again.

"Five minutes!" he shouted. "Starting now."

I nodded, and another coach, acting as referee, blew a whistle. Robbie lifted the ball with the toe of his right foot and began to make his way down the pitch, preparing to pass it to one of the others. He didn't get that far, though, because I took it off him effortlessly, slipped in and out of two midfielders, past a defender, and, in that moment, my career as a professional footballer began.

When it was over, I walked slowly toward Matt, feeling I'd done all right but not certain that I'd played quite as well as I could. I was talented, yes, but these boys were a lot better than any I'd ever competed against before. I could play alongside them, but it wasn't a foregone conclusion that I could beat them.

Still, he stared at me for a long time before narrowing his eyes, then looking me up and down, holding his gaze on my calves for a few moments. I flexed them, to emphasize the muscles, and he nodded. That's when I knew I was in.

"Tell me your name again?" he said.

9

By the second week of the trial, Catherine has done all she can to impress upon the jury that Lauren has a moral character only slightly less reprehensible than that of a war criminal. Some of her questions have been so blunt, so debasing, that I've felt ashamed to have them asked in my name.

It's probable that the jury now knows more about Lauren Mackintosh than they do about their own families. They know that she took cocaine twice in the weeks leading up to her A-levels, although they do not know that she received two A*s and an A in those exams. That she once performed oral sex on a former contestant from *The X Factor*. That she was underage when she lost her virginity, fifteen when she had her first boyfriend, and fifteen and a half when she cheated on him with his best friend. That she was in the passenger seat when her cousin was arrested for drunk driving. That her parents never married and that her father almost never saw her for the first eleven years of her life. That she's attended two football matches in the club's home ground. That she once told a friend she fancied Phil Foden. That, among the nine pictures featured on her Tinder profile, are two of her in a bikini on a beach. That she's been to Ibiza on three separate occasions. That she once kissed a girl. That she has, on occasion, gone out on a Friday or Saturday night wearing no underwear beneath her dress. That her favorite lipstick is called Brazen. That she has sent pictures of her breasts on Snapchat. That she would prefer to marry someone rich than someone poor. That she once stole some mascara from Debenhams. That she followed the

Wagatha Christie trial. That she doesn't believe in God. That she has credit card debts totalling two thousand pounds. That she's on the pill. And that she has a nut allergy.

Her parents also now know all these things about their daughter.

And yet, there is nothing she has done that I haven't done, or wouldn't do, or that Robbie hasn't done, or wouldn't do. Or that most young men or women our age haven't done, or wouldn't do. But they are not on trial, I tell myself as I stand in the dock; she is. It takes me a moment to recognize my error, and when I do, it's hard not to admire how good my barrister is at her job.

I have observed the jury throughout all of this and seen varying responses. Juror no. 1, an older lady, seems disgusted by Lauren, pursing her lips regularly at every fresh revelation. Juror no. 4, a young man in his early twenties with horrendous acne, blushes violently whenever anything sexual is mentioned. Juror no. 11, an Asian man in his mid-fifties, surprises me by how incensed he appears by Catherine's line of questioning. Once, I thought he was about to assume a barrister's role and stand up to object. Juror no. 8 falls asleep from time to time. Juror no. 7 is visibly moved by how upset Lauren grows at times. Only Juror no. 6, Dr. Freya Petrus, remains inscrutable to me. She scribbles intently in her notepad throughout proceedings, and I wonder what she's writing. Is it notes about what has been said, her thoughts about the responses, or something entirely unrelated?

It's a few days later, immediately following Robbie's testimony, that I find myself in a bathroom off the second floor, one that I know from experience is almost always empty. I've gone there not just to pee but to try to clear my mind of everything he said.

When the door opens, I glance around, and to my dismay I see Robbie's father walk in. I've avoided him since the start of the trial, only speaking to him on that first morning when our parents met, and haven't looked in his direction in the courtroom, even when I've felt his eyes on me.

I hope he'll turn around and leave when he sees me, but no, he must have planned this encounter, for, rather than approaching a urinal or entering the single cubicle, he walks slowly up behind me, as close as he can get without our touching, and stands perfectly still. I can feel his breath on my neck. I tell myself to remain calm, but the cold white tiling is before my face, and I'm worried he will slam my head against it and knock me out.

"Please go away," I whisper.

"No," he replies.

I zip myself up and turn around.

"You've been avoiding me, Evan," he says.

"I thought it was best."

"I never took you for much of a thinker."

This annoys me. I don't care how well read he is, or how much he knows about music or art. I've read books too. I can play piano. And I wanted to be a painter.

"You didn't avoid me at the Birmingham match," he says. "No, you made it very obvious then that you wanted me to notice you. I've thought about that evening a lot since then. I must say, it was quite a clever move on your part. You were hoping to have a little leverage over me, I suppose?"

"Something like that," I say.

"Twenty-four teams in the Second Division," he says. "And what, another sixty in the rest of the league?"

"Sixty-eight," I say. "And it's called the Championship."

"And yet you chose this club. The club my son plays for. You could have gone anywhere. But you came here."

He glances toward my left shoulder.

"How's the arm?" he asks.

"Healed," I tell him. "Although when I get anxious, it starts to hurt."

"How does it feel now?"

"It's aching."

"You didn't need the leverage," he says, sounding almost disappointed in me. "I meant what I said back then. That if you kept your mouth shut, then nothing bad would happen to you. You *have* kept your mouth shut. And nothing bad has happened to you, has it?"

"Well, I'm being tried as an accessory to rape," I tell him. "So there's that."

"You can't blame me for what's happening here."

"No, but I can blame your son. And you're the one who brought him up."

His jaw tenses. A memory flashes through my brain of the night we met, when he brought me back to his so-called bolt-hole near Woolwich Ferry and I unwittingly auditioned for him. The books in his hallway. The vinyl albums. The objets d'art. How I saw the photograph of his son wearing a football strip and wondered whether all fathers were obsessed with turning their sons into professional footballers. Rafe didn't seem like the sort and, of course, Lady Wolverton told us on the morning that the trial started that they had expected something different from their son. *I had always hoped he might go into medicine or the law.* Well, he's involved with the law now, but not, perhaps, in the way she'd imagined. But when I saw the photograph of him in his club kit, I stored that information away in case I ever needed it. And, one day, I did.

"I'm disappointed in you, Evan," says Rafe.

"And I'm frightened of you," I reply. "So I took out a little insurance. That's not so stupid, is it?"

"Are you in love with him?" he asks.

"With who?"

He rolls his eyes. "With my son," he says irritably. "With Robert."

I take a moment to consider my answer. The truth is, there's a lot that I hate about Robbie. I hate his smugness, his misogyny, his casual homophobia, his cruelty, his off-the-cuff racism, his taste in music, his ridiculous car, his habit of hogging the ball and not passing if he has even the slightest chance of scoring, his love of Pot Noodles and Toblerones. I hate how he silences people around him before burping, how he idolizes Nigel Farage, how he rates women on a scale of 1–10, how he imitates my accent when he wants to humiliate me, how he keeps a list on his phone of every girl he's fucked and calls it his burn list, how he never says thank you to waiting staff, how he calls the older women in the club canteen "the hogs," how he resents playing in the Championship, how he believes he's this city's answer to Lionel Messi. I hate his habit of taking selfies with his tongue out, of ordering bottles of Moët in clubs and leaving one of the reserves to pick up the tab, of standing before me in the dressing room stark naked because he knows where my eyes will go, of always wanting to go to karaoke at the end of a night out, of texting me to let me know whenever he gets laid. In fact, it's almost impossible for me to think of anything I like about Robbie. But Rafe has asked me a question, and I've never lied to him before. I won't start now.

"Yes," I say. "I am."

He looks baffled. Completely incredulous.

"But why?" he asks.

"I don't know," I admit, and for a moment I feel like laughing, as if I'm talking to a friend and not my erstwhile pimp, the man who made me money but who also subjected me to degradation at the hands of Sir. "I just do. I have, from the moment I met him. He's electricity to me."

"He's not gay. You realize that? You can't change him."

"I know," I admit. "But it's how I feel. I can't rationalize it. The truth is, I've always thought that if you can explain why you love someone, then you probably don't."

He frowns, as if considering this. He looks as if he actually feels sympathy for me.

"But your little plan has backfired, hasn't it?" he asks. "You thought coming here would protect your future, and instead you're on trial and in love with someone who will never feel the same way toward you."

I feel tears begin to form and rub my eyes, not wanting to appear weak before him.

"Do this for me," he says quietly, reaching out and placing his right hand against my cheek. I lean into it. "Take the blame."

"But how?" I ask. "There isn't even a way that I can do that."

"You're a smart boy. You'd figure it out."

"Robbie is the one accused of rape. I'm just the pervert with the camera."

"I did so much for you," he says.

I step away, walk toward the sink, turn my back on him, and let the water pour over my hands for longer than necessary.

"You introduced me to him," I say bitterly.

"To Robbie? No, I didn't. You came here of your own accord and—"

"To Sir," I say.

He's quiet now. I've silenced him. For a moment, anyway.

"I knew he'd like you," he says. "And he paid well. You were happy to take the money."

"I have nightmares about him to this day," I say. "I don't remember the faces of any of the others. But him? He's always there. I never felt like a whore except when I was with him. The things he did to me. You have no idea how depraved he was."

"I have some," he says, looking down, unable to meet my eye. So, he does feel some shame. "The boys before you . . . well, they didn't walk away without their own scars."

"And you let me walk into that, knowing what he was like? You said you wouldn't put me in any danger."

"Evan," he says. "You worked for me. I was fond of you, yes. More than I usually am of any of the boys in my employ. But it was just a job, I told you that. And you knew what you were taking on. It's not like you'd agreed to work the perfume counter at Selfridge's."

"He was a fucking animal!" I shout, my voice echoing around the room, and Rafe nods, accepts this, before exhaling loudly.

"Well," he says. "This won't count for much, but those days are over for him now, aren't they? He won't be hurting anyone ever again."

This is true, but it's small comfort.

"When it all broke," I say. "His scandals, I mean. I wondered whether you'd get dragged into them."

"I worried about that too," he replies. "But he's not stupid. I mean, he's thick, yes, but he's not stupid. You think you had a difficult childhood? Just imagine what his was like."

I'm not unaware of this. But it's no excuse.

"You think you're so different from him, don't you?" I ask.

"Of course I am," he says, offended.

"No. You're just another rich married man fucking the help."

He turns away. He doesn't want to hear this.

"Tell me what really happened that night," he says.

"You want me to tell you that your son isn't a rapist."

"Of course I do," he says, raising his voice, then glancing back toward the door. "Understand that I will do whatever it takes to prevent Robert from going to jail. Someone has to. You saw him on the stand today. He was arrogant. Dismissive. It didn't play well with the jury."

"I blame the parents."

"We need to be clear on something," he says, growing angrier now. "If Robert ends up going to prison, then you'll be going too, and there will be consequences for you inside."

"Severe consequences, I know," I reply. "I've been on the receiving end of those before, remember?"

"A broken arm is nothing compared to what you can expect if this ends badly for my son. And you know from experience that when I say something, I follow through. I am not a man who deals in idle threats."

We fall silent, staring at each other. He moves toward me. Puts his palm to my cheek again. He does care about me, I think. I could have been the son he wanted, the artist whose work he would have funded. He would have attended my openings and marveled at the fortunes my canvases sold for. We would have given joint interviews to the *Guardian*. And Robbie could have been my father's boy, the footballer, the wild man, the thug. They could have sat in his apartment watching *Match of the Day* and phoning hookers at the end of the night. I would have dedicated my Turner Prize to Rafe; Robbie his FIFA Best Men's Player trophy to Charlie.

"Are you sure it's Robert you're in love with?" he asks quietly. "Or is it me?"

I say nothing. I don't know.

"What is it you want from me, Evan? Tell me. Be honest."

I shake my head and look him directly in the eyes. "I want someone to love me," I say. "And not to hurt me. Never to hurt me."

He holds my gaze, and I can see that somewhere deep inside him there's something he doesn't want to acknowledge. The usual apathy, but for once mixed with regret and an unexpected touch of love. This, I assume, has never happened to him before. To my surprise, he leans forward to kiss me, and I let him. Father, son; son, father. They're wrapped up together in my head now and I don't care which is which. He puts his arms around me and holds me close, whispers something into my ear, and when I ask him to take me into the cubicle he wins the conversation, as every conversation must have a victor, by pulling away and shaking his head.

"Just remember what I said," he tells me, making his way toward the door. "Find a way to keep my son out of jail. Because if you both go down, only one of you can expect to come out again."

When he leaves, I lock myself in the cubicle alone, put the seat down, and weep, just like I did in the football stadium when I was a boy. I'm crying for Robbie. For me. For our parents. Even for my father. But also for Lauren. It occurs to me that the jury now believes she's a whore, even though, of the two of us, I'm the only one who has ever actually charged strangers for sex.

10

In the end, it took almost a year before I made it into the first team. My fitness levels were nowhere near the standard needed and I had little understanding of how to treat my body to prevent it from sustaining injuries. Alongside this, I had to learn how to operate as part of a team. But the coaches stuck with me. Fitness could be worked on, they knew, but talent was innate.

The sports pages picked up on my signing and were puzzled that a complete unknown, at the age of nineteen, would be signed by a Championship club, even one that seemed at no risk of promotion any time soon. There was interest in what might happen if I found my way into the first team. Finally, during our eleventh home game of the season, I was brought on in the fifty-second minute and scored two goals, one of which was pretty good, while the other was a fluke. But flukes win games, and we won that one, which brought us up to tenth in the table. The following weekend, away from home, I scored a hat trick, and suddenly my name was everywhere. A few weeks later, the manager of the Irish team came to watch me play, and soon after I got called up for the qualifying rounds of the Euros, scoring against Denmark and providing an assist in a one–all draw with Germany, although, as my father was fond of pointing out, I missed a crucial penalty against Greece.

Dad attended all the Irish home games and, after my debut, tried to force his way into the changing rooms at the Aviva to offer his supposedly expert analysis to the players on what we'd done right or wrong, but, to my relief, security kept him outside. Embarrassed, I told him never to do that again, that no one other than the manager, coaches, medical staff, and players were allowed in there, and he grabbed me by the neck, pushing me up against a wall, and told me that I wouldn't be where I was if it wasn't for him and I should show a little fucking gratitude. I apologized and crawled away.

It was around then that the club sorted out the apartment for me, and I was pleased when I was told that I would be living in the same development as Robbie. Following our first encounter, we'd become close. I'd cultivated the friendship, of course, for my own purposes, but it shocked me how drawn I was to him. Of course, it didn't hurt that he was a defender, while I was a forward, so I didn't threaten him in any way. In time, he introduced me to his agent, Neil, who approached me with relish.

"You're the dream," he told me. "Young, good-looking, a great player. Do you want to be rich?"

"Sure, why not?" I said with a shrug.

The way I looked at it was that in fifteen or so years' time, I could retire, go wherever I wanted in the world, and never have to return to the island. And if that meant having to spend those years with my studs planted in the earth, then so be it. Within a month, Neil had signed two lucrative sponsorship deals for me and promised more ahead.

A boy from the reserves, only a year younger than me, started hanging around, and I knew he was cruising me. We didn't speak, but when we passed in the corridors our eyes always met, and I recognized his desire. I asked around about him and learned that his name was Wojciech and that he'd come to the club from a team in eastern Poland. Two days after I moved into my apartment, he tracked me down as I was leaving the cafeteria.

"I hear you've found somewhere to live," he said.

"Just give me your phone," I replied, uninterested in small talk.

He took it from his pocket and held it to his face to unlock it before handing it across. I opened the Contacts tab and entered my name, address, and phone number.

"Nine o'clock," I told him.

Back home that evening, I showered and changed into sweatpants and a T-shirt. I hadn't had sex in a year, since my rent boy days had come to an end. After my London experiences, I'd avoided all physical intimacy, felt little interest in it, but, since meeting Robbie, I'd started to feel that buzz again.

Shortly before nine, I stepped out onto my balcony and leaned against the railing. At the same moment, on the other side of the courtyard, a door opened, and Robbie appeared. Below us, a taxi pulled up. Wojciech got out and glanced at the fountain and the perfectly manicured lawns, probably wondering whether he too would get to live in a place like this one day. I looked across and saw Robbie watching him, then looking back at me. He was too far away for me to read his expression. The buzzer sounded, and I went back inside and pressed the button to give Wojciech access, leaving my door ajar before going into the kitchen and chugging a bottle of beer in one go.

When we were done, I took another shower, expecting him to be gone when I emerged, but, to my irritation, he was sprawled on the sofa, one hand resting casually inside his boxer shorts, watching football on the enormous television set that came with the apartment.

"You're still here," I said, and he nodded, pulling a face when a player I vaguely recognized from the Northern Ireland squad was tackled and tumbled dramatically to the ground.

"Who else have you fucked?" he asked, glancing toward me as I knotted the towel around my waist.

"You want my entire sexual history?" I asked. "Seriously?"

"No, I meant on the team."

"No one."

"And on the reserves?"

"No one."

"Why not?"

"No one's offered. And I assume most of them are straight."

"Come on," he said, laughing a little. "No one's straight these days."

He named a couple of people. A kid who still hadn't signed his papers and a left back from the first team who spent more time on the bench than he did on the pitch. He mentioned an older man on the coaching staff too who'd tried it on with him, without success.

"We could do this again if you like," he suggested.

"I'm tired," I said.

"No, I meant another time."

"Sure."

"What about Robbie Wolverton?" he asked as I collapsed into an armchair, wishing he'd just gather his shit together and leave. I knew how Rafe had felt now, on that first night when I'd outstayed my welcome.

"What about him?" I asked. "Robbie's into girls."

"Yeah," said Wojciech. "But, you know, he has his kinks."

I tried not to appear too interested. "What kind of kinks?" I asked.

"You haven't heard?"

I shook my head.

"He likes to be watched. Needs to be watched."

I reached for the remote control and lowered the television volume until it was almost mute.

"What are you talking about?" I asked.

"He let me watch once."

"When?"

"Soon after I got here. We were at a party, and he was hooking up with some girl. He asked if I wanted to watch. Kind of insisted on it. He wanted me to film him."

I raised an eyebrow, skeptical.

"And you did it?"

"Yeah. When they went upstairs, I followed them. The girl started complaining, saying she didn't want me there, but he told her to shut up or he'd just go downstairs and choose someone else. *It'll take me less than two minutes*, he said, *I've got my pick of them.* She wasn't happy about it but didn't want to lose out. He arranged the lighting, told me exactly where to stand. It was like a master class from Steven Spielberg."

I felt myself growing hard again.

"Did you join in?"

He shook his head. "I couldn't," he said. "Not with a girl. But he wanted me to."

I thought about this for a while. I remembered how I'd asked Rafe to close the curtains in his apartment on the night of my audition and how he'd refused. He wanted the city to watch us as he fucked me up against the window. They were so alike, both of them. Father, son; son, father.

"Do you still have the video?" I asked.

He shook his head. "No, I shot it on his phone."

"So I just have your word for this."

"Why would I lie?" he asked. "You know what they say about him, right?"

"What?" I asked. "What do they say?"

"That he can only get it up when there's another guy there. It's not that he wants to fuck the guy, or maybe he does, he's a freak anyway, so who knows, but he has to be watched. They're all like that, these English guys. They spend all their time in these academies from the time they're five or six years old. They hit puberty together, and God knows what goes on between them then. In the end, they can only perform when there's other players in the room. They're literally playing to the gallery, like they do every Saturday afternoon. They need eyes on them, need someone to watch them score, to make them feel like gods. All those videos, you've seen them, players sharing a girl, watching each other, cheering each other on. They can be pretty homophobic, some of them, but most of them are gayer than we are, only they don't realize it. In Poland, players don't act like that. In Ireland?"

"And the girl," I asked, ignoring his question. "The girl you filmed him with. What happened to her?"

He stared at me, baffled by the question. "I don't know." He shrugged. "Why? What does it matter?"

When he reached for the remote to turn the volume up again, I made a grab for it and switched the television off.

"Tell me what he did to her," I said, walking over and standing before him. "In detail."

He smiled. He had a hold over me now.

"I'll show you if you want," he said, loosening my towel.

Afterward, I knew I would see Wojciech again. Not for himself, but for what he could do for me with these stories.

When he left, it was almost midnight, and he tried to kiss me at the front door of my apartment, but I pushed him away.

"Please," I said. "We're not dating."

"You won't tell anyone, will you?" he asked.

"Not if you don't want me to."

"Cool. I won't either."

"I couldn't care less whether you do or don't."

"Yeah, sure," he replied. "Until the fans start calling you faggot, and the sponsors don't want to work with you anymore."

"I couldn't care less about the fans," I told him. "And as for the sponsors, let's face it, they'd make even more money if I came out publicly. They'd kill to have a poster boy like me."

"So why don't you, then?" he asked. "If you're so brave."

"No one's ever asked," I said.

11

It's the seventh day of the trial. Lauren has given evidence. Robbie has given evidence. Everyone who was present in Robbie's apartment that night has given evidence. The gaffer has given evidence. Robbie's closest childhood friend has given evidence. A player I'm friendly with from the Ireland team has given evidence, testifying to my good character, and is now being pilloried in the Irish press and getting crucified on Twitter. He's backtracked since, naturally, pledging a month's salary to the Rape Crisis Centre in Dublin, but it's no good. He's basically fucked. And, today, I gave evidence.

Leaving the courthouse afterward, I'm stopped in my tracks when I see someone completely unexpected waiting for me on the pavement. Fr. Ifechi Onkin, the Nigerian priest who caters to his small flock of four hundred on the island, and who I have not seen or spoken to since leaving. I regret not using a different exit, but he's looking directly at me and nodding his head in greeting, so I have no choice but to go over.

"You're here," I say, extending my hand, which he takes between both of his.

"Evan," he replies. "You're surprised to see me, I imagine?"

"Yes."

"I wondered whether you and I might talk?"

Before I can answer, I see my father descending the steps of the courthouse and charging toward us, a big smile on his face. He throws an arm around Ifechi's shoulders, a gesture the priest shrugs off like a bad cold.

"Father," he says. "Is it yourself ? Why didn't you tell us you were coming?"

"It was something of a last-minute decision," he replies.

"But you've come to support us," says Dad, and Fr. Onkin's face doesn't change, neither confirming nor denying this assertion. "Were you in the courtroom earlier?"

"I was, Charlie."

"So you heard this one's evidence?" he asks, nodding toward me.

"I did."

"And what did you think?"

"The jury seemed receptive to Evan's account of what took place," he replies.

A moment later, Mam joins us. Like me, she's confused by Ifechi's presence. For some reason, an image of that last morning on the island comes back to me, her pushing banknotes into my hand and saying, *Go on now, you, and don't look back.*

"Can I buy you a pint, Father?" asks Dad.

"No, Charlie," says Ifechi, shaking his head. "I would, however, like to spend a little time with your son, if you don't mind."

"Good luck getting any conversation out of him," Dad says. "He has all the personality of a brick wall, this one. But that said," he adds, turning to me, "you did well in there today. You got the tone just right. You didn't lay it on too thick about the little slag, but you didn't let her off the hook either. You played it exactly right."

I glance toward Mam, whose expression is dark and difficult to read, but Ifechi's appearance is unsettling me, so I agree to join him.

We make our way down a narrow lane, where he indicates a coffee shop on the corner, but I see a pub a few doors further along and ask if we can go there instead. Reluctantly, he agrees. After today, I need something to help me take the edge off.

Before we go inside, I notice Juror no. 6, Dr. Freya Petrus, standing by the open door of a sports car with a boy who I think might be her younger brother, as he can't be more than fourteen. They're talking animatedly as he throws a tote bag with the phrase "The Rozelli Programme'" printed on it into the back and climbs into the passenger seat.

Walking over to the driver's side, she glances in my direction, catching my eye for a moment before turning away.

In the pub, I order a pint, and Ifechi asks for a small whiskey, but I make it a large one.

"Why are you here?" I ask him when we're both seated.

"I wanted to see you."

"Are they calling you?" I ask, and he frowns. He doesn't understand my question. "The prosecution," I say. "Have they asked you to give evidence?"

"Why would they do that?"

"I don't know. It's just—"

"There is absolutely no reason why they would do that, Evan," he says. "I can offer nothing to this trial. The prosecution doesn't even know that I exist."

Frankly, I wish that he didn't. At least not here. I want him to go back to the airport and return to the island.

"It's not my intention to cause any trouble," he continues. "You understand the seal of the confessional, yes?"

I nod. Although the school forced us to troop up the hill to the church every Thursday morning when I was a child, I never had much to confess, so I simply made things up. Ordinary decent sins. Until the day came when I found myself in such distress that I finally used the sacrament for its intended purpose.

"This is a difficult time for you," he says, and I'm tempted to laugh. "You think?" I say.

"What will you do when it's over?" he asks.

"I'll go to jail," I tell him. "Or back to the club. One or the other."

"No, you misunderstand me," he says. "I don't mean after the verdict is delivered. I mean fifteen years hence, when this trial is a distant memory and your playing career has come to a natural end. What will you do then?"

"I won't go back to the island, if that's what you're asking. I'll never go back there."

"It might call you back," he says. "Don't we all dream of returning home?"

"You don't," I say.

"I don't what?"

"Dream of going home."

"You don't know anything about my dreams," he tells me.

This is true, and I feel slightly chastened by his response. "Sorry," I say. "I've just always assumed that you didn't leave Nigeria of your own accord. That you escaped."

"What an extraordinary word to use," he replies, looking mildly offended. "I love my country very much. And I miss it."

"I couldn't even pick it out on a map, if I'm honest," I admit.

"I will certainly go home one day," he says. "Just as you will. I will be buried in the earth of Nigeria, alongside my people. And I believe that you will eventually be buried on the island. Alongside yours."

This sounds almost threatening when he says it. As if this might happen sooner than it should.

"How is your mother coping with all of this?" he asks. Only one person can guess my real reason for leaving the island, and that is Ifechi, although Mam, I think, has her suspicions. Consumed by shame, I came close to confiding in her on the night before I took my father's boat out into the waves between the island and Galway, planning to throw myself over the side when I got halfway, when I knew that I was too far from land to swim to safety. Although, in the end, I simply sat there, staring at the water, knowing that I couldn't take this final step, so hoping that it might pull me into its embrace. Eventually, Dad, Luke Duggan, and two of his friends came to find me, and I sat in their vessel, crying like a baby as they brought me back, before running up the dunes, away from the chattering crowd that had gathered in the hope of drama.

"She doesn't say much," I tell him.

"She loves you."

"She's my mother."

"She doesn't want to think badly of you."

I take a long draft of my beer. I have nothing to say to this.

"And your father?"

I offer a quick, bitter laugh.

"He doesn't care whether I'm guilty or not," I tell him. "All that matters to him is that I keep playing football. He's already been in touch with the Irish manager, you know, about the World Cup qualification campaign. He's told me that when I get off—his phrase—my place in the squad will be secure. He doesn't see what I see, though."

"Which is what?"

"The messages posted on socials."

"I don't know that world at all." Ifechi waves a hand in the air dismissively. "Fools."

"Noisy fools."

"What do they say?"

"Half the men call it a setup," I tell him with a shrug. "The other half polish their halos and say I'm a degenerate animal."

"But your text messages," says Ifechi, shaking his head, and I look away in shame. It feels at times as if everyone in Ireland and the UK has read those WhatsApp messages. If I am found guilty, it will be the callousness of them, their unapologetic misogyny and depravity, that will convict me.

"And as for the girls," I continue, "some of them call Lauren Mackintosh a slag. They say, look at the getup of her in those photos. The ones leaked from her Instagram account before it was deleted."

"And the rest?"

"They think I should be castrated."

Ifechi finally lifts his whiskey to his lips.

"As you know," he says at last, "I would never break the seal of the confessional with a third party. But I remain at liberty to discuss certain matters with you."

"I'd rather not," I tell him.

"If that was true, then you would have declined my request to join me here. You would have found an excuse to return home."

"You came all this way, Father," I say. "I do have some manners, you know."

We stare at each other for the longest time. It's obvious to me that he's waiting for me to introduce the subject. In the end, I have no choice.

"You want to talk about Cormac, don't you?" I say with a sigh, looking down at the wood of the table, which is badly scarred by the fingernails, keys, and glasses of many years. I run my thumb into one of the grooves until the point of a splinter touches the tender place beneath my nail. I hold it there for a moment, considering pushing harder.

"Yes," he tells me. "I want to talk about Cormac."

"Where is he anyway?" I ask. "Still working on his father's farm, I suppose?"

I can hear it in my voice. I want to sound contemptuous, but, instead, I sound desperate to know.

"Working on it?" he replies. "No, of course not."

I look up. For a moment, I imagine Cormac traveling the world. Working in an Irish bar in Munich. Studying for a degree in America. Teaching surfing in Australia. The idea of any of these things is painful to me.

"He's running it," says Ifechi.

I look up, surprised.

"Running the farm?"

"Yes."

"You're kidding." I didn't expect this. I thought he would have got out.

"You didn't know?" he asks.

"No."

"I don't mean about him running the farm, I mean about his father."

"I don't know what you're talking about," I say.

"Evan, Joseph Sweeney died eighteen months ago."

I'm genuinely shocked to hear this. Mam usually keeps me abreast of any gossip from the island, but she's never mentioned this, even though I spent half my childhood in the Sweeney house and considered Joe and Siobhán to be like an uncle and aunt to me. I want to be somewhere else, somewhere alone, somewhere, anywhere, so I can think about this without having to talk.

"I should go," I say, glancing at my watch. "If I look hungover in court tomorrow, it won't play well for me. It's closing statements."

"You can stay a little longer," he tells me, and I remain where I am. He's in control here, I understand that. Fine, I think. If he wants to talk, then let's talk.

"Look, what I said back then," I say. "I was just a kid. I was being dramatic, that's all."

"No," he replies, shaking his head. "Evan, I remember our conversation very clearly. And I remember the despair you felt."

"Then you're misremembering."

"You felt alone. And deeply wounded."

"No."

"You were ashamed. And hurt."

"No."

"You felt you'd lost someone that you loved."

"No."

"You told me what you did."

"I liked Cormac."

"I know you did."

"He was my friend. My best friend."

"I know that too. You grew up together."

"Yes."

"And when he lost his brother, you became his brother."

"But I wasn't his brother, was I?"

"As I understood it, he thought of you in that way."

"He could think what he liked," I say. "But it doesn't make it so."

Ifechi thinks about this for a few moments. He reaches for my hand, but I pull away. I'm not holding hands with a priest in a pub. The press pack is more interested in Robbie than in me, so I haven't had to put up with as much harassment outside the court as him, but still, there are smartphones everywhere.

"I don't know Cormac Sweeney well," he tells me, looking me directly in the eye. "And, in my position, I should make no judgments. But, Evan, I do not like him. He is a cold person. A man who thinks only of himself. He is a bully."

I feel my jaw clench in anger. I cannot bear to hear him speak these words. Not about Cormac.

"You try losing your brother when you're seven years old," I say, raising my voice, ready to fight my friend's corner. "A brother you idolized and who was only a year older than you. Then see how you turn out."

"I did lose a brother when I was seven years old," he tells me.

"Well, you're just perfect, then, aren't you?" I say, drinking a size-able amount of my beer. "A fucking saint."

"His name was Amobi."

I don't ask any questions about his lost brother. I'm not interested.

Neither of us speaks for three, four, five minutes.

"You were a very vulnerable boy, I think," says Ifechi eventually.

"We're all fucking vulnerable."

"A boy who wanted someone to care about him."

"Who doesn't?"

"I recall the word you used when you described your feelings toward Cormac."

I can't meet his eye. Because I remember it too.

"You might. I don't."

"Love," he tells me. "You said you were in love with him."

"What do you know about love?" I ask bitterly.

"Many things."

"Jesus, fine," I say, throwing my hands up as I rear back in the seat. I didn't realize, until this moment, that I was almost bent over the table, my forehead close to the woodwork. "But I was seventeen, Father. I didn't know how to deal with my feelings for him. I was just a kid."

"Do you remember what you told me when you came to confession?"

"No."

"Don't lie."

"Fine. Fuck. Yes."

"You told me that you asked Cormac to call to your house late at night. You'd suggested to him that you would go into the fields together."

"And he came of his own accord. No one forced him."

"You said that you would bring alcohol. And the marijuana ciga-rettes. You planned on your both getting drunk and smoking until you became high."

"Which is what we did."

"But it's not all you did, is it, Evan? We sat on either side of the grille, remember, and spoke for a long time. You told me what happened after that."

"Nothing happened," I insist, my foot tapping restlessly on the floor.

"If that was true, then why were you in such pain afterward? And why would you have left the island on your father's boat and contemplated taking your own life?"

"We have very different memories of our conversation, Father," I say, downing the last of my pint and staring at his whiskey, wishing I could just pick it up and finish that too. And then order five more.

"I don't believe we do. You were in such distress on the day you came to see me," he continues. "You told me how he treated you when you expressed your longing for him."

"This is all bullshit," I say, glancing back toward the bar. "Look, are we having another drink here or what?"

"You said that you woke the next day and wanted to kill yourself."

"I'll get my own so," I say, standing up. "Do you want one more, or would you prefer to just fuck off?"

"All I want is for you to admit what you told me. It was a few years ago, yes, but you know that what I say is the truth."

I remain standing. He doesn't have to remind me of anything. I remember that night very well. I remember how infatuated I had become with Cormac and how I'd come to realize that I'd felt that way about him for as long as I could recall, even before I knew what infatuation was. I remember him showing up in his favorite David Bowie T-shirt. I remember him and me getting through two six-packs of beers while smoking a bunch of joints, talking nonsense, and giggling as we got high. I remember the surprise on his face when I leaned into him. I remember how he allowed me to kiss him, the alcohol and the weed softening his reserve, for ten, maybe fifteen seconds, before he pushed me away. I remember pressing my hand against his crotch. I remember the expression on his face when he pulled away, disgust mixed with confusion, and said he wasn't interested in anything like that with me, that we were just friends. I remember trying to kiss him again. I remember him telling me to stop. I remember him shouting, *For fuck's sake, Evan, get your fuckin' hands off me.* I remember keeping going. I remember him saying, *Fuckin' Jesus, fuckin' listen to me, will you?* I remember him using both hands to push me away. I remember him slapping me when I refused to stop. Slapping me. Not even punching me, slapping me. The humiliation of that. I remember turning my face away to avoid the revulsion on his face. I remember how the soil gave way beneath me as I lay back, and wishing it could suck me down into its warm embrace. I remember worms. I remember weeds. I remember the smell of the earth and the glimmer of the stars above me. I remember his fury when he stood over me. I remember him saying how he didn't care that I was into guys, but what the fuck, did I think he was a fag too? I remember the names he called me. I remember how I tried to talk to him over the days ahead, saying I was sorry, that I hadn't meant any of it, that I'd been drunk, high. I remember him saying that he thought we were friends, but it had all been a lie. I remember him telling everyone we knew how I'd tried to kiss him. I remember the laughter, the mocking, the humiliation, the name-calling. I remember the shit on our WhatsApp groups, on Instagram, on Snapchat. I remember how, from that point on, he turned away whenever he saw me.

And I remember confiding all of this in Ifechi and telling him that I didn't want to live anymore, because I'd betrayed my best friend and he'd betrayed me in return, and I couldn't decide which betrayal was worse.

I remember every moment. I remember wanting to die.

"We are not in a confessional now," Ifechi tells me. "We are in a pub in England, far from the island of your birth, where no one can hear us. I wonder whether you want to unburden yourself to me again."

"In what way?" I ask, looking up, wishing he could help me but knowing that he can't. The memory has ruined me.

"By telling me the truth. You suffered terribly in those last months on the island, through no fault of your own. And, when you left, you were damaged. No boy of that age should feel so badly about himself. You are who you are. You were born the way you were born. You did something that felt natural to you. And you were humiliated over it. Cormac Sweeney, this so-called friend of yours, was no friend at all."

I can't reply. I know he's right, but I will not bring myself to criticize Cormac. I can't.

"So," he says at last. "Tell me the truth about what happened between you, this—"

"Ah, for fuck's sake."

"Robert Wolverton, and the young lady who has brought these terrible charges against you."

"I've been telling the truth since this whole nightmare began."

"I'm not sure that you have."

"But you're not on the jury, are you?" I ask, standing up. I look at him, wishing that he could save me, but no one can.

"Evan," he says.

"Fuck off."

"Let me help you."

"You can't."

"If you let me—"

"No."

And now my head is in my hands. I am crying. I am crying like I haven't cried in a long time. I reach out. I take his hand, as he tried to do with me earlier when I pulled away. I clasp it tightly. I wrap it in both my hands.

My sobs are so powerful, they threaten to overwhelm me.

"Breathe," Ifechi says.

"He said I was a bad friend," I say. "But I wasn't. He was the bad friend."

"He was."

"He should have helped me."

"Yes, he should have."

"He should have told me there was nothing wrong with me."

"Yes, he should have."

"But he didn't."

"No."

"Why didn't he?"

"He—"

I don't even hear. I want beer. I want whiskey. I want drugs. I want sex. I want a sharp knife. I want fifty sleeping tablets. I want anything that might take away the pain.

"Evan."

"What?"

"Evan."

"What? *What?* Tell me!"

"Evan."

I look at him. He looks at me.

I pull him toward me, my eyes on his lips, he's a good-looking man, but he pushes me away too, because they all do, and then the room grows dark and spins. I am on the island. I am in the woods with Cormac. I am on the boat. I am on the farm with Harry. I am in London. I am in Rafe's apartment. I am in Sir's palace. I am on the football pitch. I am in Robbie's bedroom with him and Lauren. I am in a courtroom.

I am on the floor, looking up at the ceiling, and Ifechi is leaning over me, slapping my face, saying, *Evan, Evan, wake up, Evan.*

Talk to me.

12

The evening after my twenty-second birthday, I was in Robbie's apartment, where we found ourselves discussing the subject I felt we'd been working toward for a long time: our fathers. When he went to the kitchen to get some more beers, I studied the framed photographs scattered around his shelves, as I had done in Rafe's apartment on the night we met, and in Sir's residence before our first encounter. In a family picture taken perhaps a dozen years earlier, Rafe looked young and handsome, while Lady Wolverton was exactly as I had always imagined her to be. Blond, trim, efficient-looking. There were two older sisters, who resembled their mother. And there, at the center of the picture, was Robbie himself, around eight years old, missing a front tooth, and smiling widely, a football at his feet. I stared at it before being distracted by another picture sitting alongside it. Rafe, standing next to Sir, on the day that he was knighted, the two of them laughing uproariously over some private joke, displaying their great white teeth and their glorious, unassailable privilege.

"I always knew he was important," Robbie told me, appearing by my side and taking the photograph from me, then studying it himself for a moment before returning it to its place. "He'd been busy for as long as I could remember. Rarely at home. Split most of his time between the House of Commons and his Chambers, although we usually traveled to the constituency house at weekends, which he hated. The day he entered the House of Lords, he sold it and never went back."

I pointed at another photograph, where Rafe was standing between two familiar figures, one looking a little grim, the other grinning like the Cheshire Cat.

"I grew up knowing Tony as Tony and Gordon as Gordon," said Robbie. "When I was a kid, I couldn't understand why everyone made such a fuss when either of them came to dinner. Robin Cook was my godfather, you know."

"Who?" I asked.

"Doesn't matter. He's dead now."

"They never came together?" I asked. "Tony and Gordon, I mean?"

"Christ, no. Dad was very good at playing them off against each other. He kept on the good side of both all the way through, while pretty much everyone else had to choose a side. But by the end, he knew the gravy train was over, so he stepped down. He didn't want to lose his seat, which he would have done in that election. Not losing has always been very important to my father. You know, he only texts me when we win a game, right? Never when we lose."

"And your sisters?" I asked.

"Ellie's an investment banker, and Honor's training to be a vet. Much more popular with the olds than me. He knows I earn good money, more than he ever earned at my age, and I think he likes the fact that I'm a footballer. Makes him seem unconventional, like those stupid socks he wears. But he hates that I play in the Championship. Still calls it the Second Division, just to belittle me. He keeps telling me I should move to one of the big clubs, Man U, Arsenal, Liverpool, like it's up to me, but that's never going to happen."

"It might," I said. "You're a good player."

"I'm all right. And your dad," he said, moving over to one of the enormous, overstuffed armchairs, opening a couple more bottles and handing one to me. "He wanted to play, didn't he?"

"He never stood a chance. He can kick a ball around, but that's about it." I didn't want to talk about my father; I wanted to talk about his. "Were your parents happy?"

"They've stayed together all these years, so I guess there must be something there. When I was a kid, yeah, they seemed pretty loved up.

But I think it's more of an arrangement now than anything else. I'm pretty sure Dad's had affairs."

"How many?" I asked.

"God knows. A man like him, with all that power. Good-looking. Wealthy. They were probably throwing themselves at him."

"Women, you mean?"

"Yeah, of course." He paused. "What else would I mean?"

"And your mum never thought of leaving him?"

He sighed and ran a hand across his eyes. "Something happened when I was around ten that nearly broke them up. I still don't know exactly what it was. All I know is Mum came home early from a trip, so I assume she caught him with someone in the house."

"But she still didn't leave?"

"No, I guess he made it up to her somehow. Although they never shared a bedroom after that. Their relationship became much more . . . professional, I suppose. They lived together, brought the three of us up, we went on holidays as a family. But it didn't seem like they were married anymore. Not in any real sense."

I thought about it. I imagined the scene that Lady Wolverton might have faced that evening and wondered who the boy was. Whether he was being auditioned too. Maybe that was when Rafe decided to buy the Woolwich Ferry flat. So he could have a place to conduct his tryouts without fear of disturbance. A thought occurred to me.

"Do they own many homes?" I asked.

"My parents? No, just the house on Connaught Square. And a cottage in Cornwall, but I don't think they go there very often anymore."

"Nowhere else? He doesn't have a flat or anything?"

Robbie frowned. "No," he said. "Why?"

"No reason."

"What about you?" asked Robbie.

"What about me?"

"Your parents. Different, I suppose."

I always recognized a thin undercurrent of superiority in Robbie's tone. As if his parents would, naturally, be complicated people with complex lives, while mine would be simple, unadventurous rural folk.

"Well, they've never exactly been sweethearts," I admitted. "Or, if they ever were, it was before my time. Dad works the farm all day, and Mam's spent most of her life regretting moving to the island. I don't have any brothers or sisters, so I don't know why she stays, to be honest. She could leave if she wanted. I thought she would when I moved away. But no. She's institutionalized."

"Are you close to them?"

"I'm not close to anyone."

He looked directly at me as if he wanted to ask me something but wasn't sure how I'd take it. One of his legs was slung over the side of the armchair, his feet bare. My eyes dwelled on them. Like me, like everyone on the team, he never wore shoes or socks when we didn't have to. Anything to let our hardworking feet breathe.

"Can I ask you something?" he said eventually.

"Sure," I said.

"Wojciech. I've seen him coming and going from yours a few times. What's that all about?"

I took a sip of my beer.

"We're fucking," I told him.

He seemed pleased that I hadn't bothered to obfuscate.

"How long has that been going on?"

"A while."

"And are you, like, in love with him or something?"

I burst out laughing. "Christ, no," I said. "He's just a hookup, that's all."

"Does he feel the same way?"

"Don't know. Don't care."

He raised his voice and asked Siri to change the music to something less high-energy than we'd been listening to.

"So is that how it's always been for you?" he asked.

"Being gay?" I asked. "Yeah."

"You've never been with a girl?"

"Nope."

"Fuck." He shook his head. "Not even, like, to try it out? To see if you might enjoy it?"

"Zero interest," I said. "I'm a gold-star gay, me."

"You know," he said, pointing a finger at me, "I had you figured out long ago."

"Really?"

"Yeah. The day I met you. When you came to the club and were all, *Hi, I want to be a professional footballer, where's my contract, where do I sign, when's my first match?* I could see the way you were looking at me. I knew it then."

I smiled but didn't say anything. Yes, I'd been attracted to him, but that wasn't why I'd been staring at him so intently, nor was it why I had worked so hard to establish our friendship.

"You were so obvious," said Robbie.

"Does it bother you?" I asked, and he took a long draft from his beer.

"Couldn't give a fuck," he said. "Why would I?"

"I don't know. This whole football world."

"No one cares about shit like that, not anymore. Shag whoever you want. The only people who'll give you stick if it comes out will be the fans in the stand. The opposition stand, I mean."

"Nothing could matter less to me," I said, which was the truth. They shouted abuse during every match anyway. Because I'm blond, good-looking, and look about twelve years old, they called me a faggot whenever I came anywhere near them. Water off a duck's back. I barely noticed their presence. I was on the pitch strictly to earn enough money to live the future I wanted, when I would neither have to run up and down a field nor work on one.

"And what about you?" I asked tentatively. "Have you ever done anything with a guy?"

He paused for a few moments and smiled. "Are you hitting on me, Evan?"

"Maybe."

"Nah, not my thing."

"So, never, then?"

"Like you with girls. Zero interest."

"OK."

"Do you have a crush on me?"

"Yes."

"You'd like to fuck me?"

"Sure."

He seemed pleased by this. I hated his ego. And yet I was drawn to it.

"Are you going to tell people? About being gay, I mean."

"Why would I?"

"I don't know. To be brave, or whatever. Footballer comes out, all that crap. David Beckham tweeting his support to make sure he's part of the story. You'd be BBC Sports Personality of the Year before you knew it."

"I don't want to be a poster boy."

"Why did you come to this club anyway?" he asked. "Of all the clubs in England, why this one?"

"You don't want to know."

"I do."

"I came because I wanted to meet you."

His smile faded a little then. It was one thing for him to enjoy the fact that I had a crush on him. It was another thing entirely to think that I might be some type of stalker. He seemed confused, even unsettled, by this revelation. But it was the truth. I had come there for one reason and one reason only. To have some hold over Rafe—and Sir—if I ever needed it.

We remained silent for a few minutes, then he put his bottle down and stood up, walking over to sit next to me on the sofa. He looked me directly in the eye, then reached out and placed both hands on my shoulders. I closed my eyes. I wanted him to start something; if it was going to happen, then it had to begin with him. He moved in close enough to kiss me, but still, I did nothing, waiting for him.

Instead, he stood up and walked toward the windows, opening the curtains so I could see across to my own building, the lights on in some of the apartments. We were exposed to them, and they to us.

"I feel like I could ask you to do anything right now," he said, looking back at me. "And you'd do it. I'm right, aren't I?"

"Probably, yes."

I could see the outline of an erection in his sweatpants. It was nothing new. He often had one in the dressing room after training or a match and, rather than hiding it, he flaunted it. He came over and stood before me for twenty, maybe thirty seconds, waiting for me to do something. He glanced back toward the windows. The smell of the earth was in my nostrils. A slow grin spread across his face.

"OK," he said, lifting his phone from the coffee table and opening the home screen. "Pick a number. Any number between one and thirty-eight."

"Why?"

"Just do it."

"Twenty-two," I said.

He scrolled down and sucked his breath in. "Oh, good call," he said. "Holly. Total slag."

"You list your girls by number?" I asked.

"It's simpler that way. Keeps them in a neat list in my contacts. I put their names, pictures, and details in after that. The best thing about Holly is—"

"I don't care," I said.

"Bro, all I gotta do is text her and she'll come over."

I stood up, relieved and disappointed at the same time. Collecting my jacket, I turned toward the door.

"Where are you going?" he asked.

"Home," I said. "Where else?"

"Stay. Try something you've never tried before."

"Me, you, and number twenty-two."

"Yeah, what's wrong with that?"

"I'm not into girls."

"And I'm not into guys. So what? We'd both enjoy it." He hesitated. "And, you know, we could—"

"We could what?"

"These little slags love to be filmed."

"Or I could stay," I said. "And you could put the phone down. And call no one."

"It's just . . . nah," he said, shaking his head. "Me, you, and number twenty-two. That's what I want. Just you and me? Nah. Doesn't work."

"Pity," I said, walking away.

It was the last time I would see Robbie before the night out after the QPR match, which led us to a bar, to a nightclub, to Lauren Mackintosh, back to this apartment, upstairs to his bedroom, and, ultimately, to a courtroom.

13

The press is out in force this morning. They know, like we do, that the verdict is likely to be delivered today. Closing arguments have been made, and yesterday, after reminding them of their responsibilities, Judge Kerrey sent the jury out to deliberate. A tense afternoon followed before we were told to go home, but now it's Friday, and the assumption is that they will return early, allowing the jurors to enjoy a long weekend.

The reporters scream questions at me as I make my way from the car to the courthouse, but I ignore them. Dad waves them away furiously, like a flock of pigeons, while Mum keeps her head down and strides forward, her arms wrapped around herself as if she's back on the island, walking along the beach with the wind from the Atlantic Ocean blowing in her face.

Inside, I see Mr. Armstrong in conversation with a colleague, and I glance in his direction, wondering whether he will acknowledge my presence, but even though he looks over, I could be a complete stranger for all the recognition he shows. Perhaps he's already mentally moved on from this case to his next one. All that's left for him, after all, is to know whether or not he's won.

I have no idea whether we will be found guilty or not guilty. Lauren was compelling in her evidence, but, while the jury was initially sympathetic toward her, our barrister did an excellent job of destroying her character. Rafe was right in suggesting that Robbie's arrogance and narcissism on the stand would have counted against us, and I think I came across as cagey, particularly when questions were asked about how I'd spent my time between leaving the island and beginning my career as a professional footballer. I've asked Catherine how long she thinks we'll get if we're convicted, and, while she was reluctant to speculate, she finally admitted that Robbie would likely be sent down for eight to ten years while I could expect five to seven. With good behavior, she added, he could be out in six and I in four.

I try to imagine what it would be like to spend that amount of time in prison. My experience of jail is limited to what I've seen on movies and television shows, and I doubt that's an accurate representation. Will I be raped in there? Given how I look, I imagine that's likely. Will I be killed? No, that seems a little dramatic. Or will it just be endlessly boring, one day of tedium following another, as my muscles atrophy and my brain turns to mush? And what will I do when I get out? My football career will be over.

Perhaps I'll get a normal job.

Perhaps I'll move to the other side of the world.

Perhaps I'll kill myself.

My parents and I return to the room where we gathered on the opening day. Mam sits down with a heavy sigh while Dad paces the floor like an expectant father. When the silence becomes too much, she speaks.

"If the worst happens—" she begins, but Dad cuts her off.

"Don't start with that, Maggie," he says.

"If the worst happens," she repeats, raising her voice now and looking toward me, "how do you think you'll cope?"

"I won't," I tell her, and she nods, because she knows her son.

"You'll just have to stay strong," she says.

"Would you shut up, woman?" shouts Dad. "You're upsetting the lad. Can we not cross that bridge if we get to it?"

"That bridge is just up ahead, Charlie," she replies, turning on him. "Can you not see it, no? Because I can. I'm looking right at it."

"That lot out there," he says, pointing toward the door, and I don't know if he's referring to the jury or the press, "know a dirty little slut when they see one. They won't destroy everything I've worked for because some filthy whore can't keep her knickers on."

Did I hear that right? Did he say everything that *he'd* worked for? There's a part of me that wants to be found guilty now, if only to spite him.

"Jesus Christ," says Mam, standing up and walking as far away from him as she can. Her arms are wrapped around herself again; this is a new form of self-preservation, I realize. "What kind of man did I marry?"

"One who did all the hard work and left you to bring up the child, and look where that got us."

"So this is all my fault?" she asks.

"Your problem is you know nothing of the world."

"My problem is I was never allowed to see any of it," she roars. "Sure, haven't you kept me locked up in that bloody house on that godforsaken island since the day you brought me there? And all the promises you made when we were courting! The places we'd go! The things we'd see! And the only places I ever went were a few threadbare shops in a village out of the Stone Age, and the only thing I ever saw was the inside of a church. Christ Almighty, the highlight of last year was the night we went to the new pub just because Tim Devlin had repainted the walls of the snug. The excitement! I could hardly contain myself!"

"Ah, would you shut up," says Dad, who can't bear to hear anyone criticize his beloved island, the center of his tiny universe. "If you hate it so much there, then you can pack your bags, for all the difference it makes to me. You wouldn't be missed, I'll tell you that for nothing. You think I'd be lonely without a wife? Sure, I'd get another. They're two-a-penny."

I bury my face in my hands, wanting to block out the sound of their arguing, the discordant music of my childhood. I wonder does Mam understand that he's right, that she can leave any time she wants. But she won't, I know that. She's trapped. Everything she has is wrapped up with him, and the land is a powerful force, especially in Ireland. He'd rather cut out his heart than surrender so much as a clod of earth to her. And how is a woman in her fifties, who has lived most of her life in isolation, supposed to survive in society, where she knows no one?

"Here they come now," says Dad. He's standing by the window again, looking down at the activity below.

"Who?" I ask.

"Your pal."

"Robbie?"

"And those fancy posh parents of his. Do you know, I'm half-minded to have a word with them before we get into the courtroom."

"Leave it, Charlie," says Mam, and this is enough to send him toward the door. He won't be told what to do, least of all by a woman. Maybe she knows this.

"I'll be back," he says as he marches out.

As much as I can't stand to be in his company, the silence he's left us with is almost impossible to bear. I haven't been alone with Mam since all this started. In fact, I don't think I've been alone with her since she walked me down to the dock on the day I left the island, when she told me to get on the boat and never to look back.

I don't know what to say to her anymore. Things have changed between us. I became a different boy than the one I was supposed to be. I wanted to be a painter. I wanted to be good. I wanted to love someone, and to be loved in return. But none of these ambitions came to be. I think, sometimes, there are people who are destined never to have anyone fall in love with them. It doesn't matter what they look like, how they behave, how much money they have, how much kindness exists in their heart. The love of another person is simply never going to be theirs. There's some aspect of them, something inherent, something indefinable, that makes people turn away. And I think I'm one of those people.

"Evan," she says finally, her voice low. I know what she's going to ask me, and I can't bear it. I feel the potential for tears—mine, not hers—and fight them back. I don't want to walk into that courtroom with red eyes. "It's time to be honest with me."

This is something she would never have said in front of Dad. He doesn't want the truth, but she can't go on without it.

"I don't mean about what happened with that poor girl, God love her," she says. "We can discuss that another day, and we will, I promise you that, when this horror show is behind us."

"Then what?" I ask.

She stares at me for a long time, as if I shouldn't have to ask.

"Cormac Sweeney," she says. "I want to know what happened the night that you and he went into the woods together."

I feel my entire body grow cold. Why this? Why now of all times? It's either the best moment in our lives to ask me this question, or the worst.

"I don't know what you're talking about," I say, looking away. "Cormac and I were—"

"Don't play me for a fool!" she shouts, slamming the palm of her hand down on the table, the sound startling me. My mother has never had a temper, and its sudden eruption startles me. "We might be only five minutes away from a jury sending you to jail for something you say you didn't do—"

"I *didn't* do it," I insist.

"But whatever verdict comes in, and whatever the truth is about that disgusting night, I want to know what happened between you and Cormac. Remember, I knew that boy since the day he was born. Sure, didn't he spend half his childhood under my feet, just as you did under Joe and Siobhán's? I need the truth, Evan, or I swear to God, I will walk out of this room right now and march headlong into the traffic below."

I'm shocked by this. It's possible that she's just being theatrical, but the expression on her face makes me realize that anything is possible. I crumble inside. She is my mother, the only person on this planet who I am certain would lay down her life for me. And she is demanding the truth. The problem is, my life, my spirit, my entire personality, has become so soiled that I can scarcely remember what that word even means anymore.

"Please, Evan," she says, quieter now. "You have to tell me."

"We had a thing," I say, too ashamed to look at her. "That's all. Nothing more."

"A thing? What do you mean, a thing? What kind of a thing?"

"We liked each other."

"You mean you liked him."

"Yes, I liked him."

"But he didn't like you."

"I thought he did."

"But he didn't."

"He was my best friend."

"But he didn't like you in that way."

"What does it matter?" I ask, looking up. "It's ancient history."

"It matters to me," she says. "I need to know."

"But why?"

"Because I have to understand the son that I raised," she tells me. "And my own part in all of this. Did you do something to him, Evan? To Cormac? Did you hurt him in some way?" She pauses. "Or did he hurt you?"

I look down again and can feel the furrowing of my brow.

"Cormac and I . . . we were so close," I say, so quietly that it's almost a whisper. "We got drunk, that's all. We got high. And we kissed. It happens."

"And then what?"

"Nothing."

"I don't believe you."

"What does it matter?" I shout, throwing my hands up in the air. "Why do you care? It was nearly five years ago."

"Did you have sex?"

"No."

"But you wanted to?"

I can't look at her.

"Yes."

"Did you try?"

"Yes."

"Did you force yourself on him?"

"Jesus, no."

"The truth, Evan!"

"As if I could have! The size of him."

"He's no bigger than you."

"He's stronger."

"Well, something more must have happened," she insists. "Because you were never the same after that night. It wasn't long before you took your father's boat out and—"

"He was mean to me," I say quietly, so quietly I'm not even sure that I said it aloud.

"What?" she asks. "What did you say?"

I sit down and stare at the carpet. "He was mean to me," I repeat.

"Mean to you? In what way?"

"I thought we were friends."

"You thought Cormac Sweeney was your friend?" she asks, raising her voice and offering a bitter laugh. "Sure, that boy never looked out for anyone in his life other than himself. My God, the way he treated you when you were growing up. The times I wanted to slap him for the things he said to you, only I'd have had Siobhán Sweeney down on me like a ton of bricks. What did he do?" I remain silent. "Evan, for God's sake," she says. "Tell me. What did he do?"

I have no choice. I'm exhausted by questions. So I tell her what happened. The truth, just like she asked for. When I finish, she's looking at me with so much love on her face that I struggle to keep my emotions together.

"Oh, Evan," she says. "They were just words. From a nasty little prick of a boy who hasn't an ounce of goodness in him and never did. Why did you let them hurt you so much?"

"It's always been just words," I tell her, feeling the tears coming now, despite my earlier determination to keep them at bay. "Everything Dad said to me from as far back as I can remember was just words too. Everything Sir said—"

"Who?"

"But their words were right, weren't they? Dad. Cormac. All those gallerists who turned down my work. They all told me the same thing. That I'm worthless."

"You're not worthless," she insists. "You're a kind and loving boy who's—"

"On trial for accessory to rape."

This silences her for a minute or two.

"So this girl," she says eventually. "Lauren Mackintosh. She's lying, yes?"

"Of course she is."

"Because I know you've been through a lot, Evan, but I can't believe that I could bring up a son who could stand by and watch while something like that took place. I couldn't live with myself if I knew that to be the case."

"I didn't," I say, reaching out to her now, and she lets me bury my head on her shoulder. "I didn't. I didn't, Mam, I didn't. It's a lie, it's all a lie. Whatever happened with Cormac is long ago now, but this, all of this, this is all a lie. She's making it all up, I swear she is. We did not do what she says we did. She wanted to have sex with Robbie, and she never objected to me filming it. I know that's not great in itself, and that you must be disgusted with me for even doing that, but I swear that's what happened. We are here, Robbie and me, because of a lie. I swear it to you, Mam. I swear it. I didn't do it."

She pulls herself away so she's looking directly at me, and I swear I have never had someone stare at me with so much intensity before.

"Just let me just get through today," I say, sitting back and emitting a sigh that seems to come from the very depths of my broken soul. "Please, Mam, just let me get through today, that's all I ask of you. After that, we can talk. There's so much more, so much that I've done that I want to tell you about. I'm . . . I'm rubbish."

"You're not," she says, crying now too. "Never say that about yourself, Evan. You're my son. And I love you. No matter what you've done."

I look up, and I know that she means what she says. No one knows me better than her, but I don't think anyone knows her better than me either. And I see it there, I see it in her eyes.

"You don't believe me, do you?" I ask. "About Lauren, I mean. You think I'm lying. You think I did it."

"I'd forgive you if you did," she says. "I'd forgive you for anything, because that's what mothers do for their sons. But you have to admit it. You have to be honest. With me, if not with anyone else."

I say the next seven words as forcefully as I possibly can.

"I. Didn't. Do. It. She. Is. Lying."

She looks away now, her expression one of terrible sadness, and places her hands together, as if in prayer. "Oh, my son," she says. "I love you, but—"

"But what?"

"I am so ashamed of you."

When Catherine leads Robbie and me into the courtroom, she seems subdued, and it crosses my mind that perhaps barristers are told the verdict in advance, but it's more likely that she, like Mr. Armstrong, is already thinking about the case she'll be arguing tomorrow, when she's finally rid of us.

As we make our way into the dock, Robbie asks how I'm feeling, but I neither acknowledge his question nor answer it. I have nothing further to say.

Judge Kerrey enters and takes her seat before nodding toward the bailiff and, a moment later, the jury members file into their seats. I glance toward my father, who is sitting alone now. Mam is gone. She could be anywhere, I suppose. Traveling back to the island. Disappearing off into another life. Walking headlong into the traffic.

As it turns out, Juror no. 6, Dr. Freya Petrus, has been elected jury foreperson, and when invited to do so she stands. The bailiff asks her whether they have reached a verdict on which they are all agreed.

"We have," she says.

The scent of the soil is almost overwhelming now. It's trapped in my nostrils, making it hard for me to breathe. The stench of the football pitch. The smell of the farm I grew up on. The stink of the forest where Cormac Sweeney humiliated me and broke something inside me.

He asks whether we are guilty or not guilty, and, before she can reply, I turn my eyes to the heart of the courtroom and imagine, for a moment, the life I might have enjoyed had my talents been in my hands rather than my feet. The art I might have created. The joy I might have given. The friends I might have made. The lovers I might have taken. The life I might have built. The happiness I might have felt.

And then the verdict is delivered.

14

Six of us went out that night. Robbie, me, our goalkeeper, Wes, and his brother, Lucas; one of the physios, Stephen, and his childhood friend, Kevin. Earlier that day, we'd played QPR and, somehow, had beaten them 6–1. With only three games left before the end of the season, and now in seventh position, we had no real chance of getting into the play-offs, but we were guaranteed a place in the top half of the table, so we had nothing to worry about or fight for. We could just run out the clock and look forward to the summer break. I'd already planned a month on the Greek islands and had been thinking of inviting Robbie along, liking the idea of posting pictures of the pair of us, shirtless and in swim trunks, on the beaches of Santorini, knowing that Rafe would see them online and be anxious about what I might reveal in a moment of drunkenness.

We started in one of the more exclusive pubs in the city, drinking beer, not yet ready for the shots and cocktails that would come later. Girls came over, wanting to talk, trying to flirt, demanding selfies for their social media accounts. Later, when we arrived at the nightclub, we ignored the queue and were ushered inside by a bouncer, before being brought to a VIP area where a gym rat stood guard, studying each girl who wanted to cross the divide and deciding who was hot enough to gain entry to the promised land.

One came over and sat by my side, and I wondered what her face might look like beneath the layers of makeup she wore. Her mountain of hair was arranged so it sat atop her head as if she'd just emerged from the heart of a tornado. She must have spent hours getting ready for the night, but to me, she looked like a mess. She told me her name; I wasn't listening. There was a boy by the bar who kept looking in my direction, and I wanted to talk to him instead.

"We had it on at work," she told me.

"You had what on?" I asked, shouting to make my voice heard.

"The game, of course!"

"Oh, right," I said. I'd already forgotten about the game.

"Congratulations on your goal. It was the best one."

"I wanted to be a painter."

"What?" She leaned closer, putting a hand to her ear, trying to drown out the music.

"I said thanks."

She put a hand on my lap, close to my crotch, and moved in to kiss me, but I stopped her. Even the idea of that mush of viscous lipstick making contact with my mouth made me nauseous. I put the palm of my right hand in her face and pushed her back.

"What the fuck?" she asked, looking shocked.

"Ask next time," I said. "Fucking ask."

"Before kissing you?" She looked baffled. It was obvious she'd never been met with such recalcitrance.

"Yes."

She took a moment to rearrange her features and to pretend that this was fine. "Sorry," she said. "It's just I really like you."

"How can you possibly 'really like me'? We only met two minutes ago."

"OK." I watched as she tried to process this. After a moment, her face lit up like we were old friends. "We could just talk, yeah?"

"Or you could fuck off," I suggested, and now she stood up, pulled what there was of her dress down so it just about covered her ass, and marched away, pushing past the bouncer and returning to her friends, probably waiting for someone else who was semi-famous to come in and try it on with him instead.

I waited a while, had some more drinks. I thought about calling Wojciech, but instead made my way over to the boy at the bar. He was talking to a girl, but he turned to me when I stood next to him, introducing himself as Logan.

"Evan," I said.

"Yeah, I know," he said. "Evan Keogh, right? I recognize you. But I'll be honest with you, I have no interest in football whatsoever. None."

"That makes two of us, then."

I gave him the smile, the smile that said *I'm interested, and I know you're interested, so what now?*

"Explain the offside rule to me," he said, and I did, and he grinned.

"Hot," he replied. "Although I didn't understand a word of it."

"I wanted to be a painter," I said, my second time tonight, and, like the girl, he didn't hear me, leaning in and asking me to repeat it. I wondered whether those words were destined to be forgotten by the universe now. People couldn't even seem to hear them when I said them aloud.

"I'm over here if you want to join?" he said, nodding toward a table where three other guys were gathered, friends of his, I assumed, and I looked back toward the VIP area and saw Robbie watching me and looking angry, as if I'd deserted him. The rest of our group, and the girls who had joined them, were all talking, but he seemed removed from them, focusing solely on me. I knew I could leave with Logan right then if I wanted, but, if I did, then I wouldn't be with Robbie.

"Not tonight," I told him. "But give me your phone."

He unlocked it, handed it across, and I tapped in my number.

"Any night you want," I told him, feeling the beers start to hit me. "Except the night before a game."

He nodded, not bothered that I'd said no. He was young, fit, good-looking, and could get any guy he wanted in any club. He had no interest in being some ridiculous male WAG. This made me even more interested in him, and, just as I was about to change my mind and say yes, I'll join you and your friends, I'd like to be with a group of gay men who don't give a fuck about football, Robbie came over and put his arm around me.

"Sorry, bum boy," he said to Logan, and his voice was already leery as the alcohol did its magic. He threw an arm around my shoulder and planted a smacker of a kiss on my cheek, which had exactly the effect on me that he knew it would. "You can't have this beautiful man tonight. We've got plans."

"A friend of yours?" asked Logan, ignoring him, disdain written all over his face.

"My best friend."

He nodded and unlocked his phone again, scrolling to his contacts. I knew what he was doing. Deleting me.

"Good luck with that," he said, picking up his drink and walking away. I watched him go. I wanted to follow. But, Robbie.

"We're going back to mine," he said.

"It's late," I said.

"We're going," he repeated. Not a suggestion. A command. "Now."

As I followed the group out of the club, I saw Robbie's right arm wrapped around the waist of a nineteen-year-old girl, his hand held low, while her left hand was tucked into the back pocket of his jeans.

An hour later, we were all in Robbie's apartment. The six of us and at least ten girls. Music playing loudly, some people dancing, some already coupling up. On the balcony, looking back into the room and trying to catch the eye of any of the guys so they would see what was happening, Kevin was getting blown by one of the girls. He looked disappointed when I turned away rather than cheering him on.

"You want some of that, don't you?" asked Robbie, coming up to me and handing me a Jack Daniel's and Coke.

"Give me a break," I said. "He looks like Shrek's ugly brother."

Robbie laughed and continued to move around the room, dispensing drinks and largesse. I thought of what he might let me do if I got him drunk enough. When I turned back, Robbie had moved toward the staircase and was standing with his back to the wall next to Lauren. She said something and he burst out laughing, then put his hand behind her head, his fingers inside her long hair, and pulled her closer, and they started kissing. I made my way across the floor as she took him by the hand, and they started to ascend the staircase. Before going up, he looked in my direction, giving me a grin, a wink, and the thumbs-up sign.

A girl came over and told me she was Lauren's best friend and Robbie better treat her right.

"I'm not his keeper," I snapped. "And you're not hers."

"It's Evan, isn't it?" she asked, nonplussed by my rudeness, and I nodded. "Do you want to fuck?" she continued, as casually as if she was asking whether I wanted a cigarette.

"I'd rather drink bleach," I replied.

"What?" she asked, looking mystified, as if she couldn't possibly have heard me right.

"Just leave me alone," I said. She took a step back and turned on me as if I'd punched her in the stomach.

"Fuck you," she said.

She walked away, and I thought about leaving. I put my drink down and looked toward the door, but, rather than walking toward it, my feet took me up the staircase, where the music was not as loud, then around the corner toward Robbie's bedroom.

It didn't surprise me that he'd left the door ajar. He was probably hoping I'd come up to watch the show. He'd practically invited me, after all. I pushed it open wider and looked at them. They'd turned off the main light, but a small lamp in the corner was on. Robbie's shoes, socks, and shirt were on the floor, along with her blouse. She was moaning slightly as he kissed her stomach, one of his fingers moving beneath a bra strap, but then she turned her head, opened her eyes, and saw me standing there.

"Fuck," she said, startled, and Robbie stopped what he was doing and looked around. He smiled at me.

"You want some too?" he asked. I said nothing, and he turned back to her. "Don't worry," he said. "He's harmless."

"Tell him to get out," she said.

"No, babe, he's fine. Let him watch."

"Fuck off," she replied, to both of us I think, but she laughed a little as she said it, as if she assumed that I'd just take the hint and leave. Instead, I stepped inside and closed the door behind me. There were just the three of us there now, and the expression on her face changed. "I mean it," she said, pulling herself up in the bed now and turning to Robbie. "Tell him to get out."

Robbie groaned and sat up, his knees on either side of her waist.

"What does it matter, babe? It's no different than watching porn."

You want a go after me?" he asked, turning to me. "Something new? You might like it if you try."

"OK, you can both fuck off now," said Lauren, growing angry now and trying to pull herself out from beneath him, but he pressed his thighs against either side of her and used his hands to pin her arms to the bed.

"Don't. Be. A cunt," he said, spitting the words at her, and I saw her grow pale, frightened, recognizing what might be about to happen and her powerlessness in the moment. She looked at me.

"Tell him to get off me," she said.

"Should I?" asked Robbie, turning to me with a broad smile on his face. "Should I get off her? Or should I get her off? You tell me what to do and I'll do it. Promise."

I stared at them both for what felt like a long time. Downstairs, "Starman" was playing loud. I closed my eyes and spoke.

"Let me make you happy," I said.

I took my phone from my pocket, unlocked it, and turned the camera to video.

"Fucking sweet," said Robbie, his face lighting up. "I knew there was a reason I keep you around."

And that's when I started filming.

I filmed as Robbie reached down and pulled Lauren's underwear off.

I filmed her trying to get out from underneath him, telling him no, that she wanted to leave.

I filmed Robbie pulling his jeans down, one hand struggling to keep her arms pinned to the bed above her head and then kicking off his boxer shorts.

I filmed her crying and pleading with him to stop, to please stop, that she didn't want this.

I moved around to the side of the bed and filmed as Robbie pushed himself inside her, turning to give me a triumphant beam as she screamed, *No, no, stop, no, stop.*

I filmed him thrusting, and I turned the camera to her face as the tears flowed down her cheeks.

I filmed them as Robbie said, "What do you reckon, Evan? This is what you want, isn't it? You're fucking loving it, aren't you, you sick fuck?" and he pressed one hand against her mouth to shut her up.

I filmed them as he pulled out and jerked off on her stomach, before collapsing on the bed next to her, when they both went quiet.

I filmed her as she slowly moved away, wiped herself dry with the bed sheet, and struggled to find her underwear, her blouse, her skirt. The way she was walking reminded me of watching *Bambi* when I was a child, the way the little deer can't walk at first, her legs uncertain what to do or whether they can even support the weight of her body.

I filmed as Robbie turned to Lauren, saying, "Give me your number, yeah? We can do this again another time?"

I filmed her wiping the tears from her cheeks and slowly getting dressed before, with quiet dignity, she opened the door of the bedroom and made her way outside, closing it softly behind her.

And then I stopped filming.

Robbie lay back on the bed, naked, his hands intertwined behind his head. I put the phone down on the bedside table, took my clothes off, and lay down next to him. Neither of us moved for a long time. I moved closer to him, letting my head rest on his chest, inhaling his scent as he kissed me gently on the forehead. He fell asleep quickly, but I stayed awake, thinking about what I had been a part of. I didn't leave the bedroom until around five o'clock the following morning, when there were still a few bodies sleeping in the living room below. Gathering my things, I left the apartment and stepped out into the cool morning air.

But before crossing the courtyard and returning home, I turned my phone off and made my way over to the flower beds at the corner of our development, to the ecological plot that I'd always liked, where the flowers and weeds were allowed to grow wild, unmolested, encouraging insects and bees to fly among them. Pushing my way into the left corner, I knelt down, and, using my hands, I dug a hole about two feet deep.

Then I buried the phone beneath the earth.

15

While I want nothing to do with the phalanx of microphones and cameras waiting for us outside the courthouse, Robbie marches straight toward them, his parents flanking him on either side, and gives a speech that he must have been working on for weeks, describing how malevolent young women target professional footballers, then cry rape when they realize their target just wanted a good time and not a lifelong commitment. He criticizes the media for portraying him as a criminal when he, in fact, has been shown to be the real victim. When asked whether he feels any sympathy for Lauren Mackintosh, he shakes his head.

"I know at times like this people usually say that there are no winners here," he says. "But I don't feel that way. Evan Keogh and I are the winners here. The jury recognized that this girl was a liar who set out to destroy our lives, and they refused to sanction it. Justice has been served. We won. She lost."

As I leave, I see my father marching toward me with his arms outstretched and a wide smile on his face, but I turn away. There's no sign of Mam. I hail the first taxi I see and tell the driver to take me directly home and to turn off the radio. I feel no sense of victory. The last thing I see as we pull away is Rafe, standing on the courtroom steps, watching me with an inscrutable expression on his face. He will leave me alone now, I think. There will be no consequences, severe or otherwise.

The club issues a statement the following morning saying that it subscribes to the rule of law, so Robbie and I are welcome back to training and, once we're match-fit again, we will be reinstated in the first team.

It remains solid in the wake of an onslaught of negative social media commentary that condemns it for standing by us.

A march takes place in the city center that weekend dedicated to victims of rape, following a path from the courthouse to the front of the football stadium. About two thousand people join in, all ages, both sexes, but it passes off relatively peacefully and most of them disperse to the pubs afterward to get drunk and see what the night holds in store for them, because, in truth, they don't really care. More worrying, however, is the rally that takes place in Dublin, where more than three times that number march from the Rape Crisis Centre to the headquarters of the Irish Football Association, holding posters of my face with a red line drawn through it, demanding that I be dropped from the national team and play no part in the upcoming World Cup qualification campaign. Unlike the club, the Irish FA announces that it has no current plans to recall me and that the player who has taken my spot during my absence is a great find who has earned his place. I feel no regret over this. I don't want to play anyway. The pay, after all, is shit.

Dad, however, is incensed, and goes on every radio station that will have him—which is most of them—to defend my good name and his. Newspapers run articles condemning him, condemning me, condemning Mam, condemning the entire football culture. For weeks I search my name obsessively on social media, reading the abuse and the hatred, which is only marginally less disturbing than the comments of the people defending me.

Something changes in Robbie in the months after the verdict is announced. Rather than being humbled by what has taken place, he becomes even more self-assured, even more arrogant, and completely invincible on the pitch. Within six months, his game has improved so much that he's signed by a Premier League team, finally achieving his dream of playing in the upper tier. Again, there are protests by people in that city, but they don't last long, and, by then, the narrative has changed. New scandals have emerged to replace ours.

My form, unlike Robbie's, doesn't change, and when the season break comes I disappear alone to Australia's Gold Coast, where no one has ever heard of me, and spend a quiet eight weeks there, considering my future. I think about giving up the game entirely, but I have a good ten years in me still to earn more than enough money to allow me to retire in my mid-thirties and live the life I want without ever needing to return to the island. And so that's the decision I make.

When the new season begins, the furor dies away quickly and normal life is resumed. I score goals. We remain mid-table. Dad comes to the occasional match and berates me for missing opportunities, which I always do, deliberately, when he's there. Since Robbie is no longer part of the team, I never have to face Rafe again. Wojciech is dropped by the reserves and goes back to Poland. This doesn't bother me. I don't need sex. Don't want it. Ever again.

I am a professional footballer.

That is my life.

And one day, that will come to an end and I will be a person without any purpose in the world.

It's almost two years later before I see Lauren Mackintosh again. I'm in London for a few days during the Christmas break and am sitting in the corner of a pub in Covent Garden, reading a book. I'm on my second pint, but the glass of my first remains on the table with a mouthful left at its base. I hear footsteps approach, and a voice asks whether she can take it away.

I glance up to say yes and realize who I'm looking at.

It takes her a few moments to recognize me in return, but then she's seeing someone she hasn't encountered since that last afternoon in the courtroom, when she slumped in her seat, placing her head in her hands, as Juror no. 6 announced the verdict. The moment of recognition lands, and she slowly returns the empty glass to the table.

"You," she says.

I stare at her, uncertain what to say.

"What do you want?" she asks, her voice betraying panic. "He's not with you, is he?"

"No," I say quickly. "No, I swear. I'm alone. I just came in for a drink, that's all. I had no idea you worked here."

She seems to accept this but glances toward the bar, where a tall, muscular man is flirting with one of his customers, as if to reassure herself that she can return to safety if she needs to.

"I'll go," I say.

"You have a full beer. Drink it. I'm not frightened of you."

I nod. A part of me wishes she will walk away; another part wants her to sit down and talk to me. To my complete astonishment, that's exactly what she does. When I have the temerity to do so, I find myself looking directly into her eyes. She is as strong now as she was when she was giving evidence.

"You moved to London, then?" I say at last, stating the obvious.

"You think I could stay at home?" she asks. "My name was all over Twitter. Anonymous accounts, of course. I couldn't go to uni anymore because of the abuse I was getting. I had to drop out."

"I'm sorry," I say, and she laughs bitterly.

"No you're not."

"I am. It's not what I wanted."

"What did you want, then?" she asks, but I have no answer to this. She leans forward. "Why did you do it? Why did you lie?"

"I had no choice."

"You did. A pretty simple choice. You could tell the truth, or you could lie. And you chose to lie."

"I would have gone to jail."

"You deserved to."

"I wouldn't have survived there."

"So you destroyed my life instead."

"I'm sorry."

"Stop saying that. You're not."

I remain silent. How can I disagree?

"It must be so easy," she says finally.

"What?" I ask.

"Going through life without a conscience."

I consider this. She's not wrong.

"Well, you got what you wanted anyway," she says with a sigh, looking away.

"Did I?"

"You're still playing, aren't you? Earning a fortune. While I've lost everything."

"Being a footballer was never what I wanted."

"No? What was it, then?"

"It doesn't matter," I say, shaking my head. "I wasn't good enough."

"Well, I was," she says. "I loved history. I loved studying it. I wanted to be a teacher."

"You still could be."

"I can't even read a history book anymore," she tells me. "It's all tied up in that time. In what you and your rapist friend did to me. You've caused me more pain than you can possibly imagine and have never taken responsibility for any of it." She takes a breath, then speaks with remarkable calm. "I know this sounds like a cliché, but it's the truth: you and that friend of yours—I won't say his name—you destroyed my life."

I look down at the table. I don't see it as a cliché at all. I believe her.

"I'm sorry," I say for the third time, aware how useless my words are.

"Then prove it."

"How?"

"Tell the truth."

"Lauren, it was two years ago. It's over. Everyone's moved on."

"It's only over because you allow it to be over," she says. "If you mean what you say, if you really are sorry, then tell the truth. There'd be a retrial. I'd be vindicated. I could get my life back. And you and that prick would pay for what you did."

I shake my head.

"I'm sorry," I tell her.

"That's four times you've said that."

"But I can't."

"You can," says Lauren. "You just won't."

Then she stands up, picks up the empty glass, and walks away. I follow her with my eyes as she takes out a towel and wipes down the bar, before smiling at a young woman who's just walked in, taking her order. Throughout the rest of my time in the bar, and even when I leave, she never looks in my direction again.

✧　✧　✧

I get very little sleep that night and take an early train home in the morning. When I return to my apartment, I take a long, hot shower before retrieving the easel that has been sitting in one of the spare bedrooms since I first moved in, along with my paints and brushes, and sit down to paint a picture. One last picture. It's not much good. I can see that. I know I don't have any talent. Not in my hands anyway. But still, during those hours, I feel more at peace than I have in a long time.

When it's completed, I go downstairs and make my way out into the courtyard, toward the area of rough grass in the corner of the apartment block. Kneeling down, I dig my hands into the earth, and it doesn't take long for me to retrieve the phone I buried there the morning after Robbie raped Lauren Mackintosh. It's muddy, but even if the handset is damaged, the SIM card inside will be fine, and someone who knows about these things will be able to retrieve the footage of the video I shot that night.

Then I walk four miles to the local police station with the phone in my pocket and hand it to the officer behind the reception desk, telling her my name, giving her my address, and suggesting that her colleagues examine its contents.

After that, I go home.

Which is where I am now.

For no good reason I can think of, I'm watching football on television. For the first time in my life, I find the game rather interesting.

And, waiting for the police to show up, which they will sooner or later, I realize the stench of earth has finally cleared from my nostrils.

I can breathe freely at last.

FIRE

1

When I was twelve years old, I was buried alive within the grounds of a construction site.

Ever since, I've been terrified of enclosed spaces and one of the consequences of this is that I always try to avoid elevators. This morning, however, workmen are repairing the staircase between the ground and first floors of the hospital, leaving me with no choice but to make my way up to the burns unit in the lift. And, to make matters worse, I'm not alone.

The boy standing in the corner can't be more than fourteen, and he appears anxious, tapping his right foot on the floor in an insistent rhythm. I try to intuit from his demeanor whether he's visiting a loved one or is here for a consultation himself and decide on the former. Next to him stands an overweight man with a heavily stubbled double chin who I assume is his father. When he catches my eye, he holds it for a moment before allowing his gaze to fall to my breasts. As we ascend through the spinal column of the building, he continues to stare, before looking up and studying my face, as if he's deciding whether or not, given the opportunity, he would have sex with me. When he looks away and yawns, I can only assume that I haven't met his exacting standards.

They exit on the fourth floor—Renal—while I continue up to the sixth, exhaling in relief when the doors finally open, a slight prickle of perspiration tickling my back. Ahead of me stands Louise Shaw, the most senior nurse practitioner and the closest thing I have to a friend here, along with Aaron Umber, a medical student who's taken the unusual step of opting for a three-month elective on my team. He's my responsibility, but for some reason his presence has irritated me since his arrival. He's never anything but polite and is both diligent in his work and focused on our patients, so I have no reason to feel such antipathy toward him, but nevertheless, I find myself snapping whenever the poor lad opens his mouth.

"Good morning," says Louise, somehow managing to control the dozen or so files that she's carrying, along with the Styrofoam cup of coffee and KitKat with which she greets me every morning. She's due to retire soon and I'm worried that whoever replaces her will not be as attentive to my needs. "Late night?"

"No," I say. "Why do you ask?"

"You look tired."

"Thank you. It's always nice to start the day being told that I look wretched."

"I didn't say that you looked wretched," she tells me, her Irish accent seeping through. "I said you looked tired. There's a difference."

"Well, as it happens, I was in bed by ten," I tell her, which is the truth, although I wasn't alone, so perhaps that accounts for any weariness I'm exhibiting. I turn to Aaron, who's watching me in that unsettling way of his, as if he suspects I'm not human at all but a visitor from another planet, and not a particularly friendly one at that. It's crossed my mind that he might have a crush on me. I'm only thirty-six, after all, and from what the media are always telling me, young men his age are consumed these days with lust for older women. Leaving aside the fact that I'm his superior, however, he hasn't a chance as he's not even remotely my type. It's not that he's unattractive—in fact, he's quite good-looking, if you like that sort of thing, with dark blond hair cut high on his head and short at the sides and sharp, gray eyes—but he's thirteen years my junior and I haven't slept with a twenty-three-year-old since I *was* twenty-three and have no intention of ever doing so again.

"What do you think, Aaron?" I ask him. "Am I some washed-out old hag?"

"You look fine, Dr. Petrus," he tells me, his cheeks coloring a little at the directness of my question.

"Just fine?"

"No, you look great. I mean . . ." He trails off, clearly uncomfortable with this line of questioning. One good thing about the contemporary world, where everyone lives in perpetual hope that they'll be on the receiving end of a remark deemed sufficiently offensive that it can be reported to HR, is that conversations between colleagues, particularly between those of opposite sexes, tend to remain professional. Which suits me fine.

"You ignore her," Louise instructs Aaron with a maternal smile before turning back to me. "You'll want these," she adds, extending the pile of folders in her arms. "Just the usual. Test results, evaluations, overnights, and so on."

"Put them on my desk, will you, Aaron?" I ask, retrieving the coffee and KitKat and watching as he scurries along the corridor. His trainers have seen better days and, as he's quite tall, his ill-fitting scrubs expose his ankles. Maybe it's the fashion these days.

"How much longer do I have to deal with him?" I ask when he's out of earshot.

"Not much longer than you have to deal with me," she says. "But, of course, after he's gone, another him will show up. Along with another me. We're all replaceable."

"Another you would be fine. Another him though . . ."

"Be nice," she says, admonishing me in the way that only she would have the courage to do. "You intimidate him, that's all. You look like a supermodel, speak like a fishwife, and, on top of that, you're his boss. That's a combination that frightens boys his age."

"He's not a boy," I tell her. "He's a man. There's a difference."

We exchange a few particulars about a skin graft I'll be performing just after lunch on a young woman who collapsed with an arrhythmia, ending up with third-degree burns from the two-bar electric heater that warmed her flat because she couldn't afford anything more. Then I make my way toward my office, hoping that Aaron won't be waiting inside for me. My prayers are answered because he's vanished off to wherever he takes himself when I'm not barking orders at him. The precision with which he's laid out the folders on my desk annoys me, and then the fact that it annoys me annoys me too. It's ridiculous that I should be so aggravated by his efficiency.

I follow through on some emails, sending quick, straightforward replies to anything that seems urgent. A conference taking place in Paris in a few months' time that has invited me to present a paper on the ethics of temporary grafts from deceased donors. A medical journal asking whether I might proofread an article on the prevalence of edemas in over sixty-fives who've suffered insult to the top two layers of the dermis. Various administrative hospital matters, including details of a meeting where I'm invited to discuss what further cuts I can make in my department to help ensure that the NHS runs on a budget of about £2.99 a day. An hour passes, and as I do my rounds at eleven thirty, which is fast approaching, I reach into my bag, grab my cigarettes and lighter, and head back toward the dreaded elevator, passing Aaron on the way and telling him to be ready to join me on my return.

It's a warm morning and I'd intended standing in my usual spot just under the shade of the awning, but, seated on a bench about twenty feet away, near the statue of the hospital's founder—who was involved in the nineteenth-century slave trade, although no one's cottoned on to that yet, so he remains in situ for now—I notice the boy from earlier. He's alone, his elbows on his knees, his head in his hands, staring at the ground. I know that I should turn away, smoke my cigarette in peace, and focus on this afternoon's operation, but when I see a boy his age in such obvious pain and showing clear signs of vulnerability, I simply can't help myself.

"Do you mind?" I ask as I approach him, and he startles for a moment, before looking up and shaking his head. His straight dark hair tumbles down to his eyebrows, a little like the Beatles in their mop-top days. His skin is mercifully free of acne, but his nails are a horror to behold. He must gnaw on them like a teething puppy with a chew toy. In fact, he lifts his left hand to his mouth as I sit, attacking his index finger with gusto, and I gently slap it away. "Don't do that," I tell him with a smile, so he knows I'm not just being a scold. "You never know what kind of bacteria you're carrying on there."

"That's what my mum says," he tells me. "She also says that smoking causes cancer."

I turn to look at him and raise an eyebrow.

"Cute," I say, taking my first drag, then blowing the smoke toward him, and he waves a hand in the air to drive it away. I hold the flame of the lighter steady for a few moments, enjoying its purple-blue splendor, before snapping the cap shut. Reaching for the pack, I offer it in his direction.

"I'm fourteen," he tells me, a note of reproach in his voice. When did teenagers become so puritanical? At his age, I would have taken one and put a second behind my ear for later.

"I won't tell if you don't."

"No, thanks," he says.

We remain silent for a few moments, and when it becomes obvious that he's too shy to talk, I take the lead. Which is fine. I'm no pediatrician, but I do know how to talk to boys his age. I've made quite a study of it.

"I saw you in the lift earlier, didn't I?" I ask him. "You looked a little upset. Was that your dad with you?"

"Yes."

"Are you sick? I'm not prying. I'm a doctor. I work here."

"No, I'm fine," he tells me. "It's my friend. He's not doing so well."

"Who's your friend?"

"Harry Cullimore. Do you know him?"

I shake my head and take another drag on my cigarette. The name means nothing to me, but then the hospital has almost 180 beds and I rarely venture far from either the burns unit or A&E. He tells me that Harry had a kidney transplant three months earlier, but it hasn't taken and he's back on dialysis now, waiting for some unlucky person to crash their motorbike or fall under a bus. He's been kept in for the last five days due to complications related to a bladder infection, and there's no sign of him being released any time soon. When he says the word *bladder*, he blushes and looks away, which is adorable.

"It's good of you to visit him," I say.

"He's my best mate," he replies with a shrug. "We grew up together." The boy is close to tears, and his helplessness touches me.

"And you?" I ask. "What's your name?"

"George," he says.

"George what?"

"George Eliot."

I laugh, unsure whether he's joking.

"What?" he asks.

"George Eliot?" I ask. "Seriously?"

"Oh yeah," he tells me, obviously accustomed to being asked this question. "The writer. I know. But she was a woman, wasn't she? And I'm, you know, not."

"That's really your name?"

He nods, and I have no reason to doubt him. It would be a strange thing to invent.

"Well, I'm Freya," I say, offering him my hand to shake. He takes it, although he's obviously uncomfortable with such an adult convention. His palm is slick with perspiration, and I try to be subtle when I wipe it on my skirt. "Where's your dad anyway? Is he coming back to collect you?"

"No, he had to go back to work. He just dropped me off and came up to say hi to Harry. I'll get the bus home in a bit. You don't work in the kidney department, do you?"

"No," I say. "Burns."

"Like, people caught in fires?"

"Among other things, yes."

He grimaces, as people often do when I tell them my speciality. Illnesses are one thing, but disfigurements, particularly those caused by fire, make people uncomfortable. They feel sympathy for the victims, of course, but they'd prefer not to witness the deformities.

"Are there things the doctors aren't telling him?" he asks. "Harry, I mean. Could you find out and let me know?"

"I'm sorry, no," I say. "I can't do that."

"Why not? He's my best mate," he repeats.

"I understand. But there are rules regarding patient confidentiality. You'll have to speak to your friend himself. Or his parents. I'm sure he'll share with you whatever his doctors have told him."

He nods. He's seen enough television shows to know the ethics that govern the medical profession. I'm aware of his eyes drifting toward my legs. He isn't any more subtle in his ogling than his father was, just less experienced in it. His tongue protrudes from his mouth, and I know that, right now, he's not thinking about Harry. He's thinking about sex. But then, to my surprise, he starts crying.

"Hey," I say, stubbing my cigarette out beneath my trainer and moving closer to him. "Are you OK?"

"Yeah," he says, wiping the tears from his cheeks. "Sorry. It's just—"

"What?"

"I don't want him to die."

I am rarely troubled by sentiment. I prefer to remain dispassionate in my dealings with patients and their families, speaking to them in ways that neither patronize nor offer false hope. I tell the truth, refusing to sugarcoat adverse diagnoses. When I have to deal with the emotions of children who have suffered in conflagrations, their skin blistered, their features distorted, their nerve endings either severed or screaming out in unendurable pain, I do so in the company of their parents and a nurse—usually Louise—along with one of the hospital's pediatric therapists, where I remain composed and professional throughout. So I'm surprised when George's tears inspire an unfamiliar and, if I'm honest, rather unwelcome empathy in me.

"I'm sure your friend's doctors are doing everything they can for him," I say.

"Do people die from kidney failure a lot?" he asks.

"It happens," I admit. "It's a serious disease. But older people, mostly. Your friend's body will be young and healthy, so he has that in his favor. It will put up a fight."

"He doesn't look healthy. His face is gray and he's all weak. Like, he can't even get out of bed on his own right now."

There's not much I can say to reassure him. The truth is, if Harry has already rejected one kidney, then he will most likely reject another. Multiple transplants cause extraordinary trauma, and bodies as young as his aren't designed to be abused. Eventually, without renal attainment, his functioning organs will be unable to compensate and they'll start to shut down. Of course, I don't say any of this to George. He wants comfort, not a professional opinion.

"It's good that you care about your friend so much," I tell him. "It's sweet."

He studiously avoids looking at me. Teenage boys never want to look fragile in front of girls or women. When they talk about us with their friends, they can be ruthless and demeaning, speaking of us as little more than bodies to be used or experimented upon for their pleasure, but when they're alone with someone of the opposite sex, their intrinsic terror and total spinelessness assert themselves. They are monsters, every one of them, utterly devoid of decency.

"I sometimes have to treat people your and Harry's age," I tell him, cautiously placing a hand on his while not wanting to frighten him away. His skin is incredibly soft. "And every one of them feels better when they know they have people who care about them. You could be out with your other friends right now, larking around, having fun. But instead, you're here. He's lucky to have you."

There's something I want to ask him, but I made a promise to myself when I woke this morning that I would never ask this question of anyone again. To break that vow within a few hours would show a total lack of willpower on my part. And so I simply glance at my watch and stand up. I need to go. Rounds.

"You take care of yourself, George Eliot," I say. Turning my back on him, I feel his eyes follow me as I walk away. He's upset, concerned for his friend's well-being, but he's still a fourteen-year-old boy and his hormones are affecting his every waking moment. Ahead of me are the sliding doors that will lead me back inside, and I tell myself to keep walking, to march through them, return to the elevator, and let him go about his day.

But that's when I think of Arthur and Pascoe, of the caves dotted around the coastline of Cornwall, of the night I almost died, and I'm defenseless. I stop, look down at the ground for a moment, then close my eyes, allowing myself a resigned sigh. When I open them again and turn around, George looks away, embarrassed at being caught staring, and I walk back toward him.

He has nothing to fear. If anything, it's me who should be afraid.

After all, a doctor in the burns unit should know better than to play with fire.

2

I've never heard the name *Vidar* before and so, as we make our way downstairs, I ask Aaron to google it. After some quick fumbling with his phone, he tells me that Vidar was the Norse god of vengeance, which feels somehow appropriate, considering the conversation I plan on having with the parents of a four-year-old child I've just finished treating.

"How are you with kids?" I ask him.

"Good in the sense that I like them," he tells me. "Bad in the sense that I can't bear to see them hurt."

"They wouldn't be here if they weren't hurt," I reply. "It's not like they come here just for the fun of it. We're not Euro Disney."

He throws me a look that suggests he's formulated an equally sarcastic reply in his head but doesn't quite have the confidence to deliver it yet.

As we approach the second floor, I relate to him the boy's past presentations. He's been treated in A&E twice over the last twelve months, once for a broken wrist (left), when he fell off his tricycle, and once for a perforated eardrum (right), after he stuck a pencil so far into his ear canal that it breached the tympanic membrane. Now, only twelve weeks later, he's back with a deep dermal burn to his right hand after supposedly pressing it against one of the hobs on the family's electric stove. There's no record of any further investigation being done into the child's well-being after the second episode, and for a third to take place in such a short time frame raises red flags.

"That doesn't seem like something a child would do," says Aaron. "Children don't seek out pain. They run from it."

"Most," I say.

"All," he insists.

"Well, yes," I concede. Anyone can let their hand fall upon a hot plate, but the body's natural aversion to trauma makes it physically impossible for it to remain there, anymore than we can strangle ourselves or force ourselves to remain under the water level in a bath. "To suffer a burn this deep, someone must have held him down."

"Jesus," he says, visibly disgusted, and his revulsion is not just performative; I can tell that he means it. "Don't you wonder what kind of person would hurt a child?"

"You obviously haven't done your peds rotation yet," I tell him. "When you do, you'll see exactly the sort of people who do things like that. Most of the time, they're called parents."

"Not always though."

"No."

The boy's father, Börje, who's Swedish, looks anxious when he sees me marching down the corridor, as well he might, because if he thinks I'm going to fall for whatever ridiculous version of events he's invented to explain what's taken place here, then he's delusional. I don't even waste my time saying hello, simply raise a finger to point him toward a nearby room, where his wife, Sharon, is already seated, cradling the boy on her lap. The child is subdued, nursing a dummy in his mouth, his eyes half closed, barely alert. Soft, wounded whimpers escape him from time to time, like an animal caught in a trap who's slowly losing the will to fight on.

Exhausted both from the medications he's been given and the ordeal he's going through, his central nervous system is working overtime to force him to sleep. When I examined the burn earlier, a large blister had already developed on the palm of his hand and the damage to the subcutaneous blood vessels had turned the skin alabaster white. Thankfully, the attending nurse had given him a shot to relieve what must have been unbearable pain, but even he, who must see harrowing injuries on a daily basis, looked upset by the child's distress. I gave instructions for the wound to be cleaned, dressed, and treated with a course of silver sulfadiazine, before asking to meet the parents privately to clarify the chain of events that led their son here.

"So, what happened?" I ask without any preamble, pausing for only a moment before adding, "This time."

A silver box sits on the table in the center of the room with tissues peeping from the top, while a portrait of the king and queen, wearing comforting expressions, hangs on the wall. This is the room where people are brought to be told that a loved one has died. It's where A&E doctors explain to shocked relatives why they were unable to save a life, directing them toward ancillary staff who can instruct them on what to do next before fleeing in search of patients still breathing. I take a seat, but Aaron, I notice, remains standing by the wall, his arms crossed before him in a surprisingly aggressive gesture. His attention is directed toward the child, who he's studying with real compassion on his face. I can't decide whether this degree of empathy will ultimately make him a good doctor or a terrible one.

"He was playing," says Börje. "Seeing how long he could keep his hand on the cooker."

The man's English is almost perfect, tinged with just a slight Scandinavian accent.

"I don't accept that," I say, shaking my head. "It's not something that anyone could possibly do, let alone a child. So I ask again: What happened? The truth, this time."

Börje glances down at the floor. A neck tattoo is visible, descending beneath his polo shirt toward his back. Ropes of some sort. I don't know what they signify. He's a powerfully built man, shaven-headed, thick-necked, muscular, shoulders straining to be released from beneath the cotton fabric. His son's file tells me that he's a construction worker, which might go some way to explain my immediate antipathy to him, as it recalls memories of Arthur and Pascoe, and the building site in Cornwall where they buried me alive. But he does not frighten me. Men do not frighten me. If anything, it's them who should feel nervous.

"He can be naughty," explains Börje, and his choice of word is another indication that he's not completely familiar with the nuances of English, for I can't remember the last time I heard a child described in such an old-fashioned way. Vidar snuffles a little in his mother's arms, halfway between consciousness and sleep. He doesn't know what's going on, only that he's suffered before, he's suffering now, and most likely he'll suffer again. This is his life. It has probably been this way since the day he was born.

"Your son has third-degree burns," I say. "There's a chance that he'll never have full feeling in his hand again."

The man's face falls. He looks frightened, traumatized, grief-stricken, all at once. Whatever fit of rage led him to do this to the boy, it has passed now, and he's witnessing the result of his actions. This will not end well for him, I tell myself, taking some pleasure in drawing out his pain, wanting to inflict as much distress on him as he has on this defenseless child. I will let it slowly dawn on him that I know what he has done and that I intend to make him pay for it. When I'm ready, I will call the police and see to it that he's arrested. I will testify against him in court, as I've done many times before. I will do all I can to ensure that he never hurts his son again.

"We should go home," says Börje, his voice trembling, and it disgusts me to witness the hypocrisy of the tears pooling in his eyes.

"No, not yet," I say, making it clear that he's not in charge; I am. "I need to know exactly what happened here. This is your last chance to tell me the truth."

"I already have," he insists. "The cooker, the electric heat—"

"A child cannot inflict that level of trauma on himself," I insist, raising my voice. "It's ridiculous of you even to suggest it."

I mean trauma in the medical sense, of course, not the emotional. Although I can only guess at how much distress this small boy has endured in his short life. He must believe that the world is a place he entered only to be hurt. He must long for release. In his mother's arms, he cries out and tries to sit up, but, to my astonishment, when she attempts to comfort him, he reaches out to his thug of a father before a burst of pain in his hand makes him explode in near-hysterical tears. I've seen this before. He wants Börje because if he can convince the man that he will be good from now on, then the man might never hurt him again.

"How long do we need to stay here?" asks the mother, Sharon, and I turn to study her for the first time. She's English, a plain sort of woman, overweight but dressing to disguise it, with dry skin and dark bags beneath her eyes. Although she's younger than me, she could pass for ten years older. I wonder how she can allow this man, this husband, this person who she once went on dates with, and laughed with, and fell in love with, and slept with, and holidayed with, and got pregnant with, and had a child with—how she can let him hurt her little boy in the way that he has.

"As long as it takes," I say, softening my tone now, for I don't want her to feel any worse than she already must. "This is the third time that Vidar has presented in a year, Mrs. Forsberg. That gives us cause for concern."

"He is a mischievous boy," says Börje.

"A mischievous boy," I repeat, shaking my head, almost laughing. I wonder where he picks up these phrases.

"But a good boy," he adds, looking directly at me. There's something in his eyes. Something pained. Something asking me to—what? Forgive him? Accept that he doesn't mean to do the things he does to his own child, but that he has no choice?

Fuck you, I think.

I will destroy your life.

I will bury you alive.

"He's tired," says Sharon, lifting the child slightly off her lap. "He needs to be in his own bed."

"No," I say. "Not yet."

"Then when?"

I turn back to Börje.

"When you tell me the truth."

"I've told you," he insists. "I've—"

"No," I say. "You can forget that. Your explanation makes no sense. So you can tell me everything now, or I can go outside and call the police and let them get to the bottom of it. It's your choice."

I turn back to Sharon, willing her to set aside whatever fear she might feel toward her husband. What violence has he inflicted upon her? I wonder. If she were to remove her clothes, what scars or bruises would I discover on her body? Using only my eyes, I try to tell her that I can protect her too, if only she trusts me.

From her bag comes the sound of a phone ringing. To my surprise, she retrieves it, answers it, and talks to the caller as if nothing that is taking place in this room matters in the slightest. And as she does so, the child remains in her arms, weeping softly, unaware of the pain that will come in the middle of the night, or the following morning, when the painkillers have worn off.

"Börje," says Sharon, passing the boy roughly toward her husband. The child is like a rag doll, his limbs flopping uselessly. "It's Sara. Take him, will you?"

"Whoever Sara is, she can wait," says Aaron, speaking for the first time since we gathered here. His tone mixes authority with controlled rage. I turn to look at him, surprised by his intervention. "This is more important."

"Sara is my boss," replies Sharon irritably, waving him away as if he's utterly insignificant. "I can't just ignore her."

Honestly, I'm surprised that she works at all. She looks like one of those women who sits at home all day, watching daytime television programs that tell her how to make tasty, healthy meals for her family, using ingredients she couldn't possibly afford, let alone source, before frying fish fingers for her son and throwing a few cheese strings on the plate. In this moment, I feel as much antagonism toward her as I do toward her husband. They deserve each other, but Vidar doesn't deserve either of them.

"When I come back," says Sharon, standing up and walking toward the door, "we really have to go." She's addressing me now like I'm the help. "So, can you just get my son everything he needs, please? His medications or creams or whatever? We can take care of him from here. We're his parents, after all."

She doesn't wait for a reply, just walks out, turning her attention back to her phone and letting the door swing closed behind her.

The room falls into silence for the best part of a minute, until:

"Help us," whispers Börje.

"What?" I ask, uncertain whether I have heard him right.

"Help us," he repeats, still beneath his breath, as if he's too frightened even to let me hear what he's saying. "Please. You must help us."

At first, I don't understand what he means, but then he glances toward the window that faces out onto the corridor, where his wife is gesticulating wildly on her phone, before standing up, carrying Vidar over to Aaron, and placing the child in my intern's arms. The boy turns his head, muttering something unintelligible, before nestling into Aaron's chest. Sharon has disappeared now, but still, Börje moves away from the window and toward the wall, where he cannot be seen from outside, before turning his back on me. Slowly, he pulls his polo shirt up, dragging the hem toward the base of his neck tattoo, exposing his back, which is covered with purple bruises and scratches. Someone has hurt him too. Someone has beaten this powerfully built man and he has not been able or willing to ward off the blows. I study his injuries. They are terrible. They need medical attention. And they are, of course, hidden in a place where others cannot see them. Once he's certain that I understand, he lets his shirt fall again and turns back to me.

"Help us," he repeats. "Please."

And it's only now that I glance outside and see Sharon marching back toward us, her face contorted with anger, looking as if she will not accept another moment of defiance from either her husband, her child, Aaron, or me.

That's when I understand what is actually going on here.

That it's not always the man who is the offender.

That women can be abusers too.

I look at Börje, but before I can say anything, Aaron pipes up.

"Of course," he says, for some reason excluding me in what he says next. "Of course I'll help you."

3

Friday evening. An empty weekend stretches out before me, which might explain why, after making my final check of postoperative patients in the late afternoon, my compulsion takes hold. I consider going to the cinema, but the idea of sitting in a darkened auditorium for two hours doesn't appeal. I could take a book to my local wine bar, but some man will inevitably approach to tell me that a gorgeous woman like me shouldn't be drinking alone, and when I make it clear that I'm not interested, he'll insist on buying me a glass of wine anyway. When I say I don't want one, he'll reply that I've probably never tried a Sequoia Grove Cambium, and he knows they have some bottles of the 2006 here, and he's not taking no for an answer. When I say he'll have to, he'll shake his head and tell me to trust him, that I'll thank him when I try it. And when I tell him to please go away, to please just leave me the fuck alone, he'll stare at me with an expression suggesting that he'd like to pin me to the wall by the throat and inform me that it's my loss, he was only trying to be friendly, and that I'd be a lot prettier if I smiled. The whole thing will leave me in such a murderous rage that it's simply masochistic to put myself through the ordeal.

In a vain attempt to ward off my urges, and knowing that this usually has a soporific effect on me, I order a meal from a local Indian restaurant, but only pick at it, leaving most of the food in the fridge to be reheated for tomorrow's lunch.

Finally, accepting my weakness, I take a long, hot shower, tie my hair back into a ponytail, and apply a little makeup before dressing in a pair of blue jeans and a simple white blouse. Hanging a sapphire pendant around my neck, I examine myself in the mirror and smile. I was a reasonably attractive teenager, but I became more striking in my twenties, and now, in my mid-thirties, I've somehow become beautiful. Almost every heterosexual doctor in the hospital has hit on me at one time or another, but I've knocked them all back. I've heard whispers that people think I might be a closeted lesbian, and it irritates me to think they believe I'd be so shallow as to conceal something of such little consequence. For a while, I invented a boyfriend as my excuse to decline invitations for drinks, visits to art galleries, or trips to upcoming concerts. My fantasy lover's name was Jesse, he was two years younger than me, a windsurfing fanatic whose man-bun was something I ruthlessly mocked but secretly adored. We met on a train when we were traveling separately toward Vienna and ended up spending the entire night wandering the city, telling each other the story of our lives. I lifted the entire plot of our romance from an old movie, but if anyone noticed they didn't mention it. Jesse and I were together for a few years, until he left me for a younger woman. You know things are bad when even your imaginary boyfriend cheats on you.

It's not that I haven't tried dating. When I was in my final year of medical school, I went out with a first-year student who was planning a career in thoracic surgery. At first, I enjoyed his company, but as I got to know him better I realized that all he cared about was the money he would eventually make, the house he would eventually buy, the luxury holidays he would eventually go on. He was only twenty but could spend an entire evening discussing his pension plan. When he announced that he'd purchased a space in a cemetery's memorial wall where his ashes would be placed after his death, and suggested we visit it together on a Sunday afternoon, I broke up with him.

Later, when I was qualified, I tried something completely out of character, having an affair with a married anesthesiologist some twenty years my senior, but try as I might, I couldn't enjoy the sex. Louise tells me that if I'm not careful, I'll end up on the shelf, like the responsible eldest sister in a Jane Austen novel, but the truth is, I'd rather tie a noose around my neck than place a ring on my finger.

I spray a little perfume on my neck and wrists and, before leaving the flat, make sure to leave my purse on the dressing table in the bedroom. I turn on the lamp in the living room as it will offer a welcoming glow when I, or we, return. Also, I check there's a can of Coke in the fridge. I hate Coke and never drink the stuff, but on nights like these it's important that there's one waiting.

The building I live in lies on the outskirts of the city, fourteen stories high, and my apartment is on the twelfth. I have far more room than I need, but a feeling of space is important to me. I can't be closed in. If the regulations permitted it, I would knock down every wall and turn it into a 2,500-square-foot studio apartment, but under the terms of my lease, internal reconstruction is prohibited. When I first viewed it, I was hesitant to commit as the estate agent informed me that it had once been owned by a well-known footballer. By a strange coincidence, I had sat on the jury for the young man's rape trial some years earlier and worried that this might prove a bad omen. In the end, however, I decided that it was too good to give up and, after all, the offense hadn't taken place here but in the building opposite.

In the underground garage, I'm walking toward my car when I see Hugh Winley coming toward me. Hugh moved into the apartment above my own earlier this year and, unlike the other residents, who tend to keep themselves to themselves, has an irritating habit of trying to engage me in conversation. I've done my best to keep him at bay while not being rude, but he's persistent. A children's television presenter, he seems to think that makes him something special, or that I should think he's something special, which I don't.

"Freya," he says, picking up his pace to catch up with me. "Where have you been? I haven't seen you in ages."

"I've been working," I say.

"Of course. Busy busy," he replies, nodding furiously and pulling at the neck of his low-cut T-shirt to ensure that I can see the definition of his pectoral muscles. "I've hardly had a minute to myself lately either. I was at a reception for the Prince's Trust last night and—"

"Can't stop," I tell him, not wanting to suffer his attempts to impress me by name-dropping whatever nineties pop star or self-aggrandizing former *Hollyoaks* actor he ran into there. "Another time, yes?"

He moves around rather deftly, inserting himself between me and the car door so I can't open it without physically pushing him out of the way. Like many men, he's not trying to appear threatening but is making it clear that he has no intention of letting me leave until he's completed whatever pathetic mission he's on.

"Actually, I'm glad I caught up with you," he continues. "There was something I wanted to ask you."

I offer a deep sigh. It's easier just to let him spit it out.

"Have you ever heard of Aladdin Stardust?"

I have no idea what he's talking about. It sounds like some sort of Christmas pantomime, but as it's only September this seems unlikely.

"No," I say.

"He's a David Bowie tribute act," he explains. "Do you like David Bowie?"

I shrug as if to say, *Of course, doesn't everyone?*

"He's meant to be amazing. He has the voice down and even has two different-colored eyes, although, to be fair, they're probably contact lenses. He's playing next Thursday at this place nearby and I wondered whether—"

"I have surgery every Friday morning," I tell him, which is untrue. "So I always get an early night on Thursdays. Sorry."

"Oh, that's a pity," he says. "Then I guess I'll have to give my spare ticket to some other lucky girl."

"I guess so," I say, brushing past him as I try to achieve something that really shouldn't prove so difficult: gaining access to my own car.

"While we're talking," he says, and I have to hand it to him: he's nothing if not determined. "Your nephew mentioned to me that he was interested in television. I told him I'd invite him on set sometime on one condition. That you came too."

He smiles at me, a dazzling smile, and I can tell that not only is he accustomed to women falling at his feet, he's absolutely convinced of his entitlement to such obeisance. He's good-looking in that boyish, non-threatening way that defines children's TV presenters, who generally look as if they were neutered at twelve, and I realize now that I've become not just a challenge, but an affront to his sense of self. He simply refuses to be rejected. I almost suspect that if I agreed to go out with him, he'd cancel at the last minute, just to prove a point. None of that matters right now, however, as I'm more concerned about what he's just said. For, after all, I'm not an aunt.

"My nephew," I repeat slowly, half a question, half a statement.

"We met in the lift last week," he tells me. "At least, he said he was your nephew. I'm not wrong, am I?"

"No, you're not wrong," I tell him. "He did mention something about wanting to work in the arts. I just assumed he meant film or theater, that's all. Not kids' TV."

His jaw clenches a little at this, but I mean, come on. This is a man who spends an hour five days a week with his right arm stuck up the arse of a glove puppet called Biggles.

"I'll let him know," I say, managing to insert myself into the driver's seat at last. "I know he's busy with school at the moment, but maybe we can set something up somewhere down the line."

"Only if you come too!" he repeats, as I finally pull the door closed and turn on the engine. He remains where he is, watching me as I drive away.

I put this encounter out of my mind as I make my way toward Ramleigh Park. It's a pleasant, balmy evening, and the sun is starting to set. Halfway there, held up by some roadworks, I glance to my left and notice a group of teenagers gathered on the street. Two boys and a girl are playing Rock Paper Scissors and she apparently loses to both, because they whoop and holler and high-five each other. When the trio walks away, turning down a side street, I wonder where they're taking her, what consequence her loss involved, and only the aggressive beeping of the car behind me when the workmen allow us to drive on stops me from pulling in and following them to protect her.

When I reach the park, I find a parking space without difficulty. A couple of pitches have been set aside for games of football. Both are occupied, the first by children aged around five or six, the second by the older boys.

I glance at my watch. It's seven fifteen, which suggests to me that they'll probably finish on the half hour. I wish I'd brought a book and am about to turn the radio on when my phone rings, an unfamiliar number showing up on the screen. I press the red button to reject it, assuming it's some cold caller, but when it rings again a few moments later I decide to answer in case it's someone from work.

"Hello?" I say, waiting for the caller to speak, but there's only silence on the other end. "Hello?" I repeat. "Who's this?"

I'm about to hang up when a voice says, "Is this Freya?" and immediately I know exactly who it is and end the call, flinging the phone away from me onto the floor of the passenger seat. I feel a burning sensation in the pit of my stomach, frightened that it might ring again, but, to my relief, it doesn't. When I finally build up the courage to retrieve it, I block the number on my text messaging service, on WhatsApp, and on the phone itself. *How did this happen?* I wonder, panicking. *How does he have my number?*

I consider going home. The combination of my encounter with Hugh and this unexpected communication has disturbed me. Perhaps the universe is conspiring to tell me that my plans for tonight are unwise. Despite the inevitable harassment, the prospect of a wine bar seems increasingly enticing, but before I can decide one way or the other, I notice that the football has come to an end and the teams are packing up their belongings. Immediately, I feel that intoxicating rush, that overwhelming thirst for revenge, that tells me I have no choice but to see this through.

The young kids leave first, whisked away by enraged fathers remonstrating with dejected five-year-olds over how they missed an open goal. The older boys follow. Some hang around in groups, some leave in pairs, sharing messages or pictures that have come through on their phones while they've been playing. Others begin walking home on their own. I scan them as they leave, waiting for the right boy to appear. I don't know who that is, but I will when I see him. It takes almost ten minutes before he turns onto the path. He's of average height for his age, and neither skinny nor muscular. He hasn't put on tracksuit bottoms over his shorts, as some of the other boys have, and carries an enormous schoolbag on his back and a training bag over one shoulder. His blond hair needs cutting—he keeps brushing it out of his eyes—and one of his knees is covered in mud. He has AirPods in, and his head is moving slightly in time with whatever music he's listening to. Most importantly, he's alone. Perhaps he doesn't have any friends. It's always better if they don't.

I turn the engine on and allow him to walk a few hundred meters ahead. As he makes his way toward the traffic lights, I drive forward and pull up, waiting for him to reach me. When he does, I roll down the window on the passenger side and call out to him.

4

The twins' names were Arthur and Pascoe, traditional Cornish names, and to this day I don't know which of them came up with the idea of burying me alive, but, as they coexisted in a strangely symbiotic state, it's possible they devised the plan together through some unspoken telepathic power without either taking the lead.

When I think of that night, there are three things I recall above all else.

My frantic longing for water. The sound of the earth as they flung spadefuls down upon my improvised coffin. And my desperate need for air as I sucked what I could through the small breathing tube they had left me with. Only one of the four elements—fire—was missing that night, but its time would come.

Growing up in Norfolk with my grandmother, Hannah, I had been starved of the company of children my own age as she didn't allow me to socialize. Although she seemed ancient to me, Hannah was only thirty-two when I was born and thirty-three when my mother, Beth, moved to Cornwall, leaving me in her care. She preferred me to call her by her given name, insisting that "Gran" made her sound like an old lady, just as my mother made me call her by hers because she didn't want people to think that she was old enough to have a child. Both had become pregnant when they were teenagers and, thinking this was the natural order of things, I assumed that I would be a mother myself at sixteen, but, thankfully, I realized that it would be cruel to bring a child into this world.

My first task when I got home from school every afternoon, regardless of the time of year, was to light the fire in the living room, a job I rather enjoyed, clearing out the ashes from the previous evening's blaze before sweeping the grate clean and re-laying it with crumpled-up pages from yesterday's newspaper, a few sticks of wood, and pieces of coal, artfully arranged, and then taking a match to it all. I became proficient and could build the flames so they would burn all night.

For two months every summer, however, I was dispatched on the train to Cornwall to spend July and August with Beth, who threw her arms around me and wept when she collected me at the station, wrapping me in her cigarette-scented embrace, telling me how deeply she'd missed me and how much I had grown, but quickly becoming irritated by my presence. By the time we reached the small cottage she rented by the sea, the tears with which she'd greeted me had been replaced by eye rolls and muttered asides if I asked too many questions, spoke too loudly, sang along with the radio, breathed too heavily, sniffed, coughed, scratched, opened the window, closed the window, did anything, in fact, to remind her of my existence. Instead of feeling welcome in her home or being overcompensated for her lack of maternal affection across the other ten months of the year, I always went to bed on my first night aware that she was counting down the days until I could be dispatched back to Norfolk.

With each passing summer, the cottage grew shabbier, while Beth grew skinnier and more wide-eyed. Her drinking and smoking, along with her habit of just picking at her food, made her increasingly gaunt, but this seemed to attract men, rather than turn them away. Every year, there was at least one new boyfriend for me to acquaint myself with, few of whom showed any interest in me, and in return I barely acknowledged their existence. There was little point, after all, in trying to build a relationship with someone who would be long gone by the time my next visit came around. There was a Derek, who sat on the sofa plucking impotently at the strings of his guitar. A Roger, who chewed his nails and spat the pieces across the room. A Dave, who told me that I'd better hope I grew into my face or no one would ever want to fuck me. A Nick, who was a Mormon, but, he insisted, a bad Mormon. A Chris, who took me for long walks along the beach with his enormous husky in tow. A Jonathan, who swore that he could have been the greatest actor of his generation, only other people were jealous of his talent and they'd ruined it for him. A Joe, who always had a can of cheap lager on the go. A Daisuke, whose family came from Hiroshima, "where the bomb went off," but who had never traveled further east than Exmouth or further west than Penzance. A Gethin, who taught me how to spell and pronounce *Llanfairpwllgwyngyllgogerychwyrndrobwllllantysiliogogogoch*, the village in Anglesey where he had grown up. A Jasper, who read voraciously but rarely got past page fifty of any book. A Tom, whose conversation always seemed to return to the death of Princess Diana, which he insisted was a murder covered up by the Establishment. And these are just the ones that I remember. I didn't begrudge their presence in Beth's life. Each new addition, each throwaway, seemed as much part of who she was as the clothes she wore, the cheap makeup she applied every morning, or the roll-up cigarettes that always protruded from her right hand like a withered extra finger. She wouldn't have been Beth without any of them.

As uncomfortable as these visits could be, I enjoyed being in Cornwall. I liked the sunshine, the fresh air, and the screech of the seagulls in the morning. I liked the local curiosity shops and the winding lanes, some of which I ran quickly down, then struggled to ascend on the way home. But most of all I liked the beach, and that summer, the summer I was buried alive, I liked the fact that I made, or thought I made, some friends.

Beth's cottage was rented to her by a local man named Kitto Teague, who also owned the much larger property next door, having inherited both from his parents. The Teague home was probably five times the size of Beth's but had been in a state of bad repair for a number of years, and Kitto was in the process of making renovations. Enormous glass windows had been installed facing down toward the sea, and the garden had been dug up and was due to be replanted. Beth's that-summer-boyfriend, Eli, who was friendlier to me than most of his predecessors, was site foreman and told me that Kitto was plowing hundreds of thousands of pounds into the makeover.

"He wants it to look like one of them *Grand Designs* off the telly," he told me. "And it might do by the time we're finished."

Beth liked to complain about the lorries that gathered outside, the delivery skips and large wooden boxes that brought new furniture in and took away the old, but there was nothing she could do about it. Her home was on Teague land, after all, and she lived in constant fear that her rent might be raised, or the cottage knocked down entirely to extend his property.

Aware of my interest in the house, Eli asked whether I wanted to see inside, and we waited until Mr. Teague had gone into town for the day, when I followed him in, studying the shiny new stove and the granite marble of the kitchen island. Some of the workers lit cigarettes as soon as their employer had left, and Eli shouted at them, saying they were causing a bloody fire hazard, and if they wanted to smoke, then they could bloody well do it down by the beach on their breaks. Even though he was younger than most of them, it impressed me to see how seriously he took his job and how attentive they were to his instructions.

Upstairs was more of a mess, but he explained the layout of the bedrooms and bathrooms and it was obvious that when all the work was finished it would be a beautiful home. I developed a fantasy that Eli would marry Beth, become my father, then divorce her and take me to live with him instead. He would build a home just like this one, only better, and I would never have to see either my mother or my grandmother again, but when I asked Beth whether she thought he might propose she just laughed and shook her head, saying she had no intentions of shackling herself to one man from here to eternity. Men, she told me, were like knickers. You needed to change them regularly.

We never talked about my real father. There was no point, as Hannah had already told me all I needed to know. That he was a lad from the year above Beth in school, a wrong 'un from a family of tinkers who were no better than they ought to be, and he'd just shrugged his shoulders when Beth told him that he'd got her up the spout, saying it was nothing to do with him if she was the town bike and how did she know it was his anyway? Half the school first eleven had had her.

"Which they hadn't," she insisted. "Not half, anyway."

He left Norfolk before I was born, and that was the end of that.

Before I met Arthur and Pascoe, I would spend my afternoons strolling up and down the beach, paddling in the water, and, on sunny days, changing into my swimsuit beneath a towel before swimming as far out as I dared, which wasn't far, as although I loved the water I had a terrible fear of sharks. (Hannah's favorite movie was *Jaws*, and whenever it was on television she made me sit down to watch it with her, even though she knew that it gave me nightmares.)

Sometimes, I would observe other families on holidays, fathers, mothers, and their children splashing around in the waves, building sandcastles, eating picnic lunches, and wished that I could be among them. I would have liked a brother or sister, someone for me to take care of, or someone who might take care of me, but when I asked Beth whether she would ever give me one, she said that she'd sorted that problem out years ago because being a mother was the hardest job in the world and she didn't intend doing it twice, even though, to my mind, she had barely done it once.

It was only a few days after Eli let me see inside the Teague mansion that I encountered the twins for the first time. I was walking down the path that led from the cottage to the beach, and they were making their way simultaneously from the other side along a carefully constructed set of steps toward the end of their garden. I watched them carefully. Two boys. I would have preferred a boy and a girl, but I'd take what I could get.

"You're the Petrus girl, aren't you?" they said when our paths crossed, and their voices were like nothing I'd ever heard before. Posh, refined, condescending. Their family roots, I knew, were here in Cornwall, but they'd been brought up in Kensington, in West London, which Beth said was where the swanks lived.

"Them Teagues," she told me, "have more money than they know what to do with. He's a big shot in some bank. Probably nicks it all from the vault."

They stood tall, both of them, although they were still growing into their looks and needed haircuts. Almost in unison, they would blow air up from their lower lips to brush their fringes from their eyes, which was when I would see the scatter of pimples dotted across their fore-heads. When they declared me "the Petrus girl," it made me feel like they were talking to a member of staff, and although I didn't like their tone I longed for their company, anything to ease the isolation, so I said yes and told them they could call me Freya.

"He's Arthur," said Pascoe, pointing toward his brother.

And, "He's Pascoe," replied Arthur, pointing back. "Don't mix us up or we'll kill you."

There was no chance of my doing that. They weren't identical and Arthur had a pronounced birthmark on his neck, just beneath the jaw-line, that looked a little like the map of the Thames that I saw at the start of *EastEnders*. I stared at it, wondering whether it was in fact a birthmark or he had been badly burned when he was younger. As I studied it his face reddened slightly, which only emphasized the deformity.

"How old are you?" I asked, and they told me. Fourteen.

"And you?"

"Twelve."

"Just a kid," said Arthur, laughing and shaking his head, and Pascoe joined in. I got the impression they were trying to mock me, but I was just a kid so I couldn't quite see how this could be considered an insult. What was wrong with being twelve? They'd been twelve themselves not so long before.

"Your house," said Pascoe, nodding in the direction of Beth's cot-tage, "belongs to us."

"It's not mine," I told him. "I just stay with Beth for a couple of months every summer, that's all. I live in Norfolk."

They rolled their eyes, as if this cast me even further down the pro-letarian ladder than they'd imagined. They asked about my father, and I told them, verbatim, everything that Hannah had told me, even using her terminology. *Wrong 'un. Tinkers. No better than they ought to be. Up the spout.* I said that I'd seen their father come and go over the last week but not their mother, and when I asked whether she would be coming down to Cornwall soon, their smiles faded. Arthur looked away, his glance directed toward the water. Pascoe watched him for a moment, appearing equally troubled.

FIRE

"Mother died," he said at last. "Just after Christmas. That's why we're here now, doing the bolt-hole up. Dad says he needs a project."

"What's a bolt-hole?" I asked, and Arthur pointed back toward the house.

"That's a bolt-hole," he told me.

I felt bad for them over the loss of their mum. The mother of a girl in my class at school had died a few months earlier in a car crash, along with the father of another. Everyone had felt sorry for them at first, but then it turned out they'd been having an affair, and, with the casual malevolence of children, our sympathy dried up instantly and the two grieving daughters, half sisters in adultery and tragedy, became sworn enemies.

"How did she die?" I asked, and, to my astonishment, Pascoe told me that his father had murdered her, but that the police hadn't found out because he was very clever and they weren't supposed to tell anyone. Arthur remained silent throughout this exchange but didn't seem surprised by it. I didn't know whether Pascoe was having me on, but I rather liked the idea of the story, so encouraged him to tell me more. "How did he kill her?" I asked.

"Well, he didn't do it himself," he told me. "That would be asking for trouble. No, he hired someone. A trained assassin. Used to work for MI5 or MI6 or one of those places. Someone who knew exactly what he was doing."

"But why?" I asked. "Didn't he love her anymore?"

"That's the thing," he said. "He loved her too much. So, when he found out that she was sleeping with someone else, he had to act. You do know what that means, don't you? Sleeping with someone else? Or are you too young yet?"

"I know what it means," I declared haughtily, holding his gaze until he turned away. We'd started studying biology in school that year, and bodily parts, both male and female, their functions, what went where, and what happened when they did, had become the most common topic of conversation in the schoolyard as we offered both accurate and absurd explanations to each other.

"You can't tell anyone though," said Arthur, squeezing my arm so tight that his fingermarks remained there for some time.

"If you do," added Pascoe, "then Father will murder you too."

"And us."

"All right," I said, uncertain whether to believe them or not but unwilling to take the chance.

"You should be grateful we even told you," he said, folding his arms and looking me up and down as if he was considering the price he might get for me on the open market. "The only thing better than knowing a secret is having one of your own."

5

Because the boy is listening to music, I have to call out to him a few times before he notices me. He startles for a moment before removing his AirPods, his expression a little anxious, as if he's expecting me to reprimand him for some inadvertent transgression.

"Sorry," I say, leaning across the passenger seat. "You couldn't help me out, could you?"

He steps closer to the car now, glancing around but remaining silent. He has surprisingly large brown eyes and long eyelashes that put me in mind of a fawn.

"I'm a bit lost," I explain, laughing to put him at ease. "You don't know where Ramleigh Crescent is, do you?"

His face relaxes now. He hasn't done anything wrong. I'm just a woman who needs directions, that's all.

"Oh, right," he says, looking down the street. "I think you're pretty close, actually. Like . . . umm . . ." He points in the direction of a roundabout. "You go down there, I think, and when you get to the traffic lights—"

"The first set?"

"Yes. Before the taxi rank." He thinks about it, putting the thumb of his left hand to his mouth and holding it there as he deliberates. It reminds me of George biting his nails on the bench outside the hospital a few weeks earlier, a memory that sends a sharp burst of anxiety through me.

That phone call a few minutes ago.

"Is this Freya?"

"After that, I think you go left," the boy continues. "Although I'm not really sure. Do you have Google Maps?" His eyes flicker toward the dashboard of my Audi A8 and move hungrily across the various screens and the white leather interior.

"You look like a boy who's interested in cars," I say, ignoring his question and smiling at him.

He nods and looks embarrassed, shuffling back on the pavement as he hitches his backpack up his shoulders.

"I couldn't ask an enormous favor, could I?"

"What?"

"You wouldn't jump in and direct me?" I ask. "I hate to play the damsel in distress but I'm just really hopeless at things like this."

He blinks, uncertain how to respond. "Umm," he says.

"I can barely find my own flat unless I'm standing in front of it," I continue. "And I've lived there for years."

"Well, I suppose," he mutters.

"You're a star," I tell him, and, before he can change his mind, I reach over and open the passenger door. Still, he doesn't move. He's probably been told from childhood that he should never get into cars with strangers, but it's not as if I'm some overweight middle-aged man trying to entice him into a Ford Fiesta with the promise of a burger and chips and a packet of Haribo afterward. I'm an attractive thirty-six-year-old woman driving a sports car. I'm hardly a threat.

"I should probably go home," he tells me. "My mum . . ." he adds, trailing off.

"Do you live far?" I ask.

"Well, I get the bus."

"Oh, buses are hopeless. They never come. And if they do, they break down or you can't get a seat. Tell you what. You help me find Ramleigh Crescent and then I'll drop you home once I know where it is. Deal?"

"Umm."

Without waiting for an answer, I sit up straight in my seat and look ahead, as if we've agreed upon this plan, and although he remains tentative, he defaults to what I can only assume is his true nature: obedience. He's a good boy, and I like that. He'll do what he's told and cause no trouble. It takes a few moments, but at last he gets in, closes the door behind him, and before he can even put his seat belt on, I pull out, almost driving straight into the path of a passing van.

"Through the roundabout and all the way to the lights?" I ask.

"Yeah, I think so."

We drive in silence at first and he keeps his backpack pressed firmly across his knees, as if it contains all his most precious possessions and not just his schoolbooks. His training bag is squashed on the floor around his feet.

"I'm Freya, by the way," I tell him.

"Hi."

I wait for him to offer his name, but he doesn't.

"And you?" I ask.

"Oh, sorry. Yeah. I'm Rufus."

"That's an unusual name. I've never met a Rufus before."

"I'm named after some singer my mum likes," he tells me.

"Rufus Wainwright?"

"That's him."

"Believe it or not, I heard him play live once," I say, a total lie, but I'm aware of the album released from the performance. "At Carnegie Hall in New York. He performed an entire concert that Judy Garland played there decades earlier."

I hope this will inspire him to ask me something about it, just to get the conversation going, but no, total silence. He probably has no idea who Judy Garland is, so I mention *The Wizard of Oz* and he turns to me and smiles for the first time.

"Oh yeah," he says. "The Wicked Witch of the West."

"That's the one."

"She always scared me when I was a kid."

I smile. He's still a kid, after all. And he was right to be scared of her.

"Well, it's nice to meet you, Rufus," I say, accepting that I'm going to have to make all the running here. I nod toward his sports bag. "You were playing football?"

"Trying to," he tells me. "I'm not very good." He hesitates briefly, perhaps wanting to impress me. "Although I did score a goal today."

"Good for you!"

"An own goal," he adds in a self-deprecating tone, and I burst out laughing.

"Well, a goal is a goal," I say. "You hit the back of the net. That's what counts."

"Tell that to my teammates. I nearly got my head kicked in."

We've reached the end of the road now and I turn left, as instructed. I know exactly where Ramleigh Crescent is and have absolutely no reason to visit it, but it's just off the main road that leads back to my own apartment building, which is all that matters. His phone rings, and he takes it out of his pocket and looks at the screen.

"Mum," he tells me.

"Are you not going to answer it?"

"No point. I know what it'll be about."

"And what's that?"

"She'll be saying that she's going out for the night and has left me five quid on the table for a McDonald's."

His answer couldn't be more perfect. No one's waiting for him at home.

"Is that a regular occurrence?" I ask, recalling how Hannah brought me up with a similarly cavalier attitude toward nutrition.

"Sometimes," he says quietly, perhaps not wanting to sound disloyal to his mother.

"Can you even get a meal for five pounds?" I ask.

"Oh yes," he replies, more confident now. He obviously knows his fast-food menus. "Burger. Chips. Shake. Chicken nuggets."

"Something for you to look forward to, then," I say. "Where do you live, anyway?"

He tells me. It's about a ten-minute drive east.

"Oh wait," he says suddenly, pointing to my right as we pass Ramleigh Crescent. "You've just gone past it."

"That's fine," I say. "I don't need to go there right now. I'm looking at a house for sale tomorrow and wanted to be sure I knew where it was in case I got delayed on my way. I'll drop you home now if you like."

"Thanks."

"But, if you don't mind, can we just stop at mine first? It's on the way."

He says nothing but starts fiddling with his fingers. "I'm not holding you up, am I?" I ask.

"Well . . ."

"You probably have plans for the evening. Meeting your girlfriend or whatever."

I glance toward him and watch as a blush spreads slowly from his neck toward his ears.

"No," he says, awkwardly.

"You don't have a girlfriend?" I ask, doing my best to sound surprised.

"No."

"A handsome boy like you? I thought you'd be fighting them off."

He gives me a shy look that mixes pride with discomfort. His right leg has started to bounce up and down, and he rests his hand on it as if he's trying to keep it steady. His legs are slim with golden hairs sprinkled around the calves.

"Sorry, Rufus," I say. "Have I embarrassed you?"

"No," he replies. "It's just—"

"Just what?"

"My best friend, he has a girlfriend," he says quickly, raising his voice a little, and I'm not sure why he's telling me this. Perhaps it's to make it sound as if he's connected to the world of sex in some way, if only at a one-step remove.

"Is she getting between you?"

"No," he says, shaking his head. "No, she's nice."

"Do you mean that you like her too?"

"Well . . . not in that way, no."

"All right," I say. I would have preferred him to be a bit more negative about her, to tell me what a bitch she is, how she's destroying their friendship, but admire the fact that he's as loyal to his friend as he was to his mother. Again, a good boy. The best kind. The safest kind.

"I should probably get home," he says.

"Hungry?"

"Yeah. And, you know, homework."

"Of course," I say. "I'll just make that quick stop at mine and then we'll be on our way."

"Actually," he says, as the lights before us turn red. "I can just get out here and jump on the bus."

"Absolutely not," I insist, prepared to press the child lock if necessary, although I'd rather not do something that might frighten him. "A deal's a deal. I promised you a lift, and a lift is what you'll get."

When we arrive at my building, I swing into the underground car park and the barriers lift when the camera reads my license plate. I can see that this impresses him. Pulling into my spot, I turn the engine off.

"I'll wait here, will I?" he asks.

"No, come upstairs. It can be dangerous sitting in car parks on your own. You never know who might come along and, I don't know, try to molest you or something." I laugh and he looks down at his feet. I notice his eyes open wide as if he's holding some complicated internal conversation with himself. "It'll only take a few minutes. I'll show you where I live. A famous footballer used to live in my apartment, you know."

He has no choice, because I offer him none, and also because I'm an adult and he's still, technically, a child. I get out of the car and stand there, waiting for him to exit too, and eventually he does. Happily, there's no one else nearby. I have a dread of Hugh Winley appearing suddenly out of the darkness, like Deep Throat in *All the President's Men*, still demanding that I go on a date with him.

We make our way toward the lift, and I inhale the universal scent of teenage boy: perspiration, anxiety, and Lynx. Closing my eyes as we ascend toward the twelfth floor, I breathe carefully, as I always do when I'm trapped in enclosed spaces. I can tell from Rufus's expression that he has no idea what he's doing here and is growing increasingly uncertain. When I look up toward the rising numbers, I feel his gaze traveling to the opened button on my blouse, where a hint of red bra peeps out from beneath the white. I reach down, as if to scratch an itch, and allow another button to pop open, pretending I don't know that it has, and he exhales a little louder before covering it up with a cough.

I lead him toward my apartment and unlock the door, standing back to allow him to enter first. The table lamp I left on earlier offers the perfect glow against the evening light that seeps in through the windows and he steps inside, looking around.

"This is really nice," he tells me, his eyes widening. He wanders over to the other side of the room, where glass doors open onto a balcony that faces an identical building opposite.

"Thanks," I say. "Do you like music?"

"Umm, I guess."

I tell Siri to play a song that relaxes me, a ballad, and he listens for a moment.

"I'm learning piano," he tells me.

"Oh yes? And how's that going?"

"It's OK," he replies, blushing again, as if he already regrets revealing any detail about his life. I can tell that he wants to talk to me, but he's a nervous, anxious fourteen-year-old boy, and every time he says something, he immediately regrets it. I leave him alone for a moment, going to the bedroom to retrieve the purse I deliberately left on my dressing table earlier.

"Sorry," I say, holding it in the air when I return. "I forgot this, and I'm nearly out of petrol. Might have to stop at a garage on the way."

Another lie, of course. I filled the tank yesterday.

"It's fine," he says. "But I should probably get home now."

"Why? No one's expecting you, are they?"

He looks at me and blinks a few times.

"You said your mother's going out."

"I know, but—"

"No, you're right. I've already taken up enough of your time. Although I am a bit thirsty. I might just grab a quick drink. Would you like one?"

He looks around the room. "Umm."

"I'm pretty sure I have a Coke in the fridge," I tell him. "Would you like a Coke?"

"Umm."

I don't go to the fridge just yet. Instead, I walk toward him. His skin is remarkably clear. I can tell that he's the sort of boy who isn't going to suffer acne and wonder what he'll look like when he's older. Right now, he's neither a boy nor a proper teenager. His face has a blankness to it that could develop into anything. He could be one of those innocent, asexual boys larking around naked in a Henry Scott Tuke painting or a tattooed thug living on a council estate and dealing drugs to children. But while he's blameless now, almost angelic, it's only a matter of time before he matures and not only recognizes his power to destroy girls in pursuit of what he wants but acts upon it. Right now, as I stand before him, some innocent twelve-year-old girl is lying on her bed not far from here, plaiting the hair of her dolls, looking up at the fairy lights that brighten her room or the luminous stars on her ceiling, completely oblivious to the fact that, one day, she'll be one of his victims.

"Let me get you that Coke," I say.

I make my way into the kitchen and take the can from the fridge, shaking it vigorously before returning to the living room and handing it to him. He looks at it as if there's nothing he wants less, but it's in his hands now so he has no choice but to open it. When he does, it explodes, of course, and his football shirt is soaked within seconds. He cries out in dismay before dropping it on a side table, where it fizzes over the top, then looks at me in mortification.

"I'm so sorry," he says, as if it's his fault that this has happened and not mine.

"Don't worry," I say, stepping toward him. "Accidents happen. But look at you, you're drenched!" He peels the polyester fabric away from his skin. "You can't wear it home like that. Take it off and I'll put it on a quick wash and dry for you. It won't take long."

His expression changes to one of pure terror. The last thing he wants to do is remove his shirt.

"It's OK," he says.

"Take it off," I insist, reaching down and lifting it from its base, like a mother undressing a toddler, before dragging it higher. He lifts his arms and I pull it up, bringing it into the kitchen, where I simply toss it on the floor. I have no intention of doing his laundry; I'm not his servant. When I return, he's wrapped his arms around his pale, white chest and is looking down at the floor.

I come closer.

"Look at you. All sticky." I press my index finger to his sternum before drawing it slowly down toward his navel. "You know what you need?"

"What?" he whispers, his voice cracking in a single syllable.

"A shower."

"I'm fine," he tells me, shaking his head quickly.

"You're not fine," I reply. "What kind of person would I be if I sent you home like this? Some kind of monster. Just like the Wicked Witch of the West." I step even closer to him now, and our eyes meet. I can feel his tension, his fear, his desire, his confusion. It's a combination that intoxicates me. I try to recall the name of the child I treated a few weeks ago, named after the Norse god of vengeance, but it escapes me for the moment.

I lower my voice, almost whispering.

"You're very shy, aren't you, Rufus?" I say. "Boys your age are usually so overconfident. It's refreshing to meet one who isn't."

Gently, I place the flat of my right hand against his chest.

Vidar, that was it. *Vidar.*

"Don't be nervous," I say, taking his hand now as I lead him toward the bathroom. "You can trust me."

6

It's not often that I find myself completely surprised, but when Aaron knocks on my office door and asks whether we might go for a drink together some evening, I'm so astonished that it takes me a moment to respond.

"A drink?" I ask, turning away from my computer screen to give him my full attention. I don't for a moment think he's asking me on a date— that would be utterly bizarre—but I'm puzzled why he'd think I'd want to socialize with him, considering how abruptly I've treated him since his rotation began.

"Yes," he says. "If you're busy, I totally understand. It's just that we only ever speak here, and I'd be grateful for an opportunity to talk in a less formal atmosphere. About my career."

I'd like to say no, to tell him that the moment I walk out the front doors in the evening, that's it, my duties have come to an end, but I need to be seen to be helpful to junior doctors; after all, they submit evaluations on us, just as we do on them. And so, fine, I tell him, somewhat grudgingly, suggesting Saturday, which will at least break up an otherwise empty weekend for me and disrupt a busy one for him.

On Friday, he emails the name of a bar in town, and when I arrive, deliberately late, I'm rather impressed to see the effort he's made. He's wearing a pair of gray jeans, paired with a crisp white shirt, and a sturdy pair of boots that matches his belt, and a brown leather jacket rests on the banquette beside him. He smells good too; colognes and perfumes are banned in the hospital, but whatever he's sprayed himself with this evening offers a pleasant scent of wood and vanilla. *Has he got dressed up just for me?* I wonder.

"Dr. Petrus," he says, leaning forward, as if to kiss my cheek, but quickly realizing that this would be an unwise move. "Thank you for coming."

"You can call me Freya," I tell him. "We're not in work now."

"Freya," he repeats, bowing his head briefly, like I'm a member of the royal family and he's greeting me on one of my engagements. "What can I get you to drink?"

I ask for a vodka and cranberry and, while he's gone, I glance around the bar. It's almost full, with most tables populated by couples or four-somes, friends on a night out. It feels strange to be in their company. Any one of them might look toward Aaron and me and assume that we're in a relationship too, and while I have no ambitions in that regard, and would shut down any advances on his part, it's not unpleasant to feel like a normal member of society for a change. This is how my life might have been, I think, had it not been for the Teagues.

When he returns with my drink and a fresh beer for him, we move seamlessly into small talk. A famous rock star has died earlier in the day, and we discuss her life and career. A scandal involving a prominent banker is growing, and he confides in me that the disgraced woman is his mother's first cousin. There's some mention of a trip to Amsterdam that he's looking forward to. And then, rather unexpectedly, he tells me this:

"You know, I applied to the hospital specifically because I wanted to work with you."

"Really?" I say, raising an eyebrow. In our profession, there are plenty of famous doctors, but I'm not one of them. Burns, the whole field of plastics in general, doesn't usually attract much attention, unlike the more glamorous arenas of brain and heart, which tend to draw physicians blessed in the former but lacking in the latter. "Why?"

"Because you're the person who made me want to be a doctor."

I reach for my glass and wonder whether he's just flattering me with an eye to advancement. For a moment, my eyes focus on his hands. He has the fingers of a surgeon, I think. Bony. Steady. Repulsive.

"I don't understand," I say.

"The Rozelli Programme," he says, and I groan, as there are few phrases that I dread as much as this. The initiative is one that the hospital introduced more than a decade earlier and involves medical professionals visiting local schools and universities with the hope of encouraging students to pursue careers in the NHS. I've been forced to take part on numerous occasions and, while I do what I can to get the pupils enthused, it's not something I enjoy. "You gave a talk to our year when we were doing our GCSEs," he continues. "You told us about patients you'd helped and showed slides of people who'd been trapped in fires. How you'd helped them get back to some meaningful form of life. Most of my friends found it a bit upsetting, but not me. I found it inspiring. I found *you* inspiring."

"Well, that's good to hear," I tell him, pleased that whatever I said encouraged him in some way. "To be honest, I've never felt very confident when it comes to public speaking. But it's become something of a requirement for surgeons and senior consultants. The Rozelli Foundation pumps a lot of money into the hospital, but they do make us dance for it."

"You spoke so passionately about what you do," he continues. "I don't want to sound melodramatic, but that day changed my life."

I can't help but smile. I'm not usually susceptible to flattery, but he seems sincere. Whatever my allergy is to him, I let it go for now.

"Thank you, Aaron," I say. "That's kind of you to say." I pause and offer a small concession. "I know I'm not always the easiest person to work with, but—"

"Your focus is on your patients," he says, cutting me off. "I know that. And I'm just some know-nothing intern getting in your way. I'd be a cunt too if I was you."

I blink, uncertain I've heard him right over the noise of the bar.

"I'm sorry?" I ask. "What did you just say?"

"I said I'd be curt too if I was you."

I remain silent for a moment, examining his face for any sign of disrespect, but he seems sincere enough.

"You're a good doctor," I tell him eventually, even though I don't have any strong feelings on the subject one way or the other. "You have a good career in front of you."

We move on to other subjects. We talk about Louise and how she'll be missed when she retires in a few weeks' time. He tells me about a thriller he's reading that he thinks I might enjoy, featuring a murderous pediatrician as its central character. I mention a film I've heard good things about, and he says that he hasn't been to the cinema in more than a year. The last time he went, he witnessed a road traffic accident on the way home and ended up testifying in court as a witness, an experience he found strangely exhilarating.

"Actually, I know that feeling," I tell him, ordering fresh drinks from a passing lounge girl. She glances at Aaron appreciatively, offering him a flirtatious smile, and to my surprise I feel like scratching her eyes out. "I served on a jury once. I would have preferred to get out of it, but in the end it turned out to be quite interesting."

"Really?" he asks. "What kind of a case was it?"

"Rape."

He pulls a face.

"That must have been difficult," he says.

"Why?"

"Well, as a woman . . ." He drifts off, perhaps sensing that, considering the times we live in, he's veering into dangerous territory.

"You're assuming it was a woman who was raped," I say.

"That's true. Am I wrong?"

"No, but you shouldn't assume."

"You're right."

"Are you a football fan?" I ask.

He nods.

"Then you might remember Evan Keogh and Robbie Wolverton."

"I do," he says. "One of them raped a girl and the other filmed it. They played for my team. My old team, I mean. I walked away after that."

"They both swore that the encounter had been consensual, and we believed them. We found them not guilty. It's not something I'm particularly proud of. We didn't feel that the prosecution had proved their case beyond a reasonable doubt, so we found for the defense."

"I read somewhere that forty thousand women report a rape to the police every year."

"Actually, it's closer to seventy thousand."

"And you didn't feel like . . . I don't know . . . making an example of them?"

"No. The truth and the facts don't always tally. But, of course, it didn't end there. A couple of years later, Keogh confessed. Went to the police and admitted everything. He even handed over the video evidence. In a way, you have to admire him for finally coming clean."

"Maybe his conscience got to him," suggests Aaron.

"Maybe," I agree. "It would be so much easier to go through life if you didn't have one, don't you think?"

"No," he says, his immediate and emphatic reply surprising me, even though this was just a throwaway comment on my part. "I think it would be horrific."

"Anyway, they were rearrested, retried, and they had no choice but to plead guilty. Wolverton's still in jail. He'll be there for another five years."

"And Keogh killed himself," says Aaron.

"Well, he was found dead in his cell. It was all a bit Jeffrey Epstein, if you ask me. It's hard to know what to believe."

We talk about this a little more, then change the subject again. I want to know more about him. I ask whether he has a girlfriend and he tells me that he does.

"What's her name?"

"Rebecca," he replies.

"Is she studying medicine too?"

"No," he says, shaking his head. "She's training to be a pilot."

I know I shouldn't be surprised by this, but I am. It's still a relatively unusual career path for a woman.

"And how long have you been together?"

"Almost two years now."

For some inexplicable reason, I feel jealous.

"How about you?" he asks. "Do you have a partner?"

His use of the word *partner* makes me think that he's hedging his bets so as not to offend me.

"I do," I lie.

"And their name?"

Their. He's still covering himself.

"Eli," I say.

"And what does he do?"

"He's a SPAD."

"A what?"

"A SPAD," I say. "You don't know what a SPAD is?"

He shakes his head, orders more drinks. I ask for a large this time.

"No," he says. "It sounds like something to do with gardening."

"That's a spade, you moron," I reply, teasing him and touching him on the upper arm. "A SPAD is a special adviser. He reports to the chancellor of the exchequer, in fact."

"That's pretty cool," says Aaron, impressed.

"Cooler than being a surgeon?"

"No, nothing is that cool. Not even being a pilot."

"Good boy," I say, patting him on the hand now, and, instead of laughing along with me, he appears annoyed by the phrase, which I only meant as a joke, and pulls his hand away.

"So have you met the prime minister?" he asks.

I tell him that I have. That we're quite friendly, in fact. That I gave him a book for Christmas and he gave me a scented candle. I enjoy building this fantasy life, just as I enjoyed creating Jesse, the imaginary boyfriend of my twenties. The more alcohol that enters my bloodstream, the better I get at lying, or at least I think I do. Perhaps I should have been a novelist. I could have spent every day inventing lives much more interesting than my own.

"I'm sorry if I've been hard on you, Aaron," I say at last, because the evening has gone much better than I expected and, to my surprise, I find that I've rather enjoyed it. "But you must recognize the importance of our work. A hospital isn't a social club, you know? We're not there to make friends. Our sole responsibility is toward our patients. So, if I've been short with you from time to time, please don't take it personally. It just means that I have to put all my attention where it's most needed. It will toughen you up."

"I'm tougher than you think," he tells me. "But can I ask, why did you choose burns?"

"I'm sorry?"

"Of all the disciplines. Why burns?"

No one has ever asked me this before. I have no parents. I have no siblings. I have no friends. I'm entirely alone in the world, so my choices have always been my own and unquestioned. I consider the question carefully, wanting to give him an honest answer.

"Because people turn away," I say at last.

He frowns. It's obvious he doesn't understand what I mean.

"If you have cancer," I explain, "everyone is on your side. They'll wear ribbons and run marathons to raise money for your treatment. You're sanctified for developing a disease over which you have no control. If you have Alzheimer's, your family has to figure out how to look after you while secretly hoping you'll have made plans for a one-way trip to Switzerland. As humans, from the moment we reach puberty, we search for beauty. We do it in our daily lives, whether we're looking at someone we want to fuck or someone we want to fuck us. But beauty is meaningless. It's nothing more than the manner in which the skin is formed over the skull. And the skull is nothing more than the way the bones have been formed in the womb. None of it means anything. Beautiful people have so many advantages. You're a good-looking guy. I know I'm an attractive woman. But have you ever wondered what it would be like to be blessed with such extraordinary beauty that, when you walk into a bar, every head turns in your direction?"

"I'm sure that happens with you," he says. "I'm not trying to be creepy, but—"

"No, I get it. And yes, it does. Sometimes. But that will come to an end soon. The elements destroy everything. Think of water. When someone drowns, and their body floats back to shore, their features are so bloated it can be difficult to identify them. Think of earth. When a body is buried, it starts to decompose immediately. Think of air. If we're deprived of it for even a few minutes, we die. Then think of fire. When someone's physical appearance is damaged by burns, we turn away, repulsed. We don't want to know."

An old Hot Chocolate song sounds over the speakers, one I haven't heard in many, many years. "It Started with A Kiss." I glance at Aaron.

For some inexplicable reason, he's laughing a little. Do I want to kiss him? I *should* want to kiss him. So why don't I? He's not exactly age appropriate, but he's not entirely age inappropriate either. No one would bat an eyelid.

My mind drifts back to Cornwall, to Arthur and Pascoe, and to the night they buried me alive. I could tell him this story. I could tell him the real reason that I chose burns as my speciality. I could tell him every-thing about my life, about who I am, about what I do, and see how he reacts. But I'm not stupid. Nor am I drunk enough to reveal the worst of myself to this relative stranger. I've sat through a trial once and have no desire to do so again.

"Twelve thousand," says Aaron after a lengthy silence, apparently apropos of nothing.

"I'm sorry?" I say.

"Twelve thousand," he repeats. "That's how many men report being sexually assaulted in the UK every year. We forgot to mention them when we were talking about rape figures earlier."

He's right too. In some ways, it doesn't surprise me that he knows the exact statistics for men but underestimates the number for women by almost 50 percent. But it disappoints me.

And just when I was beginning to think well of him too.

7

Whether or not Arthur and Pascoe's father had, in fact, murdered their mother would forever remain a mystery to me, for I never asked them about it again.

When I spoke to Beth about her landlord, she simply shrugged her shoulders, saying that she didn't know him well and that he only came by occasionally to make sure she was keeping the place in good repair. Eli was equally unhelpful, telling me that all he'd ever discussed with Kitto Teague were his plans for the renovation and as soon as the place was finished he'd be glad to move on, as Teague was a tight-fisted London sod who condescended to the locals and never got his round in.

While the house's overhaul intrigued me, I was more interested in the great pit being dug toward the rear of the mansion, looking down onto the beach, into which, eventually, a swimming pool would be installed. It was intended to be the final construction job; until then, it was being used to dispose of all the building site's detritus, and every Tuesday morning an enormous lorry came by to empty it.

"Why do you need a pool when you live so close to the sea?" I asked the twins, leaning over the side one afternoon and looking down. There was no rain that summer, and the base was a rich shade of blackish brown, a mixture of cracked earth and displaced sand that blew in overnight from the coastline.

"Because we're rich," said Arthur. "And rich people have pools."

Having never known any rich people, I accepted this as perfectly reasonable. Beth lived from hand to mouth, working in a pub most evenings and cleaning holiday homes during the season, while, back in

Norfolk, Hannah held down three jobs, a café in the mornings, a bar at night, and a fast-food restaurant on Saturday evenings, although she still never seemed to have any money.

I tried to picture what it might look like when it was filled with water, imagining the sides tiled in bright green with a mural of cartoon fish spread across the base. I wondered whether the Teagues might allow me to swim in it the following summer when I returned or whether they would keep it just for themselves.

My relationship with Arthur and Pascoe developed slowly over those first weeks, and although we spent most of our time together, I found their company as irritating as it was addictive. They liked to lord over me the fact that they were fourteen while I was only twelve, inferring that they knew so much more about the world than me, although I suspected, being poor, that I understood it a lot better than they did. Sometimes they became shy, particularly at the beach, when I slipped beneath a towel to change into my swimsuit. Then I would catch them watching me, their faces growing red when I ordered them to turn away, and they would be less confident until we were all dressed again, at which point they would reassert their dominance.

At other times, they could be aggressive, although never with each other, pushing me roughly or dragging me to the ground in a game of wrestling, covering my body with theirs, their hands mauling every part of my skin that was available to them. I would give back as good as they gave until, finally, they would jump away from me in a sudden rush, looking awkward and confused as they tugged at the crotch of their shorts.

I had only known one other set of twins before, two girls in my class in school. They were as different as diamonds and dust and didn't seem to like each other very much, let alone want to spend any time together, sitting far apart in the classroom and socializing with different groups of friends. In the two months I spent with Arthur and Pascoe, however, I don't think I ever saw either of them alone.

Once, they brought me upstairs in their house while their father was out to show me their makeshift bedroom, which contained a double bed that they slept in together. The walls were entirely bare, not a book, toy, or photograph in sight.

"What do you think of that?" asked Arthur, giving me a sordid look that I was too young to understand. I didn't think anything of it, I told him. What was I supposed to think? It was just a bedroom. Everyone had one.

"It's only for now," explained Pascoe. "When the house is finished, we'll have beds of our own."

"Although we'll still share a room," insisted Arthur.

"Definitely," replied his brother.

Sometimes, when we were rambling around the dunes, they would grow tired of my company, almost forgetting that I was there, and I might slip behind, happy to be on my own for a while. When I'd eventually catch up with them, I would discover them walking hand in hand, something I had never seen two boys do before, or sitting by the rocks, staring out to sea, one boy's head resting on the other's shoulder. If one ran off to pee, the other went with him and, at first, I thought it was because he didn't want to be left alone with me, but in time I started to realize that they simply couldn't bear to be apart. Their need to touch each other regularly, even if it was just a slap on the back or an arm around the other, struck me as strange but affectionate.

Then, one day, they told me about the caves that had been eroded into the rocks of Cornwall over centuries.

"Smugglers used them hundreds of years ago," explained Pascoe. "They came from France, bringing gold, diamonds, and whiskey with them. They had a whole crew of accomplices around the coastline so they could distribute everything and make their fortunes. But they hid lots of stuff in the caves too in case they got caught, and sometimes they forgot about it or died or drowned and it was left behind. Half these caves have hidden treasure in them if you look hard enough. It might be buried deep under the sand, or in the nooks and crannies, but it's there. When we were down here at Easter, I found a gold necklace."

I raised an eyebrow, unconvinced. It sounded like something they'd read in a book. They seemed offended by my disbelief.

"We'll show you," they said, and we walked down the hills together, descending carefully as the stone beneath our feet was sharp and unforgiving.

"You can only come here at low tide," said Arthur. "If you came in the evening, it wouldn't be long until the caves filled with water and you'd drown."

The idea of this made me uncertain whether I wanted to risk entering, just in case the tide came in early, but the sun was still high in the sky and the waves were placid so there seemed little risk. Still, something about the place reeked of danger, and my reluctance must have been obvious.

"Come on," said Pascoe, reaching out and trying to drag me forward. "Don't be a girl."

"But I am a girl," I told him.

"That's no reason to act like one," said Arthur. "Take our hands," he said, looking at his brother, who walked back and stood on the other side of me. "The whole point of coming here is to explore it together."

I was intrigued, certainly, and, unwilling to be bested by them, I finally agreed. Inside, it was brighter than I had expected, the daylight sparking into the passageway and bouncing off the glossy, sea-sprayed rocks. Tunnels led left and right with the occasional hollow allowing light to spill through from the surface. I thought of Ali Baba and the Forty Thieves and wondered whether, when I turned a corner, I might be confronted by chests filled with gold. I could fill my pockets, I told myself, and bring it all back to Hannah and Beth. Or, better still, I could run away with it and never have to see either of them again.

As we ventured further into the interior, I began to worry that we'd taken so many turns we might be unable to retrace our steps. I didn't want to appear frightened, however, so was relieved when Arthur said, "We can stop here, this is the best place."

Looking ahead, I saw a rough wall of black stone, and in front of it an area filled with sand and tiny stones, the accumulation of centuries of night waves eroding the rocks here before breaking them down into pebbles. I was glad to have reached the end and turned around, ready to return, when Arthur stepped in front of me, blocking my way, as Pascoe took up position behind.

"Not yet," said Arthur, looking me up and down, and the pupils of his eyes seemed to grow larger as he reached out to stroke my bare arm. "There's a game we like to play, but we only play it here. Where no one can see us."

"What kind of game?" I asked.

"A fun game."

"Aren't all games fun? Isn't that the point?"

Arthur and Pascoe looked at each other. They obviously hadn't expected me to be quite so provocative.

"They're meant to be," agreed Arthur. "But this one is more fun than anything we've played before. And it'll be even better with a girl."

He reached out and took my hand, pressing it to the crotch of his shorts, and when I didn't immediately remove it, he smiled and glanced toward his brother, who was watching us intently.

Looking back, I don't think I told him to stop; not that first time, anyway. It was exciting and, recalling all those schoolyard conversations, I wanted to see what it was like. It wasn't what I expected. From what little I understood, I thought it was supposed to be enjoyable for both people, but it wasn't enjoyable for me. I felt like a piece of meat, lying on the ground, while Arthur did what he wanted to it. He didn't even look me in the eye. When he was finished, however, which was only two or three minutes later, Pascoe started to unbuckle the belt on his shorts, and this time I did say no.

"That's not fair!" he cried. "You can't do it with Arthur and not with me."

"I can," I said, pulling myself to my feet a little unsteadily. I wanted to run into the water and wash myself. I felt grubby and dirty, embarrassed by what had happened. My natural twelve-year-old curiosity had given way to immediate shame.

"No!" insisted Arthur. "He's my brother. If I get to do it, then he does too."

I glanced behind me. There were several tunnels leading from where we were, and I wasn't sure which one would take me back to the beach and which would lead me further into an inescapable labyrinth.

"I'm going home," I said, turning away, but Pascoe ran ahead, cutting me off.

"It's my turn!" he shouted. "You said we could both do it!"

"I didn't!" I cried, because I'd said no such thing. "I can't, anyway. It hurt."

"Freya," said Arthur patiently. "Do you know what a tease is?"

I shook my head.

"It's when a girl leads a boy on," he explained, "but then won't go all the way. It's the worst thing any girl can do."

"It's even worse than murdering someone," agreed Pascoe.

"But I don't want to," I repeated, starting to cry now, because, while I may have been complicit in what had taken place with Arthur, I knew that I didn't want to do it again. With anyone. For a long time.

Seeing that I wasn't going to change my mind, Arthur pushed me to the ground and pulled my arms back, pinning them down. The moment violence took over, my brain seemed to disassociate itself from my body. A part of me thought that one of them would take a rock and bash my brains in, killing me like Kitto Teague had supposedly killed their mother, if I didn't give in. And so I lay there, and he did what he wanted to do.

Every day over the next month, they would collect me after lunch and we would make our way to the caves together, rarely talking now, and the same thing would happen. Looking back, I don't understand why I allowed it to continue. I didn't enjoy it, but I was worried that they would abandon me. I was twelve and desperately lonely. Thanks to Hannah's insistence on my being her unpaid servant, I'd never been allowed to have a friend, let alone two of them. Perhaps this, I told myself, is what good girls did for their friends.

Eventually, however, I decided that I'd had enough. Beth didn't notice my change of mood, but Eli did and asked me about it. I wanted to confide in him but worried that if he knew the things I'd been doing, then he would want to do them with me too. And he was so much bigger and stronger than the twins that the idea was too frightening for me even to contemplate.

When I told the boys that I wouldn't go to the caves with them anymore, they said I had no choice, that the game only ended at the end of the holiday.

"No," I insisted. "It's not going to happen again."

"And what makes you so sure of that?" asked Pascoe.

"Because," I said, "if you make me do it again, I'll tell."

This unnerved them, and I felt I had regained some power. After this, I didn't see them for three days and, despite myself, felt even lonelier than ever, wondering whether I had made a mistake. When they finally called at the cottage again late one night, Beth was out as usual and I was already preparing for bed.

"We're sorry," said Arthur, holding a bunch of flowers in his hands, and there was something about his forlorn expression that made me think that he really was.

"Really sorry," added Pascoe.

"We still want to be friends."

I looked from one boy to the other and felt a surge of gratitude toward them. They were company. And I longed for company. It only took me a moment to say that I forgave them.

"There's something we want to show you," said Pascoe, and I shook my head and said that whatever it was, it would have to wait until the next day. I was too tired.

"No, this is too good to miss," said Arthur. "It's only up by the swimming-pool pit."

"What is it?" I asked, intrigued.

"You have to see it for yourself," he told me, and, not wanting to fall out with them again, I agreed, putting on some warmer clothes and allowing them to lead the way.

The pit looked much the same as it always did. The lorry had come a few days earlier, so it was once again half full of paint cans, ripped cardboard, and enormous empty boxes. Arthur and Pascoe were standing by what looked to be a wooden chest, and from the words on the side I could tell that it must have held some of the latest furniture to arrive.

"Come down," they insisted, and when Arthur held out a hand for me, I took it and joined them. They opened the lid of the chest, and we all looked inside. It was empty. Arthur climbed in, and he didn't have to squeeze up too much to fit; it was the perfect size for a boy his age. I stared down, wondering why he was bothering. When he clambered out again, Pascoe took a turn and lay down too, his arms crossed across his chest, as if he was lying in a coffin. He closed his eyes, waited a few moments, then slowly sat up, speaking like Dracula.

"I want to drink your blood."

I rolled my eyes. It seemed strange to me that they'd dragged me all the way here just to look at an empty box.

"Your turn," said Arthur, turning to me when his brother got out, and I shook my head.

"No, thanks," I said.

"You scared?"

I wasn't. I just couldn't see the point of climbing into a box only to climb out again.

"She's scared," said Arthur, turning to his brother, who nodded.

"It's because she's a girl," agreed Pascoe, and I sighed and said fine, I'd do it. I climbed inside and lay down on my back, just as Pascoe had done, and looked up at them. In the sky was a full moon, and it caught my eye as I stared at the gray shapes dotted across it, which I decided were continents, and on one of those continents were countries, and in one of those countries was a city, and in that city were houses, and my father lived in one of those houses and he wasn't a wrong 'un at all, but was kind and lonely and missed me.

"Happy?" I asked, but instead of answering, they pulled the lid of the box over, shutting it tight. Immediately, everything went black. Shocked, I didn't even have the strength of mind to push it back up, and a hammering began from outside. To my horror, I realized that they were nailing it closed. After a moment, I found my voice and started banging at the makeshift ceiling, calling their names, begging to be set free.

"You need to think about your behavior," said Arthur casually, and then I heard the sound of earth from the pit being thrown on top of my coffin. "Don't worry, you'll still be able to breathe. We've left a hole free above you and we'll send a tube down. But you'll be in there for a while, so you might as well get used to it."

I screamed and continued to push at the roof as more soil landed and, even though I knew the chest was already at the base of the pit, I imagined the scene from outside, the entire quarry being filled with soil and me disappearing forever beneath it. I banged and banged, growing more terrified than I had ever been in my life before. This was it, I told myself. This was how I was going to die.

Buried alive.

8

It's been a few weeks since my evening with Rufus, which turned out to be far more troubling than my usual encounters.

He was clearly alarmed when I led him into the bathroom, even more so when I turned the shower on, but when I took my blouse off, he emitted some strange, petrified sound that blended confusion, desire, and terror into one. I've experienced similar reactions before, of course. Among their friends, most of these boys act as if they could put Casanova to shame, but in reality they're all completely terrified of women.

When we made it to the bedroom, he lay beneath me with such a frightened expression on his face that anyone would think I was forcing myself upon him, and when he whispered, "Please don't hurt me," I was this close to telling him to gather his things and leave. His body reacted as it should, however, and somehow we got through it. When it was over, he slipped out from beneath me and slunk to the floor, staring down at the carpet.

I left him to it, returning to the bathroom to clean up, and when I emerged, he'd at least had the dignity to drag himself to his feet and was sitting on the side of the bed, wearing his football shorts and Coke-stained T-shirt again, but still barefoot. Only now did he turn to look at me, rearing back a little as if I posed some sort of threat.

"Why did you do that to me?" he whispered.

"Why did I do what?"

"What you just did."

I watched as he reached for his socks, slowly pulling them on, and decided to ignore his question.

"You should probably leave now," I told him, which was when I realized that he was drying tears from his cheeks. "Why are you crying?" I asked. "If anyone should be upset here, it's me."

He looked at me and frowned, then tried to put his runners on but struggled with this rather basic task, possibly because his hands were shaking so much.

"You're putting them on the wrong feet," I said, going over to help him, but he pulled away.

"Don't touch me!" he shouted, so loudly that I jumped back.

"Jesus, fine," I said, holding my hands in the air. "But the left runner goes on the left foot and the right runner goes on the right. It's not rocket science."

The tears came faster now, and he ran the insides of his elbows across his eyes to wipe them dry.

"You can stop blubbing," I said. "I'm not going to press charges, if that's what you're worried about."

"What?" he asked, looking bewildered. "What do you mean?"

"I mean we both know that you took advantage of me, but I won't go to the police. You'd only end up in a young offender institution, where God only knows what would happen to you, and I don't want that on my conscience."

"But I . . . I didn't . . . it was you who—"

"As far as I'm concerned, none of this ever happened. But you should count yourself lucky. Anyone else in my place would have had you arrested by now."

He stared at me, shook his head slowly, then started crying again.

"But I need you to go," I continued. "And don't ever come back here again. If you do, I'll report you. You'll end up as a convicted sex offender. Your parents will disown you. Your entire life will be ruined. Is that what you want?"

"No," he whispered.

"Good. Well, you've been warned."

He pulled himself to his feet and made his way back into the living room, walking so unsteadily toward the front door that, if I hadn't known better, I would have assumed he was inebriated. When he reached it, he struggled with the lock and I had to open it for him. When my hand brushed his arm, he pushed me away. Then—Christ alive—the tears again.

"What the fuck is the matter with you?" I asked. "I'm trying to help you here."

"I didn't want it," he said.

"Didn't want what?"

"That. What we did."

"Then why did you do it?"

"You made me."

"Did I drag you into my car?" I asked, raising my voice now. "Because I seem to remember you opening the door of your own accord. Did I force you up to my apartment? You came willingly enough. Did I pour Coke over your T-shirt so you'd have to take it off? I don't think so. I'm pretty sure that was you. Very subtle, by the way."

"It exploded over—"

"Take responsibility for what you did, Rufus. You haven't even apologized."

"I'm . . ." He looked around, his face falling, completely disoriented.

"Look, I'm a grown woman," I said, trying to sound magnanimous. "Believe me, I'm used to the violence of men. I don't know what's going on in your life, but maybe from now on you'll realize that you can't treat girls like this. Not everyone will be as willing to forgive as me."

He nodded.

"I'm sorry," he said.

"As you should be."

He paused for a few moments, then looked at me, genuinely curious.

"You really didn't want that?" he asked tentatively.

"Rufus," I said, in as measured a tone as I could muster, "you raped me. You understand that, right? You are a rapist. That's something you're going to have to live with for the rest of your life."

He seemed uncertain what to do next, so I decided the only way to get rid of him was to drive him home. We traveled down to the garage in silence, and when he placed his bag in the back seat, he sat there too, rather than joining me in the front. For the first time, I noticed that his school backpack had two badges sewn into it. One for the city's football team—the same team whose erstwhile players I had once sat in judgment upon—and one bearing a picture of the Muppets. I felt embarrassed for him. It was the sort of thing a child would have. We didn't speak as we drove, other than him giving me quiet directions, and when I finally pulled up outside his small, terraced house, he leaped out of the car like a jack-in-the-box, disappearing inside without so much as a goodbye.

I haven't given him a second thought since then, but now, when there's a knock on my door, for some reason his face pops into my mind, even though I know it can't be him. It must be Hugh Winley, I tell myself, coming up to try it on with me again. He'll be standing outside with a bottle of wine, saying he's just opened it but doesn't want to drink alone. I'll have to be firm with him. Tell him once and for all that I'm not interested. He has a certain malevolence to him, though, that is perhaps not uncommon in children's television presenters, and I assume he'll react badly to a definitive rejection.

However, when I open the door, it's not my neighbor standing there, and as it turns out, I rather wish it was.

It is, however, a fourteen-year-old boy. When I recognize his face, my heart sinks.

Those phone calls where no one spoke when I answered. And then the one where he did, on the very same evening that I picked Rufus up from his football game.

Is that Freya?

"Hi," he says, the very definition of a shit-eating grin on his face. "Remember me?"

"Graham," I say, knowing full well that I'm getting his name wrong but not wanting him to think that I remember it. My heart is beating a little faster in my chest. I've never slept with a boy twice. I've never needed to. It's not as if I actually enjoy the experience, after all. I just want to destroy their chances of ever forming happy, healthy relationships in the future.

"George," he says, correcting me. "George Eliot. Like the writer, remember?" He walks brazenly past me, marching into the living room, followed by an overwhelming stink of cheap cologne. I stare at his back and offer a slight laugh before closing the door. If I could, I would pause the universe for a moment and think this through. Whatever made him repeatedly call me, and whatever has brought him here tonight, I need to play it very carefully.

"Did you miss me?" he asks, turning around.

"What are you doing here?" I ask, folding my arms across my chest. Although I'm wearing loungewear, my feet are bare, and I feel exposed. I can't just throw him out, because that would risk antagonizing him and children his age are extremely unpredictable. I need to figure out what he wants. And then deny him it.

"I wanted to see you again," he said. "That's OK, isn't it?"

"How did you find me?" I ask.

"Ah," he says, throwing himself down on the sofa and pulling his phone from his pocket. "That is a really good question, and I think you'll be impressed. I actually spent the last few weeks trying to remember where you lived, and I just couldn't do it. I mean, I literally walked the streets day after day trying to find this building. You brought me quite a distance from my home, didn't you? But then it finally occurred to me." He holds his phone up and waves it at me. "These things track your movements. All I had to do was go back to the night we fucked, and it would tell me where I was. It pinned it down to the exact location. I don't know why I didn't think of it before."

I flinch when he says the word *fucked*, but I'm even more disturbed to learn that smartphones track our movements. Does that mean that every boy I've ever brought here has a record of where he's been? If this is true, then it's very concerning.

"You phoned me, didn't you?" I ask. "Called my number over and over, then hung up when I answered."

"To be fair, I spoke once. But, after that, I couldn't get through again."

"I thought you were a cold caller," I lie. "So I blocked you."

"Who talks on the phone anyway?" he asks. "Old people. No offense."

"How did you get my number?"

"After we fucked," he says, and I recoil again at his casual use of the word, "you went into the bathroom but left your phone on the bedside table. By the way, just so you know, 1111 is literally the dumbest passcode ever. It's the first thing everyone tries. So I just called my own phone, then deleted the call from your log and stored you in my contacts."

I sit down in the armchair opposite him. "I see," I reply, wondering what would happen if I took him out to the balcony and just pushed him over. We're twelve floors up, after all. Every bone in his body would break, and his skull would smash into a dozen pieces. But there's always someone from the opposite building outside having a smoke, and I wouldn't get away with it. "Well, it's nice to see you again, Graham."

"George."

"Sorry, George. Yes. But why are you here?"

"Isn't it obvious?"

"Not to me."

He shrugs his shoulders.

"I'm horny."

I notice that my left hand is tapping nervously on the armrest, and I force myself to remain still. I don't want him to feel that he has any hold over me.

"That's a really inappropriate thing to say," I say, giving him my best Miss Jean Brodie.

"I mean, it would be, yeah," he says, scratching his chin, "if we hadn't already done it. But since we have, it doesn't seem so bad."

"That was a mistake," I say. "And I decided not to take it any further."

"Take what any further?" he asks, frowning.

"What you did to me," I say.

"I don't get it."

"Well, you took advantage of me," I tell him.

He laughs, which makes me want to take a baseball bat to his head.

"*I* took advantage of *you*?" he asks. "Look, I'm not gonna lie. I loved every moment of it. But it's you who did that to me, not the other way round. You're the adult. I'm the child. You picked me up outside the hospital, told me where to meet you later, collected me, brought me here. I was just visiting a mate. I wasn't, like, on the pull. Anyway, fuck that, you need to be honest with yourself, Freya. I can call you Freya, right?

It was amazing, wasn't it? I literally haven't stopped thinking about it ever since. I bet you haven't either. It's why I've been trying to find you."

"Well," I say, realizing that I need to change tack as it's obvious that he won't be easily threatened. "I'm glad you enjoyed yourself, but it was a one-off."

"No, it wasn't," he says, brushing this away and looking around the room as if he's considering moving in.

"It was."

"Nope."

I stare at him, wondering what my next move should be. I've never been put in this position before and am uncertain how to handle it.

"You need to leave," I say.

"No problem."

"Thank you."

"After we do it."

I feel a sense of panic overwhelming me. The earth is falling on my coffin, I'm searching for my breathing tube and pushing against the roof, begging Arthur and Pascoe to release me. But they're not there. They've gone home. I'm buried alive.

"That's not going to happen," I say forcefully.

"It sure is."

"It's not."

"Why not?"

"Because you're just a kid."

He throws his head back and laughs, as if this is the greatest joke in the world. "Seriously?" he asks. "I mean, come on."

"You need to leave," I repeat. "What happened then, that night, it was a mistake."

"If it was, then it's one that I want to repeat. Over and over and over and—"

"Have you told anyone about this?" I ask.

"Just my mate," he says. "My best mate. Harry. You remember Harry."

I stare at him, wondering whether he's gone completely mad.

"How would I know your friend Harry?" I ask.

"He's the one in your hospital," he tells me. "Who needs the kidney transplant."

"Oh yes," I say, vaguely remembering our conversation on the day we met.

"You can relax, he didn't believe me. And I didn't tell him who it was either. I just said an older woman had popped my cherry."

"Has no one ever told you that you're not supposed to kiss and tell?" I ask.

"I didn't kiss and tell," he says, sitting forward and opening his arms wide. "I fucked and told. Big difference. Anyway, like I said, he didn't believe me. Thinks I made it all up. Not that it matters. I know it happened, and you know it happened, and that's enough. But maybe tonight, when we're doing it, we can take a photo? So I can show him? I'll keep your face out of it, I promise. Just, like, the rest of you. Your tits and stuff. And my face in it so he knows I'm not lying."

"George," I say, trying to remain calm. "I'm not going to say this again. You need to leave."

"Or what?"

"Or I'll call the police."

He sits back now and smiles. Uses his left hand to mimic a phone being held to his ear.

"Good evening, Constable," he says. "I'm a thirty-something woman who picked up an underage boy a few weeks ago and took him back to my apartment and had sex with him. I know that's against the law, but let's just forget that for now because he's in my apartment and refuses to leave. Can you send someone over to throw him out?"

Maybe there'll be no one outside smoking. Maybe my timing will be perfect and I can simply toss him over the side.

"I'm not going to have sex with you," I insist.

"Sure you are," he replies.

"And what," I ask, "makes you so sure of that?"

To my annoyance, he makes himself at home by using the toe of his right foot to kick off his left trainer, then his left to kick off the right, revealing once-white socks that look like they've been through the washer about a thousand times.

"Because," he tells me, "if you don't, I'll tell."

9

It's late afternoon and I'm preparing for a surgery taking place in two days' time. A man named Richard Conway, separated from his wife of four years, waited outside their former marital home until she returned from work, then approached her as she put her key in the door. When she turned, he sprayed her with lighter fluid before tossing a lit match in her direction, resulting in third-degree burns to her right arm, neck, breasts, and the lower half of her face. I plan on doing a skin graft that should hopefully repair some of the damage he caused, although she will never, of course, look as she once did.

I've dealt with crimes like this more often than I can count. I've seen women whose faces have been destroyed by the men who stood next to them at an altar promising to spend their lives together. Women who know they'll never willingly look in a mirror again. Women who've gone through dozens of operations just to stop people staring at them on the street, on a bus, or in a supermarket. Wasn't it Margaret Atwood who said that men are afraid that women will laugh at them, but women are afraid that men will kill them? In Conway's case, he didn't want his wife dead; he just wanted to make sure that no other man would ever want her again.

I've invited Aaron to assist at the operation. And when I say assist, I mean observe. He's still too green to hold a scalpel, but it will be good for him to witness what takes place in theater. Louise appears pleased, if a little surprised, when I mention this to her.

"You're warming to him, then?" she asks.

"Well, I wouldn't go that far," I say. "But I'm making an effort, like you suggested. Actually, I invited him for a drink."

"You didn't!"

"I did. I thought it might help if I got to know him a little better."

"And?"

"Well, it wasn't the best evening of my life, but it wasn't the worst either. He's polite, interested, curious. His girlfriend's training to be a pilot, did you know that?"

"How would I?"

"I thought the pair of you talked."

"We do," she says. "But he plays his cards close to his chest, that one. Still, I'm not surprised he's got a girlfriend. He's a bit of a looker, don't you think?"

"Not my type."

"Too young?"

I glance at my watch and think about the final episode of a drama series that I've been saving to watch tonight. I think about my Ocado order. I think about an award-winning novel I've been reading but that I can't get to grips with. I think about anything but her question.

"With retirement looming," she continues when I fail to answer, "I wonder should I start looking for a younger man."

"You don't think Liam would mind?" I ask, referring to her husband, with whom she has a very loving relationship.

"Sure he would, but he doesn't have to know, does he? From what I read, all the twenty-something boys are mooning over older women these days. It's that pop star, what's-his-name. The lad from the boy band. Always going after them."

There's an awkward moment as she realizes that I'm not engaging with her banter in the way that I usually would.

"So, was there a spark?" she asks eventually.

"I'm sorry?"

"A spark," she repeats. "Between you and Aaron. On your date."

"It wasn't a date," I say, rolling my eyes.

"You asked him out."

"No, he asked me."

"Did you not just say, 'Actually, I invited him for a drink'?"

I'm thrown for a moment. She's right. I did say that.

"I meant that I agreed to go for one, that's all. He wanted to discuss his career in a less, you know, formal environment than the hospital."

"And when did all this take place?"

"A couple of weekends ago."

I'm fond of Louise, but the expression on her face, that self-satisfied smile, is annoying, and I regret bringing the subject up at all.

"Trust me," I tell her, "I have absolutely no ambitions in that direction."

"If you say so."

"He's practically a child," I insist. "What do you take me for?"

Perhaps my tone is more aggressive than I intended because she looks a little put out.

"All right," she says. "I was only teasing."

"Well, don't," I say.

Perhaps it will be better, after all, when she's no longer here. There should be clear lines drawn between doctors and nurses, and we've grown too familiar with each other.

Aaron is with me now, studying my surgical plan, when my pager goes off and I'm summoned downstairs to A&E. I move quickly and he follows like an obedient puppy, although he waits for the elevator while I take the stairs, which means he has to run to catch up with me when Holly, one of the more experienced nurses down here, sees me approaching and offers a quick nod of acknowledgment before handing me a clipboard.

"House fire," she says. "Thirty-two-year-old female, nine-year-old male, seven-year-old female, two-year-old infant."

I scan the notes prepared by the ambulance crews, flicking through pages, knowing exactly what I'm looking for, and taking in every relevant piece of information. When I push open the door to the area where they're being treated, a team of nurses and junior doctors is already attending to them and I'm hit with the familiar smell of charred flesh along with the equally recognizable sound of suffering, a low keening emerging from beneath gauze-covered bodies as cannulas are inserted into veins and morphine is injected to deliver some relief from the pain. I quickly establish that the mother is unlikely to survive, while the two-year-old has already been covered with a sheet and I instruct a porter to remove him to the morgue. The older children are still alive but only the girl looks perceptibly human. From behind me, a sound of deep distress arises from Aaron.

"If you're going to throw up, take it outside," I say, and he turns and runs.

Over the next hour, I prescribe medication, order tests, and do all that I can to alleviate the pain of the three remaining victims. The nine-year-old boy's organs are beginning to shut down, and all I can do is make his transition from this world to the next as painless as possible. Most of my attention needs to be turned toward his younger sister, who's suffered the least amount of trauma but whose future is irrevocably changed. Earlier today, she would have been a perfectly normal-looking child with her entire life before her. She would have gone on to meet a boy or girl someday and fallen in love. She would have broken hearts and had her heart broken. She might have taken trips to the Grand Canyon, the Great Barrier Reef, Victoria Falls. She might have become an award-winning actress, the managing director of a tech firm, or an employee in an organic-food shop. But none of those things are likely to happen now. She's too young for her skin to heal. Her life will be defined by pain and, most likely, an endless series of operations.

When Aaron returns, he's steeled himself for the wretchedness contained within this room and walks toward the boy, taking his hand in his and holding it gently. I can't hear what he's saying, but he's speaking to the child in a low, calming voice and the boy is moving his charred fingers a little, as if he's trying to squeeze my intern's hand.

Seven minutes later, he dies.

Thirteen minutes after that, his mother passes away too.

The girl is made as comfortable as possible before being moved upstairs to the specialist burns unit, where she will become my priority over the next twenty-four to forty-eight hours. When there's a moment to breathe, I make my way outside the hospital and close my eyes, throwing my head back in a desperate need to inhale some fresh air, even though I contradict this by lighting a cigarette. Three hours have passed since we were summoned downstairs, but it feels like only a fraction of that time. Aaron joins me but remains silent as he leans up against the wall.

"Are you all right?" I ask, offering him a smoke too, but he declines.

"Yes," he says. "Sorry about earlier."

"Don't be," I tell him. "Situations like that take some getting used to." I hesitate, then pay him a rare compliment.

"When you came back in, Aaron, you did a good job. I saw you comforting the boy. We might not have been able to save him, but you showed great empathy."

He offers a half smile. "I thought you said that we should keep emotion out of the job?"

"I did," I admit. "But sometimes that's impossible. We're only human, after all."

"Are we?" he asks.

"Well, aren't we?"

He shrugs. "I don't know, sometimes. Someone did that to them."

"Of course someone did."

"A man."

"Probably."

"Men like that—"

"Are less rare than you might think."

"You say that like we're the only monsters."

"You know a lot of female serial killers, do you? Female rapists? Women murdering their husbands?"

"Not many, no. But I don't think one sex is more inherently evil than the other."

I shake my head. It feels pointless arguing with him. His generation always believe they're right about everything. Their sense of moral superiority is what makes them so unbearable.

"I mean it, Freya," he says, surprising me in his use of my first name. "Think of that little boy we treated a couple of months back. Vidar. It was his mother who was abusing him and her husband."

"True," I admit.

"And I've seen some other things while I've been here."

"I'm not saying women are perfect," I say. "Or that we're always the victims. I'm simply saying that, more often than not, men are the perpetrators of violence against us, not the other way round."

"Everyone I know, all my friends, we have mothers, sisters, girlfriends, ex-girlfriends, we had female teachers, we have female bosses, we've been surrounded by women, just like you've been surrounded by men, and some of us have scars too. Not scars like they have, of course," he adds, pointing back toward the hospital, where our most recent patients lie. "Not the sort you can see. But they exist all the same."

He's speaking quietly but passionately, displaying his empathy once again, and I realize how, more than any other intern who's ever studied under me, he'll develop into a brilliant doctor. Surprisingly, I feel an almost maternal pride in him.

"You're a good man, Aaron," I say, the words out of my mouth before I even knew I was going to utter them.

He turns to me, and I expect a smile of gratitude, but instead he's frowning. He looks like he's about to say something unexpectedly aggressive, but before he can, a man approaches and introduces himself as the detective assigned to the case.

"What happened?" I ask. "Do you know yet?"

"There's history," he tells me.

"What kind of history?"

"The husband," he says, confirming what both Aaron and I had already suspected. "The wife was in a shelter. He couldn't track her down. The council found temporary accommodation for her, he found out where, came over, and set the place alight."

"His own children?" asks Aaron, looking aghast. "He'd do that to his own children?"

"She pushed him too far, I guess," the detective says. "There was a custody hearing due to take place on—"

"She pushed him too far?" Aaron asks, raising his voice, the first time since he arrived on my rotation that I've seen him express anger. "I'm sorry, but . . . what the fuck?"

"No, I didn't mean—"

"What, there's a point she can push him to, and after that he can't be held responsible for his actions?"

The policeman stares at Aaron for a few moments before turning to me.

"You might want to ask this young man to control his emotions," he says. "Those kinds of comments do nothing to help the situation."

"Fuck you," I tell him, and a staring competition begins between us. He's overweight and trying for movie-star stubble but only looks like he was too lazy to shave. I glance at his left hand and see the telltale whiteness on the flabby fourth finger of his left hand where a wedding ring used to be. There's no point arguing with men like him. Eventually, when the case is built, he'll be in touch, and I'll find myself in a court-room testifying to what took place. A prosecution barrister will tell the jury why the husband should spend years in jail for his crime, while a defense barrister will offer reasons why the jury should let him get away with it. And twelve people will decide. As I did a few years ago. They might get it right or, like me, they might get it badly wrong.

"All I meant was—" he begins, but I shake my head, cutting him off before he can say anything else.

"Dr. Umber is right," I tell him. "You can't say things like that. Three people are dead, two of them children. A fourth is in a critical condi-tion. And instinctively, whether you intended to or not, you blamed the victim. You blamed the woman."

"It was a turn of phrase, that's all."

There's no point continuing to argue the toss. He'll fight his corner to the death, men like him always do, especially when arguing with women, so I simply turn away and make my way back inside and along the corridor toward the nurses' station. Holly is still on shift and asks me how things went. I shake my head, and she's experienced enough to understand what this means without any words needing to be exchanged. Around us, gurneys pass by while outside, in the waiting room, people sit with broken arms, sprained ankles, knife wounds, all the injuries that human beings suffer on a daily basis because our skin is only so thick and our bones only so resilient and from the moment we arrive on the planet the universe is against us, conspiring to drown us, set us on fire, bury us in the earth, our spirits floating off into the atmosphere.

I'm about to return to the staircase and the comfort of my office when a fresh gurney is pushed through the doors, followed by two para-medics and a woman in her late thirties. I glance toward the patient. Around his neck I see dark purple bruises that tell me he's tried to hang himself. Emergency doctors rush toward him while I take a step back; it's not my department and I know better than to get in their way. They check his blood pressure, his heartbeat, his eyes. They place a mask over his mouth and feed him oxygen. The woman accompanying him—his mother, I assume—is distraught, telling us that she heard a loud noise from his bedroom, which turned out to be the sound of a chair being overturned. She ran upstairs, discovered him, but was too weak to cut him down. She held his legs, trying to keep him elevated for as long as she could, while he kicked and struggled against the tension of the noose he'd created for himself with his school tie. Finally, she let his legs go, reached for some scissors from his desk, and jumped on his bed to cut away at the fabric, and he fell to the ground, unconscious.

"They weren't even sharp, the scissors," she tells us, looking around at each of us in turn, her eyes desperate with fear. "Just a kid's scissors, you know? Blunt ones. For his arts and crafts. He loves his arts and crafts. He always has, since he was a child. So they're blunt. You know. For children. So they don't hurt themselves. I couldn't get them to tear away at the fabric."

I've been a doctor for a long time, and I can usually tell, simply by looking at a patient, what their chances are. This boy is still breathing, but there's little hope. He'll be placed on a life-support machine almost immediately and within a few hours, or a day at most, his mother will be told there's nothing more that can be done for him, that brain activity is nonexistent, and then she will have to make the decision to turn the machine off. In the moment of her most extreme grief, she'll be asked whether she'll allow his organs to be harvested.

"What's his name?" asks one of the A&E doctors, and although the boy's mother is the one to answer, I hear the words emerge from my lips at the same time, so quietly that the chances of anyone overhearing me are almost impossible.

"Rufus," I whisper. "His name is Rufus."

10

Lying in my makeshift coffin, I slowly began to understand that there is only one thing crueler or more virulent than a fourteen-year-old boy: two of them.

At first, I had been terrified, convinced that I would quickly run out of oxygen and die beneath the earth. The breathing tube the twins had fed through the ground worked well enough, but even so, every breath I sucked desperately into my lungs felt as if it might be my last. The darkness contributed to my panic. I heard sounds, or imagined I did. Sometimes I found myself laughing hysterically, then breaking down in tears. As the hours passed, I started to imagine that the outside world was a fantasy and that only here, inside my tomb, was reality. Occasionally, I pinched myself, wondering whether I'd succumbed to some horrible nightmare. I dozed, then woke with a shock, my hands pressing impotently against the ceiling.

I found ways to pass the time. I sang my favorite songs over and over. At school, I'd memorized the names of all the English kings and queens, from William the Conqueror to Elizabeth II, and I recited them backward. I thought of every job that began with the letter "M" and every country that started with the letter "A." I came up with the most disgusting ways to destroy the lives of fourteen-year-old boys. I decided upon the meal I would have eaten, had I known this would be my last night on earth. I composed letters in my head, one to Hannah and one to Beth, telling them what terrible parents, or surrogate parents, they had been. I counted my fingers and toes and became convinced that I had nine of the former and eleven of the latter. I tried to remember as many of Black Beauty's owners as I could. I closed my eyes and dreamed of wide-open spaces. I cried. I laughed. I made popping noises with my mouth. I think, at one point, I slept.

When I finally heard the sound of the soil being cleared from above me, I panicked again, uncertain what fresh torture might be in store for me, and when the lid was lifted at last and the morning sun shone down on my face I was momentarily blinded. As my eyes adjusted, however, I recognized the faces of the boys kneeling in the soil, looking down at me with anxious expressions. The birthmark on Arthur's neck seemed more pronounced than ever, and they appeared surprised, even frightened, when I didn't immediately leap from my improvised grave.

"Freya," said Pascoe, reaching a hand down, his voice filled with fear. "Freya, are you all right?"

I stared at his hand, uncertain whether to take it.

"Come on, Freya," said Arthur. "It was a joke, that's all. A game. Don't be mad at us."

So, this was the second game we had played. Which was worse? I wondered. One that involved my being repeatedly raped in a cave or one that saw me being buried alive? And if there was to be a third, what form might that take? Perhaps they would tie me to a wall and throw axes at me. Or take me to the top of the cliffs and hang me over by my ankles.

Slowly, I felt the warmth return to my body and I sat up cautiously, my back aching from the long hours I had spent lying in the same position. Pulling myself to my feet, I felt my knees tremble as I exhumed myself. To my right, I noticed a long steel pole discarded by the builders in the dirt and considered picking it up and bashing their brains in with it. Then I thought, *no, I'll kill just one of them. That would hurt more.* I was familiar enough with their ways to know that neither could possibly survive without the other.

"We didn't mean to leave you there for so long," said Arthur, doing his best to sound repentant. "It was only meant to be for an hour or two. But we fell asleep. Father didn't come home—we usually wake when he does—so we couldn't come back. We don't know where he is."

He looked at me as if he expected me to offer an explanation for Kitto's absence, but it was the furthest thing from my mind.

"You buried me," I whispered, my voice grainy. I was dehydrated, badly in need of water. "You left me to die."

"It was a game," he repeated, and I turned to Pascoe, who appeared far less contrite than his twin. If anything, he looked mildly irritated, as if he considered it something of a bore that I wasn't willing to laugh along at their actions. Arthur moved forward and, worried that he was going to put me back where he'd found me, I pushed him away. He stumbled, almost falling into the pit himself. I ran from them both, my unsteady legs gathering strength as I raced toward the beach. When I reached the shoreline, I ran into the water, desperate for the sea to cleanse me.

I remained there a long time, swimming much further out than I'd intended. I could swim to France if I wanted, I told myself. I could drown. I could escape them all.

On the shoreline I saw the twins waving for me to return. Their heads were pressed together, locked in conversation. I guessed that they were frightened, just as I had been frightened. Fearful of what I might do, who I might tell. There were so many ways that I could cause trouble for them, after all. The cave; the grave; these waves. Their telling me that their father had murdered their mother. I had rarely thought of this since they'd first mentioned it, but it came back to me now as I floated there, wondering whether it might, in fact, be true. If the boys were psychopaths, then it stood to reason that Kitto might be one too.

Eventually, I returned to the beach, stepping onto the sand and walking past them, ignoring their attempts to talk to me. As I made my way back in the direction of the cottage, it pleased me to think that they would spend the hours and days ahead worrying about what might happen next.

Back home, I found Beth lying on the sofa, smoking a cigarette and watching one of those Saturday-morning television shows aimed at teenagers. Scattered on the carpet were empty beer cans, and she waved in their direction, not taking her eyes off the screen, utterly oblivious to my soaking clothes, and instructed me to clear them up. She was barefoot, wearing a tracksuit, and hadn't showered yet, her makeup from the previous night streaked across her face.

"You were up and about early," she muttered, and I knew then that she hadn't even been aware of my absence the night before. From the bathroom, I heard the sound of the toilet flushing and the taps turning on, and, glancing down the corridor, I expected to see Eli emerge through the door, his usual smile on his face when he saw me. But when the door to the living room opened, it wasn't Eli who stepped into the room, it was Kitto Teague. I stared at him, unable to comprehend his presence here. He paused for a moment and frowned, as if he wasn't entirely sure who I was.

"Where's Eli?" I asked, turning to Beth, and she shrugged her shoulders, took a long drag from her cigarette, then laughed at something one of the television presenters said, before answering.

"Eli's history," she said. "He's gone. And good riddance too."

"Gone where?"

"To the unemployment office, I expect," said Kitto, sitting down on one of the kitchen chairs and reaching for his shoes. "Three weeks behind schedule," he added, his voice so refined that it seemed almost comical, as if he was putting it on. A cartoon Englishman in an American film. "That's what I get for hiring a yokel rather than bringing a professional down from London. I should have got rid of him long ago."

"Ditto," said Beth.

He walked over to the sofa and retrieved his coat, leaning over and whispering something in Beth's ear. She muted the television for a moment before looking up at him.

"I don't see why not," she replied to whatever it was he'd said. "Only, just so you know, I'm not here for a bunk-up any time you've got ants in your pants. Take me somewhere nice next time, all right? Somewhere fancy though, not just down the pub for cod and chips and mushy peas. I can get that any time."

"Let's wait and see," he replied quietly. He made his way toward me, narrowing his eyes as he looked me up and down. For a moment, I thought he might prize my jaws apart and check my teeth.

"You're friends with my sons, aren't you?" he asked, and I nodded.

It seemed pointless to try to explain the complicated nature of our relationship, which even I did not fully understand. "Do you have a favorite?"

"A favorite?" I asked, frowning.

"Yes, among the two of them," he said. "Is there one of them that you like more than the other?"

I stared at him. It had never occurred to me to separate them in any way. They seemed like a composite being to me. They had always been the twins. Arthur and Pascoe.

"Or perhaps one that you dislike less?" he continued. "Personally, I've always preferred Pascoe. Arthur can be querulous. And I find that birthmark of his unsightly. Their mother was a twin too, as was her father. It's not a Teague trait. I find it faintly ridiculous, if I'm honest. Their devotion to each other embarrasses me too. I'd prefer they fought, as boys do, not carried on as if they've got some unholy crush on each other. I'd rather hoped you might come between them, in fact. That they'd fight over you. Anyway . . ."

He drifted off for a moment and glanced around the room with a sigh, as if he was considering whether or not he should put the rent up or simply burn the place down. "Don't tell either of them I said that, will you?" He reached down and took my chin in his hands. "No one likes a tattletale." Then he leaned over and kissed me gently on the lips, lingering there for a moment while Beth watched and took a long, slow drag on her cigarette as she observed us.

"It doesn't really have to be somewhere fancy, Mr. Teague," she called out as he left. "I was only joking. The local is as good as anywhere."

He didn't reply, merely raised a hand in the air without looking back. Beth, on the other hand, wore a hopeful expression on her face. I found it surprising that she would address him in such a formal way. If they had slept together, as I assumed they had, then surely she could at least call him by his first name.

"I think I might be onto something there, sweetheart," she said, rubbing the thumb and index finger of her right hand together in the universal sign for money. Her cigarette fell as she did so, dropping onto the floor, but she didn't seem to notice as it connected with a newspaper, igniting a small but determined flame. I watched as the pages rose in anger, knowing I should say something but choosing to remain silent. It took another thirty seconds before she realized that the heat around her ankles was the beginnings of a fire, and she quickly stamped it out.

I remained in my room for the rest of the day, stretched out on my bed. Although I was exhausted, whenever I closed my eyes I imagined myself back in my coffin with the sound of the earth falling on the lid and the cramped walls closing in on me. I was only twelve years old that summer, but I was mature enough to know that I would think about what had taken place during those months for the rest of my life.

Still, I reassured myself that all was not lost. After all, there was still a week left before I was due to return to Norfolk. There was still time to set things right.

11

It's the seventh time that George has shown up at my apartment, but at least he no longer arrives unannounced. Instead, he texts when he wants sex, and I've learned that I can only get away with saying no twice in a row before he becomes threatening, leaving me with no choice but to invite him over. I take no pleasure in our encounters and have grown to despise both his smug little face and the tawdry remarks he makes, thinking they might put me in the mood. I have no idea how much porn the boy watches—quite a lot, I imagine, if his words and actions are anything to go by—but he clearly hasn't the first clue how women in the real world behave or what we want from our sexual encounters.

We don't, for example, want our hair pulled. Nor do we want to be choked. It's not a turn-on to be called by the names that men have historically called women in their attempts to demean them. We would prefer that our partners ejaculated into condoms rather than onto our faces. Rape fantasies are not an actual thing, although rapes themselves are. We're not interested in filming our encounters and subsequently uploading them to the internet, nor do we particularly enjoy watching the erotic encounters of others. Thanks to unfettered access to Wi-Fi since before he even reached puberty, however, these are clearly the things that George believes are the fastest way to a girl's heart. And to think: people used to say it with flowers.

Today, he turns fifteen, which is the final nail in the coffin in terms of any interest I might ever have displayed in him, and to my dismay he insists on spending his birthday with me, making it clear in advance that he expects me to do something special to mark the occasion. I thought this meant a cake and a present, but no, he sent me a link for a High Neck Halter Lace Bodysuit from Victoria's Secret and said that he wanted me to wear it on what he called his "special night." I did as instructed. For the time being, at least, I have no choice.

He's confided in me a few times about his home life, apparently believing that I care about his regular arguments with his father and his nonexistent relationship with his mother, who left when he was four years old and moved to Jersey, starting a new family there that didn't involve him. He visits every summer for a month, just as I did with Beth when I was a child, but he tells me that she barely tolerates his presence, while his stepfather and step-siblings actively resent him.

"Maybe we could go together sometime?" he asks, and I glance across the room from where I'm preparing his birthday dinner, his favorite and a gourmand's delight: chicken nuggets, chips, and beans.

"Go where?" I ask.

"To Jersey," he says. "To my mum's."

I stare at him in disbelief.

"Why on earth would we do that?"

"Because I'd like you to meet her. You're my girlfriend, after all, and she's my mum. You'll need to get to know each other sooner or later."

It takes all my self-control not to burst out laughing.

"George," I say, keeping my tone steady as I can't risk provoking him. "I'm not your girlfriend."

"Of course you are," he replies, looking genuinely surprised, even wounded. "We're sleeping together, aren't we?"

"That's just a physical act," I tell him. "And a private one. But we're not actually dating. We've never even been outside this flat together."

"I was thinking about that too," he says, coming over and taking my right hand in his sweaty little fist. The urge to pull it away and wipe it on my trousers is overwhelming. "Don't you think we should do something other than just, you know, have sex?"

"I'd be very happy not to have sex with you, George."

He frowns. Perhaps I'm being too subtle for him.

"Like, we could go to a film together some night. The new Trans-formers movie comes out next week."

"The what?" I ask.

"You're kidding, right?"

I shrug.

"Oh my God," he shouts, growing animated now. "It's a series of movies about these machines that—"

"How many are there?" I ask.

"Machines?"

"No, movies."

"I don't know. A bunch. We could watch all the old ones here across a few nights—I could stay over—and then go to the IMAX to see the new one. What do you think?"

I think that I'd rather dig a hole to the center of the earth with my tongue.

"Sure," I say. "Sounds like a plan."

"Great. Sorted."

He then starts talking about the Marvel Cinematic Universe, which has apparently spawned dozens of films, and says that we can start on them once our triumphant journey through the world of Transformers has come to an end.

"I can't believe you haven't seen any of them," he says, looking genuinely baffled. "Like, I thought people your age were really into cinema?"

"I like Almodóvar," I tell him. "And Woody Allen. And Jane Campion."

He stares at me in complete bewilderment, as if I've just started speaking Latin. I shake my head. There's no point explaining. To my ennui, he begins a long and erudite analysis of the virtues of Ironman, Thor, and Captain America, and it takes all my willpower to stop myself from telling him that I would rather have my eyeballs prized out with nail scissors than subject myself to any of these celluloid atrocities.

"And if we plan on going to my mum's at some point," he continues, bringing the conversation back to where it started, but sounding a little more cautious now, "then, before that, maybe I could introduce you to some of my friends."

I open the fridge door to hide my face from him as I let out a silent scream. "George," I say. "You haven't told anyone about us, have you?"

"No," he says. "I swear I haven't. You told me not to."

"You know how much trouble I could get into if any of this got out, right?"

"I do," he says, smiling now, knowing the power he has over me. "You could go to jail."

He's too young to be a good liar, and I'm reasonably confident that he's telling the truth, but at the same time, I'm also conscious that a teenage boy having regular sex with a thirty-six-year-old woman will, at some point, brag about it to his friends. He'd probably enjoy the kudos just as much as the sex itself, if not more, and it would only take a single party, two or three beers, or a joint, before he let it slip, and then word would spread from boy to boy before it found its way back to me in the form of two members of His Majesty's constabulary knocking on my front door, wanting a word.

But my confidence does not equate to certainty, which is why I brought some sleeping tablets back from the hospital this evening, crushed them, and dropped them into the bottle of beer that he always drinks when he arrives. I'm standing in the doorway of my bedroom now, watching him while he sleeps. He looks ridiculously young and innocent, his mouth a little open, his fringe falling in his eyes. No one looking at him would suspect that he's a blackmailer. They'd think he was a perfectly nice kid.

I pick up his jeans from the bedroom floor and take his phone from his back pocket, switching it to mute, and hold it in front of his face to unlock the home screen. When it opens, I take it into the living room and begin a forensic examination of its contents.

He has the same phone as me—albeit a much earlier incarnation—which makes things simple as I'm familiar with the operating system, but while I keep a very ordered home screen, collecting all my apps in neatly organized folders, his is utter chaos, a Jackson Pollock painting splashed across dozens of pages in no conceivable order. I've no idea what most of them do, but I start with the basic Messages app, which is empty. I suppose that's too old-school for him. I try WhatsApp next, and only three conversations are saved, a back-and-forth with his father, another with someone called Steven, who, when I scroll through them, seems to be his uncle. Neither contains anything incriminating. His third communicant is someone called GF, which turns out to be me, and is a complete log of every message we've shared, from my initial message on the day we first met outside the hospital to the one he sent me earlier tonight telling me what time he'd be arriving. I'm pleased that he hasn't entered me on his contacts list by name, and it doesn't take me long to figure out what *GF* means.

Girlfriend.

His social media doesn't include Facebook or Twitter—even his parents have probably given up on them—but he has Instagram, although he hasn't posted many pictures and doesn't seem to reply to any of the messages he receives, which tend to be a series of indecipherable emojis rather than actual words. I've heard of Snapchat but have never used it, and the fact that it's the first app on his home screen and has a bubble saying he has fifty-four unopened messages makes me realize that this is where most of his communications take place. I open it and try to understand how it works. The people he communicates with on there seem to have normal names, and within the messages themselves, things aren't much more literate. Thankfully, when I eventually translate them into English, none of the gibberish seems to refer to me.

Until I open one directed to *HarryCull2010.*

George has already admitted to me that he's told his friend Harry that he's sleeping with someone, but swore that he hasn't said who it is. To reassure myself of this, in recent weeks I've used the hospital's internal computer system to keep a close eye on the boy's progress. He's an outpatient now and is doing better than he was a few months ago, but he's still awaiting a second kidney transplant. Shortly after George started blackmailing me, I went down to his room one afternoon wearing my doctor's coat so he'd assume I had a reason to be there, and found him engrossed in an Agatha Christie novel. In other circumstances, I might have talked to him about how obsessed I'd been by her books when I was his age, but instead, I made small talk with him as I scanned his chart and asked how he found his dialysis.

"It's OK," he said. "I'm getting used to it."

"You're very brave," I told him. "Do you have many visitors? When you stay in, I mean."

"My mum and dad and my sisters," he told me. "And some friends."

"They must be worried about you."

"I guess," he said. "Most of them seem frightened."

"Why?"

"Because I might die." His tone was remarkably calm, and I rather admired his stoicism. "They don't know how to deal with what I'm going through."

I sat down next to him and placed a hand on the outline of his knee beneath the blanket. He stared at it for a moment, but I left it there, even when he tried to move away. "Life and death aren't things a boy your age should have to worry about."

"I don't have much choice," he said. "My best mate though, he's been really good."

"Oh yes?" I asked. This was what I had come here for. "What's his name?"

"George. George Eliot."

"Like the writer."

"Like the writer," he agreed, smiling.

"And how long have you known each other?" I asked.

"Me and George? Forever. We live three doors apart and our mums are besties. We basically grew up together."

"So he's like a brother?"

"I guess," he said.

"He cares about you?"

He looked away then, perhaps embarrassed by the question. I shouldn't have expected a child his age to be able to cope with such an emotional remark, and when one of the nurses appeared to check on him, I said goodbye and returned upstairs.

And here is his name now on George's Snapchat.

HarryCull2010

The messages go back a long way—George must save them all—and most of them are utter nonsense, barely comprehensible to someone my age, but then I come across an exchange that frightens me:

made her cum twyce 2nite, writes George.

u gotta let me know who she is

cant shed kill me

she hot?

fuk yeh

pix or it dint hapn

And then, to my horror, there is a picture. Of me. Not, thankfully, of my face, but of my body. He'd asked for one before, of course, but I'd refused him. I must have fallen asleep after some encounter, however, and he took a photo of my breasts with his own face directed to the camera, offering a wide smile and the thumbs-up sign.

u lucky cunt

hahaha

like wtf

i no

howd u even

hoes be hoes

ledge

It goes back and forth with more drivel, but as obnoxious as the conversation becomes, I'm at least relieved that he never names me and there are no pictures that could identify me.

Still, it's only a matter of time.

Eventually, a sound from the bedroom makes me hide the phone down the side of my sofa and George wanders naked into the living room, looking a little disoriented after the effects of the pills I gave him.

"Do you have some water, bae?" he asks, making me cringe inside.

"Fridge," I say.

When he makes his way toward it, I go into the bedroom and return his phone to the pocket of his jeans, glancing toward the bedsheets, which are in total disarray after our fifteen minutes of passion.

A moment later, he's behind me, his arms wrapped around my waist, and I know that he's about sixty seconds away from insisting that we have sex again. I turn around and smile.

"You're insatiable," I say.

"You love it, you filthy bitch," he tells me, pushing me down onto the bed, and I do exactly what he wants, offering no complaint, because I would prefer to comply with his wishes than find myself spending the next ten years in jail.

But really. This can't go on forever. I refuse to be a victim any longer. It's time to act.

12

The bar is quite busy but, thankfully, Louise has reserved a private area for her retirement party. I haven't socialized with people from the hospital in years, and if this gathering was being held for anyone else, the chances of me being here at all would be minimal. But Louise is the closest thing I've ever had to a friend at work, and it would be rude not to put in an appearance.

A curious thing happened on my way here. While making my way toward the venue, I saw Hugh Winley on the other side of the street, my ardent admirer from my apartment building, sitting in the open window of a separate bar with a young man of around his own age. I wouldn't have normally given it a second thought, but as I glanced in their direction, they leaned into each other and kissed. I watched for a moment, and when they separated, Hugh reached forward and placed his hand gently on his companion's cheek with an expression of total adoration on his face. Assuming he's gay, or at least bisexual, why on earth is he spending so much of his time trying to convince me to go on a date with him? I really don't understand young people anymore. I don't know whether I admire their sexual fluidity or find it utterly narcissistic.

Glancing around now, I recognize some of my fellow doctors and surgeons, along with nurses and administration staff, and for a moment feel a twinge of envy that Louise inspires so much affection among our colleagues. If I was to resign tomorrow, I can't imagine anyone showing up to wish me well. One day, of course, I will walk out of the hospital for the final time with two or three decades of empty days ahead of me. Financially, I'll be secure, but how will I fill my time? It's a thought not worth dwelling on right now, so instead I take a sip from my drink as I decide which group to join. Before I can make up my mind, however, our hostess marches toward me, arms outstretched, a wide smile on her face.

"Freya," she says, wrapping me in an embrace. When she pulls away, I notice that her pupils are a little dilated; she must have started early. "I was beginning to worry about you."

"Oh, I've been here for ages," I lie.

"See over there?" she says, pointing toward a table bearing the weight of dozens of gift-wrapped presents. "It's like I'm getting married all over again."

"Speaking of which," I say, handing her an envelope that contains a gift voucher to one of the city's most popular restaurants.

"You're very good," she says. "But I'll open it later, if you don't mind. You've written your name inside, so I know who it's from?"

"Of course," I reply. Seated on a banquette a short distance away, chatting to the head of HR, I notice her husband, Liam, a corporate lawyer who's also due to retire soon; their plan is to backpack around the world together, an ambition that I rather admire. I haven't traveled enough in my life. Perhaps that's something I could do when my time comes. "I'm going to miss you," I tell her.

"Ah, you'll have forgotten me by this time next week," she says, slapping me playfully on the arm. I don't know whether to be offended by this or not, although, if I'm honest, she's not entirely wrong.

"And God knows who they'll stick me with next," I say. "We've worked well together, haven't we?"

"We have indeed," she replies. "We've always been very professional." I find this a rather strange response, but perhaps it's appropriate. So many times over the years she's asked me about my life and my relationships outside work, and I've never been very forthcoming, which is probably why she eventually stopped.

My phone buzzes in my pocket, and I take it out and look at the screen. Middlemarch, it says. We can all use codes to hide our secrets. Louise, looking down, sees the word and frowns.

"Middlemarch," she says. "Who or what is Middlemarch?"

"Just a friend," I tell her. "No one important."

"Like the book."

"Like the book," I agree.

"And why do you call this friend after a book? What's his name? Or her name?"

I wave away the question. There's simply no way to explain.

"Have you got a fella at last, Freya, is that it?" she asks, looking giddy now, eager for gossip, and I look around in search of an exit. The music is too loud, and I feel claustrophobic. There are too many people here.

"What's he like? Is he good-looking?"

"He's no one," I repeat. "Just an acquaintance, that's all."

"You're a dark horse, I'll give you that. I've often wondered what it is you get up to at night."

"Believe me," I say, "you don't want to know."

We chat a little more, but she's the star of the night and it's not long before others come over to offer gifts, wish her well, and buy her a drink, and I soon lose track of her, thinking that I could probably have one more and then slip away, my duty done. I head toward the bar and am ordering a vodka and cranberry when I hear a voice call my name.

"Dr. Petrus!"

I look around and see Aaron seated in a corner booth next to a young woman I don't recognize. He waves me over and, for want of anywhere better to sit, I decide to join them. Unlike the time we went for drinks together, he stands up and kisses me on both cheeks, as if we're old friends.

"Rebecca," he says to his companion as I sit down, "this is Dr. Petrus. My boss."

She hesitates noticeably before saying, "Of course," and extending a hand toward me. She's neither beautiful nor unattractive, a plain girl whose features would, I think, be difficult to remember afterward, and I'm a little surprised that Aaron is dating her. Her dark hair is cut short at the cheekbones in an unfashionable attempt at a Louise Brooks bob. Her eyes, however, are quite striking, and when they connect with my own, I feel as if she's reading every thought in my head, which is rather unsettling.

"I've heard a lot about you," she tells me.

"Dr. Petrus, this is my girlfriend, Rebecca," adds Aaron.

"I told you," I say. "When we're not in work, you can just call me Freya. It's nice to meet you, Rebecca. You don't mind being dragged along to one of his work functions, then?"

"Not at all," she says. "I haven't met any of his colleagues until tonight, and he's spoken so well of Louise." A slight pause. "He's talked about you too, of course."

There's an obvious distinction being made here, but I choose to ignore it. He's probably complained about my attitude toward him on numerous occasions and she's decided to take against me. Not that her opinion matters. I already feel a similar antipathy toward her and guess that she's the dominant force in their relationship. Aaron could do so much better. I drink my vodka more quickly than I should, and before I know it he's taken a fresh order from both of us and disappeared into the crowd. I follow him with my eyes, hoping it won't take him long to be served as I'm not particularly interested in making small talk with this creature.

"So, tell me, Rachel," I say, "what is it you do?"

"It's Rebecca," she says.

"Sorry."

"And I'm training to be a pilot."

"Oh yes," I say, feigning interest. "Aaron mentioned something about that. I must admit I know nothing about that industry. Are there a lot of female pilots these days?"

"More than you might imagine," she tells me. "When I started out, there were fourteen men and three women in the training program, and now, two years later, only seven of the men are left, but the three of us are still standing."

"Well, that's something, I suppose. It was the same in medical school. The dropout rate was much higher among the men than the women. Why do you think that is?"

"I couldn't possibly begin to guess," she says, which shuts that conversation down. Clearly we're not going to bond over the staying power of the sisterhood.

"And was that something you always dreamed of doing?" I ask. "Since you were a child, I mean?"

"No," she tells me, glancing at her watch. I consider just sitting back and ignoring her, waiting for her boyfriend to return, but I'm so irritated by her now I feel like this is a challenge that I want to rise to.

"A family thing, perhaps? Was your father a pilot?"

She laughs and shakes her head. The expression on her face is impossible to read. I'm considering asking whether she always behaves this rudely toward complete strangers when my phone buzzes again. I feel a stab of irritation as I take it out and look at the screen.

I want to come over.

Not tonight, I reply quickly. I'm going into surgery. My phone will be off for the next few hours.

"Something important?" asks Rebecca, and I shrug.

"Something I need to take care of, certainly," I tell her. "I just have to figure out how."

"I'm sure you will."

"I'm sure I will. You have something between your teeth, by the way."

She doesn't, but I rather enjoy watching her suck at her gums, trying to extract whatever it is.

"Your accent," I say. "You're Irish?"

"Yes."

"Did you know Louise before, then?"

She stares at me as if I'm the stupidest woman alive. "No, of course not," she says. "There are five million people in Ireland. We don't all know each other."

Thankfully, before I can tell her to go fuck herself, Aaron returns and places the drinks on the table, glancing from his girlfriend to me and back again. It's a strange moment. I almost feel as if I'm being interviewed to join a coven, or being told the reasons why I'm being excluded from one.

"I was just asking Rachel," I say, "whether she—"

"Rebecca," says Rebecca, for the second time.

Naturally, I know her name is Rebecca. I'm getting it wrong deliberately just to demonstrate to her how unimportant she is to me.

"I'm so sorry," I say. "Rebecca, of course. I was just asking Rebecca whether her father was a pilot."

They turn to look at each other, and he retreats slightly in his seat. To my surprise, she leans toward him and they kiss. I turn away, noticing that not only are they holding hands but that they're clasping them very tightly, their knuckles whitening against the skin. My aversion toward him, which had diminished in recent times, immediately returns. I find their behavior both boorish and disrespectful.

"How about you?" asks Rebecca, turning back to me when she's finished molesting the poor boy. "Were your parents surgeons?"

"No," I say. "My mother was an architect, and my father was a mathematics professor in Cambridge."

Something in Rebecca's expression tells me that she doesn't believe a word of this and, of course, she'd be right not to.

"Are they still alive?"

"No, they died in a house fire when I was twelve."

Aaron raises an eyebrow. "You never told me that," he says.

"Why would I?"

"But a house fire. Is that why you . . . the burns unit, I mean?"

I try to recall whether I ever gave him a reason why I made this my speciality. He did ask me about it on our quasi-date, I recall, but I can't remember what I said and am anxious about contradicting myself.

"It played a part in it," I tell him. "But not the only part."

"Was it arson?" asks Rebecca.

"That's a strange assumption," I say, turning to her. "Wouldn't an accident be the more likely explanation?"

"It would, yes. But was it?"

"No, faulty wiring," I say after a pause. "A spark in the garage where the fuse box was located ignited a dozen cans of paint. We were having the house renovated at the time. Putting in a pool, among other things."

"How awful."

"It was, yes."

"But you escaped unharmed."

"I was staying with a friend that night," I tell her. "Otherwise, I would have died too."

"And did they catch whoever did it?"

"No one did it," I say, raising my voice a little. "I told you, it was an accident."

"I mean, did they arrest whoever installed the wiring? Surely there'd be a case for manslaughter?"

I stare at her, baffled by her prying. I'm not prepared to discuss this any longer, not least because the more lies I tell, the more difficult they are to remember.

"You never answered my question," I say.

"What question was that?"

"I asked what your father did. Or does."

She doesn't hesitate for a moment.

"He was the head of the National Swimming Federation in Ireland," she tells me. "He held that position for many years until it was discovered that he'd sexually abused eight young girls in his care. Eight that we know of, anyway. There was a trial. Quite a famous one in Ireland, actually. And he went to prison. He's still there, in fact."

I'm astonished by the frankness of this admission. She reaches for her glass and takes a drink.

"I see," I say, a rather impotent response on my part, but I can't quite think what else to say. "That must have been very painful for you."

"It was, yes."

"And are you still in contact with him?"

She shakes her head. "Of course not. Why would I be?"

"Well, I presume you loved him once."

"When I was a child. But now? No. I wake every day hoping to learn of his death. I'll never speak to Brendan again," she adds, and I notice she refers to him by his first name, as I always did with Hannah and Beth, removing all sense of familial connection. "Anyone who hurts a child forfeits all rights, in my opinion."

"Did he admit his guilt?" I ask. "Or was it a jury trial?"

"Why do you ask?"

"Because I'm interested. I served on a jury myself once."

"To this day he refuses to take any responsibility for his actions. His victims have to live with it though. Well, some of them, anyway."

"Some of them? What do you mean?"

"That there must be some who are dead. Girls who took their own lives."

An image flashes into my mind.

Rufus seated by the side of my bed, barefoot and trembling.

Rufus on the gurney as it was wheeled into A&E, the purple bruises around his neck from where his school tie had choked him.

The sight of Rufus's coffin in the distance a couple of weeks later, when I stood in the graveyard, hidden from view, watching as he was buried.

"I admire how willing you are to talk about this," I tell her. "Utterly unashamed."

"Why would I be ashamed? I didn't hurt anyone. Don't you think it's the perpetrator who should feel shame?"

"Of course I do. But I suppose—"

"You suppose what?"

"Well, just from an intellectual standpoint, one has to wonder what happened to your father to make him do the things he did."

"Does one?" she asks, stressing the *one*, as if I'm condescending to her. "Why?"

"In order to understand it."

"It's not something I want to understand."

"Then how do we, as a society, learn from it? How do we stop it from happening again?"

"I don't give a fuck about society," she replies. "I only care about the lives he destroyed. Those girls' lives, first and foremost. And my sister's. And my mother's. And mine."

"Of course," I say. "Look, I'm a surgeon, not a psychologist, but these things interest me, that's all. And the fact that you're so up-front about what your father did makes me—"

"It's quite simple really," she says. "Brendan was—is—a pedophile."

"But do you think he was born that way or that something happened to him, somewhere in his own youth, that led him to do the things he did?"

She hesitates now. I don't know how long she's been struggling with her family history, but it's clear that I'm asking her something she's never properly considered before.

"It's not impossible," she says after a lengthy pause, her words coming out carefully, as if she's judging the weight of each one, "that he was born with the sort of brain that meant that, one day, he would find himself sexually attracted to children. That can happen, I suppose. But surely the difference comes in the decision whether or not to act upon those urges. Right and wrong comes into it. A man—even a woman, for that matter—might have such impulses. But because most of us are moral human beings who don't set out to hurt others, we do nothing to feed them. We never would. Can a person be blamed for how they were born? No, of course not. But it's neither here nor there, is it? It's the committing of the act that matters. A man, a regular heterosexual man, might have rape fantasies that he cannot control in his imagination but that he would never in a trillion years indulge. None of us can be held responsible for the things that lurk in the darkest parts of our minds. But in our lives? Yes, we can. So whether something happened to Brendan when he was a child or not, I genuinely do not fucking care, Freya. If it did, he could have chosen to break the cycle. If it didn't, he could have chosen not to start one. But he *did* do what he did. He made that decision. So fuck him. Let him rot. I'll open a bottle of champagne when he dies."

A lengthy silence ensues, and I glance at Aaron, who has remained silent throughout this exchange, but he's looking at the floor, his brow furrowed. The resulting awkwardness is broken by Louise approaching us and, in her drunken state, planting a kiss on my left cheek and one on Aaron's right, before insisting on taking a photograph of the three of us on her smartphone.

"I knew you two would get along in the end," she says, and Aaron smiles back at her.

"We're not quite there yet," he says.

13

It was the final days of my stay in Cornwall. Since the night they buried me alive, Arthur and Pascoe had been reluctant to spend much time with me, no doubt worried that I might hold them to account for what they had done. Instead, I chose not to mention it at all, hoping they'd think that I'd either forgotten about it entirely or had experienced no traumatic effects. Only once, when Pascoe brought it up in a way that made it clear that the twins had rehearsed this conversation, did we even touch upon it.

"That was a stupid thing you did that night," he said as we walked along the beach, the two boys to my right with me by the water's edge, for they never allowed me to stand between them.

"What night?" I asked.

"You know what night. Climbing into the box like that. Sleeping in it. You might have died."

A lengthy silence ensued. So this, I told myself, was the way that they had decided to frame what had happened. As my fault.

"I know," I said at last, keeping my tone steady. "Thank you, both of you, for saving me. I don't know what I'd have done if you hadn't."

Immediately, the tension between us seemed to dissipate, and I watched as they gave each other reassuring smiles. Perhaps they genuinely thought I was so stupid that I actually believed this version of events.

"You're just a kid," said Arthur, ignoring the fact that, if I was, then he had spent much of the summer raping a child. "But you need to be more careful in the future. Especially when you go home, because we won't be there to protect you."

Later, in the village, I ran into Eli, who was sitting outside a pub with a beer, reading a newspaper and smoking a cigarette. I waved to him and he called me over, inviting me to sit down. He asked me how I was, and I told him the truth, that I missed him.

"Miss you too, sweetheart," he said, folding his paper and putting it to one side. "But your mum, she gave me the old heave-ho."

"Why?" I asked, interested to know, as it had seemed to me that she'd been lucky to find someone as nice as him.

He rubbed his thumb and index finger together.

"Money," he said. "I don't have enough for her, do I? She's got a few good years left in her yet and she's throwing the line out, hoping to reel in a bigger fish." He took a drag from his cigarette and stared off in the direction of the sea before shaking his head. "Forget I said that," he said, turning back to me with a smile. "She's your mum. I shouldn't say anything bad about her to you."

"She gave birth to me," I told him. "But that's about it. She's not my mum really."

"I never did understand why she gave you up," he said, and I repeated the hand gesture he had made to me—*money*—which made him laugh.

"Still, she was just a teenager, I suppose," he said. "Can't blame her for not being ready. I don't hold grudges. We had fun together, but neither of us saw it as anything long term. Truth is, I'm not the kind of guy who gets upset about things like that. If someone wants to be with me, great. And if they don't, well, I'm not gonna lose any sleep over it."

In my mind, I returned to my earlier fantasy that he would marry Beth and adopt me, only this time I didn't want her in the picture at all. I wanted it to be just the two of us.

"When are you going home?" he asked.

"Day after tomorrow."

"Shame," he said. "I'll miss you."

I felt myself light up from within.

"We could do something together before I go," I suggested, and he raised an eyebrow, looking slightly baffled.

"Like what?"

"I dunno. Have dinner. Somewhere fancy though, not just down the pub for cod and chips and mushy peas. I can get that anytime."

He shook his head. "Don't think that would be right," he said.

"It doesn't really have to be somewhere fancy. I was only joking. The local is as good as anywhere."

"Still," he said, looking away and glancing at his watch. "Probably not."

I felt embarrassed and confused and worried that he was going to leave. *I'm just like her, amn't I*, I thought. *Just like Beth. And I'll end up just like her too.*

"Why did Mr. Teague fire you?" I asked, anxious to change the subject.

"Because he's an idiot."

"No, but why?"

"Doesn't want to spend the cash," he said. "Happy to throw it away on sofas, massive televisions, and sound systems, but he wants all the behind-the-scenes shit done on the cheap. That's what rich people are like, Freya. Tight as fuck."

"What behind-the-scenes stuff ?" I asked.

"Electrics," he said. "Cheap cables. Cheap plumbing. Looks good on the outside, but when things go wrong, and they will sooner or later, it'll be a shit show. Still," he said, taking a long drink from his beer, "it's his money. If he wants to throw it away, that's on him. But it's a . . . what's the phrase? . . . a false economy. Ten years from now—five—he'll be pulling everything out and having to start all over again."

"You won't do it for him then, will you?"

"'Course I will," he said, breaking into a wide smile. "Work's work and a pay packet's a pay packet. If he wants me to redo that house every few years for the rest of my life, I'm good with it, as long as he pays me."

He reached for his cigarette pack, removed another, and looked around for his lighter. He stood up, went over to the next table and asked for a match from another customer, while I retrieved his lighter from where it had dropped underneath the bench and put it in my pocket. When he came back, I'd moved around to his side of the table and was sitting in the seat next to his. He seemed a little surprised by this, but I explained that the sun had been in my eyes.

"Can I have a drink?" I asked.

"Sure," he said. "What do you want?"

I racked my brain for things I'd heard Beth or Hannah order over the years and asked for a vodka and cranberry. Eli threw his head back and laughed.

"I meant a Coke or a Fanta," he said. "You're twelve years old."

"I'll be thirteen in November," I told him.

"So come back to me in November five years from now and I'll get you one then."

I gave in and let him buy me a Sprite, and when he returned, carrying another beer for himself, I set aside the straw and glass he'd brought with him and decided to drink it directly from the bottle, just as he was doing.

"You're better off without her anyway," I told him, doing my best to sound grown-up.

"Without who?"

"Without Beth. You're too good for her."

He smiled and shrugged. "She's a piece of work, that's for sure."

"I mean it. I've met lots of her boyfriends over the years, and I've hated them all. But you're different."

"Cheers."

"Do you know the caves down by the beach?"

"Sure," he said. "Why?"

"Just asking. I'd like to visit them again before I go."

"Tide'll be in soon. You better wait till tomorrow morning."

"We could go together then."

He shook his head and took a drag from his cigarette. "Sorry, kid," he said. "Starting a new job tomorrow. A smaller house than the Teagues', but I know the owner and he's all right. It'll be simple enough."

"Don't call me that," I said quietly.

"What?"

"I'm not a kid."

"All right," he replied. "I didn't mean anything by it."

"I know you didn't," I told him, reaching out my right hand and placing it on his left leg, close to his crotch, as I moved my face closer to his.

I had expected some sort of reaction—this was, after all, how Arthur and Pascoe liked to begin things with me—but I hadn't expected what happened next. It was as if he'd received an electric shock. He leaped from the seat, knocking over both our drinks and his chair, jumped back, and stared at me wide-eyed.

"What the fuck?" he said.

I stared back at him, confused by his response.

"I really like you, Eli," I said.

"Jesus, Freya," he said, running his hands through his hair and looking around to make sure no one was watching us. "You're just a child. I didn't . . . I wasn't trying to . . ." He looked both frightened and upset. "That's absolutely not what I'm looking for," he told me. "I've just tried to be a friend to you, that's all. Christ, I hope you haven't thought that I . . . that I've been trying to . . ."

He seemed so distraught that I looked away, already bored by him. Clearly, I'd made another mistake. I'd hoped he might take me away from Hannah, from Beth, from the twins. That he might be a father to me, or a dad, or a brother, or a lover. Anything. Someone who would love me. But no. He was just another person who didn't care about me in the slightest.

I stood up and walked toward him as he backed away.

"You can relax," I told him. "You're an old man, you're nothing special, and I have no interest in Beth's cast-offs."

I turned away then. I only saw him once more, at his trial a year later, when I sat at the back of the courtroom and watched him collapse in the dock when the verdict was delivered.

Served him right.

✦   ✦   ✦

I was due to get the train back to Norfolk on Saturday morning, and Beth had promised that we would spend Friday night together, presumably to make up for the fact that we had barely spent any time together since my arrival. She'd seen me at breakfast, and occasionally before I went to bed, but had barely acknowledged my presence outside of that. Even on her days off, she either stayed in bed until the late afternoon, or lay on the sofa watching rubbish TV and sending me to the village to buy food and cigarettes.

Although she promised to take me to the pub with her for dinner, I knew she'd find a reason to cancel. Kitto had been coming to ours, or she'd been going to his, almost every night for the last week and it made me laugh to think that she actually believed he was grooming her to become the mistress of the big house, like some Victorian housemaid who manages to snare the wealthy widowed duke. True to form, she told me that we'd have breakfast together on Saturday instead, giving me four pounds to go to the local burger shop for my dinner and telling me that she wouldn't be home because Mr. Teague was taking her to the pub, the one where she'd supposedly been going to take me, and afterward she'd be spending the night in his house.

I waited until late, long past one o'clock in the morning, when I saw the lights go on, and watched from the safety of the beach as Beth and Kitto returned home. Upstairs, where Arthur and Pascoe slept, remained unfinished, but downstairs was almost completed. They might have been any wealthy couple coming back from a night out together. I made my way closer, past the pit where the swimming pool would never, in fact, be installed, and watched as they stood in the kitchen, opening a bottle of wine and kissing. At one point, he pressed her up against the fridge and his hand disappeared beneath her dress. When he went to the bathroom, I watched as Beth opened cupboards, examining their contents, then looked around the room, taking everything in, probably deluding herself into imagining the changes she would make when she won her upgrade. And I continued to watch when, eventually, the lights went off and they went upstairs to the bedroom.

Another hour passed before I risked entering. It wasn't difficult to get in. Eli had keys to the property, and he'd left them at Beth's when he was dismissed from his dual positions as site foreman and boyfriend. Making my way upstairs, I carefully opened the door to the master bedroom and looked in at Beth and Kitto, who were sleeping side by side, their mouths wide open, looking ugly as they dreamed of wildly different futures. Then I went to the twins' room and stood over them. They were curled up together, Arthur's arms wrapped around Pascoe's naked torso. Leaning down, I placed a gentle kiss on both their foreheads, and they moved only slightly beneath the covers before settling back into place.

Returning downstairs, I went into the garage, where the fuse box was located, along with a dozen cans of paint and various flammable materials. From my pocket, I took out Eli's lighter, holding it in a handkerchief so my fingerprints wouldn't overwrite his, and found a bottle of methylated spirits, which I splashed around the floor. Pulling a few wires from the fuses, I lit one, and it connected quickly, igniting others, before feasting on the flammable liquid on the floor. I stepped away, watching as it burst into life. It was a beautiful sight to behold. With all the work going on in the house, I knew it wouldn't take long for the woodwork to soak up the blaze and spread toward the second floor. They'd never know, any of them. They do say that it's not the house fire that kills people, it's the smoke. All four of them would be dead before their bodies were cremated. They wouldn't feel a thing.

Before returning to the cottage, I made sure to drop the lighter in the grass, somewhere a little hidden but easy enough for the police to find. Eli deserved this. He could have saved me but had chosen not to, so he could take his punishment too.

I slept well that night, even through the sounds of the sirens from outside, which proved a good thing, as the next few days were busy as people sympathized and took care of me. The police asked whether Eli had ever touched me, and I said no, because I knew he'd be going to jail for the rest of his life anyway so didn't feel the need to add to his charges. Soon I was taken back to Norfolk, and back to Hannah, and we lived together till I was eighteen. During those years I devoted myself to my schoolwork because I knew the only way out was to win a scholarship, which, in time, I did. I'm pretty sure I said goodbye on the morning I left. And that was that. I was gone.

She's probably still alive, somewhere. After all, she'll only be in her sixties. But Beth is gone. And Kitto Teague is gone.

And most importantly, Arthur and Pascoe, those two malevolent fourteen-year-olds, never made it to fifteen, and never got to hurt anyone again.

14

The resolution to what I have come to think of as my Middlemarch problem arrives more easily than I expected.

George texts me on Sunday following Louise's retirement party, demanding sex, as usual. I tell him it won't be possible, that I have a complicated surgery scheduled for the following morning. A four-year-old child whose legs were badly burned when a deep-fat fryer fell on him from a kitchen counter. (Which is actually true.) He grumbles a bit but, showing a little decency at last, accepts this.

He messages again the following evening. I ignore his text and set my alarm for the fairly random time of 1:13 a.m., at which point I briefly wake and send an already-typed reply to explain that I've been in the hospital all night and didn't have my phone with me, but that I'm longing for him and want to see him soon.

On Tuesday afternoon, he tells me that he wants to come over at seven o'clock, but once again I don't reply. I have a plan in place, but I need to wait until Wednesday, which is always the quietest night at work.

Annoyed by my silence, he texts later to say that, as much as he'd like to hook up with me later in the week, he won't be able to, because there's a girl called Holly in his year and they're going to a film together, and he'll probably fuck her afterward, so I've missed out, and I'm going to spend every day for the rest of my life regretting that I lost him, but I have no one to blame but myself.

I don't reply.

Thirty-four minutes later, he texts to tell me that Holly doesn't exist, that he made her up, that he loves me and only me, and that eleven months from now, when he turns sixteen, we can get married, and that he'll do anything I ask of him if we can just meet up.

I don't reply.

Seventeen minutes later he texts to tell me that he's going to report me to the police for having sex with him when he was underage. He's planning on taking me to court and making sure that I'm sent to prison, then suing me for ten million pounds for emotional distress.

I don't reply.

Eight minutes later, he sends me a dick pic.

I don't reply.

Fourteen minutes later, he tells me that he's really sorry for everything he's said so far, it's just that he knows that he and I are meant to be together, like in that film *Romeo and Juliet*.

I don't reply.

Two minutes later, he tells me to go fuck myself.

I don't reply.

Eighteen minutes later, he tells me that the only reason he fucked me was because he felt sorry for me.

I don't reply.

Thirty seconds later, he tells me I'm a prick-tease.

I don't reply.

Seven minutes later, he tells me that a teacher in school called Miss Woods blew him in the art room during first break.

I don't reply.

Eleven minutes later, he sends me a video holding the second and third fingers of his right hand in front of his mouth, his tongue pushing through.

I don't reply.

Four minutes later, he tells me he's going to tell his dad everything.

I don't reply.

Twelve minutes later, he sends me a link to a YouTube video of Billie Eilish singing "Bad Guy" and says this is his favorite song of all time.

I don't reply.

Six minutes later, he asks whether I've watched the latest season of *The Summer I Turned Pretty*.

I don't reply.

Nine minutes later, he says he's always wanted to go to Venice and maybe we can go there over the summer.

I don't reply.

Twenty-one minutes later, he tells me that I'm a pedophile and I should be castrated, which is too baffling a suggestion to even consider replying to.

Six minutes later, he tells me that he's never loved anyone as much as he loves me.

I don't reply.

Thirty seconds later, he tells me that I'm an incredible person and I should stop running. (I have no idea what I'm supposedly running from.)

I don't reply.

Five minutes later, he tells me that if I don't call him, he's going to take a taxi to the American embassy, then run as fast as he can toward the guards standing outside holding his PlayStation controller in his hands, and they'll be so freaked out that they'll probably shoot him dead.

I don't reply.

Nine minutes later, he sends me a video of a dog whose master has come back from serving in Afghanistan and the dog goes completely crazy when he sees him. **I love dogs but I don't have one,** he tells me.

I don't reply.

Four minutes later, he says he's about to take a piss and can we Face-Time while he does it.

I don't reply.

Eight minutes later, he tells me he's going into the hospital tomorrow to report me.

I don't reply.

Twenty minutes later, he says he's just ordered a Deliveroo. Chicken nuggets, cheese-loaded chips, and a Sprite.

I don't reply.

Nine minutes later, he tells me he's been watching Joe Fazer videos online and do I think he should work out more and build bigger muscles like Joe, who, he tells me, is inspirational.

I don't reply.

Fifteen minutes later, he tells me that if I was with him right now, he would strangle me with his bare hands.

I don't reply.

Twenty seconds later, he tells me that when he kills me, it will be painful, it will be with a knife, that he'll stab me slowly, repeatedly, pushing the knife in and out of different parts of my body, and he'll get away with it too, because he's too clever to get caught.

I don't reply.

Four minutes later, he asks me which female movie star I'd fuck if I had the chance.

I don't reply.

Seven minutes later, he says that if it was the other way round, he'd fuck Penn Badgley.

I don't reply.

Nine minutes later, he tells me that he was only joking, he's not gay.

I don't reply.

Twelve minutes later, he tells me that he doesn't mean there's anything wrong with being gay, that one of his best friends has already come out and he's cool with it, but it's not something he'd be into himself.

I don't reply.

Eight minutes later, he tells me he's thinking of reading *The Mill on the Floss*, so he'll have something to talk about when people mention his name.

I don't reply.

Six minutes later, he says he's stoned.

I don't reply.

Two minutes later, he tells me that he's not stoned at all, that he was just making that up to impress me. He asks whether I remember him refusing my offer of a cigarette on that "incredible" day when we first met.

I don't reply.

Seven minutes later, he tells me that he thinks there's something wrong with him because he's never not horny.

I don't reply.

One minute later, he tells me that I'm a cunt.

I don't reply.

Eighteen minutes later, he tells me that I mean absolutely nothing to him, that he's had a lot better.

I don't reply.

Three minutes later, he asks what's it like to be a frigid bitch.

I don't reply.

Four minutes later, he tells me that I'm obviously a lesbian.

I don't reply.

Eight minutes later, he says that he's thinking of getting a tattoo of my name on his arm.

I don't reply.

Ten seconds later, he asks can he come over.

I don't reply.

One minute later, he tells me that if I don't answer his call, he's going to phone the *Daily Mail* and tell them how he was sexually abused by an old woman.

I don't reply.

Seven minutes later, he sends me a photo of a ham, cheese, and onion toastie he's just made. **Just call me Gordon Ramsay!** he adds.

I don't reply.

Eleven minutes later, he tells me he's thinking of signing up for the army when he turns sixteen, even though his dad wants him to take his A-levels and then go on to uni.

I don't reply.

Four minutes later, he asks me what the fuck are the royal family all about? Like, it's 2024.

I don't reply.

Two minutes later, he asks me whether it's difficult being so fat and ugly.

I don't reply.

Nine minutes later, he says that in his film studies class in school they're watching *Death in Venice* and have I seen it? It's, like, a hundred years old, he tells me, but it's pretty good. Last week, they watched *Chinatown*, which he says was fucked up. He's not sure, but he thinks the dad had sex with the daughter, but it was too confusing and there were no action scenes other than when some little French guy slit the main guy's nose open with a knife. You're a very nosey fellow, kitty-cat, the French guy said. That's how I think of you, Freya. My kitty-cat.

I don't reply.

Thirteen minutes later, he says he feels sorry for my patients because I must be the worst doctor in the history of the universe and anyone I treat will probably die.

I don't reply.

Two minutes later, he tells me I have cellulite all over my face.

I don't reply, but at least this makes me laugh.

Eight minutes later, he says he's going to sleep, that he's tired, but that he loves me.

I don't reply.

One minute later, he texts:

Talk tomorrow, luv ya sexy x

I don't reply.

When the night of the long texts finally comes to an end, I realize I have no choice. I can't allow this to continue any longer.

They say that the easiest way to hide something is to do it in plain sight. Which is what I do. The following evening, I message to apologize for not responding to any of his messages, telling him I had an emergency surgery, turned my phone off, and just fell into bed exhausted when I got home. I feel the same way, I tell him. That the age difference between us doesn't matter. That he's the best lover I've ever had. That when I look to the future, all I see is me and him together. That I only want to be with him. And then, finally, I tell him that I want him to come to my flat at nine o'clock tonight and that I'll make it up to him for keeping him waiting so long.

He replies with a series of indecipherable emojis that I don't have the energy to translate into English, but I assume they mean he's pleased by my suggestion, then throw my phone on the sofa, make some pasta, listen to some music, do some prep for an operation coming up three days later, and wait for him to arrive.

"Hi, bae," he says when I open the front door, and it takes every ounce of my willpower not to rip his throat out right then.

"Beer?" I ask.

"I'm not in the mood for a beer," he says. "Do you have any Jack Daniel's?"

"Sure," I say.

"I'd, like, literally kill for a JD," he says.

I try not to laugh at his utter absurdity and make my way toward the kitchen.

"How do you like it?" I shout, as if he's a whiskey connoisseur.

"On the rocks," he says, and I wonder does he even know what that means. I pour a healthy measure into the glass, add some ice, then a substantial amount of the oxycodone and morphine I lifted from the hospital's dispensary earlier, before bringing it out to him.

"I'm sorry about all those messages," he says, looking a little embarrassed. "I was just . . . having a bad night, that's all."

"Don't worry about it," I say, smiling. "I was flattered. They made me realize how much you like me."

"I don't just *like* you," he says, and I notice that he's sipping his whiskey in tiny amounts so he doesn't have to actually taste any of it. I need him to actually drink it. "I *love* you, Freya."

"And I love you, George," I say. He beams.

"We're really going to make this happen, aren't we?" he asks.

"Absolutely," I say. "It's time to tell people. Your dad. Your mum. Your friends. Everyone."

"They're gonna lose their fucking minds," he says.

He tries for another sip of his Jack Daniel's, but he's losing the battle.

"Oh wait," I say, standing up. "I forgot the Coke."

"What?"

"No one drinks Jack Daniel's straight," I tell him. "You need some Coke in it."

I reach out to take his glass, and he nods. "Yeah, I didn't wanna say," he replies, looking relieved.

I go to the kitchen and open the fridge, where my trusty cans of Coke are waiting for me, and pour a decent amount into his glass.

When I hand it back to him, he sips it cautiously, but the Coke overpowers the taste of both the whiskey and the opioids, and he makes much better progress now.

It only takes about thirty minutes before he starts to have difficulty breathing and then, as I watch, he falls to the ground and suffers a stroke. I do a little work on my laptop, answering a few emails and updating some events on my calendar as he stares at me in terror. His eyes are focused on mine, consumed by fear, but I do nothing to help him. As it happens, I become so involved with the case studies I'm reading that I don't even notice when he dies.

A doctor wearing a white coat and carrying the appropriate lanyard can get through any door in the hospital. I've worked there for years. I know where the CCTV cameras are and where they're not. I know the circuitous if rather convoluted journey I can take to wheel a gurney from the loading bay into one of the service elevators and bring it to the morgue, where there are thirty cold lockers, only half of which are ever occupied, without fear of my actions being recorded.

When George's body is eventually discovered, no one will have the slightest clue who he is or how he got there.

When I get home, I scrub the flat clean of his presence and have a drink myself, finishing the bottle of whiskey. This whole experience, coupled with what happened with Rufus, has forced me to rethink my lifestyle completely. *How many boys' lives have I ruined, anyway? A hundred? Two hundred? That's probably enough.*

Maybe it's time to stop.

15

Since my twelfth summer, I have been consumed by fire, laying waste to everything and everyone around me. Today, when I wake, things feel different. Enough has happened. Too many risks have been taken. It's time to quench the flames forever and find some form of peace.

I've taken a week's holiday, and it feels strange to return to the hospital and for Louise not to be there. Her replacement is a nurse around my own age, Michael, who I don't know terribly well but with whom I've never had any issues, so I resolve to stay positive in the hope that we can build a relationship as strong as the one that she and I enjoyed. He's waiting for me when I exit the staircase on the sixth floor, today's files in his hands.

"Good morning, Dr. Petrus," he says, offering something that resembles a slight bow. There's no coffee or KitKat, but I can train him on this.

"Good morning, Michael," I say. "And welcome to your first day in your new role."

He smiles and acknowledges this, holding the files out for me.

"In future," I tell him, "you can just give these to Aaron or whatever intern I'm lumbered with at the time. My preference is that they're laid out on my desk when I arrive every day."

"Of course," he says. "And just so I know, how much longer will Dr. Umber be on rotation with you?"

"Two more weeks, I think. After that, I'll be running solo for a few months before they inflict someone else on me."

I take the files and head down the corridor toward my office. Once inside, I place them on my desk and turn on the computer, feeling a sense of calm. George's body was discovered in the morgue early last week, and, as expected, no one has been able to figure out how it got there, although his father had reported him missing to the police. They eventually put two and two together, and he was identified by his mother that same evening. An investigation has been launched, but everyone is completely baffled as to what took place. Naturally, I'm steering clear of it all, and I'm certain there's nothing that can trace him back to me. I wiped his phone back to factory settings before removing the SIM card, then incinerated both. One last fire.

As for Rufus, well, he's survived much longer than I expected. In fact, rather annoyingly, he's still alive. However, there's no brain activity and the hospital wants to turn his life support off, but his mother is fighting this, unable to accept that her son is, in real terms, already dead. Apparently, she's hired a lawyer to ensure that the boy's machine is kept on.

It's late afternoon and I'm checking on one of my postoperative patients when Aaron appears at the door to the ward. He's been absent all morning, which is unlike him, but I've grown more tolerant of his presence these days and decide not to reproach him. Instead, I offer him that very rare thing—a smile—although he doesn't reciprocate.

"Dr. Petrus," he says. "I wonder could we talk privately? In your office?"

I'm a little surprised by his tone, which is rather serious, but I nod and tell him of course, that he can go there now if he wants, and I'll follow in a moment. I watch as he makes his way down the corridor, and I go to the bottled-water machine for something to drink. I have a strange premonition that the conversation ahead of us will be an uncomfortable one.

I wait a few minutes before following him and, once inside, I'm surprised to find him standing by the window, staring out, which seems rather audacious instead of sitting opposite my desk. I have to press past him to get to my own chair, and he's almost surly as he steps away. I point to the chair and, almost reluctantly, he sits.

"So," I say, glancing toward my computer screen and moving the mouse to make it seem like I'm simply too busy to give him my full attention. "You wanted to talk?"

"Yes," he says. "You know I only have two weeks left, right?"

"I do. I hope your time here has proved interesting and educational?"

"It has." He pauses for a moment. "You're a very fine doctor."

I acknowledge this with a slight nod of my head. "Thank you," I say.

"I mean it," he continues. "Probably the best I've worked with on any of my rotations. You're efficient, quick to diagnose, although you don't rush to judgment. You show great compassion toward your patients. It's one of the things that I find so contradictory about you, Freya. You're quite a complex individual, really, aren't you?"

I frown. Am I? Perhaps I am. But I don't really have any interest in a character analysis from him. I choose not to react to his use of my first name at work.

"We all are, I suppose," I reply. "Is this what you wanted to talk to me about, Aaron? I mean, I appreciate your kind words, but—"

"No, I wanted to talk to you about the Rozelli Programme."

I sit back in surprise. This is the last thing I expected.

"Oh, right," I say. "If you're going to tell me that my talk in your school is what made you interested in becoming a doctor, then you've told me that already."

"No, it's not that," he says, shaking his head.

"You want to take part in the program? I can certainly put you in touch with the facilitator. But, to be honest, they usually want people a little more advanced in their careers. Although I don't particularly see why that has to be the case. I'm sure you could—"

"I don't want to take part in it," he says. "I was a student on it, remember?"

"Yes," I say, growing weary now. "Look, Aaron, what's all this about?"

"You came to our school. You made medicine sound like a vocation."

"It is a vocation," I reply.

"You said that everyday doctors and nurses save lives. That it's the most important job in the world."

"I still think that."

"I was very, very shy back then, but I was so inspired by the things you said that I plucked up all my courage to talk to you afterward. You were kind to me. Encouraging." He takes a deep breath, as if he's been holding this in for a long time. "I was only fourteen years old at the time."

I stare at him. Something stirs inside me, and I feel a slight pain in the pit of my stomach. From the day he arrived, I knew there was something I didn't like about him, something that made me deeply uncomfortable in his presence, but I could never quite put my finger on what it was.

"Do you remember the night we went for a drink together?" he continues. "At one point, I started laughing. Because of the song that was playing."

"I have no idea what you're talking about," I say.

"'You don't remember me, do you?'" he sings quietly in a rather tuneful voice.

"I'm glad I was helpful to you," I say.

"Oh, you were the polar opposite of helpful," he says.

I look down at my desk. The screen saver on my computer screen has kicked in and, as it always does, a random word from the dictionary, with its definition, is scrolling across the screen.

Element : One of the four basic building blocks of matter.

"I don't know why you're telling me all this," I say, and he shakes his head.

"Yes, you do," he replies. "I can see from the expression on your face that you do. Please don't play the innocent. It's sort of pathetic."

"I don't know what you think you remember," I say, and he raises a hand to silence me. For the first time since his arrival in the hospital, I obey him without question.

"I remember everything," he says. "Every minute of that evening. How you told me that you had some textbooks that were suitable for boys my age who were interested in a career in medicine. You offered to loan them to me. I was so excited. You said they were back in your flat, but you could drive me there and lend them to me."

"Just stop," I say.

"It all seemed fine. Exciting, even. You were treating me like an adult. And you were so hot." He laughs a little. "I mean, you still are."

"Aaron."

"But then we got to your flat and there were no textbooks, were there? You gave me a can of Coke. Do you remember that? And when I opened it, it exploded all over me. I was soaked. You made me get undressed. You said you'd wash my T-shirt. The next thing I knew, I was in your bed."

What does he want from me? Money? That can be arranged.

"Did you object?" I ask coolly. "Or did you enjoy it?"

He pauses and considers this.

"I enjoyed it in the moment," he tells me. "But then I was just a child. Only fourteen. It didn't take long for me to feel that I'd done something wrong. Something I wasn't ready for. Within a few months, I'd changed completely. I felt I'd lost something I wasn't ready to lose. And I don't mean the obvious. I mean something far deeper. My innocence, I suppose. My childhood."

He takes a long, deep breath, as if he's been waiting a long time to say this phrase, which, I suppose, he has.

"You raped me, Freya."

A mixture of fear and horror runs through my body when he uses this word.

"Don't be so melodramatic," I tell him. "It's obscene that you would use that word for something in which you were entirely complicit."

"I don't know if you care about this or not, but I wasn't able to have a normal relationship for years. Even now, with Rebecca, things aren't quite as they should be. Sexually, I mean. Because of you. Because of what you did to me. The funny thing is, I still wanted to be a doctor," he continues, looking toward the window. "So I went to university, studied medicine and, in time, tracked you down. I wanted to learn more about you. To see you in action. To understand what kind of person would do something like that to a child. Before I—"

"Before you what?"

"Before I go to the police."

There's a lengthy silence. But I'm not ready to concede just yet.

"And you honestly think they'll believe you?" I ask.

"Who knows? But they'll be obliged to investigate it. I told my best friend at the time. And we've talked about it on and off over the years. He's willing to give evidence. I think you know him, actually."

"How would I know your best friend?" I ask, utterly baffled by this.

"And I can't have been the only person you did it to, can I? There must be others. I assume the police have some way of exploring that. Once they start, who knows how many will come out of the woodwork."

"You have no idea what they did to me," I say.

"Who?" he asks, frowning. "What who did to you?"

"The twins."

He stares at me blankly.

"Do you want money?" I ask, knowing what his answer will be.

"Christ, no," he says. "I don't want a penny from you. That's kind of insulting, actually."

"Why did you wait?" I ask him. "You've been working here for months now. Why did you wait so long?"

"I wanted to get to know you a little," he tells me. "To be honest, I only intended working with you for a week or two. But then there was Louise. I could see how close you were, and she was retiring soon anyway. I thought I'd see the internship through until she was gone." He sighs, as if years of pain have come to an end, slaps his hands down on his knees, offers a half smile, and stands up. "Anyway. There we are."

"Sit down," I snap. For the first time since he arrived at the hospital, I don't want him to go away.

"No," he says calmly. "I've said all I needed to say. It's time now."

"Time for what?"

"To report you. First to the authorities here in the hospital. Then to the police. I've already made an appointment. I imagine they'll be in touch." He glances at his watch and, to my surprise, simply leaves my office without another word.

I stare at the closed door, trying to figure out what to do next. In a moment, I'm on my feet, running toward it, flinging it open, and am charging down the corridor after him. I pass Michael, who raises an eyebrow in surprise, and see Aaron stepping into the elevator. He turns around and smiles as he sees me rushing toward him.

And that's when I realize that he's not alone in there.

There's another man standing next to him. Someone who, I assume, has been waiting in the corridor throughout our conversation, knowing that today is my day of reckoning.

They're both looking at me.

I'm ready to give up my fear of enclosed spaces. There are bigger things to be frightened of. I charge toward them, ready to rip the doors apart with my bare hands if I have to, if only I can get to talk to them both, to explain, to stop them doing what they're going to do.

But it's too late.

Aaron turns away. He has no interest in ever looking at my face again.

And his best friend, Hugh Winley, places a comforting arm around his shoulder.

As the doors close, he whispers something to him and Aaron nods and smiles again, before exhaling heavily.

I leave the hospital a few minutes later, knowing that I'll never set foot here again. I don't know when the police will show up. Maybe this evening. Maybe tomorrow. But it will be soon, and when the process begins, I know how it will end. Everything will come out. They won't care about what Arthur and Pascoe did to me, they'll say that I'm a grown woman who made my own choices. I'll be struck off. I'll go to jail. Perhaps they'll even trace Rufus or George back to me. If they do, I'll spend the rest of my life behind bars. Maybe I'll suffer the same fate as Evan Keogh, the boy on whose jury I sat. Found mysteriously dead after a supposed suicide but probably the victim of something more sinister.

I consider my choices. I could go straight to the airport and buy a plane ticket, but I don't know which countries have extradition treaties with the UK and which don't. It would probably take less than two minutes on the internet to find out, but what's the point? It would just keep all of this going and, honestly, I'm so tired.

I could kill myself. I've thought about that before but know that I don't have the courage to do what needs to be done.

I could get disgustingly drunk and, for a few hours at least, I might feel happy, before the nightmare begins.

I glance at my watch. It's just gone three thirty. I get in my car and drive ten minutes south, in the direction of a local school that gets out around now. I slow down when I see the boys making their way home and wait until I find a suitable one, walking alone, young, vulnerable, and innocent.

I slow down.

I pull over.

He's moving closer and closer, almost in sight now.

I close my eyes and take a deep breath.

I think of Arthur and Pascoe, who raped me and buried me alive.

I think of Aaron, Rufus, George, and all the other boys I've taken home with me over the years.

My finger hovers over the button that will lower the window on the passenger side. I wait until the boy is almost parallel with my car.

Only then do I make my decision.

AIR

1

In an ideal world, I would be spending my fortieth birthday in a bar overlooking Bondi Beach, a beer in my left hand, a woman I love by my right, while friends tease me about my receding hairline. Instead, I'm standing near Gate 10 in Sydney Airport, preparing for twenty hours in the air with only a recalcitrant teenage boy for company. But who among us lives in an ideal world?

Granted, it's early in the morning, but I'm disproportionately irritated when I emerge from the gents to find that Emmet is not seated where I left him, his bright yellow backpack abandoned on a chair next to my own. I look around, my gaze darting between sleepy-eyed passengers, cleaning staff, and airline crew, all making their way through the concourse.

It's not the first time I've lost my son. When he was five, I let go of his hand for a moment in David Jones on Castlereagh Street, and it was almost thirty minutes before I found him again, sitting in a corner of kitchenware, with the patience of an obedient puppy, his cheeks streaked with tears but hopeful that his master will return for him sooner or later. Most parents are at their most protective when their children are infants but I'm the opposite, having become increasingly vigilant since he turned fourteen a few months ago. I can't help myself. I know the dangers out there for boys his age.

A woman stops before me, probably noticing the uneasy expression on my face. "Are you all right?" she asks.

"It's my son," I tell her. "I told him to wait for me but—"

"I thought it was something like that. Look, I'm not on duty, I'm catching a flight, but I'm a police officer and can help if you like. When did you last see him?"

"Just a few minutes ago. I went to the bathroom and—"

"How old is he?"

When I tell her, she studies me with a mixture of incredulity and pity.

"Oh, for Christ's sake," she says. "I thought you meant a toddler. He'll be around here somewhere. You can't lose teenagers, as much as we might want to sometimes."

A moment later he appears from behind me. He must have followed me into the bathroom and used one of the cubicles.

"What?" he asks when I glare at him.

"This is him?" the woman asks, and I nod.

"Yes."

"Then I'll leave you to it," she says, walking away.

"I didn't know where you were," I tell him when she's out of earshot.

"I needed to go," he says slowly, as if speaking to someone of limited intelligence, a tone he's increasingly adopted with me in recent times.

"I asked you to wait with the bags."

He rolls his eyes. If this gesture was ever to become an Olympic sport, he'd be Australia's number one hope.

"Can I get some chocolate?" he asks. "I didn't have any breakfast."

"You said you weren't hungry."

"Because you got me out of bed at three in the morning. Of course I wasn't hungry."

I made sure we had everything packed by yesterday afternoon so there would be nothing for either of us to do but take quick showers when our alarms went off, but the taxi still picked us up from North Bondi at three thirty. Neither of us uttered a word on the way to the airport, Emmet wearing completely superfluous sunglasses along with the AirPods that have become my mortal enemy. But it's important not to get the day off to a bad start. We're going to be in each other's company for an extended period and if we're going to survive this trip without killing each other, then it's down to me, as the adult, to adapt to my son's mood swings.

"An apple might be better," I suggest, knowing exactly how this will be received. "Or maybe we could find some ham and cheese croissants."

"Nah. Chocolate. I need some for the plane too."

"Fine," I say, leading him toward a Relay, where he loses himself before a wall of processed sugar. He's always had a sweet tooth but never seems to put a pound on. If I ate half the trash that he does, they'd have to wheel me home. I watch him from behind, his bare legs bronzed and slender from spending so much time at the beach, and recall when my own body was as slim and athletic as his. I'm still pretty fit, for my age, even if the belt buckle is starting to loosen by a notch. I run and I surf, although Damian—Emmet's closest friend—recently said that what I do isn't surfing at all, it's controlled drowning, which set them both off in near hysterics of laughter. That said, Emmet isn't as tall as I was at that age and, at only five foot seven, remains shorter than most of his friends. Although he'd never articulate it, I suspect he's hoping for a growth spurt soon. He recently bought some dumbbells, trying to add some muscle to his lean frame, and he's started buying enormous tubs of protein powder that he's adding to his morning milkshakes.

I make my way toward the magazines, where I pick up a copy of *GQ*, a crossword book, and the *Sydney Morning Herald*, scanning the headlines quickly. Turning away, my eyes land on a table holding a selection of the latest fiction, and at its center is a pile of the new novel by Furia Flyte. A miniature cardboard cut-out of the author is propped up, showing her with her head turned coquettishly to the left, an enigmatic smile on her face. She's dressed entirely in white, which only accentuates the blackness of her skin, and her arms are wrapped around her body. Something in the pose seems a little strained, as if she's uncomfortable connecting her beauty to her work but has been convinced to do so.

"It only happens with women," she told me once, when I quizzed her about the machinations of the publishing industry.

"Maybe because all the men are ugly," I suggested, and she shook her head, listing four or five male novelists who she considered handsome, none of whom I had ever heard of but who I looked up online afterward to see what they wore, how they styled their hair, how they presented themselves to the world, looking for tips as to how to model myself on them so that she might fall for me as I fell for her. Studying their author pictures, and the pained expressions on their faces as they stared into the middle distance, looking for all the world as if someone had asked them to explain Fermat's Last Theorem, they seemed more constipated than anything else.

Being confronted by her image now, however, feels like a punch to the guts, a complicated blend of lingering desire and anger. Since its publication, I've done all I can to avoid Furia's book—her fourth— which hasn't been easy, as it's been heavily promoted. Her picture has appeared on the front page of weekend supplements and, driving into work, I've occasionally been forced to turn off the radio when she's been announced as a guest. I haven't even set foot in a Dymocks store since Christmas for fear of being confronted by it and, while I've never been a big reader, I usually have a thriller on the go. But some masochistic urge forces me to pick it up now and read the blurb on the back. I already know the basic story, which concerns the relationship between an indigenous female drover in nineteenth-century Western Australia, a traveling magician, and the magician's wife, and I grit my teeth as I read the synopsis. I can't bring myself to turn to the dedication or acknowledgments pages so return it to the pile. Just as I do, a woman's hand reaches out to lift it.

"You haven't lost him again, I hope?" she asks, and I realize it's the policewoman from earlier.

"No," I say, nodding across the shop, but Emmet's pulled another disappearing trick, causing me a fresh burst of irritation. "Oh, for fuck's sake," I mutter.

"Perhaps you should keep him on a leash."

"It would make life a lot easier."

"I'm just teasing," she says. "I have one of them at home myself. A teenager, I mean, not a leash. So I know what they're like. Bloody nightmare, most of the time. Sweetest kid on the planet till puberty hit and then, bang, Hannibal Lecter without the charm. I've basically decided to stay out of his way until he turns twenty. Maybe twenty-five."

Looking around, I discover him standing before a display of neck cushions. He's placed one around his neck, and I know that he's going to ask me to buy it for him. Sure enough, he trots my way, holding it out like a peace offering, one that I'm expected to pay for.

"Dad," he says, but I cut him off. There's no way I'm spending eighty dollars on something so pointless.

"No," I say.

"But—"

"Emmet, no. There'll be plenty of pillows on the plane. Those things aren't even comfortable. They just look like they are."

He glances toward the woman and, perhaps because she's present, decides not to make a fuss. He notices the book she's holding, however, and an opportunity for payback presents itself.

"You should buy that," he tells her. "It got great reviews. Well researched. Unreliable narrator. Literally everyone is reading it."

"Literally everyone isn't," I say, making inverted comma symbols in the air, but he saunters away without catching my eye, a self-satisfied smirk spreading across his face as he returns the cushion to where he found it.

"He doesn't seem that bad," she says, turning to me, but I say nothing. It's hard not to admire my son's ability to offer a *fuck you* without actually saying the words.

"No, he's a total charmer," I reply, laughing a little to myself.

Over the Tannoy, I hear an announcement that our flight will begin boarding shortly and make my way toward the till, paying for more chocolate and gelatinous sweets than any human being should consume in a month.

"And these," says Emmet, appearing by my side now and throwing in a party-size bag of Honey Soy Chicken crisps, enough to feed a family of four.

"For fuck's sake," I say. "You do know there'll be food on the plane, right?"

"It's always smart to bring your own supplies."

It's simpler just to buy what he wants. After all, I'm tired. I'm anxious. I'm undertaking a journey that might prove to be an enormous mistake. And yet, despite my early morning crankiness, as we head toward the gate I feel a desperate desire to pull my son into an embrace, to press his body against my own and explain to him how important the next few days will be for both of us. I can't, of course. If I even tried to touch him, he'd push me away in mortification. And this from a boy who once loved nothing more than cuddling up to me while we watched Pixar movies on a Saturday evening; one who would often crawl into my bed in the middle of the night until he was nine or ten, lying in the empty space next to me while he fell back asleep.

The truth is, he wouldn't even be here now if he'd had any choice in the matter, but he's still at an age where I have some semblance of authority over him. He wanted to stay home alone, which was an absolute nonstarter, then tried to persuade me to allow him to bunk with Damian while I was gone. Another no.

So he's here. But under sufferance.

One final drama before we board.

A security guard is standing by the seats we were occupying earlier, staring at our backpacks. For all the fuss I created about Emmet remaining with them, they slipped my mind when we went to the store. The guard, who looks as if he should be studying for his HSC, not in full-time employment, turns to me, and my first thought is that I could help him with his acne if he asked. I'm not a dermatologist, I'm a child psychologist, but I remember enough from my days in medical school to know exactly the treatment that would sort his problem out.

"Are these your bags, sir?" he asks.

"Yes," I say. "Sorry. I went to the bathroom and then my son wanted something from Relay. I should have thought."

The boy glances at Emmet.

"Is this your father?" he asks.

"I've never seen this man before in my life," says Emmet and I roll my eyes.

"Oh for Christ's sake," I say.

"He just came over and started talking to me and—"

"Emmet, shut up."

The guard looks from one of us to the other. He may be young but surely he can see the resemblance between us.

"Fine, he's my dad," says Emmet, chuckling a little, which at least makes me smile. I like to hear him laugh.

"Can I see your passports?" asks the guard, and I take them from my back pocket and hand them across. He takes an eternity to compare the names and photos to us and I'm this close to asking him whether there's a problem but restrain myself, knowing there are few places in the world worse than an airport to create any sort of row. One false move and that's it, you're not only off the plane, you're on a no-fly list for life.

"You know you shouldn't leave bags alone like this?" he asks eventually. "They're a security risk."

"I know," I say. "Sorry. I'm barely awake."

"Do you mind if I take a look inside them?"

He asks the question politely enough, and I want to say yes, I do mind actually, but if I do, he'll probably summon a colleague and before I know it, both Emmet and I will be taken to private rooms to be interviewed separately. Thirty minutes later, our plane will be taxiing down the runway while we're left behind. And we simply cannot miss this flight.

"I don't mind at all," I say, a fake smile plastered across my face, and he studies me for a moment before unzipping my rucksack. There's not much in there. My laptop. A printout of a paper I'm writing for a medical journal. A Lee Child novel. Some breath mints and hand sanitizers. My irritation rises again, however, when he reaches for Emmet's bag. This feels like more of an intrusion—I don't like him invading my son's privacy—but, thankfully, his belongings are even less threatening than my own.

"Just be aware next time," he says, standing up to his full height now. "When bags are just slung around the place, they're a security risk."

"That's what I told my dad," says Emmet. "But he never listens."

"And I'll just check your boarding passes," he says then, and it takes all my strength not to tell him to go fuck himself, but the first-class passengers are starting to board now so I have no choice but to unlock my phone and open the on-screen wallet.

"Aaron Umber," he says, reading my name. "And Emmet Umber," he adds, swiping across. They're perfectly in order so, somewhat reluctantly, he hands them back. "Have a safe flight," he adds in a tone so severe that it comes across more like an order than a pleasantry. As if he'll return to charge us with some crime if we don't.

"Thank you," I say, making my way toward the boarding gate, where the woman behind the desk is now summoning business class passengers forward.

"Sir," says the guard before I can get more than six steps away from him, and I turn around.

"What?" I ask, raising my voice in frustration. Honestly, at this point I've had enough, and my temper is rising. I keep some Valium at home for emergencies and threw a few in my suitcase in case the week ahead proves more difficult than expected. I should have added one in my backpack. "For heaven's sake, what is it now?"

"Haven't you forgotten something?"

I frown, uncertain what he means, then realize that Emmet has returned to the very seat where I originally left him. He's put his AirPods in again and probably isn't even thinking about the time. I bark his name and he jumps up, obedient for once, and follows me. I feel a sense of relief when both our boarding passes scan at the desk without further incident.

As we make our way along the gangway toward the plane itself, it occurs to me that he hasn't wished me a happy birthday yet.

2

Although Emmet has communicated through little more than a series of feral grunts since being dragged from his bed this morning, I can tell that he's impressed by the business class cabin. He's undertaken the Sydney–Dubai return flight annually since Rebecca relocated there a decade ago, but always in economy. Despite working for the airline, which would have arranged an upgrade for her without any difficulty, she insisted that it was wrong to waste such advantages on a child. Let him wait until he can appreciate it, she said, and it didn't seem to be something worth arguing about, particularly as there was always a steward or stewardess assigned to look after him.

Although he's never refused to go, I've been conscious in recent years that he's grown less enthusiastic about these trips. It won't be long before he snubs them entirely, which will be her problem, not mine. It's not the lengthy flight that bothers him; it's the anger he feels toward his mother, a rage that's been smoldering within him for some time now, probably since puberty hit. It doesn't concern me unduly. After all, it's to my advantage that he shows little interest in the world outside of Sydney, where the beach and our home in North Bondi is central to his sense of well-being,

"Nice, right?" I say as we sit down. The cabin is laid out in a 1–2–1 formation, and I've booked a central pair with a privacy barrier that can be raised between us.

"Pretty cool," he admits, offering a small concession to the comfort of our surroundings before ruining the moment by glancing to his left, in the direction of an empty single seat. "Do you think anyone's sitting over there?"

"Why?"

"If no one takes it, could I move?"

I blink, telling myself to take a breath before replying. There are moments when I think there is nothing more difficult in this world than being a parent to a teenage boy.

"But why would you want to?" I ask.

"Because it's better. There's a window."

"How about just enjoying the seat that I booked?"

"I'm just asking."

It pisses me off that even here, in such luxurious accommodation, he'd still prefer to move as far away from me as possible. I'm fairly immune to the sense of entitlement that kids his age have but I do feel that the occasional *thanks, Dad* wouldn't kill him.

"I don't think so," I say. "These planes are all organized through weight distribution. They don't like it when someone changes seats."

"You honestly think something terrible is going to happen because a sixty-five-kilo boy moves across the aisle?"

"Sixty-five kilos?" I ask, trying to suppress a smile. He's fifty-five at most. The look of complete outrage on his face when I say this sends a knife through me, and I regret it immediately, recalling his attempts to bulk up his muscle mass. "It would probably be fine," I say, hoping to salvage the moment. "But wait a bit, yeah? They're still boarding. Someone might take it still."

He nods, accepting this, and we start to settle in, arranging our belongings. I store my backpack, removing my laptop, phone, and book, before examining the menu and small bag of cosmetics that awaits every passenger on their chair. Emmet is doing the same, studying the tiny tubes of moisturizer, deodorant, toothpaste, and lip balm with care. Along with his attempts to grow stronger, he's become increasingly concerned with his skin in recent months, and I've noticed a range of serums and moisturizers making their way along the shelves of his bedroom, a liquid army prepared to repel the advance of pimples, although so far he appears to have been lucky in that his skin remains blemish-free. Next, he picks up the television control and starts scanning through the endless list of films and TV shows on offer, removing a small notebook from his backpack and scribbling down various titles. This is a boy who loves nothing more than a good list, tracking every book he reads, every film or TV show he watches, his daily steps, his weight, even a record of the best waves he catches. Although he's unaware of it, I invaded the privacy of his phone recently and was shocked by what I discovered there—it's one of the things I'm hoping to discuss with him on this trip—but I've never seen inside his laptop and imagine it holds any number of complicated spreadsheets, along with God knows what else. For a time, I wondered whether there was an element of OCD to his relentless list-making, but I think being organized simply calms him, offering him the illusion that he's in control of a life that has, on occasion, been badly disrupted.

"You know there's a shower on this plane, right?" I ask him, and he turns to me with a skeptical expression on his face.

"No way."

"It's true. Up toward the front. Only for the first-class passengers, but still. Can you imagine? Taking a shower in the air?"

He considers this.

"What if there's, like, turbulence? Wouldn't you get thrown around?"

"Maybe the stewardess would come in and save you."

Once again, the words are out of my mouth before I can take them back, and I tell myself that I need to think before speaking over the days ahead. It's a crass comment, after all, sexist and outdated, and he blushes at the idea. At home, even on the hottest days, he never takes his T-shirt off anymore. And yet, at the beach, he's always in just his swimmers. Perhaps there are different rules of conduct by the water.

"There's a bar too," I add, pointing toward the rear of our cabin. "We have access to that, so we can go down there at some point if you like."

He thinks for a moment, as if deciding whether there is something he could object to about this, but, finding nothing, says, "That'd be fun," and I grasp at this small concession. I'd imagined him placing his headphones on his head and either submerging himself in films or sleeping throughout the thirteen hours that lie ahead of us. It's not that we need to be locked into constant conversation, but it would be nice to feel that we're not completely ignoring each other.

"What's going on here?" he asks. "Are we rich suddenly?"

"What?"

"I mean, all of this," he says, looking around. "How come you're splashing out?"

"We're not *rich* rich," I tell him. "But, you know, we're comfortable. And honestly, if we have to spend so long in the air, I thought we might as well do it in style. It's not like you ever ask for anything."

"I didn't ask for this."

"No, but I bet you're glad that I did it."

"Could be worse," he says, returning to his notebook and scribbling something down before flicking through the monitor again. He stops at a miniseries from a few years back about a young Greek swimmer in Melbourne with aspirations toward the Olympic Games, reads the summary carefully, and makes a note of it.

Since childhood, Emmet has been a natural swimmer and, in more recent years, he's also become a skilled surfer. For a time, Rebecca and I called him the Bish: half boy, half fish. At first, she didn't want him anywhere near the beach, didn't even want him to learn how to swim, but I managed to persuade her that this was not just unreasonable but irresponsible. A child simply cannot grow up in Sydney without spending half their lives running in and out of the waves. She of all people should know the dangers that water holds for the uninitiated. Now Emmet knows the waters of Bondi like the back of his hand, could tell you the different currents you might encounter every few feet from Backpackers' Rip to Buckler Point and, along with his friends, has walked from Spit Bridge to Manly a dozen or more times, stopping at every beach along the way for a swim.

For a few years, he made vague references toward the Olympics himself, ambitions that are sadly implausible. He'll never be tall enough, his feet will never be large enough—they remain a stubborn size seven—and he has no more chance of making it to the Games than I have of performing on Broadway. But, to my relief, he hasn't mentioned this in a while, the word *lifeguard* popping up in his vocabulary more frequently of late, an idea that I'm encouraging. Although cautiously, of course; too much enthusiasm on my part will only turn him against it.

A stewardess appears carrying a tray holding glasses of champagne, water, and orange juice. Despite the early hour, I choose the champagne, and she apologizes that, as we're still on terra firma, it can only be Bollinger. Once we take off, she assures me, we'll be switching to Dom Perignon. I try not to laugh and tell her that's fine, I'm happy to slum it in the meantime. On the other side of the aisle, a young man is carrying a second tray, and when Emmet reaches for a glass the steward glances toward me.

"Just an orange juice," I tell Emmet, and he does as he's told with one of his trademark sighs. If any of his lists includes the multitudinous indignities he has to endure as my son, I'm sure this latest one will make it onto it.

Further down the plane, I notice the door to the cockpit open and one of the copilots emerges, stepping into the toilet cubicle toward the front of the cabin. I recognize him immediately as one of Rebecca's colleagues from when we first moved to Sydney all those years ago, and I retreat into my seat a little. I can't imagine him scanning the cabin when he emerges, but if he does, I don't want him to notice me. Whenever our paths crossed in the past we always got along perfectly well, but I know that if we catch each other's eye now, he'll feel obliged to come over and say hello and I'd prefer that he didn't. No one is supposed to know that Emmet and I are here, after all. Thankfully, when he reappears, he makes his way back into the cockpit without so much as a glance in our direction.

The cabin is starting to fill now, and a young woman in her early twenties approaches the empty window seat, the one Emmet had ambitions toward. She has the most extraordinary good looks—I'd be willing to bet that she's a model—and appears to be dressed for a fashion shoot rather than a long-haul flight. My first thought is that while we're living it up in business, she looks aggrieved that she hasn't been upgraded to the private suites of first. A middle-aged man a few seats away jumps up to help her store her hand luggage in the overhead compartment and she thanks him, her oversized sunglasses remaining firmly on her face throughout their interaction. He tries to make small talk, but she dismisses him politely before sitting down and kicking her shoes off. The body-hugging outfit she's wearing is ridiculously short, barely reaching beneath her thighs, and her legs are bare and tanned.

I notice Emmet watching her, and it's not because she's taken the seat he wanted. His tongue is pressed against his upper lip, his eyes are open wide, and I realize in this moment that my son is straight. To date, he's never expressed an interest in either sex to me, but I've always instinctively felt that he might be gay. I was, perhaps, relying on age-old clichés that are probably as insulting as they are redundant, but despite his water-based athleticism, he was always an incredibly sensitive child, eschewing team sports or any games that involved roughness of any sort. Part of a small, tight-knit group of equally delicate boys, he's always seemed happier either in their safe company or on his own, reading books and watching esoteric, foreign-language films. His taste in music too has always tended toward sensitive female singer-songwriters or gender-defying young men. It's strange how a simple, unexpected moment can inform a parent about such an important aspect of their child's life, but the fact that he can't keep his eyes off the woman tells me that I've been incorrect in my assumptions. Is it wrong of me to feel a certain relief? Of course his sexuality wouldn't matter to me in the slightest but the world, life itself, I think, is difficult enough without adding an unnecessary layer of complexity.

I try to imagine him flirting with a girl and find the idea close to preposterous. There were girls in his friendship group when he was younger, but over the last eighteen months, they seem to have peeled away a little, the business of puberty forcing a temporary division of the sexes. I daresay that many of those I knew as children, the ones who ran in and out of our home barefoot and screaming, will reappear in my life in the fullness of time as girlfriends in a year or so. It will be interesting to see how they've changed, and whether one of them will break my son's heart or have her heart broken by him. I think he's incredibly handsome, but then I'm his father, so it's natural that I consider him to be the most beautiful boy in the world. But what if those girls, or others, feel differently? What if his romantic life proves unhappy? The idea of him suffering any sort of pain sends an almost insupportable ache through my body. I want to keep him safe from all of that. In an ideal world, I would keep him young forever, protecting him from all hurt. In that same world, someone would have done that for me. But my training also teaches me that to wrap him in cotton wool will serve only to stifle him and prevent him from growing into the man that he should become. It's a conundrum for me, one that I am struggling to solve.

The model—assuming she is one—perhaps aware that she's being observed, turns around, removes her sunglasses, and fixes her eyes on my son, who turns away quickly, pulling a book from his bag and burying his face within it. He blushes again, a slow surge of scarlet rising from the base of his neck into his cheeks and ears, and he doesn't look left or right in the minutes that follow, ignoring the cabin crew as they collect our empty glasses, not paying attention to the safety demonstration, and keeping his eyes firmly on the page as the plane taxis down the runway to take off.

We have thirteen hours in front of us, after all. And then, after we make our connection, a further seven hours in the air. Then finally, one further journey by train and boat until we reach our destination, where we might be welcomed or rebuffed. There will be plenty of time to talk.

But should I have thought this through more deeply before booking our tickets? Perhaps, but there was so little time to make a decision I could only do what I thought was right. At some point, I'll have to confess to Emmet that the only people who know we are undertaking this journey are he and I.

That we haven't, in fact, been invited.

3

Rebecca and I met in the rather unromantic setting of a chain coffee shop in the heart of England where, due to the lack of available tables, we found ourselves seated across from each other. I couldn't stop myself from glancing at her repeatedly, then looking away before she could notice me and object.

"You keep staring," she said eventually, barely looking up from her laptop, and I recognized the slight tinge of an Irish accent in her voice.

"Sorry," I replied, blushing a little. There was no other way to put it, so I decided to go with the truth. "It's just . . . how shall I put this? You're incredibly beautiful."

Her eyes opened wide, perhaps in surprise that I would say something so unflinchingly intimate, and her hesitation gave me time to make my opening gambit.

"If I can guess your name," I asked, "will you let me buy you a drink?"

She frowned now, cocking her head to one side as if to decide whether I was a normal person or potentially deranged.

"We haven't met before, have we?" she asked, and I shook my head. "But you think you can guess my name."

"I'm absolutely certain of it."

"All right, then," she said, reaching across and offering her hand, which I shook. The skin of her palm was soft, but I could feel slight calluses on her fingertips. I was this close to asking her how long she'd been playing guitar but worried I might start to sound like a would-be Sherlock Holmes. "Deal. And if you get it wrong, what do I get?"

"The question's irrelevant," I told her. "Your name's Rebecca."

She sat back in her chair and stared at me, then looked down at the table, which held a notebook, a pen, and her laptop, but nothing with her name written on it.

"It is," she agreed.

"So there's a pub I like across the way," I told her, smiling. "A deal's a deal, after all. You can't renege."

Ten minutes later we were seated in a quiet booth with drinks before us.

"So are you some kind of magician?" she asked. "Like Harry Potter?"

"Harry wasn't a magician," I said. "He was a wizard. Totally different career path."

"Then how—"

"The Wi-Fi wasn't working in the coffee shop," I explained. "So I connected to a hot spot on my phone. There were only three others available: *Rebecca's iPhone*, *Matt's iPhone*, and *Toby's Android*. And I was pretty sure you weren't Matt or Toby."

"Clever," she said. "I suppose you better tell me your name, then."

"You don't want to guess?"

"You look like a Ryan."

"Is that a compliment?"

"Ryan Reynolds. Ryan Gosling. Ryan Philippe. I mean, it's hardly an insult. It's not like I called you Donald."

"Aaron," I told her, shuddering slightly. "Aaron Umber."

We flirted some more, and when the conversation grew more serious, she told me that she was from Dublin, although she hadn't lived there in a few years, while I confessed that I'd never set foot outside my hometown, except for a brief trip to Edinburgh with my parents when I was twelve. She seemed surprised that I was attending medical school in the same city in which I'd grown up.

"I feel safe here," I explained, a strange admission considering it was only a few miles from where we were sitting that I'd experienced the trauma that had caused me so much damage. "And you? What brought you here?"

"Love," she replied with a shrug. "I followed a boy. It didn't work out. He's backpacking somewhere around South America now, last I heard. He left, I stayed."

"Sorry," I said.

"Don't be. Turns out I feel safe here too."

"And that's important to you?"

"Oh, it's the most important thing in the world."

Somehow, within a few days, we were officially dating. The first girlfriend I had ever had. I fell in love quickly, partly because I felt genuinely happy in her company and partly because I was so sexually inexperienced that I didn't know how to control my feelings. At the time, I was on rotation with Dr. Freya Petrus in the burns unit of the local hospital, and the pressure of working under her, along with witnessing the trauma of patients who had suffered terrible life-changing injuries, was proving pretty stressful. Rebecca's generally calm nature soothed me.

"Are you a good swimmer?" she asked one evening, a question that seemed curiously random to me.

"I'm a terrible swimmer," I admitted. "In pools, I always stay in the shallow end. I need to feel the ground beneath my feet. I've never even been in the sea."

"I'm glad," she said.

"Glad that I've never been in the sea?"

"Glad that you're not a swimmer."

"All right," I said, uncertain why that might be the case.

Which was when she told me about her father, Brendan. About the things he had done, not to her, but to her sister and to others. About the effect this had had on her life and the troubled relationship she bore with her mother ever since the facts of the case had been revealed.

In turn, I told her about Freya. About what took place when I was fourteen. Naturally, these were emotional conversations, but what we didn't do, and what we should have done, was talk about how both these experiences had affected who we were as a couple because, from the start, sex was a problem. In our first six months together, we only made love a few times, deferring to chaste hugs and something—shyness, embarrassment, self-loathing—made us too nervous to discuss the foundations of such inhibition.

During our second year together, we moved to London, where Rebecca continued her training to become a pilot while I qualified as a child psychologist. Conferences and symposia were held regularly around the country, and it was at one of these, in Birmingham, that I found my commitment to her challenged for the first time.

I had gone to a bar with a fellow student, but he'd hooked up with another attendee, leaving me on my own. I had no desire to return to the hotel so remained there, drinking alone. A young woman approached and sat down opposite me, saying that she'd spent the last thirty minutes hoping my name was Justin.

"Why's that?" I asked.

"Because I've been stood up by a guy called Justin," she explained. "A Tinder date. So I've been sitting over there feeling sorry for myself and wishing you were him. Actually, you're better looking anyway."

I didn't quite know what to say. I wasn't used to compliments.

"Have you been stood up too?" she asked.

"Sort of. I was out with a friend, but he met a girl, so he ditched me."

"He just left you on your own?"

"I don't mind."

"Yes, you do. I've been watching you. You look lonely."

"Well, I'm a solitary person for the most part."

"Solitary people bring books with them when they go for a drink. You're empty-handed."

A waitress came over, and this seemed like the moment when we would either say goodbye or decide to have a drink together. She waited expectantly, and torn between reluctance and desire, I asked whether she would like to join me.

Over the next hour she told me stories of her life while asking very little about mine, and I couldn't decide whether this was a relief or simply narcissistic on her part. Her name was Kylie, she said, named for the singer, her parents being obsessive fans who'd met at one of her concerts. She was twenty-four years old and worked as a receptionist at a talent agency that represented well-known actors, writers, and musicians. When she told me the names of some of the people who crossed her path on a daily basis, she did so without any sense that she was name-dropping, speaking of them with neither affection nor contempt and sharing no gossipy stories. She didn't want to stay there forever, she added. She was saving to buy a mobile dog-grooming van in the hope that she would one day own an entire fleet.

"I love dogs," she told me. "So much more than I love people."

"Most people do."

"I have a five-year plan and—"

A startled expression crossed her face, and she turned her head a little to the right, covering it with her hand.

"What's wrong?" I asked.

"It's him," she whispered. "It's Justin."

I glanced across the room and saw a young man standing there, looking around, clearly searching for someone. He appeared harried and sweaty, as if he'd been running. I didn't have much sympathy for him. He was almost an hour late, after all.

"If you want to go," I began, but she shook her head.

"I don't," she said. "He had his chance. And I'm here with you now."

I smiled. Talking to a random girl in a pub excited me. Flirting. Seeing where things might go. The manner in which, once in a while, one of us would reach over to touch the other's hand to emphasize a point we were making, leaving it there for a little longer than necessary, skin touching skin.

"Tell me when he's gone," she said, and I kept an eye on the hapless Justin while trying not to make my interest too obvious. He took his phone from his pocket and started tapping away.

"Quick, put your phone on silent," I told her, and she did so just before it could ring. She ignored it and, throwing his arms in the air as if none of this was his fault, he gave up and left.

"That'll teach him," she said, watching as he departed. "You only get one chance with me."

"I'll bear that in mind. Me, I'm never late for anything. If I'm not exactly where I'm supposed to be when I'm supposed to be there, then the chances are I'm dead."

"That's cheerful," she said, lifting her glass and clinking it against mine.

We spent the next hour chatting about the usual things—books we'd read, movies we'd watched, places we'd like to visit—and then:

"So you probably have a girlfriend, right?" she asked, and I was uncertain how to respond. Yes, I had a girlfriend. A girlfriend of two years. But a girlfriend who never touched me and who I was afraid to touch. I considered saying that my relationship status was complicated but couldn't bear the sound of the cliché.

"There is someone," I admitted cautiously. "But I'm not entirely sure what we are to each other."

"Do you love her?"

No point in lying.

"I do," I said. Because I did.

Beneath the table, her leg stretched out and when her right foot—bare, removed from her high heel—brushed against my calf, I knew that I was powerless. I wanted sex. Not just for the act itself but because I wanted to behave as other men my age behaved. I wanted to feel normal.

We drank some more, then went to another bar. Then to a club, where we danced. I think I surprised her by being quite good at it.

"Not just a pretty face," I told her when she commented on this, enjoying this different version of Aaron that I was creating for her benefit. A confident Aaron. A desirable Aaron. A sexy Aaron.

We kissed, and during that kiss, the song changed, "Can't Get You Out of My Head" pounding insistently through the speakers, everyone on the dance floor bursting into a spontaneous *La La La, La-La-La-La-La*. Kylie pulled away, looking at me in amusement, and asked whether I'd asked the DJ to play it. I insisted that I hadn't, pointing out that I hadn't left her side since we'd arrived. But I had, of course. I'd gone to the bathroom. And I'd requested it on the way back.

We danced some more, kissed some more, and then, at last, I glanced at my watch. Almost three a.m. The club would be closing soon.

"It's late," I said.

"Time for bed."

I nodded, looking around, uncertain what to do. Having missed out on all the rites of passage that train people how to behave in such moments, I felt absurdly anxious. In life, I was seen as a successful, confident young man. But emotionally, I was still a stunted fourteen-year-old boy.

"You can come home with me if you want," she said.

An image of Rebecca came into my mind. My feelings for her were deep and true. I loved her, I wanted her, I longed for her. But without sex, what were we to each other really? And so I gave in. We hailed a taxi. In the back seat, we kissed some more. I was conscious of the driver, who was tactfully ignoring us, probably accustomed to such late-night shenanigans, but didn't like the idea of being observed in such an intimate moment so I pulled back, preferring to look into her eyes and talk quietly, stroking her cheek with my thumb.

When we reached her flat, my excitement was equaled only by my apprehension. I wrapped my arms around her, enjoying the curve of her back beneath my hands. I grew excited by the deep sigh that escaped her lips when I placed my fingers beneath her blouse to stroke her skin. It occurred to me that I had never given Rebecca an orgasm and that for so long all of my own had been self-induced. Another thing we had never spoken of. I was so stirred by Kylie's arousal that I needed to pull back for a moment.

"Are you all right?" she asked.

"Fine," I said. *I'm normal*, I told myself. *I'm normal.*

"You look like a fifteen-year-old who's about to lose his virginity."

Normal. Normal. Normal.

"Slow down," she said when I reached for her again. "Shall we have a drink first? A nightcap?"

"Sure," I said, a little relieved as she made her way toward the kitchen.

"What would you like? I have wine, beer. I might have some whiskey somewhere if—"

"Maybe just a soft drink? I've probably had enough alcohol for one night."

When she came back, she turned off the main light so only a table lamp illuminated the room with its soft glow. "Is a Coke OK?"

I nodded, and she handed the ice-cold can to me. An image of Rebecca ran through my mind, as did the certainty that if I went through with this, I would surely repeat this behavior time and again in the future. I would become a man that I didn't want to be. A liar. A cheat. A serial betrayer. But I felt such strong desire that I was lost.

And then I opened the can.

It must have been shaken somewhere along the way because it immediately exploded, Coke drenching my top.

"Oh shit!" she said. "Sorry!" I put the can down and looked at my shirt, now stained and sticky, pulling it away from my skin.

"I can help you with that," she whispered, reaching forward to undo the buttons, and in that moment, I was taken back nine years, to Freya's apartment, a wide-eyed schoolboy uncertain what to do as she told me that I couldn't possibly go home with my uniform in such a state. That I should take it off and she'd run it through the washer-dryer for me.

Won't take more than an hour, Aaron. In the meantime, you can jump in the shower.

When her fingers touched me, I reared back, stumbling over the side of an armchair.

"Are you all right?" she asked, surprised by my behavior.

"I'm fine," I said, looking around, trying to find the light switch. It was too dark in there. I was frightened. I couldn't breathe. The flat was too small. I needed to get out.

"Where are you going?" she asked, as I grabbed my jacket and lurched toward the door. I fumbled with the lock, and she opened it for me, before stepping back in fear. "I'm sorry," she said. "Did I do something to upset you?"

I shook my head, unable to answer, and ran down the staircase, only glancing back to see her face, bewildered and alarmed.

Not normal.
Broken.
Completely broken.

The following year, on a weekend break to Barcelona, Rebecca and I sat outside a bar off the Ramblas, and I asked her to marry me. I expected her to say no. In retrospect, I think I wanted to provoke her into breaking up with me, for her to recognize that the three years we'd spent together, those wasted sexless years, had been a mistake but one that could be set right if we separated now. After all, we were both still young enough to start over. To my surprise, however, she agreed without hesitation, and that was it, we were engaged.

We celebrated for the rest of the weekend. With alcohol. With good food. With walks and sightseeing and selfies. But physically, with nothing more than the occasional chaste kiss.

I had gone to Spain with the deliberate intention of proposing, convincing myself that things would improve after we made this commitment. Perhaps I wanted to lock her down, so she wouldn't leave me, and I wouldn't be alone. A half-life was all I merited, I told myself. I didn't deserve what came so easily to other men. Who, after all, would want to touch someone as soiled as me?

It would be quite a few years later before the possibility of something more would present itself and I would become overwhelmed by real desire.

Rebecca and I might have met in the most boring place possible, but when I first laid eyes on Furia Flyte, it was in a much more exotic setting.

4

Emmet has cocooned himself into his seat, kicked off his trainers, pulled a blanket over his body, and is lost inside a subtitled French language film. I'm not surprised he's chosen this over the multitude of Hollywood movies available on the in-flight entertainment system. From childhood, he's displayed a quietly intellectual bent, with books and cinema proving almost as important to him as swimming. A poster for Visconti's *Death in Venice* hangs on his bedroom wall at home, while his shelves are filled with a mixture of manga and classics. Only last May I found myself walking along Walsh Bay midafternoon and spotted him emerging from one of the pier theaters during the Writers' Festival, carrying several books in his hands. I felt instinctively that I shouldn't call out to him and waited until he'd disappeared out of sight before crossing the road to see whose session he'd attended. It made me wonder how many other things went on in my son's life that I knew nothing about.

Sensing me looking toward his screen now, he glances over and presses the button to raise the privacy barrier between us. I give him the finger, and as he disappears from sight, it's good to hear him laugh aloud.

I eat, enjoy some more champagne—the Dom now, may the gods be praised—and watch a couple of episodes of an American comedy show. Despite the length of the flights, I've been quite looking forward to my enforced absence from the world, and even though my chair could not be more comfortable, I decide to stretch my legs and make my way toward the bar area. A few seats are available on the left-hand side, and

I settle into one, asking the steward for a beer. When it arrives, I open my laptop; there's a few emails I need to attend to before I can fully put my Sydney life to one side for the week. Most are related to children I work with, follow-ups with clinicians or parents, in one or two cases correspondence with the police or the Children's Court of New South Wales, and I compose each one carefully, consulting my notes, then save the document in that child's file before placing the reply in my outbox. The Wi-Fi works fine up here, but I'd prefer to reread them later for clarity's sake and send them en masse a couple of days hence. I'm lost in thought about a ten-year-old boy who's suffering debilitating nightmares and who I've been treating for five months now, when a woman takes the seat next to mine. I'm barely aware of her at first, but when I look up from my screen, I realize that she's not a complete stranger.

"You're suspiciously alone," she says, and I laugh.

"I swear I haven't lost him," I say, holding up my hands. "He's up there, watching a movie."

The steward, who bears an uncanny resemblance to a young Paul Newman, approaches and she orders a glass of champagne, which arrives quickly, half a strawberry floating at the top. Her eyes follow him as he returns behind the bar.

"Working?" she asks when her attention returns to me. I'm no slouch in the looks department, but Cool Hand Luke has me well beaten.

"Just catching up on a few things," I say, closing my laptop and extending a hand. "I'm Aaron by the way. Aaron Umber."

"Charlotte Billings."

"I'm sorry about earlier," I say. "I might have been a bit snappy in the airport. Early morning and all that."

"You're fine. And I do understand. I'm about to have seven blissful days away from my son while his father looks after him. A little break from his tantrums is just what I need. How about you? How long are you staying in Dubai?"

I tell her that I'm not, that we have a connecting flight there, and when I reveal the reason for our journey, she says all the right things but asks no further questions.

"You said you're a policewoman?" I ask.

"A detective, actually."

"Impressive."

"And you?"

"A psychologist. I work with children."

"That probably comes in helpful with . . . sorry, what's your son's name?"

"Emmet. We named him for his aunt Emma."

"Your sister?"

"His mother's."

"They must be close."

I choose not to tell her that not only did my son never meet his aunt, he wasn't even aware of her existence until recently.

"I try to avoid analyzing him," I continue. "He doesn't like it when I do."

"Well, at least he's a reader. That speaks well of him."

I frown. "How do you know he's a reader?"

"He told me about the Furia Flyte novel, remember?"

"Oh yes."

"Actually, I've read a couple of chapters since boarding," she continues. "He wasn't wrong. It's very well written. And the story's interesting. I've never known much about drovers."

I nod but remain silent.

"Have you read it?" she asks.

"No," I say, shaking my head. "I'm not a big reader, if I'm honest. The occasional thriller if I want a bit of escapism."

"You should give it a try. There's this interesting detail about how—"

"No spoilers," I say, feigning a smile and hoping that she'll let the subject drop. The last thing I want to talk about is Furia.

"Fair enough. Still, it's always good to see boys that age reading, isn't it?"

She catches Butch Cassidy's eye and points toward both our glasses, which are almost empty. It's not long before they're refilled. "Billy— that's my son—he wouldn't know one end of a book from the other. It's all football and cricket with him. And now, of course, girls have entered the equation, so that's made life even more delightful."

She waves a hand in the air, as if she wishes she could simply magic all her son's interests away and return him to childhood.

"How old is he?" I ask.

"Fifteen."

"Then it's only natural."

"Oh God, I know. And it's not as if I wasn't expecting it. I was no saint at that age myself, so it's not like I have a leg to stand on. But things seemed simpler when we were growing up, didn't they? More innocent. On the rare occasions Billy graces me with his company these days, he just sits there tapping away at his phone with an expression on his face that makes me wonder what the hell kind of messages he's getting."

I understand that concern. It's something I've been dealing with increasingly in recent years with my patients. I've had more than one child sitting in my consulting room, tears rolling down their cheeks as they've told me how they're being excluded from chat groups or private accounts. A single negative emoji placed beneath one girl's beach photo left her so upset that she refused to attend school for a month. A sixteen-year-old boy whose friend request on Instagram had been ignored for two weeks had become withdrawn and sullen. It's a subject that's been preying on my mind lately as it relates to a problematic issue that Emmet and I need to discuss.

Two weeks ago, while we were watching TV together, Emmet stood up to use the bathroom. He left his phone on the sofa next to me, and despite every fiber of my being telling me not to, I lifted it and scanned quickly through his messages. They were mostly indecipherable, written in some form of English that must have made sense to him and his friends but was like Greek to me. I was about to put it back when it occurred to me to check his photos. They were mostly pictures of Bondi Beach, a few of his friend Damian surfing, but as I scrolled further back, I found something that made my stomach sink.

Three semi-naked photos.

None, thankfully, featuring his face but I knew his torso well enough to recognize that they were of him, the shots starting at his lower lip and ending with a view of his pubic hair. Who were they taken for, I wondered? A girl he was talking to? A boy? Or someone else? An adult who had contacted him through a chatroom or an app, masquerading as a teenager? When I heard the toilet flush, I had no choice but to return the phone to where he'd left it, but those pictures have haunted me ever since, and despite my training, I haven't found a way to talk to him about them. The invasion of his privacy would understandably incense him. So I've been forced to remain silent even though, every time he lifts his phone in my company, I wonder about the messages he might be sending or receiving.

"Sometimes I think having a daughter would have been easier," Charlotte continues, and I snap back to the moment. "But then you're faced with other problems, aren't you? Girls are so much more vulnerable than boys."

"You think?" I ask, dubious about this.

"Oh, I know," she replies. "Remember, I was one once, so I know what it's like. The sheer impossibility of getting through the day without suffering some form of harassment. Seriously, from the age of about twelve. That's when it starts. Then every minute you're out in public, in a bar, wherever, it just goes on and on. I'm forty-two now and I'm still not out the other side of it. Twenty years in the New South Wales police has given me the skin of a rhino, but it pisses me off."

"Things can be difficult for boys too," I suggest.

"The poor lambs," she says, unconvinced.

"They can," I insist.

"Look, I'm sure there are some who face similar difficulties, but I don't think the two can be compared." She raises her voice at the barman, who jumps slightly—ironically, he's been scrolling on his own phone, which I imagine is against airline policy—and orders two more drinks without asking me.

"I should slow down," I say. "I don't want to get dehydrated."

"Oh, come on," she replies, placing a hand on mine and squeezing it. "You're on holiday."

"Well, I'm not," I remind her, pulling it away. I hate people touching me without asking. Or huggers. They're the worst.

"Oh yeah. Sorry. I forgot. But still. I hate drinking alone. Actually, who am I kidding, I love drinking alone, but we're, what, thirty-five thousand feet up in the air? Might as well be sociable."

The steward brings the drinks, and as he puts them down before us, she gives him an unsettling pat on the thigh. "Thanks, darl," she says, and I notice his jaw clench a little as he steps away. He doesn't appreciate her touch either, hasn't asked for it, doesn't want it.

"I mean, if we are, in fact, that high," she says. "I don't really know."

"37,532," I tell her, and she turns to me in surprise.

"What?"

"We're 37,532 feet in the air. Actually, 37,618 now."

"How the fuck do you know that?"

I point toward a large television screen on the wall facing the bar, and she looks at it. A number in the lower left corner, beneath a map of our flight plan, indicates our height and position. We haven't left Australian airspace yet; it looks like we're somewhere above the Gibson Desert.

"Clever boy," she says, turning back to me with a smile. "Anyway, what were we talking about? Oh yeah, you think that life can be just as difficult for boys as girls."

"I do," I tell her, choosing my words carefully. "The thing is, because of my job, I've seen a lot of things that I wish I hadn't."

"And you think I haven't?"

"No, that's fair, I'm sure you have," I say, acknowledging this. "You've probably seen worse."

"And you've probably ended up dealing with the same kids whose lives have been fucked up by the cunts I arrest."

She's speaking a little loudly now, and an elderly couple on the opposite side of the cabin glances over, offended by her language. I feel judged by them and want to let them know that we're not together, that she's just a stranger who's engaged me in conversation.

"That said," she continues, "while teenage boys are just a bunch of horny dickheads, teenage girls can be just as bad. They'll do anything to impress the smug little bastards. And the boys know that, so they take advantage of it. I can't remember how often I made a fool of myself at that age over some guy. He always looked like a soapie, spent every free minute in the water, then just wanted to get into my pants so he could tell his mates all about it. I mean, you know what it was like. You were a teenage boy once. It's not real if they don't get to brag about it. That's one of the reasons social media is so important to them, isn't it? People want to show off. Sportsmen filming their gang rapes on their mobile phones. And Zuckerberg, Musk, all those weird little men who couldn't get girlfriends in college, it's given them a platform. A place they can make it clear how much they fucking hate women. And enable those who hate them even more to become president."

"Maybe I moved with a different crowd," I say quietly.

"In Sydney? I doubt it. They're all the same."

"I didn't grow up in Sydney," I tell her. "I only came to Australia when I was in my early twenties."

"Doesn't matter. Boys are the same all over," she says, dismissing this. "I hate to say it, but Billy's just like that too. And he's got his father's looks so he's catnip for the girls. Come on, Aaron, be honest with me. What were you like when you were fifteen? I bet you were a right little runaround."

"I really wasn't."

"Then what were you?"

I search for the right word and settle on: "Isolated."

"The shy and sensitive type?"

"A late bloomer," I offer, wishing I could extricate myself from this conversation. "Girls weren't really on my radar at the time."

"I bet you were on theirs."

To my surprise, I feel myself blushing slightly.

"Don't worry," she says, bumping a shoulder against my own. "I'm not hitting on you. As it happens, I have a boyfriend. Six years younger than me. Abs of steel. A jawline that could slice cheese. Billy can't stand him, and my ex-husband hates him even more, but that's their problem, not mine."

"You know, you're quite critical of him," I tell her.

"Of who? My boyfriend?"

"No. Of your son. Of Billy."

She rears back a little in the seat and stares at me, clearly surprised by this remark. She looks away, then lifts her glass and drains it, even though it's more than half-full. This time, the barman doesn't need to be asked; he's been watching us and comes over with the Dom, keeping a certain distance from her while offering me another beer. I take it but don't open it yet.

"That was a shitty thing to say," she says when we're alone again. "Especially from a guy who can't keep track of his own son from one moment to the next. I thought we were just chatting. Kidding around. Comparing war stories."

"We are," I reply, wondering whether I have, in fact, crossed a line. She's getting drunk but I've been matching her glass for glass, so I'm probably not fully aware of the impact of my words, and the altitude probably doesn't help.

"Like, I love my son."

"Of course you do."

"I'm not some sort of psycho."

"I didn't mean to imply that."

"Well, it's how it came across."

"I'm sorry," I say. "Honestly, I am. It's just . . . I find that when parents consistently speak about their children in negative ways, it affects them. The kids, I mean. They sense your disapproval. But you're right, I spoke out of turn. I wasn't trying to be rude. Just offering a professional thought. I should probably save it for my consulting room."

She nods, considering my apology, and I watch as she decides which she'd enjoy more: pursuing an argument or holding on to a drinking companion. In the end, she chooses the latter.

"All right," she says with a shrug. "And maybe you're right, I should lighten up about him. I didn't have much experience of parents myself so I can't even blame them. Mine were killed in a plane crash."

I raise an eyebrow and stare at her.

"It's true," she says. "I was just a child at the time. Five years old. They were taking a holiday together to mark their tenth wedding anniversary and left me with my gran in Parramatta. I was only supposed to be staying with her for a week but ended up not moving out till I finished high school."

"I'm sorry," I say.

"It's fine. I don't remember them very well, and it was so long ago. But for some reason, despite that, I've never felt any fear of planes. If anything, I actually love flying. Maybe I have a death wish. You're the psychologist. Don't you think that's strange?"

"A *child* psychologist," I say, correcting her.

"Well, I was a child then."

"But you're an adult now."

"Do we really change that much?"

"I think so. I feel that whatever happens to us when we're kids lays the foundation for the life we'll come to have. If we have a happy childhood, then we're more likely to become functioning adults. Not in every case, obviously, but it's more probable. And if we have an unhappy one, well, it's the same result. As children, we don't have the emotional resources to deal with trauma. As adults, it becomes a little easier. We've learned coping mechanisms. Did you get help to process your grief at the time?"

"Nope," she says, shaking her head. "We just got on with things back then, didn't we?"

"We did," I agree. "Unfortunately."

"Talking about what happened to me, to them, people would have said I should just be pleased that I hadn't been on that plane too. Your boy's lucky. If something shit's going on in his life, at least you have the training to recognize it. With Billy, I worry that it's something that I did. His father and I, well, we didn't have what you might call an amicable parting. We still take chunks out of each other whenever our paths cross, and it's been years since we split. Do you and Emmet's mother get along?"

"My contact with my ex-wife is minimal."

"And her contact with him?"

"Even less."

"That's unusual."

I nod.

"Still, he's a good kid, I can tell," she says, finishing yet another glass and raising her hand for another. "Trust me, I have a nose for these things. He'll be all right. He's cute too," she adds, and I feel something like an electric shock reverberate through me.

"I'm sorry?" I say.

"I said he's cute."

"Who's cute?"

"Your son. He's a good-looking boy."

"He's fourteen," I tell her.

"I know he's fourteen," she says, slurring her words a little now. "I'm not saying I want to fuck him. I'm just saying he's a looker, that's all. Those eyes! He'll be a heartbreaker, that one."

She glances at her watch, then realizes how quiet I've grown and frowns.

"What?" she asks. "Why are you looking at me like that?"

"It was nice meeting you," I say, standing up and lifting my laptop from the table before starting to make my way toward the aisle.

"What?" she calls after me, raising her voice now, and a couple of people in the seats I pass turn around to see what the commotion is about. "What the fuck did I say?"

5

I manage some sleep, and when I open my eyes, the partition between Emmet's seat and my own has been lowered. He's sitting in the lotus position, his screen turned off, reading, but he sets his book aside when he sees that I'm awake. I expect him to raise the barrier again immediately but, no, he must be feeling bored because he gives me a look that says, *Talk to me*.

"How long was I out?" I ask.

"About three hours."

I sit up and stretch my arms. It wasn't a long sleep, but I feel pleasantly refreshed. I wander down to the bathroom, making sure not to catch Charlotte's eye as I pass her seat, clean my teeth, wash my face, and when I return, he's massaging one of the mini tubes of moisturizer into his forehead and cheeks.

"You're gorgeous," I say.

"Do you know that woman?" he asks.

"What woman?"

"The woman you were sitting with at the bar. You were talking to her in the airport too."

I didn't realize that he'd seen us and wonder whether he'd come down to join me, then changed his mind when he found us chatting.

"No, I never met her until this morning," I tell him. "We just struck up a conversation, that's all. Why?"

"You're at a very vulnerable age. I don't want anyone taking advantage of you."

I laugh, as he's simply parroting back to me a line I've said to him several times over the last year. I always enjoy it when he takes the piss out of me. It reminds me that there's still something of the fun-loving kid hidden away beneath the stroppy teen.

"Can we go down there?" he asks.

"Down where?"

"To the bar."

I'd actually prefer to settle back with a movie now, but since he's actually asking to spend time in my company, I won't pass up the opportunity. We stand and make our way down opposite sides of the aisle, passing passengers snoozing behind their eye masks, and meet up just beyond the galley.

It's quiet now and we don't have to sit side by side at the wall as the table that allows passengers to sit facing each other is unoccupied. Perhaps a shift change has happened because Paul Newman has been replaced by a young woman whose hair is drawn into a complicated arrangement on her head. When we sit, she approaches and asks what she can get us.

I don't feel like another beer, so order a gin and tonic, while Emmet, with supreme confidence, orders a Tiger. There's a moment between the three of us. The stewardess can see that he's young but he is accompanied by his father, so unlike her colleague at takeoff, she chooses not to object. Emmet is deliberately not looking at me, and I remain silent until he glances up. We're both smiling.

"One," I say, pointing a finger at him and laughing. "Just one, all right?"

I don't know whether drinking with my fourteen-year-old son is the worst thing a father can do or the best. All I'm certain of is that we're thirty thousand feet above the earth, and the normal rules of life need not apply up here.

"It'll knock me out," he says in his defense.

"You didn't sleep when I did?"

"No, I watched another film."

"Well, we still have about six hours to go," I say, glancing at the screen on the wall. "Even if you only get three or four, it'll be better than nothing. You must be tired."

"Not really. Maybe. Sort of? I don't know what time my body clock is at."

"A little sleep would do you good. Otherwise you'll be exhausted for days."

"I'm used to flying to Dubai."

The stewardess, whose name tag reads Noémie, returns, carrying a tray with our drinks, bowls of nuts and crisps, and a chocolate muffin in which a single candle has been placed. I stare at it in surprise, then turn to Emmet, who's grinning.

"Happy birthday," he says.

It takes me a moment to appreciate the significance of this. He obviously organized it with her while I slept, and I'm so moved that I feel tears come to my eyes.

"You thought I'd forgotten, didn't you?"

"I wasn't sure."

"Obviously we can't have naked flames on board," Noémie tells me. "So it's an LED candle. You blow it, and somehow it goes out. Don't ask me how. Witchcraft, probably."

I make a wish, do as instructed, and, sure enough, the flame disappears.

"Thank you," I say to Emmet as we clink our glasses.

"I'm just glad that you're still mentally competent and can walk unassisted," he tells me. "Considering how ancient you are."

"Forty's not that old!"

"Welcome," he says, stretching his arms wide and doing a more than decent impression of Richard Attenborough, "to Jurassic Park!"

This is as happy as I've felt in a long time. As he takes a sip from his beer, which has arrived in a mercifully small glass, his face betrays no aversion, so I assume it's not his first. Of course, he has a life outside of mine. He has friends. Friends I've known since they were in Nippers together. Good kids, for the most part, and whatever mischief they get up to is not something that worries me unduly as they're generally quite responsible. The worst thing they ever do is stay down at the beach when the lifeguards have gone home for the night, but they're all experienced swimmers and no one is ever left in the water alone.

"So," I say, sensing that he's open to a more meaningful conversation than the feral grunting of morning time. "How are you feeling about all of this?"

"All of what?"

"This," I say, looking around. "This trip. Where we're going. What we're doing. Why we're doing it."

He blows out his lips.

"Let's just say, I've made my peace with it," he replies, and it's hard not to laugh at his use of such an adult phrase. I try to contrast who I was at fourteen with who he is now. I was happy. I had friends. I had parents who loved me. I was growing interested in girls. I liked soccer. My father and I attended all the home matches of our local football team, only returning our season ticket when two of the players were charged with rape. And then, one day, Freya Petrus came to our school as part of an outreach program from the local hospital, trying to engage young people with the idea of working toward a career in medicine, and afterward, when I told her how much she'd inspired me, she took me home with her and my life changed.

Emmet, however, is different. He's not quite as carefree as I was at that age, but perhaps the times don't lend themselves to that. Other than swimming and surfing, he doesn't care about sport. So far, he has shown—at least to me—no interest in girls. And until I saw those photos on his phone, I assumed that he had not, as yet, had any sexual experiences. But there's clearly something going on in his private universe that I don't know about, but that I need to uncover. If I am to discuss it with him, I will have to choose my moment carefully.

"Well, whatever happens," I tell him, "I'm glad you came."

"You didn't give me much choice."

"You didn't put up too much of a fight."

"Gets me out of school for a week."

"True," I say. "How is school anyway?"

"What do you want to know?"

"Anything you want to tell me."

He glances to his right, toward the window that looks out onto the dark night sky, and shrugs.

"It's school," he says. "It's fine."

"Adults usually say that life was so much easier when they were children," I tell him. "When we had no responsibilities, no bills to pay, no wives, husbands, kids, all that stuff. I think we forget that it's just as difficult being a teenager as it is being an adult. A different set of difficulties, yes, but they feel as important."

"Not for you."

"What do you mean?"

"Well, your childhood was great, wasn't it? I mean, I know Gran and Grandad died young, but you were an adult by then. Your teenage years were OK."

It's my turn to look away now. I've always known that the day might come when I would talk to him about what happened to me at his age, but for all my training in this area, I've never quite known how to approach it, worried that it might change his view of me in some way.

"I had my issues."

"Well, my childhood wasn't exactly a Disney movie."

"I've done my best."

"I didn't mean you," he concedes, his tone softening. "I meant Mum."

I decided a long time ago that I would never say a negative word about Rebecca in Emmet's presence. Granted, I've never gone out of my way to praise her either, but I knew that it would be a mistake to say or do anything that could be interpreted later as my way of turning him against her. Such behavior would only rebound on me in the future.

"Your mother loves you," I tell him.

"My mother could barely pick me out of a lineup."

"Emmet, you must remember—"

"I don't want to talk about her," he says, cutting me off, and I decide not to push this topic any further. I'd prefer to return to the more cheerful conversation that we were having earlier.

"A gym," he continues after a moment.

"What?"

"This plane has a shower, a bar. What it needs is a gym. Thirteen hours? You could get a good workout in."

"I guess," I say.

"Just a small room with some dumbbells and a treadmill," he continues. "That'd be cool."

"I think people would spend more time at the bar," I tell him.

He nods, but I'm reminded of how he's been throwing himself into exercising lately, although it doesn't seem to be having much effect on his body, which remains stubbornly slender.

"What I said about the woman you were talking to—" he continues.

"Emmet, I swear I just met her!"

"I know, I know. I was just kidding about that, but can I ask you something?"

I nod. "Sure."

"Like . . ." He hesitates, sounding nervous. "Why don't you have a girlfriend?"

I'm taken aback by the question. I can't recall him ever asking something so intimate of me.

"Well, it's not as if I wouldn't like one," I say, weighing each word carefully.

"Then why don't you? Like, you're ancient but you're not gross or fat or anything. And, as much as it makes me want to throw up, some of my girlfriends think you're not the most repulsive dad out there."

"Good to know," I say, laughing a little. "The truth is, I was never very good at relationships."

"You found someone to marry you."

"And look how that turned out."

"That wasn't your fault."

"It was as much my fault as your mother's," I insist. "Maybe even more."

"I doubt that."

"We were too young."

A strange expression crosses his face.

"What?" I ask.

"It's just . . . I wondered . . ."

"Wondered what?"

"Like, I don't know if you have . . . I mean, sometimes I've wondered whether you might have some secret life going on that I know nothing about. A woman you hook up with." He hesitates, avoiding my eye. "Or a guy maybe."

I sit back in surprise. "Emmet, I'm not gay," I tell him.

"Are you sure?"

"Pretty sure, yes."

"It just seems weird that you never date anyone, that's all."

"If I was gay, I would tell you I was gay."

"OK," he says. "That's a relief."

"You're *relieved* that I'm not gay?" I ask, surprised that he would say such a thing. It's out of character for him to express any kind of prejudice.

"No," he says quickly. "Not that. I mean I'm relieved you haven't felt that you had to lie to me about something like that. Jesus. Come on. What do you think I am?"

He looks genuinely mortified that I could have misinterpreted him, and I hold a hand up to acknowledge this. After all, Damian came out to him only a few months earlier, and if anything, it seems to have brought them even closer. Emmet's invited him for even more sleepovers than usual since then, which I think is his way of expressing unqualified support, a move that's impressed me.

"It would be nice to be in a relationship," I admit, as much to myself as to him. The truth is, all these years, I genuinely have either been working or bringing him up and haven't had much time to date, although it's not as if there aren't plenty of parents in the class WhatsApp group who would have taken Emmet anytime I asked. And a few single mums who've seemed open to the idea of going for drinks. "I just . . ." I don't know how to finish this sentence. "Maybe one day," I say finally.

"Well, don't leave it too late," he replies, and I'm about to laugh but I can see from the expression on his face that he genuinely means it.

"You don't want me to be alone," I say quietly.

"I don't want you to be lonely," he clarifies.

I nod, and there's an awkward silence between us.

"I'm sorry about earlier," he says eventually.

"About what earlier? There's so much to pick from."

He smiles.

"In the bookshop. Talking about Furia's book like that."

"Oh. That."

"It was early. I was tired, hungry, and grouchy."

"It's fine." I wait a few moments before asking a question that I'm not even sure I want him to answer. "Have you read it?"

He hesitates for a moment, then shakes his head.

"No."

"It wouldn't bother me if you had. You like books and everyone's saying how good it is. You said it had an—"

"Unreliable narrator, I know."

"That's why I thought you might have. Where did you even pick up such a phrase?"

"In English class. And, you know,"—he pauses, takes a sip from his glass—"in the reviews."

"You've read the reviews?"

He looks slightly embarrassed. "A few of them."

"OK."

I don't quite know how to feel about this. Was he hoping they'd be negative or positive?

"Have *you* read it?" he asks me, and I give him a look that says, *What do you think?*

It occurs to me that, since he's asking such intimate questions of me, perhaps this is a good opportunity to turn the conversation back on him.

"So, speaking of girlfriends," I begin, saying each word slowly so as not to frighten him away. "Is there anyone that you like?"

He opens his eyes wide and looks as if he'd be perfectly happy for the cabin door to burst open right now and suck us both out into the night sky.

"I'm not having this conversation," he says.

"So you can ask me about my love life, but I can't ask about yours?"

"Correct," he says. "Got it in one."

"OK but, joking aside, if there is someone, at school or down the beach or wherever, someone you like, you could talk to me about her." I sense an opportunity to tease him as he teased me. "Or about him."

"You think you're so funny," he says, rolling his eyes, but he can't help himself, he smiles.

"I do," I admit.

But while we're on the subject, why do you have semi-naked pic-
tures of yourself on your phone? Who asked for them? Who did you
send them to?

We've finished our drinks, and Noémie asks if we'd like another round.
It's completely irresponsible of me, of course, but I see a hopeful look on
my son's face, so I nod and say yes. Maybe I'm getting him liquored up
so that he might open up to me even more. It's reckless, I suppose, but
God knows there are worse things an adult can do to a boy his age. The
stewardess gives me a look that says, *I know I've been complicit in this,*
because the boy charmed me when he told me about your birthday, but
this is his last one.

"What will you do when I'm gone?" he asks when she returns behind
the bar.

"Gone?"

"Like, in a few years' time when I'm out of the house."

"Why, where are you going?"

"Uni," he says with a shrug. "I suppose."

"Oh, right. Then."

"What will you do?"

I've never given much thought to the fact that it won't be long before
I'm back where I started, before I even met Rebecca. It's narcissistic, but
the thought flashes through my head that I'm a good man, with a good
career. I've kept my body in decent shape, and I'm reasonably attractive.
Some might say that I'm a catch. So why the fuck *don't* I have someone,
other than my son, to go home to? Why is it that I haven't had sex in so
long? Why have I never been to bed with anyone other than my rapist
and my ex-wife?

"Dad," he says, and when I look up, he's staring at me with a concerned expression on his face. "Dad, what's wrong?"

I shake my head, confused by the question.

"What?" I ask him. "What do you mean?"

"Dad, you're crying."

6

Although Rebecca and I were both keen to keep our wedding ceremony small, particularly as I didn't have any family of my own, it surprised me how reluctant she was to extend an invitation to her mother. Some years earlier, Vanessa had spent a year on a small island off the west coast of Ireland and, after returning to the mainland, had quickly emigrated to Boston, where she found work in a library. In time, this led to a position with an independent publishing house. Eighteen months later, she married the director of that company. Rebecca chose not to attend their service, feigning illness, but Vanessa, by contrast, decided to come to ours, flying to England with her new husband in tow, and inviting us to dinner in their hotel.

I liked my future mother-in-law immediately. She had a quiet dignity to her, an engaging blend of confidence, vulnerability, and mettle. Her short dark hair was peppered with unapologetic gray, and although she was dressed smartly, I guessed she was the sort of woman who cared about her appearance up to a point, but wasn't going to waste too much time worrying about it.

Her and Rebecca's reunion proved predictably uncomfortable, Vanessa reaching in for a hug that was awkwardly received. Introductions followed between stepdaughter and stepfather, a burly American named Ron who came across as a gentle, thoughtful man, and who made an immediate effort with us both. Despite her misgivings and stated intention to remain standoffish, I could tell that Rebecca grudgingly recognized his sincerity. As a couple, Vanessa and Ron seemed happy, touching each other's arms from time to time and laughing at each other's jokes. Despite being an entire generation older than me, I felt envious of their easy companionship.

It could scarcely have been a more inappropriate thing for me to consider, but I guessed they had a far healthier sex life than Rebecca and I did.

"Are you a reading man, Aaron?" Ron asked me over dinner, and I confessed that I wasn't particularly, that my student years had left me with very little time for anything other than professional textbooks. He asked the same question of Rebecca, who usually had a novel on the go, before producing a small tote bag from beneath the table containing copies of some of the new books he was publishing that season. Years later, I found this same collection on a shelf in our living room and discovered an anthology containing a story by Furia Flyte. When I flicked through it, I discovered notes written in the margins in Rebecca's hand. If she had known at the time of reading the role the author would play in the end of our marriage, I wonder how different those notes might have been.

"I still find it astonishing that you're training to become a pilot," Vanessa remarked over the main course, and Rebecca, on high alert for anything that might be considered a slight—possibly even hoping for one—bristled.

"Why?" she asked. "What did you think I should become?"

"It's not that I *thought* you should become anything. It's just that it's an unusual job for a woman, that's all. Historically speaking. When I was a girl, it would have been unthinkable."

"There was a female pilot on the plane coming over to the UK," remarked Ron.

"True," she said, leaning forward and lowering her voice. "And, of course, the moment she made the announcement—you know the one at the start when the pilot welcomes the passengers and says their name is so and so and the flight time will be however long it will be—there was a groan from some of the men in our cabin. One even said aloud, *I hope you can all swim because we'll be landing in the middle of the Atlantic Ocean*, which he obviously thought was hilarious."

"She turned around to him," said Ron, nodding toward his wife proudly.

"I did," she admitted.

"She told him off."

"I did!"

"She said, *What's the matter with you? It's not as if she'd be given control of the cockpit if she didn't know the clutch from the brake. Show some respect!*"

"There's no clutch on a plane," said Rebecca.

"Well, obviously I know nothing about that sort of thing. But I thought, for heaven's sake, it's the twenty-first century! Do we still have to deal with men who hold such outdated ideas?"

"Personally speaking," said Ron, "if I'd had a daughter, it would have knocked my socks off to see her go into a traditionally male industry and show them who was boss."

"The industry itself isn't traditionally male," replied Rebecca. "It's just that over the years the women who've worked within it have mostly been reduced to serving food and drinks."

"Would you have liked children?" I asked him, and he nodded enthusiastically.

"Oh yes. Very much. I just didn't meet the right woman when I was the right age, that's all. I had my share of relationships, of course, some good, some not so good, but things never seemed to work out for me on that front. Until Vanessa came along, that is."

He reached across and took her hand, squeezing it gently.

"And by then, we were too old to go down that road."

"Ron has quite a tight-knit group of nephews and nieces," said Vanessa. "They came to the wedding," she added pointedly. "They've been very welcoming toward me."

Rebecca remained silent, forking a carrot and chewing on it meditatively.

"I put all my paternal longings into those kids," said Ron, and I could see his eyes light up as he described them, two boys and three girls, the lives they were living, the boyfriends and girlfriends they had, the ambitions still before them. One was working in his publishing house, and he hoped that she might take it over one day. "So I've no regrets. I think life works out the way it's supposed to." He turned to Rebecca now. "The truth is, I thought I was going to be a confirmed old bachelor for the rest of my days, and I'd made my peace with that, but then I met your mother. I thought I was happy until then. Turned out, I didn't know what happiness really was."

He looked at Vanessa when he said this, and when she placed a palm gently against his cheek, I felt a strange joy for them. Their affection was so natural and blissful.

Later, they asked where we were hoping to go on our honeymoon and I told them we'd planned four nights in Florence, then three nights in Venice, and Vanessa immediately suggested that we should come to Boston instead.

"The fall is particularly beautiful there," she added. "It would be a great time to visit."

"The fall?" asked Rebecca, in as sarcastic a tone as she could muster. "You mean the autumn, right?"

"Sorry," she said, laughing a little. "I've turned into such a native. I say things like *sidewalk* and *elevator* these days."

"And *dude*," added Ron, and Vanessa turned to him in outrage, denying that she'd ever called anyone *dude* in her entire life, but then he made a reference to a young writer whose publicity campaign she'd been working on, and she admitted that yes, she might have called him dude once, but she'd had one too many cosmopolitans at the time so it shouldn't be held against her.

"He won a Pulitzer, you know," added Ron.

"Who did?" asked Rebecca.

"The writer," he told us. "In no small part because of your mother's hard work. You should be very proud of her. She's a smart cookie."

Vanessa remained silent throughout this commendation, taking a sip from her glass of wine, her cheeks flushing a little. I could tell that she was pleased by the compliment, and proud that it was clearly deserved.

"It's like you're a different human being entirely," said Rebecca, and it was difficult to tell from her tone whether she meant this in a positive or negative way.

"How do you mean?"

"It's hard to say," she replied, shaking her head. "It's like you're not Vanessa Carvin anymore. Not the one I grew up with anyway. You look like her, for the most part. And you talk like her. But you're different."

"Well, many years have passed, so naturally I've changed. It happens."

"You're not even Willow Hale."

I turned to look at Rebecca, uncertain what she meant by this, and Vanessa exhaled a small, sad sigh.

"I'm surprised you even remember that name," she said.

"Who's Willow Hale?" I asked.

"Willow Hale was the name my mother assumed when she ran away and left me."

"I didn't run away and leave you, Rebecca," replied Vanessa in a measured tone. "If anything, I ran away and left *me*. And I messaged you constantly. I woke up every morning wondering whether your picture would still be on my contacts list or not. If her picture was there, Aaron," she said, turning to me, "it meant that she was open to me messaging her. If it was gone, then she'd blocked me. It was very random from one day to the next. Honestly, there were times I didn't even want to look because of how hurtful it could be."

I turned to look at Rebecca, but she didn't meet my eyes. She'd told me about the island, and why her mother had gone there, but not about her pseudonym or their lack of interaction during that period.

"I came to visit," she said.

"You did," agreed Vanessa. "For a night."

"What was it like?" I asked. "The island, I mean."

Vanessa breathed in deeply and I could tell that she was searching for the right way to describe it.

"Life-changing," she said eventually. "Peaceful. Full of strange, wonderful, difficult people. I'm not sure that I'd be sitting here today if I hadn't gone there."

Our small group fell silent then, and finally, to break the tension, Ron asked about my plans for the future. I told him that I hoped to work with children who'd suffered some form of trauma in their lives.

"And you'll stay here?" he asked.

"We haven't made a decision about that yet."

"It's an expensive city, from what I'm told. Especially if you plan on having children."

"We don't," said Rebecca decisively, which was news to me, and I realized that we'd never discussed the topic of becoming parents. I suppose I'd always taken it for granted that this would happen in time. I turned to look at her, trying to keep the surprise off my face, and she deliberately stared into the bowl of her wine glass, swilling the contents just enough that they touched the peak of the rim without spilling over.

"I couldn't bring a child into this world," she continued. "I just couldn't. I think about what your first husband did,"—Rebecca never referred to Brendan as her father, just as her mother's first husband— "and I think about what happened to Aaron when he was a boy—"

"What happened to you when you were a boy?" asked Vanessa, looking at me.

"And I simply refuse to bring another human into such a world. If he or she could just be born as an adult, then that would be fine. But they have to go through childhood first, don't they? And one way or another, someone will fuck them up. Or just fuck them."

Vanessa muttered something under her breath and looked away, her jaw tightening. I sensed there were emotions that she wanted to express but that she was uncertain how they might be received. Ron took a sip from his beer while I stared down at my meal. Eventually, Vanessa repeated her question, and in as brief a way as possible, keeping my language plain so as not to turn the evening any darker than it had already become, I explained what had taken place in my life when I was fourteen.

I know he meant well.

I know he was only trying to lighten the mood.

I know he simply didn't understand the experience I had gone through, but that was when Ron said:

"Jesus. When I was that age, I would have given my left arm to be seduced by an older woman."

The moment the words were out of his mouth, I think even he knew that he'd said the wrong thing. Vanessa froze, as did Rebecca. He closed his eyes, and they remained that way for about ten seconds while everyone at the table remained silent.

"I'm so sorry," he said at last. "That was such a dumb thing to say. Obviously, I have no understanding of what you went through or the effect it had on you."

"He didn't say he was *seduced* by an older woman," said Rebecca, her voice rising now, her tone enraged. I noticed a couple at a nearby table turning to look in our direction. "He said he was *raped* by one. There's a big fucking difference, Ron."

"I'm very sorry," he repeated, reaching his enormous hand across the table and placing it atop mine, an intimate gesture that I found strangely comforting. "I'm a big stupid American who speaks before he thinks."

"It's fine," I told him because I knew that his apology was sincere. I'd heard men say things like this before. The same men who would insist that if a thirty-two-year-old man even glanced in a lascivious way toward their fourteen-year-old daughter, they would gladly serve a life sentence for their murder.

Vanessa took her husband's left hand, leaving three of us physically connected. Only Rebecca held herself apart.

"I'm sorry, sweetheart," Ron whispered to his wife, and she gave him a quick kiss as he looked around the table, his brow furrowed. "I know what Vanessa suffered. And, of course, I know what happened to Emma. So it's not something to make light of. Maybe that's one of the things that brought you two together?"

Oh Ron, I thought. *Stop speaking. Please stop speaking.*

Rebecca put her glass down, firmly, and placed her hand against her forehead, holding it there.

"It's a terrible world we live in," he continued. "I had such a happy childhood myself. I hope you've found a way to make peace with what happened to you, Aaron."

"Well, I try not to allow it to affect my life any deeper than it already has," I replied quietly.

"That seems very sensible," said Vanessa. "If you don't mind me asking, what happened to the woman? Did you report her?"

"Only a couple of years ago. By which time, she'd done a lot of damage to other boys. I should have done it earlier."

"You can't blame yourself for that."

"I know, but I regret my delay."

"And was she punished?"

"Yes. Arrested, charged, tried, and incarcerated. She admitted to it all. And worse."

"What could be worse?"

"Suffice to say she won't be setting foot outside prison again in her lifetime."

"Well, that's something."

"Please don't ever mention my sister's name again," said Rebecca quietly, looking down at the table. Her tone made it clear that she'd spent the last couple of minutes seething over Ron's remarks.

"Rebecca," said Vanessa.

"I mean it. You didn't know her. You never met her. So please don't speak about her as if you have any understanding of who she was or what we lost."

I turned to her, pleading with my eyes for her to stop, but her attention was focused solely on him.

"I won't," he replied, his tone entirely sincere. "And I apologize for doing so. I didn't realize it would upset you this much, but I do now and will keep it in mind in the future."

I could feel the tension in her simmering away, longing to boil over. Her fury that he was being so reasonable and refusing to participate in an argument. She wanted to tear into him, this substitute father, someone who might soak up the rage she felt toward her real one, but he simply wasn't giving her the opportunity.

"Perhaps Aaron and I should go for a drink in the bar," he suggested finally, looking down at our plates, which were empty now. "You two ladies haven't seen each other in so long. You could probably do with a little time to catch up without us boys getting in the way."

I felt a sense of relief when Vanessa nodded.

It was more than an hour later before she rejoined us, telling me that Rebecca was waiting for me in the lobby.

"She's not coming in to say goodbye?" I asked, and she shook her head.

"No, she just wants to go home."

I said my goodbyes to both and made my way toward the door. Before I could leave, however, Vanessa caught up with me.

"Aaron," she said, standing close to me. "I want you to know that I love my daughter very much. I would lay down my life for her if I had to. And obviously I've only just met you for the first time tonight, but from what I've observed, you seem like a kind, thoughtful young man. She's lucky to have you. But, out of consideration to you, can I offer you one piece of advice?"

"Of course," I said.

She took both my hands in hers, clutching them tightly, and looked me directly in my eyes.

"Don't marry her," she said. "You're a fool if you do."

7

We both sleep through the last few hours of the Dubai flight and emerge, slightly groggy, into the airport, where we shuffle toward our next gate for the short layover. Slumped in our seats, I'm scrolling through my phone while Emmet is staring into the distance, lost in thought. His hair is a mess and he's compulsively running his fingers through it, giving off a definite air of anxiety.

Without a word, he wanders off to the bathroom, leaving his bag and phone on the seat next to me, and, a minute or so later, when it buzzes, I glance toward it, where a message from Damian has popped up. U made ur mind up yet? it says, and I frown but don't touch it. If I did, Emmet would surely reappear just as I'm looking at it. Still, I can't help but wonder what he's referring to. It doesn't take long for me to find out, however, for when my son returns, he has a rather determined expression on his face. He sits down, looks at the phone for a moment, reads the message, taps a quick reply, then puts it in his pocket before clearing his throat. When he speaks, his tone suggests that he's been thinking about what he's about to say for some time and is fully prepared for an argument.

"Dad," he says.

"What's up?"

"There's something I need to tell you."

"OK."

"Only you can't be angry with me."

Perhaps he wants to talk about the pictures on his phone. It's not the ideal time to discuss them, but it would certainly be a lot easier if he brought the topic up rather than me having to introduce it. I've spent more than a year counseling a boy only slightly older than him who gave in to a sextortion scam on Snapchat, clearing almost $3,000 from his parents' bank account before they discovered what was going on and reported the incident to the police. Although, thankfully, the pictures and videos he sent to his blackmailer never made it into the public domain or to his list of contacts, as had been threatened, he remains utterly traumatized by the incident, which went on for months, and a chill spreads through me as I wonder whether Emmet has found himself in a similar situation.

"Go on," I say.

"No, you have to promise."

"Just tell me."

He takes a deep breath, then exhales slowly.

"I'm not getting on this plane."

Of everything I might have anticipated, this never occurred to me. But at least it's not as bad as what it might have been.

"I'm sorry?"

"I said I'm not getting on this plane. I'm not going any further. I'm staying here."

I turn to look at him, to see whether he's serious. If there's one thing I've learned over the years from my patients, it's the importance of remaining calm when someone says something that is clearly designed for a reaction.

"Emmet," I say, glancing at my watch. "Boarding is due to start in about fifteen minutes, so you don't really have much choice. We've done the long part of the flight already. This is the shorter one. We'll be there before you know it."

"It's not about the length of the journey," he tells me. "I'm just not going, it's as simple as that. You go if you want to. But I'm staying here."

"What, here in the airport? For the next five nights?"

"You can book me a hotel room," he says. "It's Dubai. There's thousands of them."

"And five nights in one of them would cost more than this entire trip."

"Oh, please," he says, rolling his eyes. "You're loaded."

"I'm not loaded," I say. "But that's hardly the point. I'm not leaving you on your own in a strange city. We agreed to make this trip together, remember, you and me? We have to be there for her."

"Why?" he asks.

"Why what?"

"Why do we have to be there for her?"

It takes me a moment to come up with what I realize is an unsatisfactory, and possibly dishonest, answer.

"Because if things were the other way around, she'd be there for you."

"Like she's been in the past, you mean?"

He throws his head far back over the seat, staring up at the ceiling, remaining silent for a moment, as if he can't quite comprehend the duplicity of adults. I know he's telling himself that he'll never be the same when he's older. But he will. We all are.

"You see your mother regularly," I tell him, and he laughs bitterly.

"I see her once or twice a year at most," he replies. "It's not like she goes out of her way to spend time with me."

"You spend a month with her."

"Wrong. I come here for a month but I spend most of it sitting on my own in her apartment, reading books, watching movies, or down in the pool, while she's flying around somewhere. When she does bother to show up, she's either too tired to hang out with me or can't think of anything for us to do. Last time, she came back from Singapore after three days away and seemed to forget that I was even staying there. I literally came out of my bedroom to say hello, and she screamed like I was a burglar. I swear, it took her a minute even to recognize me."

"She was probably jet-lagged, that's all."

"Pilots don't get jet-lagged," he replies with utter certainty, and I have no idea whether this is true or just something he's read online.

"She's your mother," I say.

"No. She's your ex-wife. There's a difference."

I can only imagine how deeply it would hurt Rebecca if she heard this remark—it reminds me of how she always referred to Brendan as Vanessa's ex-husband—and there's a part of me that wishes she had. Because as fortunate as I've felt at being my son's primary guardian, it's shocked me how small a part Rebecca has played in his upbringing.

Emmet was only four years old when the whole mess with Furia led to the end of our marriage. When it became clear that the infidelity would prove to be the closing act of our relationship, the plan had been that Rebecca would remain in Sydney and he would divide his time between us. I had grown to love Australia, my practice was there, and I had neither reason nor inclination to return to the Northern Hemisphere. And for the first twelve months, this arrangement worked reasonably well. But when the airline reorganized its pilot's schedule, it made more sense for her to relocate to their hub in Dubai, and I was worried that she'd want to take Emmet with her. He was settled in school, had his circle of close friends, was thriving at Bondi's Nippers Club, and I felt it would be cruel to remove him from that. The pain of the betrayal had left things raw between us, however, and I was uncertain how Rebecca would respond to my suggestion that Emmet remain in my custody full-time, assuming she'd refuse, but to my surprise, she agreed, even expressing a sense of relief that she was free to live her own life. While her selfishness troubled me, I had no intention of challenging her on it. After all, had she insisted on taking him, and had the courts permitted her to do so, I would have had no choice but to follow her. But no, she just left him.

Last year was the first time Emmet asked whether he could cancel his visit—he was distraught at the idea of being torn away from his beloved beach over Christmas—and I used my dwindling authority to insist that he go, because I wanted him to maintain a relationship with his mother. I'd already anticipated that he would put up more of a fight this coming year, and that, at fifteen, he might even win, but because of the circumstances that have brought us to this airport now, I assume that visit won't be happening anyway.

Ahead, I notice an airline employee preparing the desk and another relocating the stanchions that separate the queues for first, business, and economy passengers. There's simply no way that I'm leaving him here alone.

"Emmet," I begin, but he raises a hand and cuts me off.

"I mean it," he says. "Honestly, Dad, this isn't a sudden decision. I've been thinking about it ever since we boarded in Sydney."

"Oh, that long? Wow. A whole thirteen hours."

"And I don't want to go any further. Look, I know Dubai pretty well and I'm not a little kid anymore. All you need to do is book someplace on your phone. You can do it right now; there's free Wi-Fi. It doesn't have to be any place fancy." He smiles a little, hoping to charm me. "I mean, not a dive though. A pool would be nice."

"A pool would be lovely," I agree. "As would a penthouse suite, a gym, a sauna, a massage, and twenty-four-hour room service. But none of those things are going to happen."

"Not for you, maybe."

"Not for you either."

"I'll be fine," he says, looking me directly in the eye. "I'm fourteen."

"When you say 'I'm fourteen,'" I tell him, "my response is you're *only* fourteen. The preposition matters."

"*Only* isn't a preposition," he says. "It's an adverb."

He's probably right. He's the reader, after all, not me. Around us, I can tell that the other passengers are sensing the impending boarding announcement as they're starting to gather their things, preparing to rush the gate like a pack of feral dogs the moment someone so much as taps the microphone.

"Can I be really honest with you about something?" says Emmet, and I nod. "Of course."

"And you'll hear me out?"

"I'll hear you out."

He takes a deep breath and points toward the gate. "There is nothing, absolutely nothing, that will make me get on that plane," he says. "Nothing you can say, nothing you can do. If you cause a fuss, I'll throw some sort of fit, and security will have us both removed. So it's this simple: you can organize a hotel room for me and go on to Ireland alone, or we can both return to Sydney right now, together. It's your choice. I'm sorry. I had planned on seeing it through. Honestly, I had. And I feel bad about leaving you to do this without me. This isn't something I planned, and I'm not trying to let you down. Especially today. On your birthday.

If it's still your birthday." He pauses for a moment and frowns. "Is it still your birthday?" he asks. "I mean, with the time difference, is it still today? Or yesterday? Or—"

"Emmet!" I snap. Global time zones are the last thing on my mind right now.

"Sorry. OK. Anyway, my point is I don't see why I should give her this when she's given me nothing."

"Other than life, you mean."

He crosses his arms defensively and shakes his head. I've dealt with a lot of children and teenagers throughout my career, and they can be difficult in any one of a thousand ways. Another parent might panic at a declaration like this, and I will admit I'm starting to grow unnerved as we're under severe time pressure. But I have to remain calm.

"You must want a better relationship with her," I say.

"I used to. I don't really care anymore."

"Don't say that."

"Why not?"

"Look, she's a complicated woman. You don't know what she's been through."

He laughs. "What?" he asks sarcastically. "What has she been through? As far as I can see, she's done everything her way, always. Made her own decisions. Let us both down."

I remain silent. Of course, he knows nothing about the realities of Rebecca's past. We've both kept that from him.

"She doesn't love me, Dad," he continues, and I can see tears forming in his eyes. "Not like you love me."

"She does," I insist. "She just doesn't know how to express it, that's all. She's damaged. We're both damaged."

"You're not."

"I am, Emmet."

"How?" he asks, sounding intrigued now, perhaps hearing something in my tone that tells him that he might not know me quite as well as he thinks he does, but I shake my head.

"That's a conversation for another time," I say. "Right now, we have bigger things to worry about. We have to go. We *have* to."

"Why?"

"Because—Jesus!—I loved her once, Emmet, that's why. Very much. Very deeply. We got married. We planned a life together. And we created you."

"So you go, then. You be there for her if it's so important to you."

"Not without you. No. I know you're angry with her but—"

"I have no feelings about her one way or the other," he says, the crack in his voice showing that he's almost overwhelmed by the complexity of his emotions and his inability to negotiate them. The jet lag is probably only adding to his stress.

"And you have every reason to feel that way," I continue calmly. "But trust me, now is not the time to act upon those feelings. This is a moment in life when your mother needs you. She needs both of us, whether she realizes it or not. And she will be glad that we're there."

He stares at me. I sense a chink in his armor. I've found myself in moments like this before, in professional settings, and know that I just need to prize it open. Very carefully.

"The loss of a parent can cause people to think differently about their lives," I tell him. "I've seen it many times in my work."

"You work with children."

"And sometimes children lose their parents. Jacob lost Jackie, remember?"

He looks away and swallows, considering this. Jacob is one of his closest friends, part of the gang he hangs around with at the beach, a boy who's spent countless nights sleeping in the top bunk in Emmet's bedroom since they were kids. His mother passed away from cancer just over a year ago and Jacob has handled his grief admirably.

"I remember," he says.

"And you were there for him. You and Damian. And Shane and Maxie. I've watched you all. I've seen how much you've helped him."

"Cos he's our friend."

"And Rebecca's your mum. She'll be thinking about you now, I know she will."

He turns to look at me. He wants reassurance.

"How do you know that?" he asks.

[421]

"Because I understand people. I'm trained to understand them. It's the one thing I know I can do well."

What feels like an endless silence lingers between us, and when he speaks again, his determination seems to have diminished a little.

"If she'd wanted us to come," he says, "wouldn't she have said so?"

"That's not her way. You don't know her like I do."

"Of course I don't," he says, bursting into a bitter laugh. "I barely know her at all. That's the problem."

"And this is an opportunity to start rectifying that."

"That's on her, not me."

"You're right. You are absolutely right. And one day, I have no doubt that you and she will sit down and discuss your relationship. When that day comes, you'll be able to tell her that you flew halfway across the world at this crucial moment because you wanted to support her. I'm not trying to pit you against each other, you know I've never done that, but trust me, that is a card you'll be able to pull out of your deck when the moment arrives."

"I shouldn't need a fucking card," he whispers, wiping tears away now. He's an emotional boy, he always has been, but he hasn't cried in front of me in a long time. When something upsets him, he tends to take to his room.

"No, you shouldn't," I agree, knowing that I can't put an arm around him, even though I want to. To pull him close would be to push him away. "But you have one."

"She didn't even speak to me on the phone," he says, his tone softening.

"Perhaps she was worried that you'd say no to coming."

"I would have said yes."

"And you *did* say yes. You said yes when I told you what had happened. When I suggested we go over. You said yes then."

"Only because I knew you wouldn't have let me stay home alone. Even though I'm fourteen."

"*Only* fourteen," I repeat. "The preposition—"

"Adverb!"

"Jesus, fine! The adverb! The point is, you *did* agree, Emmet. You agreed instantly. You want to go; I know you do. Even if you're nervous about what awaits us at the other end. You want to be there for her."

The announcement comes. First-class passengers can board now. We still have a few minutes until business is called.

"No," he says, looking down at the floor.

In front of us, I notice another family—a husband, wife, and a boy about my son's age—stand up and gather their hand luggage. They look so full of energy and excitement that I assume they're traveling directly from Dubai and haven't endured a thirteen-hour flight already. As they leave their seats, the mother throws an arm around her son's shoulder, kisses him on the cheek, and they walk on together in perfect content-ment. The boy turns to her to say something, and she bursts out laughing. I see Emmet watching them too, and he looks desolate.

Once again, he points at the gate.

"I'm sorry, Dad," he says, shaking his head. "I really am. I promise, I'm not doing this to hurt you. Or to hurt her. But there is absolutely no way that I'm getting on that plane to Dublin. None. You either book me a hotel here, a flight home, or I just sleep in this airport for the next five nights. It's up to you."

8

We had only been back in England from our honeymoon a few months when we received an unexpected visitor. I was reading through some case notes at home when the doorbell rang and I opened it to find a man standing outside, in his early seventies I judged, with a slim build and a few scraps of gray hair dragged mercilessly across his crown.

"You must be Aaron," he said, and I was a little taken aback that a stranger should know my name.

"I am," I said.

He extended a hand. "We haven't met," he said. "I'm Daniel. I work with your wife at the airline. Nothing as exciting as what she does, I'm afraid. You wouldn't be safe with me in the cockpit! No, I'm in Human Resources. I'm sorry to drop by unannounced, but there were a few documents that I needed her to sign and I'm away on holiday for the next two weeks and since your house was on my way home, I—"

"Oh, right, of course," I said, standing back and ushering him inside. "Sorry, please come in. She's just taking a bath though, so it might be a few minutes."

"No problem. I'm happy to wait if you're happy to have me."

We made our way into the living room and I tried not to notice how carefully he studied everything in the room, the books on the shelves, the paintings on the wall, the magazines on the coffee table, as if he was considering renting a room from us.

"Very nice," he said quietly, more to himself than me. "Very nice indeed."

"Can I make you a cup of tea?" I asked.

"You could, yes, but would it be very rude if I asked for something a little stronger? Only it's fierce cold out there tonight and I'm not as young as I used to be."

"I might have a beer in the fridge," I said.

"Maybe a whiskey?"

It seemed like a slightly forward request from a guest, but I offered to look, walking into the kitchen where, hidden away at the back of a cupboard, I found an unopened bottle of Bushmills.

"Water? Ice?" I asked, standing in the doorway and displaying it to him.

"We won't disgrace it with dilution," he said, and I poured him a glass, neat, bringing it back with me and leaving the bottle on the table between us. The scent of it, one I rarely experienced, brought me back to my childhood, to my own father, who had always enjoyed a glass of Glenfiddich on Friday nights when I was a child. It was a comforting memory.

"You won't join me?" he asked, and I shook my head.

"Better not," I said. "Work in the morning."

"Did no one ever tell you that it's the height of bad manners to leave a man drinking alone in your home?"

His tone was just on the polite side of confrontational, and he wore such a disturbing smile that I was left feeling rather unsettled. He continued to stare without so much as raising his glass to his lips so, when I realized that he actually meant it, I returned to the kitchen and took a bottle of Heineken from the fridge.

"That's much better," he said when I returned. "I can enjoy my drink now. You have a lovely home," he added, looking around.

"Thank you," I said. "We're only renting, of course, but in time—"

"Wasted money."

"I'm sorry?"

"I said, wasted money. Filling a landlord's pockets when you could be paying your own mortgage."

I looked at him, uncertain how to respond to this.

"When I was a young man," he continued, "when I married, there was no such thing as renting. I went from my parents' house to my marital home. I never gave a penny to anyone else, other than the banks, who fleeced me, of course, because that's the nature of the beast, but I paid it all off before I turned fifty and then what was mine was mine. Or at least I thought it was."

I was glad of the Heineken now and took a long swig from it, feeling a slight sense of relief that there were a few more in the door of the fridge if I needed them.

"You're a doctor," he asked after a moment. "Did I hear that about you?"

"I am, yes."

"What kind of a doctor, if you don't mind me asking?"

"Psychology. Child psychology to be precise."

"Child psychology," he said, musing on this. "Freud," he added, apropos of nothing.

"Well, Freud was a psychoanalyst," I replied. "I'm more of a—"

"Obsessed with sex, wasn't he? Freud, I mean."

I shrugged.

"I think that's rather a clichéd notion of his philosophies, to be honest."

"Thought everyone wanted to murder their father and sleep with their mother. Like that lad over beyond in Denmark."

I stared at him, uncertain to whom he was referring. Was there some appalling psychopath emerging from Copenhagen that I'd missed out on?

"Hamlet," he said, leaning forward and enunciating the word carefully, as if he was on the stage of the Globe itself.

"Oh, right," I replied. "Of course. Yes."

"Can I ask you a personal question? Is there good money in psychology? Or child psychology?"

I didn't quite know how to answer such a peculiar question.

"Relative to what?" I asked.

"Oh, I don't know," he replied. "Relative to being a GP, for example."

"Well, it's not really about the pay scales," I told him. "We all know the NHS runs on too little as it is. Everyone says how much they love it, but no one wants to pay for it."

"Would you not think of going private, no?" he asked, and I realized now that he was Irish, although his accent was not particularly strong. "Would there not be more money in that?"

"No, I don't approve of private healthcare."

"Do you not?" he said, raising an eyebrow. "May I ask why?"

"Because I don't believe that patient care should depend on a person's wealth. Especially when it comes to the well-being of children. Every person has the right to the same level of support, regardless of their circumstances."

"You don't think that if a man, for example, has worked hard all his life and earned a good living that he should be entitled to spend his money anyway he wants?"

"Sure," I replied. "And if he wants to spend it on luxury hotels, first-class flights, fancy cars, or a season ticket to his favorite football club, then I say good luck to him. But should he be allowed to jump the queue for medical attention? I think that's a bit more complicated. Morally speaking, I mean."

"That sounds like socialism to me," he replied, frowning. "Which, in my experience, is a luxury only those with a few quid in the bank can afford. But then, perhaps you're one of those very people."

"I think, perhaps, you overestimate our financial situation," I said, trying to sound lighthearted, and he glanced around again, a raised eyebrow suggesting that he wasn't sure he was. Our home might have been rented but it was in a good part of North London, after all, and was expensively furnished. My parents had owned their house and been scrupulous savers, and so when they died, I inherited more than enough to get a good start in life. The only reason we were still renting was because we hadn't yet decided whether we wanted to remain in London or move abroad.

"In a perfect world," said Daniel, "you must wish you were unemployed."

I sat back, baffled by why he would say such a thing.

"Because," he continued, sensing my confusion, "if no one had any need of you, then all the little children would be happy. There'd be no one looking for the help of a child psychologist."

I thought about it. It was, to be fair, a reasonable point, one I'd never considered before.

"You don't have children yourself, do you Aaron?" he asked, and I shook my head. "When you do, you might have a different attitude about private healthcare. Should one of those children fall ill, God forbid, you would want them to receive treatment as soon as possible. Even if it meant that some poor unfortunate child who'd been ahead of you in the queue got left behind. It's human nature. We look after our own first."

I could have protested but suspected he was probably right. I wasn't naïve enough to think that principles had a peculiar habit of disappearing when confronted by brutal reality.

"By what you say, I assume you're a father," I said, hoping to lighten the mood. He finished his whiskey and held his glass out to me with a smile. I took this as his signal that he wanted another, so lifted the bottle and duly refilled it.

"I am," he said, his voice quieter now, more reflective. "I was blessed with two but, sadly, we lost one."

"I'm sorry to hear that."

"There is nothing more unnatural in this world," he said, looking directly at me and pointing a finger in the air, "*nothing* more unnatural than for a parent to lose a child. No man or woman should ever have to experience that level of grief."

"No," I agreed, glancing toward the closed door that led to a corridor, which, in turn, divided our bedroom and spare room on one side from the bathroom on the other. I hoped to hear the water rushing from the bath, knowing the sound would bring Rebecca to us within a few minutes.

"And are your parents still alive, Aaron?" he called after me when I went back to the kitchen to retrieve a second beer for myself.

"No," I replied, when I returned.

"They must have died young."

"My father suffered a heart attack in his forties. My mother developed cancer a few years later and, unfortunately, it was late stage by the time it was diagnosed."

"Siblings?"

I shook my head.

"So you're all alone in the world."

"No," I said. "I have Rebecca."

"Of course, of course," he replied, nodding his head. "But you have no one of your own to fall back on."

"Again, Rebecca."

"No one of your own blood, I mean."

I sighed. He seemed determined to have his way on this. "I suppose not," I said.

"The little boy that Santa Claus forgot."

I frowned. I had never thought of myself in quite those terms before.

"It's a good thing you met Rebecca so," he said. "She's a wonderful young woman."

"She is," I agreed.

"Can I ask you a personal question?"

This was the second time he had asked this, and I felt we'd already gone well past polite small talk but nodded cautiously.

"If you had to describe your late parents in a single word, what word would that be?"

I thought about this for a little before answering.

"Successful," I said eventually.

"Now that's a very strange reply," he said. "Successful in what way? In their work?"

"In a sense. You said that the worst thing that can happen to any man or woman is to lose a child, and I don't disagree with you on that. But, by the same token, the best thing that any man or woman can do in life is to be a good parent. To give their children a happy childhood. And my parents did that. They were kind people. They loved me, they took care of me. Always made me feel worthwhile." Perhaps the beer was getting to me because I added: "There was a time, in my teens, when I struggled with life. During those years, I wasn't always as kind to them as I might have been. But they never pushed me away. They were always in my corner, even when I gave them cause to run far from it. So the reason I say 'successful' is because they took on the most important role in the world and did a great job at it."

He nodded his head. "Now that's a lovely thing to say," he told me. "And if they're listening from up there in heaven, then I imagine they'll have a smile on their faces hearing such generous words. I only hope my daughter, my surviving daughter that is, will be able to say the same thing about me someday. And that, in time, when you're a parent yourself, you'll follow their example."

"I hope so," I said. Since our night out with Vanessa and Ron around the time of our wedding, Rebecca and I had never discussed her comments regarding not wanting to bring a child into the world. We should have, of course, but I hoped that it had simply been a throwaway remark, one designed to hurt her mother. I still assumed that one day we would have kids of our own. Although, of course, to have a child would require actually having sex.

"Still, at least you're married," continued Daniel, betraying a little more of his accent now. "Which is the right way to be. All these girls today having babies with no sign of a ring on their fingers. There's a cheapness to them, don't you think? A lack of self-respect."

"I don't think people care about those sorts of things anymore," I said.

"That's because the young behave like animals," he replied, leaning forward, his face darkening. "And we allow it. God created marriage for a reason."

"God didn't create marriage," I told him. "Man did."

He waved this away dismissively.

"A child should have a father and a mother," he insisted. "And that father and mother should be joined in the sacrament of marriage, a sacrament, I might add, that no court order can dissolve, even if the world thinks otherwise. Don't you agree with me, Aaron?"

"No," I said firmly. "If a child has two parents who love each other and remain together, then that's obviously a good thing, but whether they're married or not seems neither here nor there. And a parent can bring up a child alone and do a great job. Ultimately, it's about love."

"My wife and I waited," he told me, tapping a finger against his nose, as if I was to keep this piece of intelligence to myself. He poured himself another healthy shot of the whiskey and held it to the light, looking at it admiringly. "Or rather, I waited. She had a history, I'm sorry to say. One that I was willing to overlook, which is as much to my shame as it is to hers. When I met her, she'd already been with other men. Only a few, she told me, but who's to say? Women lie. You know that as well as I do. It's in their nature. They are inherently deceitful. Especially when they're trying to trap a man, and she trapped me well and good, so she did. Oh, for a stupid woman, she was very clever when it came to snaring her catch. It took a long time for us to conceive a child, and it wasn't for want of trying, oh no. Let me assure you, Aaron, that relations between us in those early years were as regular as they were convivial, but month after month we were left disappointed. Let's go to a doctor, she said, and I did as I was told because is there anything that a man wants more than a quiet life? So we went to the doctor, a lady doctor, mind you, and didn't she—the lady doctor, I mean, not my wife—didn't she suggest that it might be my fault that we were having no success. If I wasn't a man who'd been brought up to respect the fairer sex, I'd have given her a good slap for her troubles and there wouldn't have been a jury in the land that—"

He broke off for a moment when he said this and took a long breath, closing his eyes. I allowed the silence to linger, not wishing to say anything.

"Anyway, rest assured, I never laid a hand on her. And, as it turned out, it wasn't my fault at all. There was nothing wrong with me. Or her, in fact. It was just God's way of making us wait so that we would love our children even more when they finally arrived. And He knows that we treated those girls like they were princesses of the royal blood. There was never, let me tell you, two little girls who were loved more."

He took a longer swig from the whiskey now, and I could tell that he was growing drunk. Somewhere at the back of my mind, an idea started to suggest itself to me, but like a ship lost at sea on a dark night, it was still partly hidden by fog.

"When you do have children, Aaron," he said, "may the good Lord see fit to bless you with sons. What is it that fella in *The Godfather* says, when he visits the Don at the wedding? The lad who ends up sleeping with the fishes. *May your first child be a masculine child!* Good strong boys who can look up to you and take after you. I loved my girls, I did, but a house full of women with their potions and their notions, their concoctions and their gossiping, and their bras and their panties hanging out on the washing line every afternoon, it can be too much for a man. A taunt. Something to get him all riled up. No, a man needs sons, that's the truth of it. And a man like me, in my position, with all I had to give, should have had sons. Sons would have stood up for me in my hour of need and not abandoned me like the women in my life did. That woman I called a wife and those girls I called daughters and who made up the most despicable lies about me. Have you ever had someone make up a despicable lie about you, Aaron? Have you ever had to endure a calumny that blackens your name and your reputation forever? There is nothing worse, let me tell you. When someone says that you've done a thing that you would never in a million years do, not unless you were invited to anyway, and the world hears about it and it turns on you and it says abominable things, well, it's like no other form of torture. You won't have had that happen to you, of course not, you're just a young man yet, but in time you might, so if you become a father, and I hope you do, then please God, may your first child be a—"

I sprang to my feet, upsetting the table, and he reared back, looking at me in surprise.

"Get out," I said, a feeling of nausea overwhelming me as I finally realized who my visitor was, and that he had no more connection to Rebecca's airline than I did. To my right, I heard the bathroom door open, then the bedroom door, and knew that Rebecca would be with us shortly.

"But why should I leave?" the man asked, holding his hands out to me like a supplicant. "A man has a right to see his daughter."

"You lost all your rights after what you did."

"Eleven years rotting away in Midlands prison with nothing to do but stare at the four walls all day and try to get from breakfast to dinner without having the head beaten off me by murderers and rapists and drug dealers because they needed someone to look down on, and who else, only Muggins here, Muggins, who was stitched up by his whore of a wife and his slut of a daughter, who he'd given everything to, who he'd worked every day of his life for, and who abandoned him when he needed them the most. Don't you think after something like that happens that a man has a right to look that bitch in the eye and ask, why did you do that, darling girl, why did you do that to me? Don't you know that everything I ever did was for you and your sister, that I loved you both, that I would have laid down my life for—"

The door opened, and Rebecca stepped into the living room in oversized pajamas, running a towel through her wet hair.

"Are you hungry?" she asked. "I feel like some Thai food if you—"

She paused, obviously surprised to find someone else in the room with me, probably embarrassed that he would discover her in her nightwear, and I could tell that it took a few moments for her brain to catch up with her eyes and recognize who had invaded her place of safety under false pretenses.

Her scream was a sound that haunts me still.

9

Whether it was my argument about Jacob's late mother, my suggestion that he would one day be able to express to Rebecca how he'd been present when she most needed him, my refusal to book him a five-night stay in a Dubai hotel, or the exasperated tone of an unimpressed airline representative telling us that the doors would be closed in the next sixty seconds with or without us, Emmet finally agrees to board the plane. Throwing his hands in the air, he offers a series of furious expletives and storms ahead of me, taking his seat without another word.

This time, we're on opposite sides of the cabin so don't have to interact during the flight, which is probably for the best. Once we're in the air, I stand up to look across and see that he's immersed in another film, a blanket pulled over his body so only his eyes and the top of his head are visible. With the exception of a couple of trips to the bathroom, when we pass by without even acknowledging each other's existence, neither of us leaves our seats until we land in Ireland just over seven hours later.

It's early afternoon when we arrive at our hotel in the center of Dublin. As we've been traveling for twenty-four hours, I've reserved a room here for the night, so we can rest before undertaking the final leg of our journey. When we step inside, Emmet stares at the two single beds with a frown before turning and asking for his key.

"Here," I say, handing him one of the cards the receptionist gave me when we checked in.

"What's my room number?"

"I'm sorry?"

"My room number. Or is this one mine?"

It takes me a moment to understand what he's getting at.

"It's both of ours," I tell him. "We're sharing."

He drops his head low and groans in despair, as if he can't quite believe that I've brought this latest indignity to his door. He sounds like he's in actual pain.

"For fuck's sake, Emmet," I say, raising my voice and allowing myself to grow crankier now that our flights are behind us. "It's just for one night. What does it matter? We're going to be fast asleep in a few hours anyway."

"I don't like sharing rooms."

"You share a room with Damian all the time."

"That's different. He's my friend."

"Well, feel free to go downstairs and book a separate one for your-self if you have a spare four hundred euros in your wallet. But if you don't, then pick left or right and maybe lay off the complaining for five minutes, all right? Cos I'm tired, jet-lagged, and have had enough of it."

He opens his eyes wide in surprise. This is the first time I've dis-played any annoyance since shaking him awake in North Bondi some twenty-seven hours ago, and perhaps he's realized that he's lost any power he had over me now that we've finally arrived on the other side of the world. The truth is, I haven't the energy for any more of this behavior. It doesn't help that the closer we get to the island, the more anxious I'm growing over whether this has been a good idea or not. Particularly as there's still something I haven't told him.

We each take a shower, and while I emerge in a towel, planning on changing in the room, he takes his fresh clothes with him into the bath-room so he can dress in there when he's finished. It displays a curious need for modesty considering I see him in his swimmers on the beach on a regular basis. But it's different circumstances, I suppose. Lying on my bed, idly scrolling through my emails, I notice his phone charging by the side table, and hearing the sound of running water, I can't help myself. I reach for it and go straight to his photos. None of the recent pictures are in any way incriminating, although, to my surprise, he's taken a photo of me while I was asleep on the Sydney–Dubai leg, where I look rather at peace, a half smile on my face at whatever dream I was having. Moving to his messages, I can see this same picture has been forwarded to Damian, only edited so a drawing of a penis emerges from my forehead, which in turn has led to a series of nonsensical emojis from his friend. Despite myself, I laugh.

When he reappears fully dressed, his hair wet, I suggest a walk around the city, and he looks at me as if I've proposed that we go salsa dancing. I read this as my cue that it would be in both our interests to spend a little time apart, so tell him that, regardless, I'm going out to explore, will probably find somewhere for a meal later and will text to see whether he wants to join me.

"So you won't be coming back here first?" he asks, and I shake my head, happy to leave him in peace.

"No. And if you'd prefer to just stay in and order room service, that's fine too. I mean, it'd be a shame to miss out on seeing some of Dublin, but if you need some alone time   "

"I do," he replies quickly.

"OK," I say, knowing exactly how he feels.

"I'm sorry about earlier," he adds as I reach for my jacket, perhaps feeling an impulse toward harmony now that he knows he won't have to be in my company for a while. "In Dubai, I mean. I was just tired. And a bit nervous."

"It's OK," I say, not wishing to revisit that moment. "I'll see you later."

As I leave, I notice a Do Not Disturb sign hanging on the inside of the door and pick it up.

"Shall I put this outside?" I ask and he nods.

"Thanks."

Although Rebecca was born in Dublin, and lived there until moving to England in her early twenties, I've never been to Ireland before and wander the city center, glancing idly in the windows of shops, before entering a bookshop, thinking I could probably do with buying a couple more thrillers to get me through the days ahead and the eventual flight home. The gods are clearly intent on tormenting me, however, because as I step inside, I'm confronted by a tower of Furia's novels on the New Releases table. It's piled high—it really is turning into a global phenomenon—with a sticker on the front proclaiming that it's "soon to be a major motion picture" as opposed, I assume, to a minor one.

Unlike the edition I saw in Sydney Airport, this one is resplendent in hardcover and bears a different jacket. As I study it, a young woman pushes a trolley laden with books toward the next table.

"Have you read that?" she asks, and I shake my head. "We can't keep it in stock."

I glance down. There must be thirty copies here at least, so clearly they can.

"What's it about?" I ask.

Of course, I know exactly what it's about, but I'm interested to know how she'll describe it. I remember Furia once telling me of a creative writing tutor who had asked this question of his students about the books they were writing, but insisted that they reference neither the plot nor the characters in their reply. She turns her head in the direction of a staircase, giving my question some thought.

"I think it's about selfishness," she says finally, then nods, apparently satisfied by her response.

"It's a love story, I assume?"

"Why would you think that?" she asks. "Because it's written by a woman?"

"No, because most novels are."

"Do you really think so?"

"I do," I say. "Art is generally about love, one way or another, don't you think? Every book. Every song. Every film. All of us trying to live with it. Or get over it. Or wonder why we've never had it. Not necessarily love in a sexual sense. Love between parents and children. Love for a place."

She remains silent, considering this. Her expression suggests she'd like to contradict me but can't quite decide how.

"Who's the selfish one anyway?" I ask. "In the book, I mean."

"They all are," she replies. "The main characters—she's a drover, which is—"

"I know what a drover is."

"You're Australian?" she asks, and I nod. I might not have been born there but I have permanent residency, after all, so I consider myself a native now. "I can hear it in your accent," she tells me. "Anyway, she breaks up a marriage. Although it was an unhappy marriage."

"And that makes it OK?"

"Well, it's more complicated than that. There are three people at the heart of the story, and they hurt each other at every turn. But they've all been hurt themselves in the past, so somehow we forgive them. In the end, the reader just wants everyone to survive and be happy. And of course there's the unreliable narrator, which is what everyone talks about."

"And do they?" I ask.

"Do they what?"

"Survive."

"That would be giving it away."

"I just want to know if things work out for them," I say. "A writer once told me that was the reason she wrote fiction. To give people happy endings."

"Sorry, no spoilers," she tells me. "You'll have to finish it to find out."

I arrive back at the hotel much later than intended, check on Emmet, who's in a deep sleep, before going down to the bar, sitting with Furia's book before me, unable to open it. I drink more than I should—perhaps my body is out of sync after the last couple of days—before eventually making my way a little unsteadily toward the elevator. I suspect that tomorrow morning I might regret not having gone straight to bed.

It's been many years since I've slept in the same bedroom as my son, and I find his presence strangely comforting. He's sleeping in a T-shirt and boxer shorts, his right arm slung over the side of the bed, his left leg sticking out from beneath the duvet. Part of me feels slightly disconcerted by how beautiful I find him. There were moments in his childhood when I found him so utterly perfect that it was difficult not to weep when he came running toward me. When I would bring him to

Nippers, I would study his small body and fear that I was fetishizing his splendor. I wanted him to stay that way forever, never to change. And it seems as if it's only now, in moments of repose, when he's not being a pain-in-the-ass teen, that his childhood flawlessness is momentarily restored.

I suppose I looked like him once, long ago, too. Utterly innocent.

Maybe that's why Freya chose me.

It's just gone noon when we check out, and happily, Emmet has woken in good spirits, while I, on the other hand, feel a little rough. He seems almost excited when we board the train at Heuston Station, heading in the direction of Galway.

"Don't," he says when he sees me smiling.

"Don't what?" I ask.

"You're thinking about my trains," he says, and I laugh, despite myself.

"Yes," I admit. "Those bloody things."

At the age of five, only a year after Rebecca left, Emmet became obsessed with toy trains, constructing an elaborate system of railway lines that ran around our home: carriages, signals, tiny buildings, and miniature figures everywhere. Every birthday and Christmas, it was the only thing he wanted. It was a harmless hobby, although I had to make my peace with how much of the apartment they took over. And then, one day about three years ago, I came home to find his entire collection disassembled, boxed up, and placed for sale on eBay. He sold it to a collector for a surprisingly large amount, and I found myself missing them afterward. For all my professional training, it took a while for me to recognize that their loss signaled the end of a special period in our lives. When I suggested this to him a few weeks later, he buried his head in his hands and pleaded with me, for the thousandth time, not to psychoanalyze him.

"Here's the difference between you and me, Dad," he said. "You see me selling them as a sign that I'm getting older, which means you're getting older, so you're thinking about your mortality and the fact that, one day, you'll die. While, for me, it's much less complicated. I just want a better board and a couple of hundred dollars in my bank account for the summer."

"Wow," I said, as I tried to take this in.

"And I didn't even have to spend seven years in medical school to figure that out," he added with a grin.

It was hard to argue with that assessment.

Now, as this real-life train makes its way across the country, through Kildare, Tullamore, and Athlone, we're at ease with each other, chatting about inconsequential matters. Only as we pass through Ballinasloe, with less than an hour to go, do I dare to ask how's he feeling now about seeing his mother.

"Fine," he says, noncommitally.

"Your enthusiasm is overwhelming."

"Whatever."

"Don't *whatever* me," I say. "It's complicated being a parent."

"Sure."

I can see from the expression on his face that his anger with Rebecca is what's making him try to provoke me. It crosses my mind that he'll probably be a father himself one day, and when that happens, he'll be good at it. Each year as he's advanced through the Nippers colors, from red to brown, he's shown himself to be particularly concerned with looking after younger children, encouraging them, watching out for their safety in the waves, and lending them a helping hand whenever needed. It's one of the things that makes me think his idea of becoming a lifeguard is a good one.

It was only six months ago, during that conversation, that I told him about his aunt Emma, who drowned off a Wexford beach when Rebecca and her parents were holidaying there decades earlier. He was shocked by this revelation—he'd never even known that she existed—and I could see that it left a deep impression on him. Later that day, he phoned his mother to ask about her, and she refused to engage in the conversation, insisting that Emmet return the phone to me, when she read me the riot act.

"He's our son," I told her. "He had to know sometime."

"You didn't tell him anything else, did you? About why she did it?"

"Of course not."

"Do you think I should?" she asked, her tone softening.

"Well, not over the phone."

"Obviously not."

"But maybe next time you see him?"

There was a lengthy silence.

"I don't want to bring that darkness into his life," she said. "You haven't brought yours into his either."

"Maybe he needs to hear it," I suggested. "So he can understand both of us better. He's not a child anymore."

As I'm recalling this, out of the blue, Emmet says, "Dad, there's something I need to tell you."

"Go on," I say, snapping back to the moment.

"It's about yesterday evening."

"What about it?"

"When you left me alone in the hotel."

My mind spins in a dozen different directions. I know I was gone far longer than expected—and, in the end, I never bothered to text him, assuming he would contact me if he wanted to meet—but surely nothing untoward could have taken place during my few hours of absence.

"What about it?" I ask nervously.

"It's just . . ." He hesitates, and takes a deep breath. "The thing is—"

"What? Just spit it out."

"I nearly . . ."

I'm ready to shake him now to get whatever it is out of him.

"Nearly what? Just tell me."

He looks out the window, shakes his head, then turns back, looking down at the table that separates us and scratching it awkwardly with his thumb.

"I nearly had a threesome."

I'm not certain that I've heard him right. How is that even possible? He knows absolutely no one in Dublin. And he's only fourteen. The same age I was when—

"All I needed," he adds, "was two other people."

There's a few moments of silence before he bursts out laughing, collapsing back in the seat, his knees pressed up against his chest. It takes me a minute to get the joke, and when I do, I can't quite believe that he'd prank me like this, but I find myself laughing too, unable to stop. Tears roll down both our faces, and some of the other passengers turn to look at us in irritation. I would like to preserve this moment forever. The two of us, on this train, heading toward Galway, laughing over the silliest joke I've ever heard in my life.

"God, I miss the beach," he says a little later, looking out as the green fields pass us by. "My body literally feels like it's drying out."

"I miss it too, actually."

"I will never live anywhere but Sydney."

I expect to feel pleased by this declaration, but as much as I want to keep him close, I also want him to explore the world, something that I've failed to do in my life so far. A thought occurs to me that I still could. No matter what Emmet says, I'm not Jurassic. I'm only forty. So I'll be forty-four if and when he goes to uni. That's still young.

"There are beaches in other countries," I tell him. "I'm pretty sure the oceans stretch around the planet."

"Long term, I mean," he replies. "When I'm really old and settling down. Like, twenty-seven or whatever."

I stifle a laugh.

"Well, at least we're going to an island," I tell him. "You can probably swim there."

"Can I ask you something?" he says.

"Sure."

"Furia."

"What about her?"

"Do you think . . ." He pauses and bites his lip as if he wants to ensure that he phrases this exactly right. "Do you think that if you'd never met her, then you and Mum would still be together? And that she wouldn't have abandoned me?"

I've never heard him use this particular word before to describe his estrangement from Rebecca. Would he prefer to lay all culpability for his parents' breakup at Furia's feet? I can't say that I blame him, but I don't want to lie to him either. It would be unfair to both of them, and to him too.

But it's not the time to answer.

"Can we have this conversation another time?" I ask him. "It's a long story, and we're too close to Galway. But I will talk about it with you, I promise."

He sighs, then nods his head, before taking his AirPods out, putting them in his ears, and looking out the window. I silently curse myself. I've fucked up again.

10

Neither Rebecca nor I had ever been to Australia, but two years after we married, she was offered the opportunity to complete her training in Sydney and we made the decision to relocate.

Although it stretched our budget, we chose to rent an apartment on Waruda Street in Kirribilli for a few months while we got to know the city. Our balcony faced directly onto the Opera House, and there were mornings, as we breakfasted, when I felt an overwhelming sense of well-being, an inner peace that I hadn't experienced in a long time. One night, drunk, we even had sex—a rare treat—and, as fate would have it, that was the night Emmet was conceived.

Rebecca reacted to her pregnancy better than I expected, given her previous determination not to bring a child into the world, and we might have gone on like that forever, two companionable people in a sexless relationship, bringing up their son, had Furia Flyte not entered our lives.

We first met at a birthday party when Emmet was three. We had quite a small circle of friends, as Rebecca's schedule once she was qualified left little time for socializing, and I was alone with him much of the time. I formed good relationships with the parents who helped out at Nippers, growing friendly with another set of parents, Belinda and Jake, a full-time lifeguard who proposed to teach me surfing. Their son, Damian, had bonded with Emmet on their first day in Kindy, and the two boys had rarely lost sight of each other since.

Eventually, it seemed sensible that we should all meet, and we began with a Saturday lunchtime date in the Ravesis, a lively spot that afforded views of the surfers making their way toward the beach. Somewhat to my surprise, Rebecca and Belinda hit it off, and I saw a side to my wife that I hadn't often observed before. Carefree, relaxed, unencumbered by the past. She liked Jake too and a comfortable friendship developed, pushed along by our sons' growing bond.

Jake's thirtieth birthday party took place in a nightclub in Bondi. Having lived in Sydney for a few years by now, I was accustomed to beautiful people. Hardly a day went by when my head wasn't turned by the women who passed me on the street. But in my life I had never laid eyes on anyone as beautiful as the woman I met there. I'd never even imagined that such women existed.

When I first saw her, she was standing alone by a trestle table, sipping from a glass of champagne and looking out toward the sea. Her skin was a dark ebony, her hair shaved close to the skull, allowing her extraordinary bone sculpting to come to the fore. Rebecca had vanished into the crowd, and I found myself gravitating toward her.

She looked at me rather coolly as I advanced and I guessed that she was not unaccustomed to men approaching her, but, after all, we were at a private party, which meant that we must both have some connection to the hosts.

"Can I join you?" I asked.

She nodded, and we fell into conversation easily. When she threw her head back and laughed at some remark I made about the latest government crisis, I felt a premonition, and a strong desire, that this would prove more than just a random encounter.

We exchanged details about our lives. I told her about my job, and she confessed that, while she currently worked in a theater, she had aspirations toward being a writer. Possibly a playwright. Possibly a novelist. Possibly a screenwriter. Possibly all three. She'd published some short stories, she told me, including one in an American anthology, and had had a one-act play produced at the previous year's Sydney Festival. She betrayed neither narcissism nor false humility as she talked about her ambitions, admitting that she'd already written a novel that had been rejected by publishers.

"Fuckers," I said.

"No, it wasn't good enough. They were right to turn it down."

"And you're working on something else?"

"Always."

"Will this be the one?"

"I'm twenty-nine," she told me with a shrug. "And my plan was always to get published before I turn thirty, so that ship's probably sailed. But there's nothing else that I want to do with my life than tell stories."

"Why?" I asked.

"Because unlike in the real world, when a writer invents characters, we get to decide how their stories end. Happy or sad."

"And which do you favor?"

"Oh, happy," she told me without hesitation. "Always happy. Readers need to feel that there's hope."

"For the characters?"

"No. For them."

I felt a deep desire to tell her how beautiful she was but restrained myself. But it wasn't just her face or her body to which I was attracted. It was deeper than that. I wanted to know her in every way that you can know a person.

"I haven't even asked your name," I said when we were on our second glass of champagne.

"Furia," she said, extending a hand. "Furia Flyte."

"Sounds like a pen name."

"I know. But I swear it's real. And you?"

"Aaron Umber."

"Your accent," she said. "You're not from here, are you?"

"No," I said, telling her a little about the city where I'd grown up.

"I haven't traveled much yet. Although I'd like to."

I'd almost forgotten that I was at a party. It seemed like we were just two people who'd met in a club and been drawn to each other. I couldn't be certain that the attraction was mutual, but I felt it was.

After we'd been talking for around forty minutes, Rebecca joined us, introducing herself to Furia, who looked at me with a disenchanted expression on her face, as if she was both surprised and unsurprised that

I had failed to mention the existence of a wife. The conversation became stilted then, and I looked over the balcony toward the waves crashing onto the shore, feeling a desperate urge to throw myself into the water and swim out as far as I could.

It was Rebecca, however, who brought Furia back into our lives a few weeks later. We had a spare ticket to a concert, and she suggested offering it to her.

"Why?" I asked. "We barely know her."

"Actually, I had a coffee with her on Tuesday."

I was startled by this admission, and immediately envious, having spent a lot of time since Jake's party trying to contrive a reason to meet again while my wife had simply done the sensible thing and phoned her up.

"Why did you do that?" I asked.

"Because we got along and exchanged numbers," she replied with a shrug, as if it was the most obvious thing in the world. "Why, didn't you like her?"

"She seemed fine," I said.

"I mean, we don't have to," she told me. "We can invite someone else if you prefer."

"No, it's fine," I replied. "It would be nice to see her again."

Furia replied to Rebecca's text invitation with a yes, and I spent the days leading up to the gig obsessing over what I would wear.

"Have you done something with your hair?" Furia asked when we found a small bar for drinks after the show had ended.

"He's had it styled," said Rebecca, a mocking note creeping into her tone. "He usually just gets it cut, but this afternoon he had it styled apparently."

"It looks good," she replied, her eyes meeting mine.

"Thank you," I said.

"You haven't added highlights, have you?"

"Christ, no," I told her. "I'm not some aging boy band member. I'm naturally blond but it lightens even more during the summer."

Standard conversation followed, questions about Emmet, asking how Rebecca and I had first met, and soon, the subject of whether she was seeing anyone arose. My heart beat a little faster in my chest as I waited for her reply.

"Not right now," she said. "I think I've sworn off men."

"Really?" asked Rebecca. "Why?"

"Cos I'm fucking sick of them. Every guy I've been with has done something to let me down. I just think I've reached the point where I'm wondering whether I need the hassle. They're either using apps on the side, looking for nothing more than a shag, or they're married. Or all three. The truth is, we only really need a man in order to have a child. And even then, they're pretty much disposable afterward."

"None taken," I said, and she smiled.

"I think I just need to mix it up a bit," she continued, looking around the bar as if she hoped the right man might be sitting somewhere nearby just waiting to introduce himself. "No more fuckboys. I need to try someone different to my usual type."

"Like who?" I asked, ready to transform myself into whatever that might be.

"I haven't figured that out yet. Not an Aussie, that's for sure. Someone with experience of life outside Sydney. One of the benefits of writing, if I ever get published that is, will be the opportunities I'll have to see the world. Maybe I'll meet someone amazing in, you know, Argentina or Denmark or someplace like that."

"Of course you'll get published," I said.

"How do you know? You haven't read anything I've written."

"I offered."

"No you didn't," she said, and she was right, I had merely thought it on the night we met but considered it too forward to ask.

"Well, I'm offering now," I said. "I'd love to read your work."

"Aaron," said Rebecca, "all you ever read is thrillers."

"Then it would be good to broaden my horizons, wouldn't it? Obviously I wouldn't be able to give you any great critique but, I mean, if you'd like a reader, then . . . I know it's a very personal thing . . ." I let the sentence drift away, conscious that I might be sounding a little ridiculous.

[448]

"Well, thank you," said Furia, reaching over and placing a hand atop my own and squeezing it. "That's kind of you. Let me think about it."

I ordered more drinks and went to the bathroom, looking myself in the mirror and throwing some water on my face. Although I was only in my twenties, so was still a young man, I couldn't help but think that this is how it must feel to be young, an experience that seemed to have passed me by. The only real difference, after all, between me and a fifteen-year-old virgin going on his first date was that when a kid that age was trying to impress a girl, he didn't usually have his wife sitting between them.

When I returned to the table, Furia and Rebecca were locked in conversation, and for a time it felt as if they weren't even aware of my presence.

"Have you been on a plane that Rebecca has flown?" asked Furia, turning to me eventually, and I shook my head.

"Not yet, no," I said. "When she's away, I'm home with Emmet."

"And would you trust her?"

"Well, she's a terrible driver," I said. "So I'm not sure."

"No I'm not," said Rebecca, frowning.

"You are."

"You've never said that before."

"Sparing your feelings."

"I'm a perfectly safe driver," she insisted, turning to Furia.

"Try being her passenger."

"I don't know why you're saying this. It's simply not true."

"Relax," I told her. "I'm just teasing."

"Well, stop. I don't like it."

There's nothing more uncomfortable than couples arguing in public so I bit my tongue, particularly as I couldn't quite understand why I was saying something that was actually completely untrue. The evening ended soon after and, true to form, Rebecca and I, on the verge of a row, went to bed without exchanging another word.

A week later, I contrived to be near the University of Sydney and met Furia as she was coming out of a seminar. I pretended that this was a chance encounter before inviting her for a drink. We went to a bar in Redfern where the sun bore down as we sat beneath canopies in a beer garden, sunglasses on so we didn't have to read each other's eyes. We talked for a long time, quite intimately, and then:

"Can I ask, what happened to you?" she asked me in a cautious, gentle tone.

"How do you mean?"

"You have a . . ." She thought about it, searching for the right phrase. "You have a sadness inside you, Aaron. I saw it the night we met at Jake's birthday party. And—I don't mean to be rude, it's not a criticism—but an emotional immaturity. You look younger than your years too, which is odd. It's like you're stunted in some way."

The phrase hit home. I was still the awkward boy approaching Freya after she explained the benefits of a career in medicine to my school group, telling me that if I was interested in learning more about her profession, then she had some introductory textbooks in her apartment that she could loan me, and I could come home with her and borrow them.

"Something happened to me," I told her carefully. "Years ago now I was just a kid at the time."

"Something sexual, I assume?"

"Yes."

"At the hands of a man?"

"No, a woman."

She sat back and nodded, considering this.

"That's unusual," she said.

"It's actually more common than you might imagine. No one talks about it, except to joke about it."

"Do you want to tell me more?"

I shook my head. "Another time, perhaps. When we get to know each other better."

"Isn't this exactly how we get to know each other better?" she asked. "By talking about things like this?"

"Honestly, it's too sad a story. And this is too beautiful a day. I'd prefer to just sit here with you and not sing any sad songs."

"Tell me about Rebecca, then."

"What would you like to know?"

"Are you happy with her?"

My vacillation probably said it all. I simply couldn't think of a truthful answer to the question.

"She's very beautiful," she said eventually.

"She is," I agreed.

"And smart."

"Yes. But—"

"But what?"

"I don't want to frighten you away by saying something too intimate."

"I don't mean to pry. Don't say anything that makes you uncomfortable."

"She doesn't love me," I said immediately, expressing something aloud that I had always known but never had the courage to admit aloud. "And I don't think she ever has. I don't think she knows what love is."

"Men always say things like that," she said, sighing, and I worried that I was disappointing her by sounding like a cliché. "It's always the woman's fault."

"No, I didn't mean—"

"It's OK."

She turned away. A young couple was walking down the street hand in hand, the reverse of us in that the boy was black and the girl was white, he with his head thrown back in laughter at something she was saying.

"Why would you say such a thing about your own wife?" she asked.

"Too," I said.

"Too? I don't understand."

"I say *I love you*, but she says *I love you too*. It's never the other way around. She never initiates it."

"Perhaps she thinks it goes unsaid."

"It should never go unsaid."

"Do you still sleep together?"

"That's all we do," I told her, laughing bitterly. "Sleep together. Physical intimacy has never been much of a thing between us."

"How come? You're hot. She's hot."

I felt thrilled by the compliment.

"She makes me feel worthless," I continued, uncertain why I was opening up like this. *Did I want her to pity me? To take me home to her apartment and fuck me?* "Ugly. Unattractive. Unworthy. I'm still a young man, Freya. I want someone to look at me and want me. Why shouldn't I have that? Others do. You must get it all the time. Why shouldn't I have that? What's wrong with me?"

"Furia," she said.

"What?"

"You called me Freya."

"No I didn't."

"You did."

Trying to read her mind, I wondered whether she was looking into the future, at what might happen between us in a week, a month, a year, ten years, if this connection grew deeper and she became the catalyst for the end of my marriage. Whether she was imagining what it might be like to be naked with me, as I was imagining what it might be like to be naked with her. I stretched my arm out, leaving a hand on the table, hoping that she would give me some signal, place hers atop mine as she had after the concert. She seemed to be considering it, because she stared at it for a long time before deciding against. Perhaps, when Rebecca had been present, it had felt like an inconsequential act whereas here, with just the two of us present, it would take on greater significance. Or perhaps it was because it was my left hand, and my wedding ring was visible on my fourth finger.

"Be honest with me, Aaron," she said. "Because whatever is going to happen next depends on the answer to this question. Do you believe that you and Rebecca have a future together? Do you want one?"

I took a long time to answer. I could physically feel my heart beating in my chest. The fact that she was even considering being with me made me hard. But I couldn't answer. I failed in this crucial moment and, after a minute or two of silence, she looked away, raised a hand to the waiter, and asked for the bill. As usual, I simply didn't know how to behave.

As we left, however, I took hold of her arm and asked her why she had asked me that question. She took off her sunglasses and looked directly at me.

AIR

"Because I don't want to be responsible for breaking up a marriage if there's a chance it can survive. Or if it should survive."

I took a chance.

"It can't. It won't," I told her. "You want to know something? The night before we got married, Rebecca's mother said something to me that I've never forgotten."

"What was it?"

"She said, don't marry her. You're a fool if you do."

"Her own mother said that?"

I nodded.

"Wow," she replied. "That explains a lot."

"Does it?" I asked. "What does it explain?"

She shook her head and said that we'd talked enough for one day, that she had some thinking to do, and before I could remonstrate with her and ask could we move on somewhere else, a taxi passed, she raised her hand, hailed it, and was gone.

We didn't see each other for some weeks after that but began exchanging text messages. These were not casual messages but were almost always about the status of Rebecca's and my relationship. Whether we were getting on better, spending time together, having sex. I began to worry that Furia was using me, or us, as research for a novel she was writing, but I didn't want to challenge her in case it led to her cutting me off.

What's happening with us? I asked in one late-night text, and although I could see that she had read it immediately, it took her more than an hour to reply.

I'm worried that I'm going to hurt you, she replied eventually. And you've been hurt enough already.

I'm willing to risk it.

Finally, one night, racked with desire, I showed up at her apartment building, pressing the buzzer to tell her that I was downstairs. Rather than inviting me up, however, she took the lift down to the lobby, looking both angry at my intrusion and also rather anxious.

"You can't just show up here like this," she told me.

"I needed to see you."

She glanced around, and a thought—a terrible thought—occurred to me.

"Do you have someone upstairs?" I asked. She shook her head, but I could tell that she was lying and felt almost sick with jealousy. "You do, don't you?"

"Fine. I do. I have a life, you know. And I don't answer to you."

"So much for having sworn off men. You never said there was anyone else in the picture," I said, furious with myself to hear the obvious emotion in my voice.

"You never asked. I don't know if you realize it, Aaron, but all we ever talk about is you. Your life. Your marriage. Your son. Your career. Your past. Your pain. We never talk about me at all. You never ask."

"That's not true," I insisted, surprised that this was how she saw me.

"It is," she insisted. "You tell me all the things that are wrong with your relationship, but you never talk to Rebecca about it. You speak to me like I'm your therapist."

"I speak to you like someone I'm in love with."

She reared back at this, looking shocked, which astonished me. She couldn't possibly have been surprised by this.

"Aaron, you barely know me."

"But I want to. I mean it. I'm in love with you."

"Oh for God's sake."

"You're all I think about."

She shook her head, looking pissed off, which, in turn, pissed me off.

"Are you writing about me?" I asked angrily. "About us? Is that what this has all been about?"

"No," she said, wrapping her arms around her body defensively.

"Then just tell me. I don't understand what it is that you want from me."

"I don't want anything."

"Then what has all this been about?"

"All of what?" she asked, raising her voice angrily.

"This," I said in exasperation, looking around as if the lobby of her building was the ground floor of our private home. "Everything that we've built between us."

"We've built nothing between us, Aaron. I told you early on that I'm not interested in men anymore. That I'm sick to death of men and their fucking bullshit. Bullshit like this. I want something different."

"Then why do we meet? Why do we text? You say all I ever talk about is me and the state of my marriage, but that's all you seem to be interested in, as if you've been trying to decide whether or not you should be the person who comes between Rebecca and me."

"That is what I've been trying to decide," she said.

"I don't understand," I said, utterly baffled, because she seemed to be contradicting herself at every turn.

"I've spent a lot of time thinking about this. And I've realized that I should. You're not right for each other. You're not. You'll never make each other happy. And you're both too young to be living such loveless lives. You both need more."

"So you are interested, then?" I asked.

"In what?"

"In me."

She buried her head in her hands and groaned loudly before looking back at me.

"No, Aaron, I'm not. For one thing, you've lied to me."

I took a step back, a chill spreading across my body.

"What have I lied about?"

"Do I need to spell it out?"

I stared at her. I knew what she was referring to but couldn't bring myself to admit it. And my mind was spinning as I tried to understand how she could possibly know.

"You're a kind man, Aaron," she continued. "A decent man. And I have nothing but sympathy for what you've been through. But I'm not interested in you in a romantic sense and that's never going to change. The truth is, I'm in love with someone else."

I felt as if I was about to stop breathing.

"So all of this has been for nothing?" I asked. "You've just been leading me on?"

"I've been leading you absolutely nowhere. You've just been walking behind me all this time, trying to keep up, and you haven't seen what's been staring you in the face."

Before I could say anything more, the bell above the elevator sounded and the doors opened. Emerging barefoot, wearing only a pair of denim shorts and a T-shirt, a figure emerged, looking from me to Furia and back again.

My brain couldn't immediately comprehend how this person was here. Or why. It simply didn't make any sense.

Furia turned around, saw her, and looked down at the floor.

"I'm sorry," said Rebecca, looking almost relieved that the truth had finally been revealed. "This wasn't how either of us wanted you to find out."

11

A man named Cian Ó'Droighneáin picks us up from Galway Harbour in a small boat and tells us that it won't take more than an hour to reach the island. I see Emmet visibly spring to life, like a wilting flower, when he's close to water again. Somehow, the waves of the Atlantic Ocean look and smell different to those that lap toward Bondi, Manly, Coogee, or any of the other beaches I'm familiar with from Sydney. Even as the spray splashes across my face, it tastes different on my tongue. Darker, more threatening, offering a warning that travelers pass through its current at their own risk. I wonder how many souls it has claimed over the centuries in revenge for intrusion. For Emmet, however, who lets his right hand to rest within it, it's a return to his comfort zone after the lengthy plane and train journeys, as if he has reverted to the warmth and sanctuary of the womb.

The Bish. Half boy, half fish.

Before leaving Sydney, I located a small cottage online and booked it for three nights. A taxi driver waiting by the port drives us up a winding road toward it, depositing us with little ceremony by the front door. The owner of the lodging, one Peader Dooley, has emailed to say that I will find a key beneath a plant pot by the front door, and he is true to his word. Stepping inside, I'm struck by the musty smell and I suspect it hasn't been occupied in some time. Opening the windows, I turn the light on—a single bare bulb hanging from the ceiling—and look around, surveying the room, which is either a kitchen that houses a living room or a living room that houses a kitchen. It's hard to tell. Emmet, frowning, is focused entirely on his phone.

"There's no Wi-Fi," he says, his tone one of utter disbelief. "Dad, there's no Wi-Fi," he repeats, louder now.

"Should I call the police?" I ask and he stares at me for a moment, as if he thinks I'm genuinely suggesting this, before rolling his eyes. "We're in a fairly isolated place, Emmet," I tell him. "It's possible there won't be any Wi-Fi on the island at all."

"None?"

"I mean, it's possible."

"How do they survive?"

It does seem a little disconcerting to be so removed from the outside world—even I'm willing to admit that—but it wasn't as if I had many options. There were no hotels, and this was the only cottage available. I leave him to make his peace with digital isolation and take a look in the bedroom, where I'm greeted by a single bed. Before Emmet can notice it and start screaming like a banshee, I tell him that I'll sleep on the sofa and allow him his privacy.

"Do people actually live here?" he asks, sounding amazed, as if he's just walked onto the set of a historical movie.

"Well, it's a rental," I tell him. "So probably not all year-round."

"But what about the other houses?"

"I don't know," I say with a shrug. "They're probably a bit more up-to-date."

He starts taking photos on his phone, and I know he wants to send them to Damian or one of his other friends with some sarcastic comment attached but then realizes that, without Wi-Fi, to do so would cost him a small fortune.

"Look, we'll make the most of it," I say cheerfully. "Communing with nature and all that."

He opens his mouth to protest but recognizes that this is exactly the sort of sentiment that he would generally endorse, so remains silent.

"Right," I add, assuming that we're done with the complaints for now. "Do you want to wash up or shall we just head straight out?"

"Where are we meeting her?" he asks.

"Who?"

"Mum."

"Ah," I reply, realizing that I can't delay this revelation any longer. I've been putting off telling him, but it really can't wait. "You might want to take a seat."

He does as instructed, collapsing into a threadbare armchair that, even from where I'm standing, has a faint feline scent to it, looking a little anxious.

"Go on," he says.

"The thing is, I probably should have mentioned this before, but your mother doesn't actually know we're coming."

There's a lengthy pause while he takes this in.

"I'm sorry," he asks, shaking his head as if he can't quite make sense of my words. "What?"

"She doesn't . . . I didn't tell her."

"What do you mean you didn't tell her?"

"I don't really know how else to put it."

"But how could you . . . why not?"

"Well, it's not as if we talk that often."

"No but . . ." He raises his voice and throws his arms in the air. "She invited us, didn't she?"

"Not in so many words. When she phoned to tell me the news, she simply said that she was coming here for the funeral and to let you know that your grandmother had died. She didn't actually say that we should travel over for it."

Emmet's eyes open wide.

"Dad," he says, trying to control his emotions. "We've flown halfway across the world! What if she's not even here?"

"Of course she'll be here," I tell him. "The funeral is tomorrow, after all. Where else would she be?"

He shakes his head, trying to make sense of this.

"So she didn't want us to come?" he asks, more of a whisper now.

"It's not so much that she didn't want us to come," I explain. "It's more that she didn't specifically say that we should."

"What if she's angry?"

"She won't be."

He shakes his head, unconvinced, and looks around in despair.

"This is insane," he says, as much to himself as to me. "I should have been taken into care years ago. You're both nuts. You're both completely fucking nuts."

I stifle a laugh. He doesn't sound so much angry as perplexed, and to my relief, he's not responding to the news as badly as I feared he would. I make my way over to the sink and turn the tap on. The water runs a hideous brown for the best part of a minute before turning clear. I pour a glass and sip it cautiously. It's cold, fresh, and delicious.

"So how do we find her?" he asks, his tone exhausted but resigned.

"Well, as far as I understand it, there's only about four hundred people on the island. And a single village at the heart of it. So I don't imagine it will be all that difficult. We could check the local pubs, and if we can't find her there, then someone will probably be able to point us in the right direction."

"Fine," he says. "Either way, this will make a great story for my therapist in years to come."

"I can probably recommend some good names if you like."

He walks past me without even acknowledging this remark and goes into the bathroom, while I unpack our cases and leave some clean clothes out for him on his bed. I hear the shower running and decide to go outside until he's ready and look around.

It's beautiful here. Green, hilly, natural. In the distance, I hear the sound of sheep, although looking around I can't see any. There's a good view of the ocean and a well-worn path leading down toward it. I could imagine a person sitting outside in the sunshine, reading a book, leaving the world behind them. It's an attractive idea. Glancing to my right, I notice a raised farm on the hill next to the cottage, where a man around my age, tall and blond, is leaning on a fence, smoking a cigarette. He raises a hand in greeting and I raise mine too, considering whether I should wander over to say hello, but before I can decide he turns and disappears out of sight.

"You ready?" says a voice from behind me, and I turn to see my son, who looks refreshed, having changed into the jeans and T-shirt I laid out for him.

"Sure," I say.

"And remember, if this goes wrong, it's on you."

I nod, and we make our way along the path that, I assume, will lead us toward the village at the heart of the island. He turns to look in the direction of the beach and asks whether he can go swimming later, and I tell him that it might be dangerous at night, but there's no reason why he can't go down there in the morning before the funeral, and he seems satisfied by this.

"What was she like anyway?" he asks as we walk along.

"What was who like?"

"Your mother-in-law."

"You mean your grandmother."

"I didn't have enough of a relationship with her to call her that."

"Nor did I. Maybe we should just call her Vanessa."

"OK."

"I only met her a couple of times," I tell him. "We went for dinner a few nights before your mum and I got married. And then we saw a little of her during that week. After that, our paths never crossed again."

"Why not?"

I shrug. "Things were complicated between them. You know that."

"Yeah, but no one's ever explained to me why. Is it just a family thing with us? Mothers who aren't interested in their kids, I mean?"

I take a breath. Perhaps now, on this brisk but sunny afternoon, in such a peaceful place, it's time to explain to him the darker aspects of Rebecca's childhood and teenage years, because God knows it's unlikely she'll ever do so herself. Maybe it will give him a better understanding of her and allow him to forgive her neglect.

"What?" he asks, when I stop for a moment and press my thumb and index finger to the corners of my eyes, trying to decide.

"If you want the answer to that question," I tell him, "then I'll give it to you. But it's not pretty."

He hesitates only briefly, before nodding his head.

"I want it," he says.

And so, as we continue to walk, I tell him the terrible story of his grandfather, Brendan Carvin, and the effect his actions had, not just on the eight little girls who he raped, but on his wife and daughters too. It takes some time and I'm surprised that he listens without interruption.

When I reach the end of my narrative, however, the part that sees Vanessa arrive on this island many years earlier, he stops and sways a little, like a drunken man.

"Are you all right?" I ask him.

"I need to sit down for a minute."

And he does. Simply collapses onto the grass, as if his legs have given way beneath him. He presses his knees close to his chest and wraps his arms around them, his head buried low, as if he's trying to make himself appear as small as possible.

"Why did you never tell me any of this before?" he asks eventually, his voice so quiet that I have to struggle to hear him.

"You were too young. It's not the kind of thing you can talk about to a child."

"My grandfather," he says, looking up, tears forming in his eyes. "He did things like that?"

"He wasn't your grandfather," I tell him. "Other than in a purely biological sense. He was just a man you never met who married a woman you never knew and fathered a daughter who gave birth to you."

"So my grandfather."

"You know grandfathers," I insist. "You know lots of your friends' grandfathers. They're different men. Good men. Kind men. Brendan Carvin was not one of them."

"What if anyone finds out?" he asks, his voice cracking. "My friends. People at school." He hesitates for a moment. "Girls."

"No one will," I promise. "He's dead now."

"Really?"

"Yes."

"What happened to him?"

"A heart attack, I was told. So trust me, this isn't something that anyone will ever associate you with. You don't even share a surname."

"Did he hurt Mum?" he asks, and I shake my head.

"He didn't abuse her, if that's what you're asking. But your aunt, Emma, yes. He raped her. Repeatedly."

"And then she drowned."

"She took her own life," I say.

He turns his head to the right and vomits onto the grass, quickly and violently. There's not much in his stomach to throw up, and soon it's just dry heaves. I place my hand on his back to comfort him but he shrugs me off and I step away, allowing him to come to terms with these revelations himself.

Time passes; a lot of time, I think. And then, finally, he rises, takes a deep breath, and looks toward the center of the island. I can read my son well. I know what he's thinking.

He wants to be with his mother.

"Let's go," he says.

The village is even smaller than I'd imagined. A few shops. A church. And, at either end of the street, two pubs.

"Let's try here," I say, walking toward the closer one. We step inside, where we're met with the eyes of twenty people, all of whom end their conversations immediately and turn to stare at us, like we're two naïve strangers wandering across the moors in a horror movie, unaware of the dangers we might face when night falls. I look around, taking them in, but Rebecca isn't among them. In fact, there are no women here at all. "Let's try the other one," I say, but Emmet places a hand on my arm.

"Can we just stop here for a bit?" he asks. "I just . . . I need to . . ."

"Of course," I say. After everything he's just learned, it's not unreasonable that he needs a little time to collect his thoughts. He takes a seat at a table by the wall, and the barman walks toward us.

"What'll it be?" he asks, and in deference to where I am, I order a Guinness. I glance at Emmet, and he looks up.

"Make it two," he says.

I wonder what the barman will say, hoping that his response won't diminish my son, but he appears nonplussed and simply nods before returning behind the bar to pour the drinks.

"Another thing for you to tell your future therapist about," I tell him. "The holiday I turned you into an alcoholic."

"I don't think I'll be calling this a holiday," he says.

It takes a long time for the drinks to be delivered, the pints sitting on the counter for so long that I think the barman might have forgotten us, but soon he tops them off and brings them over. I take a sip of mine, relishing the taste. I've never been much of a Guinness drinker, but it turns out that it's true what they say: it's better in Ireland. Emmet takes a longer draft, and it's obvious that it's taking all his willpower not to spit it out across the table.

"People actually drink this stuff?" he asks.

"They say it's an acquired taste. I can get you a Coke if you want."

He shakes his head and brings it to his mouth again, taking a smaller sip this time. "When in Rome," he adds.

We drink silently and companionably for a while and I glance around at the pub, which is tastefully decorated and seems like the model for the kind of pre-bought Irish pubs that appear in cities around the world. Some of the patrons, I notice, are still throwing covert glances in our direction, as if they're nervous that we've brought the Plague with us.

"I get that she went through a lot of shit," says Emmet eventually. "Vanessa, I mean. But none of that had anything to do with me. So why did she never want to meet me?"

I let out a deep sigh. "Honestly, I can't answer that," I tell him. "I liked her when I met her so I was always surprised that she didn't want to build a relationship with you. But things were so troubled between your mother and her. There was the occasional rapprochement over the years, but they never lasted very long. It always felt that any peace existed purely to be a foundation for another war."

"It seems insane that the closest I'll ever be to her is when I'm at her funeral. And why is it here anyway? Why did she want to be buried in this crazy place?"

"It's not a crazy place," I say, offended on behalf of the island, to which I already feel an unexpected connection. "I know we've only been here a few hours, but don't you think it's sort of beautiful?"

He shrugs, but I can tell that he doesn't wholly disagree.

"I can't remember the full story," I explain. "Rebecca explained it so long ago. But after her husband's trial, Vanessa came here—I don't know why; to recover maybe?—but it became important to her in some way. Maybe it healed her. She'd lost a daughter, remember. And, one way or another, she'd lost a husband. The entire foundation of her life had been ripped apart. All those years of marriage. All the secrets. She told me about it herself, when we met."

"What did she say?"

"That the first thing she did when she came here was to change her name. Remember, she'd been through a very public scandal. Her husband was well known in the media world through his associations with the Swimming Federation and the Olympics and so on. She didn't want anyone to connect her with the things that had happened. Willow was her middle name and Hale her maiden name, so that's the name she adopted. She might have only spent a year here, but I think she considered it to be the most important of her life."

"But no one will be able to visit the grave."

"The islanders will."

"And her husband? What's his name? Rick?"

"Ron. And I have no idea. You'll meet him later, I expect."

"Did you meet him?"

"Again, very briefly."

"And what was he like?"

"He struck me as a decent man."

The barman passes by, throwing a few logs on the fire, and when he walks past us again, I stop him to ask whether he knows a woman named Rebecca Carvin.

"No one by that name living here," he tells me.

"She's visiting for a few days," I tell him. "For a funeral."

"Ah, that'll be Willow's funeral," he replies, blessing himself. "Try the old pub. End of the street. I saw them all heading that way earlier."

"Right, thanks," I say.

"I knew her a little," he adds before walking away.

"Rebecca?" I ask, surprised.

"No, Willow. She used to come in here for soup and a sandwich at lunchtime. She had a right go at me one day when I was pouring out my troubles to her. I can still see her, sitting across from me, giving me hell about what she called the endless selfishness of the middle-aged man who does what he wants and leaves his wife to pick up the pieces." He pauses for a moment, and I notice him glance at the fourth finger of his left hand, rubbing it slightly with his thumb. "She set me straight that day, I'll tell you that. I never forgot it."

I'm not quite sure how he expects me to respond to this, but before I can think of an answer he has moved on. I make my way toward the bathroom and throw some water on my face, looking myself directly in the mirror, like a character in a film. When I return, I nod to my son and we stand up and leave. It's still warm outside, despite the setting sun, and as we make our way along the street, we attract more curious eyes. A teenage girl passes us and I notice how she looks at Emmet appreciatively, an unknown, handsome, tanned boy in her small community, and he offers her a small smile in return. I need it, because I'm growing increasingly nervous, my stomach churning in anxiety about the reception we'll receive when we arrive at the old pub.

When we reach the door, I pause and take a deep breath, as if I need to summon all my courage to push it open. Before I can commit to the moment, however, Emmet places a hand on my arm and I turn to look at him.

"Dad," he says.

"Yes?"

He hesitates.

"Just to say. I know this has probably been the world's worst fortieth birthday."

"You're not wrong there."

"But . . ." And here he avoids my eyes, looking down at the ground beneath our feet. "You've been a great dad." He bites his lip, embarrassed, and says the words that I've spent my life longing to hear, a phrase without the word *too* at the end. "So, just to say . . . I love you. And I'm glad you brought me here."

I tell myself not to ruin the moment by hugging him like a maniac. Instead, I simply nod and mentally record the moment, which I know I will relive many times in the future.

Then we push the door open and step inside.

This pub is filled with people, music, and conversation. I look around, and it doesn't take long for me to notice a table toward the rear, where the big, burdensome body of Ron is sitting, sipping a large whiskey. He's wiping his eyes.

Next to him, dressed immaculately, her hand on his arm, is Furia.

And opposite them both, speaking animatedly, is Rebecca.

She happens to glance in my direction, then frowns, as if she doesn't quite recognize me. It's not dissimilar to my own reaction all those years ago when I discovered her in that apartment building in Sydney, her brain taking a moment to catch up with the reality before her.

It's only when our son steps out from behind me that she puts both hands to her mouth in astonishment.

She stands up slowly, leaning on the table to support herself, before making her way across the floor to greet us.

I remain where I am, allowing Emmet to approach her first.

They meet somewhere in the middle, and he takes the initiative, wrapping his arms around her, hugging her close to him, and she embraces him in return.

It seems obscene, like a voyeur, to watch any further, so I turn away, but not before seeing how she has buried her face in his shoulder, her tears mixing with his.

12

On a small island like this, so isolated from the world, it surprises me that the priest who conducts the funeral service is not Irish. In fact, as I come to learn, he's Nigerian but has spent much of his life far removed from his native soil. The church, however, is almost empty. Ron, Rebecca, and Furia sit in the front pew on the right-hand side of the aisle, while Emmet and I take our places on the left. Perhaps a couple of dozen islanders are scattered in the benches behind us, but I suspect most are here simply for the mass itself or to get out of the house. Two, however, catch my eye. The neighbor who waved to me from the farm next to the cottage earlier, who's dressed in a formal black suit and sits upright in his seat, occasionally brushing his blond hair out of his eyes. And a woman sitting in the very back row, who looks careworn, as if she is struggling with the very business of existence.

In his eulogy, the priest tells us that he remembers Vanessa from the time she spent here all those years ago.

"She called herself Willow Hale back then," he says. "And I was fortunate at the time to get to know her and to learn a little about her life. My feeling was that she was a woman both running away from and toward something. She was looking for healing, and I hope that during her exile with our island community, she found some. As many of us later discovered, she had experienced a troubled period prior to coming here, but when she left, I think her soul had been restored, at least a little. Her time in America subsequent to this was filled with joy, not least because of the happiness she found with her husband, Ron." He offers a small nod in the direction of the man, who acknowledges it. "But when I learned that Vanessa wanted to be buried here," he continues, "I will confess that the request moved me tremendously. We did not stay in touch after she left, but I can only assume that something of the serenity of this place remained with her forever."

He hesitates for a moment, as if he's uncertain whether he should say what he plans on saying next, glancing briefly toward the woman in the back row, as if to seek her approval. Or at least her understanding.

"Many years ago," he continues at last, "I found myself in London in the company of a young man who had grown up in this place, and while we had a drink together, I remarked to him that eventually, I would be buried in the earth of Nigeria, alongside my people. It was something I believed at the time but I'm certain now that this will not come to pass. For, like Vanessa, I intend to make my final resting place here, in this peaceful paradise. Vanessa made many choices in her life, as we all do, some of which she may have regretted, but this, perhaps, was among her best."

Afterward, making his way around the congregation, he shakes my hand, introducing himself as Fr. Ifechi Onkin.

"And you?" he asks.

"Aaron Umber," I tell him.

"You're Australian?"

"Sort of."

"And may I ask how you knew Vanessa?"

"Her daughter Rebecca and I were once married," I explain. "That boy over there, holding her hand, that's Emmet, our son."

He looks over and takes in the scene, nodding his head.

"And were you close with your mother-in law?" he asks.

"Former mother-in-law," I say, correcting him. "And no. Not at all. In fact, I only met her a couple of times."

"Well, I'm sure she appreciated your presence here."

"No offense, Father," I reply. "But I'm not a religious man. I don't really believe in the afterlife. I think we get one shot at all of this, and we do our best, but when it's over, that's that. So I don't think she'll have any feelings about it one way or the other. She's gone."

"No, you misunderstand me," he says, reaching across, placing a hand on my arm, and smiling widely. "I wasn't referring to Vanessa. I was talking about Rebecca. It's she who will have been grateful that you traveled so far. Your marriage might not have been a success but I daresay you've cheered her immensely by choosing to be part of today, and by ensuring that your son is present. I can see the gratitude on her face. It offers a fine counterbalance to the grief."

Our son.
      Last night, when we returned to the cottage, I felt relieved at how well the evening had gone. Emmet had put aside all his resentment, remaining next to his mother throughout, even chatting amiably with Furia, who later stood at the bar and had a drink with me, where I congratulated her on the success of her novel.

"It's doing so well," I told her. "I see it everywhere."

"Thank you," she said. "It's taken me a little by surprise, if I'm honest."

"A good surprise, though."

"Of course."

We stood there, rather self-consciously, and finally, to break the silence, I nodded across the room toward the woman who had once been married to me and was now married to her.

"So how's our girl doing?" I asked tentatively, hoping she wouldn't be offended by my choice of pronoun, but if anything, she seemed pleased by it, touching my arm for a moment and squeezing it affectionately.

"All right, so far," she said. "You know just as well as I do how things were between them. I don't think the mourning period will be a lengthy one, but there are issues that remain that she still has to work through. She'll spend years doing that, I imagine."

"Well, she has you to help her with that. And Emmet."

"It was so good of you to bring him."

"It seemed like the right thing to do."

"I told her to invite him, but she was terrified that he'd say no."

This takes me by surprise.

"There's something I should probably let her know," I say, pulling her away from the bar a little to a quieter spot. "On the way here, I told him about the past. About Rebecca's father, I mean. And Emma. All of it."

Furia breathes in deeply and considers this.

"OK," she says.

"I don't know if it was my place or not, but in the moment it seemed right."

We both glance over to where Rebecca and Emmet are huddled together, and it looks as if he's scrolling through photos on his phone—probably pictures of his surfing activities and his friends—and her face is bright with joy, as is his. He says something, and she bursts out laughing before putting an arm around his shoulder, and for a moment, he lays his head there. Furia turns back to me.

"It was right," she says.

Later, before going to bed, Emmet and I sat at the kitchen table together, drinking tea, and he asked a few more questions related to the revelations of earlier. It was a conversation he would have with Rebecca at some point in the future, he told me.

"You didn't say anything about it tonight, did you?" I asked, and he shook his head.

"Oh God, no. Totally not the right time."

"It looked like you were having fun together."

"As much as you can at a wake," he said with a shrug. "But I'm glad we came. And I'm glad you told me what you told me. It explains a lot of things. I mean, there's still a lot I need to understand about it, about her, about both of you, but—"

"Then there's something else," I said.

"What? About Mum?"

"No," I said, shaking my head. "About me." We'd come this far, after all. If there was ever a time to unearth all the secrets that had caused so much trauma in our lives, then this was it. And so I told him of the things that had happened to me when I was fourteen and how badly they had affected me over the years that followed. I hoped it would go some way to explaining why I could be so overprotective at times.

He listened carefully, never interrupting, and showed no sign of embarrassment throughout what was a lengthy and difficult conversation, centered around such an intimate topic. When I reached the conclusion of my tale, he looked down at the table for a long time, his brow furrowed, and neither of us spoke for quite some time. I guessed that he needed to think this through, to reframe me in his mind as someone who had gone through a childhood trauma and spent twenty-six years trying to come to terms with it. I could tell that he found nothing salacious about it but recognized what had happened for what it was. A crime.

"There's something I need to ask you," I said finally before we said goodnight. "I saw something, a few weeks ago, on your phone. I wasn't prying. Well, I suppose I was. But I didn't mean to. It was a stupid, thoughtless act on my part. I shouldn't have looked. But I did."

He frowned and sat back in his chair, looking slightly alarmed.

"Some photos," I said. "Some photos of you."

"My phone is full of photos of me."

"More . . . intimate photos. Of your body."

"Oh fuck," he replied, putting a hand to his mouth, blushing from the base of his neck to the tips of his ears.

"I shouldn't have looked," I repeated. "I'm sorry. But since I did, I need to know why they were there. Who were you sending them to?"

His eyes opened wide now. "Sending them to?" he asked. "No one! Jesus! As if!"

"Then why did you take them?"

"Because I'm so skinny, Dad. I've been trying to build muscle. I want to keep track of my development."

"And you needed to be naked for that?"

"It's not as if you could see my . . . anything."

"They weren't far off."

"But far enough!"

"You're not talking to anyone online, are you? Someone who asked for them?"

"Oh my God," he said, burying his head in his hands. "You are the weirdest man alive."

"That might be true. I just don't want anyone taking advantage of you."

"No one is. I promise."

"You can understand why, though, right? After what I've told you about what happened to me?"

"I can," he said. "But still. This is really embarrassing."

"I'm sorry."

"Can we just never talk about it again?"

"All right," I said. "But you promise that you're telling me the truth?"

"I promise," he confirmed. "I'm a skinny fucker, that's all. And I want to bulk up. You've seen the protein shakes. And the weights. I want to build some strength, that's all." He smiled and looked a little bashful. "Like, I wouldn't mind, you know, having a—"

"Having a what?"

"Like, you know. A girlfriend."

"Oh. Right," I said. "Of course. And you need muscles for that?"

"Well, they don't hurt. We live in Bondi, for God's sake. You've seen what the guys there are like."

"So when I asked you on the plane about whether there was anyone you're interested in?"

"Let's just say I have a few options," he told me, and I burst out laughing at the cheeky expression on his face.

"Lucky you."

"I mean, if you need any tips . . ."

"Yeah, thanks," I said. "I'll know who to call on."

We finished our tea and finally he yawned, saying that he was tired and should go to bed.

"But when we get back to Sydney," he added tentatively, "maybe we could all spend some time together. Me, you, and Mum. When she's traveling through, I mean. Would that be OK?"

"Of course. I think it would be a really good idea."

"And Furia too?"

I nodded. "Of course. She's part of our family."

He stood up, came around the table, and leaned over, hugging me, something he hadn't done in more than a year, before walking away and closing the door to his room quietly behind him.

After the burial, when everyone else has made their way to the new pub for drinks and sandwiches, I find myself wandering around the graveyard, reading the names on the headstones and studying the dates. Some go back a hundred years or more while others are more recent.

It's a fine day, the sky is cloudless, and I feel a welcome sense of calm. The woman I'd noticed earlier in the back row is standing before one of the plots, laying flowers, and she turns to me as I approach her.

"A sad day," she says, the standard greeting on such an occasion. "He gave a lovely service though. Ifechi, I mean. We were lucky to get him. Lucky to keep him for so long too. He's been a good friend to me."

I glance toward the grave that she's tending.

"My son," she says before I can ask. "Evan."

"He died young," I add, noticing that the poor boy passed away before the age of twenty-five.

"He did."

"You must miss him."

She nods, as if she hardly needs to express how much.

"I met Vanessa, you know," she says. "A long time ago now, of course. And I won't pretend that I knew her well. But I always remembered her."

"You were on the island back then?" I ask.

"Oh, I've been stuck on this island since I was first brought here as a bride. I thought of moving away after my husband died, but I couldn't leave Evan on his own."

I glance at the stone again and am surprised that his is the only name inscribed on the granite. Evan Keogh. It rings a bell somewhere in the far corners of my memory, but for now I can't place it.

"I didn't let them put his father in here with him," she says, guessing the question that's running through my mind. "He's somewhere over there, in the far corner."

She nods toward an area where the graves are far less well tended. I can't help but wonder what led her to separating the pair.

"He died young too," she adds. "Well, for these times anyway. In his early sixties. Only a few weeks after Evan, as it happens."

"What happened to him?" I asked. "If you don't mind me asking."

"To Charlie? Someone hit him with an axe."

I blink, uncertain that I've heard her right.

"I'm sorry?"

"I said, someone hit him with an axe," she repeats. "It was quite the story at the time, although it probably wouldn't have traveled to as far away as wherever your accent is from. He had the head nearly separated from his body, would you believe. No one ever found out who did it. It was during the tourist season, so it was probably some ne'er-do-well from the mainland. Someone with a grudge against him. He'd made a few enemies in his time, had my husband."

"So he wasn't caught?"

"You're assuming it was a man."

"Well . . ." I begin.

"But no, whoever did it covered up their tracks very well. In the end, the Gardaí had no choice but to leave the case unsolved. It's one of life's little mysteries."

She smiles, as if she's explaining the conclusion of a crime novel she enjoyed.

"Right," I say. "That must have been very upsetting for you."

"They tried to pin it on me," she continues. "On account of it being our axe. But sure the only fingerprints on it were Charlie's, and he was a big man. I said it to the Gardaí at the time, I said do you think a fragile thing like me could lay a fella like him low? I wouldn't have the strength for it."

"No," I say, wondering whether I've run into the local lunatic. "I imagine not."

She takes my hand and speaks quietly. "I'd have had to have a fierce hatred in me to build the strength for such a deed."

I stare at her, and at last she releases me and her tone changes, as if none of this conversation has even taken place.

"She was kind," she tells me then. "Vanessa, I mean. There was a day, oh a long time ago now, when poor Evan went missing. He was only a boy at the time, around sixteen, and the whole island thought he had drowned. She brought me a cup of tea when I was standing in the dunes, my heart sinking in fear, and, unlike all the rest of my neighbors, she wasn't being ghoulish about it."

"She lost a daughter to drowning herself," I tell her.

"Yes, I heard that after she left, when we all found out who she really was. I expect that's what made her so considerate toward me. Mothers recognize each other's pain."

"And your son?" I ask. "Was that how he—?"

"Oh no. He returned safely that day, although maybe he'd have been better off lost to the water considering how his life played out for him afterward. There are times I think it was a miracle that I held on to him for as long as I did. Sometimes I feel as if God has been punishing me my entire adult life but, no matter how hard I try, I can't understand what I ever did to offend Him. It's not fair, is it? Life. You'd wonder whether it's all worth the bother."

She shakes her head sadly, then places a hand atop her son's gravestone, before walking on with a sigh, her head bowed as she makes her way toward the gate that opens onto the laneway and that in turn, I assume, leads to her lonely home.

T he sun is setting.

I make my way down to the beach and watch the waves as they lap toward the shore. Before me is the Atlantic Ocean, sweeping southeast in the direction of Tierra del Fuego, where it will make the bend for the Pacific and travel onward toward Sydney, Bondi, and home.

A sound from behind makes me turn, and I watch as Rebecca makes her way toward me. She's barefoot in the sand, and I'm glad that she's come alone. Taking her place next to me, we both remain silent for a few moments, staring out toward the horizon.

"I remember when my mother told me she was coming here," she says eventually without any preamble. "And how angry I felt. The trial had just ended, of course, and we'd had such a terrible year. I felt she was abandoning me when I needed her most. It's why I punished her. Blocking her number and unblocking it repeatedly. And then, one day, I just showed up out of the blue. She was so surprised to see me."

"She talked about that," I reply. "The night we met for dinner before our wedding."

"Did she? I don't remember."

"Yes."

She turns to me now.

"Thank you," she says.

"For what?"

"For coming here. For bringing Emmet. It never even crossed my mind that you would do such a thing. When I saw you in the doorway of the pub, I couldn't believe it."

She reaches out and we take each other's hands, recalling the good times we shared over the years, the laughs, the nights out, the jokes, the hangovers, the work conversations, the tears, the confessions, the traumas, the love.

"I don't want to have the same distance with him as I had with her," she says, sighing deeply as she turns back toward the waves. "I need to spend more time with him."

"You do."

"I've told myself that I wanted to protect him. From me. From all the anger inside me. But last night, the way he took care of me . . . Furia told me that you told him."

"You're not angry?"

She shakes her head. "No," she says. "Not at all. If anything, I'm glad you did."

"I told him about me too."

"Really?"

"Yes."

"It was the right time. He'll go back to Australia changed, I suppose, but perhaps in a good way. You've done a good job, Aaron. Better than I ever did. He's lucky to have you. I'm lucky that you're our son's father."

I feel tears form behind my eyes. It is so peaceful here, just the two of us. It occurs to me that, after Emmet, Rebecca remains the most important person in my life. Someone who I would—quite literally—travel halfway across the world to support.

"I noticed you chatting with Furia," she says after a moment, smiling.

"Yes, I made a pass, but she was having none of it."

She laughs.

"You're happy together?"

"We are."

"I'm glad."

"Thank you."

"She gave you what I never could."

She doesn't reply, but I can tell from her expression that she knows I'm right. I've spent so long lying to myself about what went wrong between us that it's time for me to face the truth.

"All those years we spent together," I say, "you needed more than my words. More than my endless romantic gestures. You needed someone who would touch you. God, it's not like you didn't tell me often enough." I take a deep breath and just say what needs saying. "You needed sex. You needed to feel loved in that way."

She nods.

"I did, Aaron."

"I've spent years telling myself that it was the other way around. That it was you who didn't want to touch me. I've lied to myself, to my therapist. Because I couldn't face it. I'm that thing that Emmet talks about."

She frowns. "What thing?"

"The unreliable narrator."

"It wasn't your fault, Aaron," she tells me. "It was hers. I won't even say her name."

"I know. You begged me to seek therapy, and I refused. I should have listened. I've never allowed myself to truly believe that I didn't have a part in all of that. To accept that I was the victim. I've never given myself a chance to heal. And that wasn't fair on you. Or Emmet. Or our family."

"It's not too late," she tells me, putting an arm around my shoulder and pulling me close. "That woman destroyed a piece of you, and you can't allow her to keep doing so. She's in prison for the rest of her life, and you're only forty. You have more than half your life ahead of you, all going well. Emmet told me that you're still single."

"I am."

"That there hasn't been anyone since I left."

"There hasn't."

She steps away now and looks me directly in the eye, placing her hands on my arms.

"I'm going to tell you something now, Aaron," she says. "And I want you to listen. Because I mean it. Because you're my friend."

I nod.

"You deserve to be loved."

W hen night falls, I find myself back on the beach, alone on the sand. It's dark now. The moon is out. Stars stud the sky. I close my eyes and take a deep breath of the cleanest air that has ever filled my lungs.

Slowly, I take off my clothes and walk naked toward the water, wanting to plunge deep down into the waves. I stay beneath the surface for as long as I can before bursting through the surface, gasping for air. I brush the hair out of my eyes and look back toward the island. I've swum a little further out than I expected but, while I may be a terrible surfer, one of the benefits of living in Sydney all these years is that I've become a strong swimmer. The water is calm too, so I know I'm in no danger. In the distance, smoke is rising from the chimneys of the cottages where fires have been lit. But I'm not ready to return just yet, so float on my back, looking up at the blackness above me. I think about my conversation with Rebecca from earlier and know how right she was. Freya Petrus stole so much of my life, and I simply can't allow her to lay claim to another minute. I refuse to be her victim any longer; I want to be her survivor. But how?

It's then, out of the night sky, that a voice seems to whisper in my ear. The voice of a woman I met only a few times and whose body is now settling into its eternal coffin, deep in the earth of a church graveyard no more than a couple of miles from here.

*D*on't go home, Aaron, she tells me.
     Not yet anyway.
Stay here. Stay on the island.
For a few months. Perhaps even a year. Move into the cottage.
Heal.
Grow strong.
Allow Rebecca and Emmet the space to find each other again while you're away. And when you're ready, when the time comes, go back to Australia and start over.

And yes, I tell myself. This is exactly what I will do. I'll tell them both in the morning and hope that they'll be happy for me. A year at most. Rebecca can base herself out of Sydney during that time, and when she's away for work, Emmet can stay with Damian's family. They'll be happy to have him.

I must remain on this unlikely rock, this final outpost of human life before the Atlantic Ocean stretches toward America, and prepare for my second life, one that I will embrace when I feel the strength and confidence to do so.

I plunge back down now, blocking out all the noise of the world around me, but keep my eyes open, staring into the dark black depths of the water, feeling the tug of the earth, the fire within me, and the air that remains in my lungs.

I'm not there yet, but one day I will be. At one with myself, at one with the universe, and—finally—at one with the elements.

Acknowledgments

For all their advice and support, many thanks to Simon Trewin, Laura Bonner, Paloma Velasco, Matt Georg, Bill Scott-Kerr, and the team at Transworld UK and to Tim Duggan and the team at Henry Holt in the United States.

I'm grateful to Niamh Cusack, Dane Whyte O'Hara, Anna Friel, and Colin Morgan for their wonderful narrations of the audio editions.

About the Author

John Boyne is the author of *The Boy in the Striped Pajamas*, which has been adapted for film, theater, ballet, and opera. His many international bestsellers include *The Heart's Invisible Furies*, which was a Book of the Month Club Book of the Year, and *A Ladder to the Sky*. His work is published in sixty languages. He lives in Dublin.